DRIVE ME
crazy

Carly Robyn writes contemporary romances with heart, heat and humor. When she's not writing or reading, you can find her spending time with her family, scrolling through TikTok, exploring Chicago's restaurant scene with friends, watching a Grand Prix, taking a million pictures of her dogs or binge-watching anything true crime-related while drinking a Diet Coke.

Follow her on social media for updates: @carlyrobynauthor.

DRIVE ME
crazy

CARLY ROBYN

PENGUIN BOOKS

PENGUIN BOOKS

UK | USA | Canada | Ireland | Australia
India | New Zealand | South Africa

Penguin Books is part of the Penguin Random House group of companies
whose addresses can be found at global.penguinrandomhouse.com

First published in the United States of America by Blue Dog Press 2024
First published in Great Britain by Penguin Books 2024
003

Editing by Lawrence Editing
Custom Illustrations by Lorissa Padilla Designs
Printed and bound in Great Britain by Clays Ltd, Elcograf S.p.A.

The authorized representative in the EEA is Penguin Random House Ireland,
Morrison Chambers, 32 Nassau Street, Dublin D02 YH68

A CIP catalogue record for this book is available from the British Library

ISBN: 978–1–405–96924–6

www.greenpenguin.co.uk

MIX
Paper | Supporting
responsible forestry
FSC® C018179

Penguin Random House is committed to a
sustainable future for our business, our readers
and our planet. This book is made from Forest
Stewardship Council® certified paper.

For my mom.
You're the reason I love stories and the reason I believed in myself enough to write this one.

AUTHOR'S CONTENT NOTE

This book is written in a light and humorous style but does touch on subjects that might not be suitable for everyone. Mentions of anxiety, panic attacks (one on-page), explicit language, sexual assault (past, off-page), self-medicating with alcohol and drugs, references to absentee parents, and death of a parent (past, off-page) are present in the novel. It is a slow-burn, open-door romance that portrays sexual content and is meant for readers 18+. Please take note!

The focus of this work is on the fictional characters and events within the Formula 1 racing world, and deviations from the current Grand Prix schedule and tracks are intentional for storytelling purposes.

PLAYLIST

Late Night Talking | Harry Styles
Take a Chance on Me | ABBA
Kiss Me More | Doja Cat ft. SZA
Foreign Land | Emily James
Swim | Chase Atlantic
Feel Again | OneRepublic
I Don't Care | Ed Sheeran & Justin Bieber
King of My Heart | Taylor Swift
We Are the Champions | Queen
No Control | One Direction
I Like Me Better | Lauv
Thinkin Bout You | Frank Ocean
Burnin' Up | Jonas Brothers
Lasting Lover | Sigala, James Arthur
Stronger (What Doesn't Kill You) | Kelly Clarkson

ONE

ELLA

IT'S SO cold out that my nips could be classified as weapons of mass destruction. I walk down the sidewalk, shivering against the biting chill as a light layer of snow dusts against my shoulders. My winter jacket is a lot better at making me look like an extra-fluffy marshmallow than keeping me warm.

Buildings stretch toward the night sky and cast eerie shadows onto the cars careening down the street at a breakneck speed. When I first moved to the city—hell, even a few months ago—the sight of the skyscrapers and classic yellow taxis brought a smile to my face. Now they serve as mocking reminders that the concrete jungle thoroughly whooped my ass. And not in the kinky spanking kind of way. More in a that-hurt-so-badly-I'm-never-sitting-again way.

I would've been more than happy to ghost everyone in Manhattan, but Poppy insisted on a proper send-off. It's the only reason I'm dragging my ass to her place in twenty-degree weather. When I finally arrive, I'm so focused on thawing my frozen fingers that I walk straight into a Hot Wheels piñata.

Oh my God.

Poppy's entire Midtown apartment has turned into a race

car enthusiast's wet dream. Signs reading "Yield to Party" and "Race in Progress" cover the walls, and checkered flags hang from the ceiling. The only thing indicating this isn't a four-year-old's birthday party is the excessive amount of alcohol in the kitchen.

I spy my best friend through the red, black, and white balloons floating around aimlessly. My mouth falls open, but no words come out. She's propping up a life-size, custom cut-out of Formula 1 legend Blake Hollis with his arm draped over some unknown woman. A woman who just so happens to have my face photoshopped over hers. *Lord help me.*

Blake looks gorgeous as per usual, but nothing ruins a pretty face more than a bad attitude. It's no wonder his team wants to have a biography written and released in less than a year. He needs as much good PR as he can get after last year's train wreck of a season.

I'm studying the display, contemplating how I'd look if I were supermodel tall with boobs faker than Monopoly money instead of five-foot-two with run-of-the-mill B-cups, when Poppy pulls me in for an organ-crushing hug.

"Ella! What do you think?" She twirls in a circle, arms above her head. "Perfect, right?"

"It's perfectly on theme," I agree, taking another bewildered look around. It's over-the-top, but then I wouldn't expect anything less. Poppy has the impressive ability to hyper-focus on a project to the point where it surpasses even the highest of expectations. It's annoying as hell when her projects happen to be my love life and floundering career, but I'll admit her apartment looks good. I wouldn't mind turning Blake's cardboard body into some type of dart board, though.

Jack bounces over from where he's sitting on the couch. He looks like he just walked off the cover of a billionaire romance novel with his perpetual smirk. He greets me with a one-armed hug before turning to Poppy. "Can I be done blowing up balloons?"

"I thought you loved blowing." Batting her piercing blue eyes, she flutters her lashes innocently. "That's why I gave you that job in the first place."

"Ha." He rolls his eyes, a teasing quirk at the corners of his mouth. "I do. I just prefer it be muscular blonds with daddy issues instead of balloons."

The conversation snowballs into Jack's latest dating mistake on a long list of many. He'll probably be Poppy's new project once I'm gone. I swallow the lump in my throat, trying not to focus on how much I'm going to miss them.

As if she can sense the chink in my armor, Poppy sighs dramatically and says, "It's not too late to back out and look for another job in New York."

I'm not sure how many times we can have this conversation before my head implodes. Two more times tops. Maybe. I throw my arm around her shoulders and gently shake her.

"It's definitely too late for that. I'm going," I confirm. A cold thrill goes up and down my spine. "And it's a phenomenal opportunity."

When I reached out to my mentor, George Phillips, for advice after leaving PlayMedia, I'd been expecting some career guidance. Instead, he offered me a job to be his feet-on-the-ground co-author for Blake's authorized biography. I haven't done much writing since my podcast, *Coffee with Champions*, blew up and I'm excited to get back to my roots. After what happened, the thought of podcasting, or even being in a recording room, makes my body flood with panic. I don't want to be constantly reminded of that. But writing? That's a safe space. It doesn't hurt that I'll be halfway around the world, either.

"Fine," she huffs, crossing her arms over her chest. "But

then you have to promise me you'll find out how many *Sports Illustrated* models Blake's slept with."

I hit a balloon floating by at her and she quickly swats it away from her raven black hair to avoid any static aftermath. Poppy's not big on sports, but she's big on celebrity gossip, and Blake's one of the athletes whose prowess has earned him international notoriety and prestige.

"Those aren't the questions he's going to want to answer, Pop," I tell her. Blake's extremely private. There's also a slight chance I'm already on his bad side after comparing his partying last year to Paris Hilton circa 2006. I don't think asking the McAllister driver his body count is going to earn me any brownie points.

"You're no fun." She sticks out her lower lip. "At least confirm the rumors that he has a huge dick."

"I'd like to know that one, too," Jack agrees with an aggressive head nod. "Honestly, if you could make a comparison chart of every driver's dick size, I feel like that would be really beneficial to us all."

Resting my face in my hands, I let out a groan. "Can I please have a drink before either one of you says *dick* again?"

A wicked grin spreads across Poppy's lips as she leads me into the kitchen. She's created a menu of drinks and snacks with Formula-One-themed names. I take a small sip of my McAllister Martini, cringing as the strong taste burns my throat. This isn't a martini; it's a hangover in a glass.

"I hate him," Poppy announces to no one in particular. "It's *his* fault you're leaving."

She says it so casually that it takes me a moment to realize who she's talking about. Connor Brixton. She refuses to call him by his name. I wish she wouldn't refer to him at all. *Adios, au revoir, and arrivederci, motherfucker.*

"I left PlayMedia of my own accord," I remind her. Digging my fingernails into my palms, I shrug my shoulders. I didn't have much of a choice, but at the end of the day, I quit; they didn't make me leave. "Can we not talk about this?"

"Ella, c'mon. You left—"

"Poppy," Jack warns, cutting her off. "We're supposed to be having fun and clearly Ella doesn't want to discuss it."

I shoot him a grateful look, but he and Poppy are staring each other down like parents in a bitter custody battle. Now would be a great time to snack on some Pit Stop Popcorn or Crash Test Chips, but they're on the other side of the counter.

"You're right. Sorry," Poppy acquiesces after a minute. She focuses her attention back on me. "Do you think Blake's listened to your podcast?"

My shoulders tense, but I don't bother reminding her that it's no longer my podcast. "I'm assuming he's looked me up. It's not hard to put two and two together."

"I'm sure he knows it was all in good fun," Jack reassures me.

I didn't say anything untrue or outrageous about Blake on my show, but I did poke some fun at his messy performance last year. My podcast was listed under sports and comedy for a reason. How could I *not* make a joke about him driving into more panties than wins? I'm praying George is right and Blake won't care that I made a few subjectively funny remarks about him.

"Pop, should we give El her present?" Jack changes the subject. "Before people arrive?"

He sips his drink, a Jump Start Gin and Juice, with a glint of mischief in his eyes. Poppy disappears, arriving back momentarily with a gift bag covered in race cars. No shocker there. It's filled with a variety of fun tchotchkes, but it's the last few items that really surprise me.

"Condoms." I blink rapidly. "You got me condoms."

I take a closer look and see the phrase *Save Fuel, Ride a Driver* embossed on the foil wrappers. My drink sputters out of my mouth, nearly hitting Poppy's chest.

"So?" Jack asks, staring at me with undisguised amusement. "What do you think?"

"That you two are certifiable." I hold the roll out in front of me. The ones in red foil are apparently cherry flavored. *Yum.* "I don't think I'll be using these, but I appreciate it."

Formula 1 drivers are infamously known as fuckboys. *No, thank you.* I'm twenty-seven years old. If I still felt like playing mind games and faking orgasms, I could walk into any bar within a five-block radius of my apartment. I want to be swept off my feet, not swept under a rug after a one-night stand.

"One final thing," Poppy says, pulling a lipstick out from the bottom of the bag. "Open it!"

I'm praying it's not a bright red color because regardless of what she says, it just doesn't work with my complexion. My eyes widen as I twist the bottom of the tube. I was way off base considering it's a goddamn knife.

Poppy claps her hands together. "Now you're protected from STDs *and* attackers!"

"Condoms to screw men"—I laugh, twisting the tube so I don't accidentally stab myself—"and a lipstick knife if they try to screw with me."

Jack chuckles with a wink. "London's not going to know what hit 'em."

"Neither will Belgium," Poppy adds. "Or Australia. Or Japan. Or any of the other places you're traveling to."

I clink my red plastic cup against hers in agreement. Twenty-one cities in fifty-two weeks. If that kind of time and distance can't help me move on from what happened, I'm not sure what will.

TWO
BLAKE

MY ANGER MANIFESTS itself in one of two ways. I either lose my temper and yell at people or stay so quiet that they're uncomfortably on edge. Right now, it's the latter. I can see the silence wrapping around Keith and George like a scratchy blanket. I'd feel bad, but I'm certain if I talk, one of them will leave this meeting with a black eye.

"Keith tells me you're not happy with my co-author," George finally says, sipping his cappuccino calmly. "What are your concerns, mate?"

"This has to be some sort of a joke, right?" The sharpness of my voice leaves no room for questions. "You didn't seriously hire her."

My anger doesn't seem to shake George. Instead, he seems rather amused. He takes another sip of his coffee, his cool gaze meeting my fiery one. I want to take the mug out of his hand and break it into a million fucking pieces.

"Need I remind you of George's contract?" my manager interjects. "He can employ whomever he pleases to help him given the tight deadline."

"I've read the damn thing," I argue. Well, my lawyer has,

but semantics. "My team has to approve anyone he hires *at least* two months in advance."

"Ella was vetted and approved back in December, Blake," Keith confirms. "You just refused to have a conversation regarding the book until now."

"She questioned my abilities as a driver and then said it's no wonder my head's not in the game on the track since I'm too busy getting head off the track," I snap. "Did you think I'd be happy about that? What experience does she have besides a stupid podcast? How is she even remotely qualified to write a biography? Do we even know if she's literate? This is bloody ridiculous. I'm not spending the season with her, so you need to find someone else."

"Nope," Keith says, shaking his head at me. "Don't try to sabotage this. We wouldn't even be having this conversation if it weren't for your manic desire to kill your career."

"I didn't ruin my career." I narrow my eyes at him. I'm aware I wasn't on my best behavior last year, on or off the track. "I'm still signed with McAllister and all my sponsors. Plus, even bad press is good press, right?"

"Bad press? Blake, you partied so much you don't remember throwing hotel furniture into a pool. The paparazzi caught you screwing a chick, who may have been a call girl might I add, in the back seat of a limo. That's not bad press, that's just fucking *bad*." Keith's thin lips purse into a straight line, brows furrowing together. He always does this when he's exasperated, and it looks like two angry caterpillars moving across his face. "You may still have your contracts in place, but don't pretend like they didn't warn you to clean up your act this season or you're out. You don't think Thompson would jump at the chance to take your spot?"

"Listen, Blake," George cuts in before I can respond. "No one's out to get you. We're doing this biography to remind the world and your team why you're the best and why they're lucky to have you racing and representing them. You know if I didn't have other commitments, I'd be the one spending the season with you, but I'd need help regardless. We're doing everything from A to Z in twelve months. It's all hands on deck, and that includes Ella."

I've known George since my early days of karting. He's one of the only journalists I actually like. He's respectful and doesn't ask ignorant questions just to get a rise out of me. We've grown close over the years and rather than write about what a mess I was last year, he showed up at my house uninvited to see what he could do to help. If I didn't trust George, and if it wasn't him working on this project, there's no way this book would be happening.

"She said Formula 1 must've required me to get a special license to behave so idiotically," I remind them.

Keith looks down at his Rolex. It was my apology gift after last year. "Are you done with your temper tantrum?"

I clench my jaw and nod, wanting to know why the bloody hell they hired her more than I want to yell.

"She's qualified, Blake," George says. "And she's good. Really good. Ella's the type of person you want helping us."

He pulls out a folder and slides it across the table. I warily open it to find Ella's résumé inside. Taking it out, I lean back in my chair and start reading. Ella Gold. From Chicago, lives in New York City. Well, lives until she follows me around like a damn mosquito. Graduated summa cum laude with a bachelor's degree in Journalism and then went on to get her master's. Interned at the *Big Ten Network* and *The New Yorker*. Worked as a sportswriter and podcast host at PlayMedia, a digital sport, entertainment, and media brand, until late last year.

George even printed out some of her work for me to look at. He clearly came prepared. *Wanker.* Her interview with Olympian swimmer Lilly King is annoyingly fantastic. Her story on Rafael Nadal losing to Novak Djokovic in the 2021

French Open Semifinal is even more annoyingly fantastic. And her article on my Monaco Grand Prix win from a few years back is just obnoxiously fucking fantastic. Objectively and subjectively. *Shit, shit, shit.*

"Why her?" The articles sit in front of me, each one of them read. "There's a long list of other experienced journalists and writers who haven't talked shit about me."

Keith stares at me like I'm crazy. Fine. The list isn't *that* long; it's rather short.

"You trust me, right? That's why we decided to work together on this?" George tilts his head, daring me to disagree. "So then trust me when I say she's the right person for the job."

I take a deep breath to control my frustration. "How do you even know her?"

"She studied abroad for a semester when I was guest lecturing. She was in my class—Advanced Issues in 21st-Century Sports and Media. We've kept in touch, and I knew she'd be perfect for this."

"She said I treated the Baku circuit like a game of Mario Kart last year."

"She's not wrong." He lets out a long, low chuckle. "You drove like a maniac."

I flip him the bird. He's right and I hate being wrong.

"Give her a chance, Blake. She's a brilliant writer and one of the only people I think can put up with your smart ass for an entire season." He gives me a pointed look.

I push my thumbs into my temples, trying to relieve the tension headache this conversation's giving me. "I don't like this. Not one bit." I hate how whiney I sound. Like my nephew when I tell him it's bedtime, but he's not finished playing with his action figures.

"Yeah, well, I don't like having to clean up your mess." Keith shrugs. "Get over it."

An incoming call from my sister interrupts my manager's next rant. She's the one person I'll drop everything for and they both know this. I excuse myself from the room to take the call.

"Well, well, well. If it isn't my favorite sister," I answer.

"If it isn't my favorite brother." Neither of us has much competition considering we're each other's only family, but the familiar greeting makes me smile. "So…the season's starting soon."

"Really?" Sarcasm drips from my voice. "I would've never guessed. Great reminder, Ashley."

She sighs through the phone, making her annoyance clear. "Don't be a jerk."

I can't help but chuckle at my niece's small voice shouting in the background that *jerk* is a bad word. A *very* bad word according to Millie.

"Sorry. I'm just tired and pissy about the biography."

"I'm excited about it," she says. "It'll let people get to know the real Blake instead of the A-R-S-E you make yourself out to be."

"Yeah, maybe." I don't bother mentioning that my problem with the biography is that I don't want people to get to know the real me.

"How do you feel?" she asks. "And don't say fine because that's what you said last year and then you got penalized after purposefully causing a crash, Blake."

It wasn't on purpose; I was just trying to sneak past Harry Thompson and it backfired. Horrendously. "We're not getting into this again, Ash."

She doesn't push me any further, no doubt to avoid World War III. I've been a ticking time bomb this past year, known to blow up at the slightest comment. God knows she got hit with enough shrapnel. It turns out mixing antidepressants and loads of alcohol isn't a great idea. Who knew?

"Did Finn and Millie get my postcard?" I ask, my voice softening. My niece and nephew love getting snail mail and I try to send some as often as possible, even when we're in the same city. The last one I sent had their favorite cartoon pig eating a macaron in front of Big Ben.

"Yep! They just sent you back a hand-drawn card. It's very…unique."

I snort at the descriptor. Unique is a nice way to describe their artistic abilities. Finn's triangles will put his future Geometry teacher into cardiac arrest, and Millie exclusively uses orange because she "feels bad it has to share a name with fruit." My sister's an interior decorator, but her penchant for color-coordination and clean lines hasn't manifested in her children.

"Finn tried to draw you two juggling at the circus, but it looks more like"—she cuts herself off with a laugh—"you know what? I'm not going to ruin the surprise. You'll know exactly what I mean when you see it."

"I'll be on the lookout for it," I tell her with a small grin. "I have to get back to my meeting, but I'll come over for dinner soon, okay? Tell everyone I say hello."

"Dinner sounds lovely," she replies. "Be safe, okay?"

I mumble goodbye before sinking against the wall. If it could just swallow me and spit me out into the depths of hell, that'd be greatly appreciated. This season is make it or break it, and right now I can't afford to break down. If I've learned anything from last season, it's that I need to do a better job keeping my emotions in check and off the track.

THREE
ELLA

THE FEW WEEKS after my goodbye party fly by. The flight to London does not. Probably because I spent all six hours panicking. I managed to calm down and remind myself why I was doing this by the time the wheels touched down. The glass of champagne—*okay, or three*—probably helped.

George lives in the suburbs outside of the city but has a two-bedroom "flat" in Shoreditch—a trendy and posh London neighborhood according to Poppy—where I'm living in between races. I only spend two days in London before flying to Bahrain for the first race weekend. I'm still adjusting to the time change, so the absolute last thing I want to do when I land is work out. Yet here I am, lugging my overweight suitcase down a never-ending hallway. I seriously have no idea where my room is; this hotel is a labyrinth. No Midwestern corn maze could've prepared me for this.

"Mom." I sigh as I turn down another hallway. I think I've already walked past these rooms. "Please don't friend request Blake. I haven't even met him yet. And I'm pretty sure the Facebook account you sent me is fake. Do you know how many people probably pretend to be him?"

"He doesn't have to accept!" she protests. "I just want him to know you have a caring mother looking out for you, so he better watch himself."

"Yeah, Mom, because you come off super intimidating on Facebook."

She posts inspirational quotes and reshares feel-good videos from the news. Nothing about her Facebook page screams "I'll kick your ass." My dad, on the other hand? Maybe. But my mom? Try again. The only thing she's likely to scare is trick-or-treaters if she's wearing a mask.

"Aha!" I stop in front of 4033. "Finally found the room."

"Be sure to check under the bed and behind the curtains to make sure the room's secure."

"Of course." I've seen way too much *Law & Order: Special Victims Unit* to not check for creepy men hiding in my hotel room. "I'll call you later, okay? Love you!"

"Love you more, honey."

I hang up the phone and use the card reader to enter the room. Holy hell. The suite is sleek, modern, and bigger than my NYC apartment by an embarrassing amount of square feet. And I had a decent-sized place, by Manhattan standards anyway. I feel like I'm on an episode of *International House Hunters*. Except instead of having a two-million-dollar budget as a button collector, I have no budget as a biographer! But don't worry. I'm willing to make that work in order to stay in this probably very expensive room in Bahrain.

Even though I'd flown first class, my muscles still ache from inactivity and I practically sprint into the shower. The high pressure of the hot water kneads the tension out of my shoulders, and I leave the bathroom in a euphoric state. I curl up in the king-sized bed, eat a room service dinner, and pass out wondering if the hotel sells sell full-sized bottles of their lavender lotion in the gift shop.

.   .   .

I WAKE up with a pit the size of a watermelon in my stomach. Today's the day I meet Blake.

I can do this.

I hope.

I'm too nervous to eat, but I head to the breakfast buffet at the hotel to make myself a to-go coffee. With my caffeine boost —and the detailed instructions Blake's manager Keith emailed me—it's easy to find the conference room we're all meeting in. Of course, when I walk in, Keith is nowhere to be found. The only person there is Blake. And I'm not sure if it's the jet lag speaking, but holy hell this man is drop-dead gorgeous.

Taking a calming breath, I paste a friendly smile on my face and say, "Hi, I'm Ella." I stick out my hand in introduction. Blake stares at it for a few seconds before quickly shaking it. I'm praying he doesn't notice how clammy my hands are.

His chocolate-brown eyes roam over me as if he's undressing me in his mind. The eye contact is aggressively brazen but somehow doesn't cross the line of being creepy. Someone needs to turn on the AC immediately because I'm starting to sweat. Photos don't do him justice. His unruly dark brown hair makes it seem like he woke up from a nap right before the meeting and let me tell you, bedhead looks good on him.

"Coffee," he grunts. *Well, at least he said something.*

Blake reaches out and grabs the Styrofoam cup from my hand. *Excuse moi?* Before I can tell him I didn't bring him coffee and he just hijacked mine, he takes a large sip. His face says it all and he wipes his mouth with the back of his hand. Serves him right.

"That's mine," I state plainly.

"I thought you brought me coffee."

"Why would you think that?" I'm not his assistant. We've never even met. How am I supposed to know how he likes his coffee?

"As a peace offering," he explains with a shrug. "Since you said you're not sure how my helmet fits considering my ego makes my head twelve sizes too big."

He doesn't bother hiding the cold contempt in his eyes. Oh boy. There goes my secret hope that he hadn't heard that episode of *Coffee with Champions*. This is going to be *fun, fun, fun*.

"Your head looks pretty normal-sized today," I comment coolly.

"You ragging on me to millions of people probably deflated it a bit."

That's a bit of an overestimation. My podcast may have hit number five on Spotify's podcast charts at one point, but millions? C'mon. I'm no Joe Rogan…or Connor Brixton.

"I also talked about the amount of raw talent you have," I remind him.

"That's not anything I haven't heard before. I know how talented I am."

I take back what I said about his head looking normal-sized. It's inflating right in front of my eyes.

"You insulted my driving," he fumes, his chiseled jaw tensing. "And me."

"I discussed you in one episode of a podcast that's no longer a thing. I apologize if I hurt your feelings, but I wouldn't have accepted this job if I didn't think you were remarkably talented."

"You shouldn't have accepted the job." He narrows his eyes. "Not sure why you did."

Jeez. Make a few critical comments about a guy and he acts like you've mortally wounded him.

"No offense, Blake, but grow a pair and get over it. I know for a fact there are women who've said way worse things about you. I read the tabloids."

I swear one corner of his mouth twitches, but it's gone just as quickly as it appears. Blake's publicist Marion walks in wearing the exact shade of red lipstick I was praying Poppy didn't get me. Her shirt's wrinkled and smudges of residual mascara sit under her eyes. I don't blame her. I know she's been working overtime to help Blake's image. The fact that she secured a book deal so quickly is astonishing. I can only imagine how overwhelmed she feels by it all.

"Nice to meet you in person, Ella!" The crow's feet at her eyes fold as she smiles. "I'm glad to see you two are already getting acquainted with one another."

The open defiance of Blake's glower tells a different story. He'd rather get acquainted with the casket he hopes to put me in. I should've added something stronger than almond milk to my coffee. Maybe Jameson?

Keith waltzes in moments later looking like a very handsome Daniel Craig during his James Bond era—rugged and weathered, but in an extremely sexy way. He's got the whole salt-and-pepper look going on even though he's in his late thirties. I wouldn't be surprised if Blake kickstarted his grays. If that starts happening to me, Blake can pay my salon bills.

Marion video conferences George in before starting a "team" meeting. I nod along as she talks, taking notes on my computer. It's not anything new. Even though George hired me, I still had to meet with both Marion and Keith before being *officially* brought on board. The life of Blake Hollis is nothing to joke about, after all.

Blake doesn't say much except a few mumbled "hmphs" and "sure, yeahs." It's impossible not to stare at him. I wonder if he's ever broken his nose. There's a slightly crooked curve in the middle. He catches me looking at him and shoots me a wink. *Who fucking winks at someone?* Especially after our conversation, if you can even call it that.

It disarms me, turning my cheeks the color of Marion's lipstick. I fight back the urge to blurt out that I was only staring because I'm concerned that if he keeps scowling, he's going to need Botox by the time he turns thirty next year. I avoid looking in his general direction for the rest of the meeting, especially because I can feel his eyes fixed on me.

MCALLISTER'S TEAM is huge with just over two hundred people. That's not even including those based out of their headquarters in London. This means I have a lot of names to learn and a lot of people to meet. I throw on a McAllister shirt courtesy of Keith, slip on my cute new necklace—which is actually a lanyard I have to wear in order to get access into the paddock—and am on my way. Day two, here we go!

The air is electric as everyone gets ready for the first race of the tour. I've never seen anything like it before. Engineers, mechanics, drivers, media—anyone and everyone seems to be here. They buzz around, never stopping in one place for too long. I quickly realize this is not the time to interrupt people to introduce myself. The team's too focused on making sure Blake and McAllister have a successful Grand Prix.

I'm wandering around aimlessly when a girl in a McAllister shirt that matches my own blazes a path straight toward me. Before I know what's happening, she's pulling me into a hug. *Um, hello to you too, strange woman.*

"Ella! It's so nice to meet you! I was worried I wasn't going to be able to introduce myself before the race. I've been running around like a bloody chicken with its head cut off. I'm glad I found you, though. There are so many people, but it was easy to spot you since there aren't too many women around here. Not sure if you noticed that or not. You've worked in sports before, so you're probably used to the testosterone overload. How's your first day here? Or have you been here for a few days? I can't remember."

She's talking so quickly it's hard to keep up. She could've just asked me to join her pyramid scheme and I would've dumbly nodded. Her dark blond hair blurs as she suddenly steps a few feet away, stopping a pair of guys walking past us. *What is happening?* Blondie poses the two guys for a photo, snapping pictures of them on her camera. I take a moment to study her. She looks like she should be in front of the camera instead of behind it with her heart-shaped face, high cheekbones, and perfectly pouty lips.

"Sorry about that!" She bounces back over to me. Her British accent is unbelievably posh. "They've been impossible to find, so I had to get a photo while I could. I'm Josie Bancroft, by the way. I do content creation and brand management for McAllister."

I stick out my hand for her to shake. "I'm Ella Gold, but you seem to know that already."

"Everybody knows who you are, babes." She shoots me a dazzling smile. As if proving her point, a few mechanics walk past us, waving at Josie and giving me a knowing head nod. "You're the writer-slash-journalist-slash-saint working with Blake this season. The one who said someone should take the stick out of his ass and hit him over the head with it."

Yep, that's me.

Josie takes over as my handler/fairy godmother and makes all the necessary introductions. I've known her for all of an hour and I can already tell she's a force to be reckoned with.

She walks me through the team's motorhome in the afternoon. Formula 1 motorhomes are million-dollar structures that get built, broken down, and rebuilt at every single race. It's the team's base for race weekends and is an equally productive and entertaining environment. There are rooms for meetings, a cafeteria, multiple bars, a barista. Plus, each driver has their own hospitality suite. It's a five-star hotel condensed into two floors and a rooftop.

We're sitting on said rooftop, away from the noise and

crowds, when Josie asks how meeting Blake was. I fill her in on our conversation.

"He's every bit as charming as he is caustic," she says, not at all surprised by my recap. "You get used to it. He keeps his inner circle really tight, so it takes him a while to warm up, but once you get to know him, he's actually a decent guy."

"Is he as man-whorish as he seems?"

She starts singing Elvis's "Hound Dog," much to my amusement.

"He sleeps with more groupies than John Mayer," Josie says nonchalantly. "Taylor Swift could write nine albums from one night with Blake. I wouldn't know firsthand, but that's what I've heard."

It's official. Josie is my new favorite person.

"They're all like that, though," she adds. "Theo—he's Blake's driving partner—says the only things they need in life are points, podium wins, and pussy."

The water I've just taken a sip of comes spraying out of my mouth. I'm the last one to be offended by a dirty mouth, but yikes. I tell Josie she can easily get that trending on Twitter. #PointsPodiumPussy. *Go, team, go!*

"My boyfriend wants me to wear a chastity belt around these guys and I don't blame him." She winks at me. "I can tell we're going to get on quite well this season, Ella."

I already miss Poppy and Jack, so the idea of having a new partner in crime, especially one who's feisty, brings a smile to my face. I have a feeling I'm going to need someone like Josie to make it through this year unscathed.

FOUR
BLAKE

THE MOMENT I arrive at the sponsor event, I feel it—the excitement pulsing through the air, the energy flowing through the room. Man, I love it. Everyone is hopeful about their chance at victory. With no points distributed and rivalries from the previous year ignored, we all focus on the current season rather than the last. I smile as I survey the room. After a disastrous season last year, I'm ready to be back. New season, new mindset. I'm going to protect the throne that's rightfully mine and add another World Championship to my roster. Fuck anyone who tries to take it from me.

The first event of the season is always overly extravagant. Limousines and expensive cars queue up outside the hotel as guests wearing expensive diamonds and luxury watches sip champagne inside the ballroom. It's the usual crowd of snobby, rich white men looking like penguins in their too-tight tuxedos. They're trying to relive their youth by living vicariously through us—which means giving us money. Not that I'm complaining. Their money allows me to drive the best car for the best team. It also buys absurdly large ice sculptures.

"Hey, hotshot," Theo calls out from the bar. "Fancy a bevvy?"

I snake my way through waiters quietly sharing hors d'oeuvres and sidle up next to my driving partner. He's sipping a Cosmo with no shame, his navy-blue eyes dancing with mischief.

"If it isn't my favorite Formula 1 fuckboy." I slap him on the back in greeting. People find it odd that Theo and I are so close. Formula 1 is one of the only sports where your teammate also happens to be your biggest competitor. But the two of us have known each other since we were kids. He's one persistent motherfucker and wouldn't leave me alone until I agreed to be his friend. We've grown up racing together and rather than turn the competition into a bitter rivalry, we use it to push ourselves to become better drivers.

He rubs a hand over his beard-stubbled chin. "I prefer Formula 1 'fuckman' rather than 'fuckboy.'"

"I'll consider it once your balls drop," I tease.

Lucas, an AlphaVite driver, appears on Theo's other side. His usually shaggy dirty-blond hair is slicked back, the silver rings on his fingers glinting from the crystal chandelier dangling overhead. "Speaking of balls, how was your winter break, Theo?"

Theo had been spotted getting lovey-dovey with a famous model in Cannes, only to be seen making out with an up-and-coming movie star in Paris a few days later. An ugly social media war had started between the girls, rivaling an episode of reality TV. He found the entire situation amusing.

After the end of last season, I'd forced myself into hibernation, meaning I hadn't joined the off-season party circuit with my friends. I'd needed time to reset and refocus.

"Who cares about that when Blake still hasn't pointed out who George's lovely writer is," Theo says, eyeing the room.

He and Lucas both scan the crowd, pointing out a handful

of old, grumpy-looking men. I've failed to tell them about Ella. The amount of shit they're going to give me is not something I'm looking forward to. PlayMedia is the end all be all of everything sports-related in America, and Luc's an avid listener of Connor Brixton's *Trash Talk* and Ella's *Coffee with Champions*. He's the entire reason I even heard her Formula 1 episode.

"I bet it's that one." Lucas points to a short and stout bald guy.

"Oh! Good guess." Theo nods while running a hand through his nut-brown hair. "I love his handlebar mustache. I was thinking it's the bloke by the door. The lanky one that sort of looks like a green bean?"

"You're both so wrong," I grumble resignedly.

Scanning the room for Ella, I find her easily. She's quite impossible to miss; I'm surprised I'm just now noticing her.

"Wait." Theo chokes, placing his pink drink on the bar. "She's the journalist?"

I give a short nod, unable to take my eyes off her. She looks absolutely stunning in a floor-length black dress with her dark brown hair falling in loose waves down her back. The outfit she wore to our meeting the other day hid the fact that she's got a great body with curves in all the right places. It's one I wouldn't mind having naked underneath mine. She's the perfect combination of sweet and sultry, and it seems like I'm not the only one who's noticing.

She's deep in conversation with Josie. It's no surprise that Josie's taken Ella under her wing. She's been with McAllister for a few years and knows everybody and everything. I like Josie. We're not the best of friends, but we're friendly enough. Theo's tried getting with her, but she's loyal to her boyfriend, Andrew. One of my favorite pastimes is watching her shut my driving partner down.

"Dude." Lucas's jaw drops to the floor, his usual cool, calm, and collected demeanor disappearing. "Do you know who that is?"

"Blake's writer, duh," Theo answers with an eye roll. "He just said that, mate. Listen up."

"That's Ella Gold…as in the host of the *Coffee with Champions* podcast."

I don't bother mentioning that the podcast is no longer around, so she's no longer the host.

"The one who said epically hilarious things about Blakey Blake?" Theo nudges my arm. "When the hell were you planning on sharing this with us?"

"Never," I mumble under my breath. Clearly, that was wishful thinking.

My friends sip their drinks, giving Ella a look I know all too well. *Hell no.* I momentarily tear my gaze away from her to glare at them. "She's off-limits, mates."

Theo tilts his head at me in amusement. "Are you staking a claim?"

I roll my eyes and ignore the question. I don't do relationships and my friends damn well know this. I've been walked away from too many times to think anyone would want to stay, so hit it and quit it tends to be my strategy. I'm more than satisfied. If there're no expectations, no one gets hurt.

Lucas and Theo aren't able to pester me for much longer before we're herded to our respective tables. I'm stuck sitting on the end next to Marion while Ella's place card seats her between Theo and Andreas, our team principal. I watch from across the table as they talk amongst themselves.

The dinner is just as boring as I remember. The head of the FIA makes a speech, some sponsors talk, and a few team principals make a toast. Shortly after dessert is served, Ella sits in Marion's now-abandoned seat and greets me with a sexy-assin smile. Her eyes are the color of the caramel apples I used to get with my sister at Camden Market growing up. A swirling mixture of green, brown, and gold.

Apparently, she's decided to pretend our entire conversation from the other day never happened. George wasn't fucking around when he said she doesn't tolerate big egos. I'm more than happy to put that to the test, though.

"Good first night back?" she asks.

"Mm-hmm." I eye the glass in her hand. "I didn't peg you for a rum and Coke girl."

"That's because I'm not." She shakes her head as color blooms across her cheeks. "Last time I drank rum, I tried getting into my apartment with my credit card instead of my key."

A chuckle vibrates through my chest.

"It's Coke Zero," she confirms. "I'm more of a Diet Coke girl, but I'll take what I can get. Since I'm a lightweight and this is my first big event...I figured it'd be best to stick to pop."

"Pop?"

"Soda. Sorry, Midwest habit. I'll most likely call your trainers gym shoes at some point, too." She takes a sip of her drink, the pink lip gloss she's wearing leaving a mark.

"So," she says, leaning forward like she's sharing a secret. "Were you pretending I was the chicken?"

I stare at her with fascinated confusion. *Huh?* I was definitely looking at breasts, but they were hers, not the chicken's. From the way her dress accentuates her chest, it looks like she has a great rack. Perky and firm. I wonder if her nipples are classic pink, pale coral, or cherry red.

"You were stabbing at it pretty aggressively," she explains, thrusting the tumbling hair back from her eyes. "Either no one ever taught you how to properly use a fork and knife or you were using it as a voodoo doll."

The throaty laugh I release catches me off guard. "No, I wasn't voodoo-doll-ing the chicken. I'm just not hungry."

I don't add that the emergency anti-anxiety meds I took earlier suppressed my appetite. The weight of everyone's expectations is sitting heavily on my shoulders and I needed something to take the edge off.

Ella plucks the untouched dinner roll from my plate, ripping off a small piece before popping it into her mouth. She doesn't even bother buttering it.

I blink rapidly. "How do you know I wasn't saving that for later?"

"Were you?"

"Well, no. But who steals someone's dinner roll?"

Ella throws her head back in unabashed laughter, the sound wholesome and seductive at the same time. "You just said you weren't hungry, and it's hardly called stealing. This isn't *Les Misérables*."

She opens her purse to take out her phone and I can't help but notice the pepper spray nestled next to her lip gloss. She's a pretty woman traveling to foreign countries, so it makes sense, but I have insane security who can do a lot more damage than a small canister can.

"Oh, wow, it's late," she comments to herself. "I'm going to head up and get some sleep. Jet lag and all of that. See you tomorrow?"

I give a quick nod, not able to stop the mixture of incredulity and exasperation I'm feeling. Don't really have much of a choice but to see her tomorrow. Her arse looks damn fucking fantastic in her dress as she sashays away, completely unaware of the looks of appreciation it's garnering. At least I'm looking forward to seeing *that* tomorrow.

The hour before any Grand Prix is the most hectic. The hour before the first Grand Prix of the season? Absolute fucking mayhem. What people see on TV are the drivers casually rolling onto the grid, ready for the race. They don't see the behind-the-scenes. Mechanics giving the car last-minute checks, engineers running through strategy, and the media buzzing around, asking annoying questions. The garage is the heart of the entire team and it's bumbling with everyone running by and shouting in organized chaos.

Sixty minutes: I do a few final stretches and reaction drills, while my team preps the generators and cooling fans for the grid.

Forty minutes: The pit lane opens, and I exit the garage with my mechanics and their equipment. Fans cheer from the stands, the sound like music to my ears. I do a quick installation lap around the track, familiarizing myself with track conditions and noting any last-minute adjustments that'll have to be made.

Thirty minutes: My engine powers off and I'm pushed to my grid position. I hop out of the cockpit and head to the front of the grid for the formal procedures, as the mechanics on the grid check my car, measuring and monitoring what they can. I calm my rapidly beating heart as Bahrain's national anthem plays.

Twenty minutes: Josie and the rest of McAllister's marketing team run around my car, snapping photos that I'm sure I'll see on McAllister's social media accounts later today. Journalists circle my car like vultures, asking questions I'm able to ignore thanks to my headphones.

Fifteen minutes: I get back into my car, my gloved hands resting steadily on the steering wheel. A sense of calm envelops me. Nowhere else in the world do I feel like I'm most myself.

Ten minutes: Everyone but the drivers, start crews, and FIA officials leaves the grid. My chest expands, a lightness fluttering through me.

Seven minutes: My team performs their last-minute checks before removing the tire blankets and lowering my car from its stand.

Five minutes: Personnel and staff exit the grid, leaving just the twenty drivers—my competition, my friends, my enemies. My whole world is condensed into one two-hour circuit.

Three minutes: We take our formation lap, trying to simultaneously warm our brakes and tires while cooling our engines. I perform a bite point find to help with my clutch control before driving into the grid again. I'm upfront in pole position, where I belong.

One minute: The five red light start sequence is initiated. The first light on the starting gantry flicks on. Let the countdown begin. The race engineers buzz in the radio attached to my ear. *Let's go, let's go, let's go.*

Forty-five seconds: Another light goes on. The excitement of the crowd drowns out the sound of my engine.

Thirty seconds: Three lights now illuminate the starting gantry. My helmet obscures the smile radiating on my face. I'm ready to go.

Fifteen seconds: The fourth light turns on. I can't tell if it's me or my car vibrating with energy.

Ten seconds: I hyper-focus on the track ahead of me as the fifth and final light switches on.

Five seconds: The calm before the storm. My fingers drum against the wheel. A burst of anxious energy appears just as quickly as it dissolves.

Zero seconds: All five lights extinguish, signaling the start of the race. It's go time, baby. I'm ready to remind the world who I am and what I'm capable of.

FIVE
ELLA

IT'S ONLY the first Grand Prix of the season, but I'm already addicted to the visceral feeling it elicits. The hum of the cars, the vibration as they whiz by, the cheers from the fans, the smell of burning rubber and fuel. It's a high I imagine no recreational drug can ever compare to. It's mesmerizing, the cars shooting by in a technicolor blur.

I stand in the garage with the pit crew to watch the race. Mechanics don their helmets, armored with their tools, ready for any emergency pit stop. Guests crowd toward the TV in the back, fighting for the best view. Most of the action is in the midfield where the drivers battle it out to secure points for their teams, but everyone in the garage is focused on the McAllister men.

The reckless driver from last season is gone and forgotten, replaced by the Blake Hollis fans scream over and sponsors fight for. He's devastatingly fast. His charming smile and devilishly handsome good looks are an easy distraction, but he's a cold-blooded killer. All of these drivers are impressive, but there can only be one winner, and Blake's talent speaks for itself.

Blake keeps his lead for the first thirty laps. Theo's not far behind him, with Everest's Harry Thompson and AlphaVite's Lucas Adler close behind them, aiming for a top position. The pendulum swung back and forth between Harry and Blake last year, and a win for Blake will hopefully set the tone for the season. The thick anticipation in the garage prohibits much conversation besides the occasional cheer or curse. The 191.5 miles leave room for a lot to happen and no one wants to jinx anything.

Blake takes a pit stop at lap thirty-six. *Holy shit.* I've never seen something happen so quickly in my life. Before I can even take a step forward, he's zooming back out of the pit lane, new tires fitted and ready for the second half of the race. Two point four seconds...it took the crew two point four seconds to change his tires. Want to know what I can do in that time? Nothing. Literally nothing. I can't even say my full name in that time frame.

The sixty-four laps end with Blake securing his first win of the season. Everyone in the garage storms out to the fences, shouting and whooping as Blake hops out of his car. It's the boost of confidence McAllister's brooding Brit needs. Soon enough, the drivers are back in the garage, elated grins lighting up their faces.

Theo takes off his helmet and shakes his head, beads of sweat flying at me. *Gross.* Although Blake's been tactfully ignoring me, Theo's been more than happy to step in. He's been my personal Formula 1 tour guide for the past few days. He's shown me around the motorhome, given me pointers on who'll be most helpful with the book, and let me ask him questions about his car. I like him a lot. He's got major golden retriever vibes—friendly, high-energy, and always running around. It doesn't hurt that he's extremely handsome.

"Impressed by my skills?" Theo winks at me.

"Never doubted I would be." I take a step back to avoid

more sweat hitting me. "Third place is a podium win. Ain't too shabby, my friend."

"Oof." He stumbles back as if stabbed in the heart. "Just a friend, babe?"

Blake overhears us as he walks past and slaps his friend on the back of the head.

"Winning first isn't shabby either, Blakey boy." Theo turns to me with a sheepish look on his face. I'm sure Blake's given him an earful about me being here. "He's not usually such a wanker."

I shrug, pretending I don't care. Blake may not want me interviewing him, but he can't avoid the journalists at the post-race press conference. It's the first one of the season, so I have no doubt I should be there taking notes.

I'm looking for an open chair when I spy Josie. I climb over lots of knees and feet before sliding into the empty chair next to her.

Her dark brown eyes shoot me a knowing look. "How's Blake been? Any better?"

"Let's just say I've made no progress whatsoever."

She sighs sympathetically. "Imagine trying to get him to sit down for a YouTube Q and A. My new personal hell. He's so crabby sometimes."

"I'm sure press conferences aren't much better."

I nod toward Blake, who is not so subtly pretending Harry, who placed second, isn't next to him at the long table at the front of the room. The two racers' rivalry is well-known and almost came to blows last season. I talked about it in great depth on my podcast last year. I don't think Blake dislikes Harry as a person; I just think he hates that Harry was there to pick up the pieces when he struggled. Now there are two Brits competing on two of the best teams—one veteran with a sultry smirk, one newbie with a sweet smile.

Josie starts singing "Macho Man" by the Village People.

I've learned that she loves incorporating song lyrics in place of actual sentences. Blake briefly glances in my direction, a slight frown appearing when he notices me. I bet if I asked him what superpower he wants, he would say teleportation. That way he could send my ass back to New York.

The press conference starts off with all the usual questions.

How do you feel about the race?

Were you confident in your starting grid position?

Were you surprised by the pace of any of the drivers?

How does it feel to be back?

I'm starting to zone out just as a reporter asks, "Thompson, how does it feel to place podium during the first race of the season? You made your mark last year with some solid wins over who some are calling your biggest competition. Do you think this is a precursor to what the rest of the season will look like?"

Now I'm on high alert. Harry chuckles and rubs a hand over his chin. He's twenty-three years old, but his clean-shaven appearance makes him look even younger.

"Well, I'm not sure I'd say Hollis is my biggest competition. I'd like to think I'm my own biggest competitor. But it's only the first race of a long season, so we'll see what happens."

I mentally applaud him on his neutral answer.

"Blake," a different reporter asks. "Last season you said Harry was, and I'm quoting you here, 'a low-budget knock-off version' of you with 'driving skills equivalent to a senior citizen at night after a glass of wine.' Do you still feel the same?"

I cough to cover up a laugh. His comment may be rude, but it's kind of funny.

"I'm way better looking than Thompson, so I doubt I would've compared us." Blake grins at the reporter before taking a sip of his water. "And Theo's nan just passed her driver's test at the age of ninety…not much of an insult."

His deep voice and British accent are quite the panty-dropping combination. I accidentally lick my lips. Although his answer is a complete non-answer, it's much better than anyone was expecting. Given his change in demeanor from last season's press conferences, it's clear he's been through some extensive media training in the past few months. Good job, Marion. I'm pleasantly surprised by his carefree tone and relaxed smile. Now, if only he would act that way toward me.

I GAVE Blake his space during Bahrain, but we're in Australia at Grand Prix number two and he's still avoiding me like I'm the flu and he's unvaccinated. Blake is the founder, president, and most active member of the Go Fuck Yourself, Ella Club. I feel like I'm going to have to Guantanamo Bay him in order to get him to talk. I've never waterboarded someone before, but if it comes to that…I plead the fifth. He's almost thirty, yet his emotional intelligence is closer to that of a three-year-old. This shouldn't surprise me, but it annoyingly still does. I don't think men exist. They're all boys.

I've had other people to interview—mechanics, engineers, the marketing team—but Blake's going to have to sit down with me sometime soon. He can't keep dodging me forever. I've got a book to write and he's got an image that needs rehab.

The days leading up to the race, I follow him from a safe distance. He barely has a second to himself. The team arrives on Thursday to settle in and attend the first sponsor event of the weekend. Fridays are filled with practice and technical debriefs where the team evaluates the setup of the car and its performance. Saturday is more practice and then a warm-up before qualifying the car. It's a stressful day because if Blake makes a single mistake or suffers a mechanical issue during his qualifying lap, he can find himself starting the race from the back of the grid. If he lands in one of the top three positions, he attends a special press conference and then attends more debriefs, more press conferences, and another sponsor event. And this is all before the actual race day.

I spend the night before the Grand Prix tossing and turning. I give up on falling back asleep and scroll on my phone until my alarm goes off at 6:30 a.m. I've been trying to work out every morning to give my days some structure. My therapist suggested I find an activity that lets me feel in control; I chose exercise. It's become an outlet for me. An added perk is that the stronger I get, the more capable I feel of defending myself.

I'm allowed to use McAllister's facilities as long as I'm not obstructing or distracting the drivers. Turns out, I'm not the problem this morning, Blake is. He's working out with Sam, his performance coach, at the other end of the gym. I didn't realize I purchased tickets to a gun show this morning, but there Blake is, showing off his arms like the weapons they are.

Can there be a rule about the drivers distracting others in the gym? How does he manage to make *sweat* look hot? His gray shirt is drenched and it's making me warm even though I haven't started my workout. There's no way I'm going on the treadmill while Blake is five feet away from me. I don't want him to think I'm following him around before his day even starts. Neither of them notices me, so I sneak over to a mat behind the free weights. Looks like today's going to be a light day.

My spot has a great vantage point because I can see and hear them without being spotted. And you bet your ass I turn the volume down on my earbuds to listen to what they're saying. Blake seems at ease, which is nice to see. Sam's been part of Blake's teams for years. It's his job to make sure Blake's in the best place mentally and physically to perform at his peak. It looks like last year didn't scare him off because he's still Blake's right-hand man.

I attempt some leg exercises and crunches, making sure anything I do keeps me hidden below the height of the weights. I'm not looking my best thanks to a rough night of sleep. I have bags under my eyes, and they definitely aren't designer. Oscar de la Renta? More like Old Navy.

I'm resting on my back, sprawled out like a starfish, giving myself a minute of rest in between sets, when a shadow crosses over my face. I glance up to find Blake hovering over me. My body freezes. Not because I'm scared, but because I can see directly up his shorts. Thankfully, he's wearing compression shorts, but I really can't handle the view this early in the morning…or probably ever.

Blake tilts his head as if trying to figure out if I'm doing some new yoga stretch before asking, "Why are you here?"

I roll my eyes. "To knit a blanket. Obviously."

What the hell else does one do in a gym? His eyes stay trained on me as I readjust so I'm sitting cross-legged. Feeling unnerved by his stare, I blurt out, "Why did the cheeseburger get a gym membership?"

Really, Ella? A dad joke?

I wait for him to answer, which he soon does. "Um…why?"

"To get bigger buns."

I'm about ready to knock myself out with a dumbbell so I don't have to die from embarrassment when Blake lets out a low chuckle. The sound reverberates off the gym walls and sends goose bumps up my arms. Definitely blaming my hardened nipples on the air conditioning and not his laugh.

"Hey, Ella!" Sam positions himself next to Blake and shoots me a friendly wink. "We're about to grab breakfast if you want to join us. If you're done working out, that is."

I hop up with ease. The hopeful look I give Blake goes unnoticed, but I don't care. Breakfast with him is the most progress I've made. He's quiet the entire walk to the motorhome. I can see the muscles in his neck ticking in irritation. It's clear he's not happy I'm crashing their breakfast. Too bad, so sad. He's going to be a lot unhappier when I eat at the pace of a snail to drag out our time together.

Chef Albie claps his hands together as he notices me behind Blake. "Ella! I can't believe you're back after I almost killed you yesterday morning."

I'd tried Albie's French toast and he put so much maple syrup and powdered sugar on it that I almost choked to death. Blake's eyebrows rise in surprise at our familiarity.

"It still tasted better than anything I could ever make," I reassure him.

Albie nods at Blake. "She's a good taste tester."

Thank you for the vote of approval, Chef. He fills my plate with every carb imaginable. It's stacked with potatoes, a new and improved French toast, a croissant, a crepe filled with Nutella and strawberries, and a breakfast burrito. I can eat maybe a third of this. His eyes are definitely bigger than my stomach.

Blake slyly eyes my croissant as we situate ourselves at a small table in the front of the motorhome.

"Want some?" Half lands on his plate before he can respond. "If anyone needs to carb up, it's you, not me. I don't think my crunches even burned a sesame seed."

He shrugs his shoulders. "I don't know, the walk over here probably burned off a few poppy seeds, at least."

The man makes jokes!

Sam spends the entirety of breakfast asking me about what I've been up to. I know via Blake's calendar that all he's done is spend time at the McAllister team HQ in London, using the simulator to prepare for this weekend. I spent the week in London as well, but George went with Blake to talk to the team so I could explore my new home base. Josie doesn't live too far away and was more than happy to show me around. I swear it's like someone shoved a battery up her ass. The girl does not run out of energy.

Blake seems floored to learn I've been here since Monday considering he only flew in yesterday afternoon.

"I've been spending time with the pit wall engineers," I explain coolly. "I figure that until you decide I'm not public enemy number one and actually let me do my job, I may as well get to know the rest of the team."

Sam nearly chokes on the eggs he's shoveling into his mouth. Blake doesn't seem to appreciate me calling him out based on the way his nostrils flare. *Whatever.* If he takes the time to get to know me, he'll quickly learn I don't back down easily. I've interviewed some of the douchiest sports players and worked in a boy's club culture for the past four years. His attitude is nothing I haven't dealt with before.

"I don't think you're public enemy number one," he huffs, his voice quiet and tense.

"Blake." I raise my eyebrows. "If your looks could kill, I'd be dead already."

I focus on cutting my crepe, not bothering to watch his reaction. I have a feeling it involves an icy glare.

"I just don't like people digging into my life."

"Well"—I sigh—"you probably shouldn't have agreed to partake in the book then."

His brown eyes narrow to slits while his lips form a hard, thin line. A brilliant idea suddenly hits me. I'm trying not to bounce in my seat with excitement, but I can't help it. I've never been great at hiding my emotions. There's a reason I'm not an actress.

"How do you feel about a little wager?"

His forehead puckers in thought. "Depends on what it is."

"You place podium later today," I offer before revising my idea. "No, scratch that. You place P1, and you can interview me instead. If you place anything but P1, I get to ask you anything I want."

The intrigued look in his eyes lets me know he's in. He's going to try to place podium regardless of this bet and we both know it, but I also knew he wouldn't back down from a challenge. When's he going to learn that neither will I?

SIX

BLAKE

THEO LOVES ELLA EVER since he learned that she said girls try to climb him like they're koalas and he's a eucalyptus tree. He's mentioned this about three times in the past week even though I heard it myself when I listened to her podcast. Her comment doesn't surprise me since I've seen firsthand how girls fall over Theo's Australian accent and larger-than-life personality.

He'd love to have someone write his biography considering he's the most open person in the world. He gives more details than anyone would *ever* want or need. A reporter once asked what he eats before a race and he somehow managed to turn that into a debate over which mythical creature he could win a fight against. He landed on a unicorn, in case you were wondering. Needless to say, that reporter doesn't ask him as many questions now.

He's been hanging out in my suite before the race, badgering me with questions to try to get inside my head. *Do you like Ella? Did she tell you about when she met Tom Brady? When she interviews you, does she write shit down or does she record you? Have you lied about anything to see if she'll call you out on it?* He peers at me, waiting for details, but I don't offer anything.

"You need to relax." He laughs at my scowl. "Ella's a cool bird. You'll like her if you stop being a moody asshole. Name one girl who knows what a bite point find is or can easily talk about the aerodynamics of downforce."

"Ella's a sportswriter. That's her job." I aggressively sip my water, drips splashing onto my chest. "And I'm sure lots of girls know that. Don't be sexist."

"Some may say Formula 1 is sexist," he replies casually.

Excuse me? Formula 1 is sexist? I'm not saying he's wrong, but this is the man who asked if the Chinese food we were ordering had any misogyny in it. He meant MSG and somehow confused the two. Lucas almost cracked a rib from laughing so hard.

"Did you know that out of almost one thousand Formula 1 drivers who have raced in a Grand Prix, only two of those have been women?" he continues. "How wild is that?"

Shock weaves its way through my body. I'm debating calling a doctor because a concussion is the only reasonable explanation for Theo's sudden interest in this topic.

He looks at me before adding, "And out of all female journalists, only twenty-one percent write about sports."

Theo's talking as if this is the most normal conversation we've ever had. As if five minutes ago, he hadn't asked me if he could pop a woman's breast implant by grabbing it too hard. So, excuse my confusion.

"I'm glad she's teaching you how to be a productive member of society, Theo."

"I promise she'll surprise you if you give her a chance."

"Why are you so obsessed with her?" I snap in annoyance. I'm starting to not like how buddy-buddy the two of them have gotten after a few fucking race weekends. He even got coffee with her and Josie in London over the weekend. I know I haven't exactly made it easy on her, but she's supposed to be spending time with *me*, not Theo.

"I like her, Lucas likes her, Josie likes her, Sam likes her," Theo answers. "You're the only one who seems to have an issue with her, mate. She poked some fun at you on a podcast —who cares? You're a big boy."

"If I agree to spend an hour or two with her, will you stop talking about it?"

I don't mention Ella's little wager. She wins either way because it'll force us to spend time together, but if she's going to spend the season asking me things, I won't say no to a chance to return the favor. No one likes being asked questions that can trigger painful memories or scratch at secrets that are best kept locked away.

"Yes, but I'm going to fact-check you and ask Ella so you can't lie your way out."

He sounds like Keith and Marion. Both have been texting me nonstop, asking how things are going. Spending time with Ella will probably be more pleasant than having to tell my team that I've been making her job near impossible.

"Fine." I roll my eyes. "Now drop it."

He answers me with a thumbs-up. I slip my earbuds back into my ears to indicate I'm done with the conversation. He takes the hint and heads back to his own suite, most likely to play video games.

Curiosity finally beats out bitterness and I've been listening to *Coffee with Champions*. I started from episode one last week and am already on episode twenty-one. It's a damn good podcast. Even I can admit that. It's equally educational and entertaining. Ella interviews everyone from the coach of the Giants, to an ESPN correspondent, to the agent of three very prominent football players. The podcast series abruptly ends with no reason as to why. Ella's a great writer, but she fucking shines as a host. So, my question is…what the fuck happened?

. . .

SWEET, sweet victory. There's nothing better than a
champagne spray from P1. I check my phone during the press
conference after the Australian Grand Prix, catching up on
texts and emails, when a new message pops up. I didn't give
Ella my number, but clearly someone did.

> FROM: ELLA GOLD
>
> Congrats on the win! I should be the one asking
> you the questions, but a deal's a deal.
> Breakfast at 10 a.m. tomorrow?

I spy her sitting in the second row, writing something on
her iPad with her stylus. She's wearing an oversized McAllister
shirt and ripped jeans with "gym shoes." I quickly text her
back.

> BLAKE HOLLIS
>
> That works. Just so you know, it's not very
> professional to be coloring on your iPad during
> a press conference.

> ELLA GOLD
>
> I'm actually doing a puzzle, but coloring isn't a
> bad idea. Want me to draw you a picture? I'm
> great at stick figures.

A smile tugs at the corners of my mouth before I can stop
it. Ella was everywhere this weekend. Talking to the engineers
about the DRS. Asking the pit crew questions about the tires
we were using for the race. Hanging out with the staff in the
motorhome. There's no avoiding her and her fucking infectious
laugh.

Lucas nudges me in the arm, telling me I was just
asked a question. *Oh fuck.* I wasn't listening to a single
word.

"I didn't quite catch that." I apologize with a head nod. "Could you repeat that, please?"

I'M surprised to find Ella already at breakfast when I arrive. Thanks to Theo's never-ending Instagram story, I know she went to a bar to celebrate with the team. Going out with Theo takes about a year off anyone's life, so I'm surprised she's alive and well. I'd been banking on a hungover and unpleasant Ella.

She greets me with a small wave. "Morning!"

Her hair is tied back into a messy ponytail and the glasses she has on can only be described as grandmum inspired. She's in biker shorts and a Queen shirt. I wonder if she researched what kind of music I like and wore that shirt to win brownie points being that I'm a huge Freddie Mercury fan.

I slide into the seat across from her and a waiter fills the empty cup in front of me with fresh coffee. It's a good thing I like my coffee black because Ella is pouring the entire carafe of milk into her own cup. No wonder why it tasted so horrible when I drank it a few weeks ago.

"Saw you went out with Theo last night. I definitely thought you'd be late."

"Nope. I'm a professional and I'm always on time." Her mouth twists into a knowing smile. "Plus, this is the first time you've willingly been in a room with me, so I wouldn't dream of being tardy."

I ignore the comment and take a folded sheet of paper out of my pocket. Before going to bed last night, I took some time putting together a list of questions for Ella. Some easy, some uncomfortable, some to push her buttons.

She whistles in appreciation. "I'm thoroughly impressed, Blake."

I ignore the compliment and get right down to business. "First question. Why'd you take a job working for me?"

An arched eyebrow flicks up in amusement. "Technically, I work for George. My job just happens to be you."

Touché, Ella. Touché.

"Why'd you leave your job to spend the season with a guy you barely know?"

"For you to be influential enough for people to want to read about your life? That's impressive, not to mention brave. I'm excited to be a part of that. And I left my job before deciding to take this job. They're not mutually exclusive."

"Why'd you leave, though?" I press.

I tried searching online to see if something scandalous happened and didn't find much. PlayMedia announced the end of the podcast on their social media pages but gave no reason as to why. Some fans speculated on Twitter, although it's clear their guess is as good as mine.

"Does it matter?" She tries coming off casual, but her tone is snappy.

"Why should I be honest with you if you're not honest with me?"

It comes out harsh, but I don't apologize. If I'm expected to share my life story with her, she can cough up one detail about hers.

"It doesn't matter why I left, Blake. I just did."

Ella leans back in her chair, observing me with a cautious gaze. Part of me wants to dig deeper, but a sliver of guilt works its way through my body. I've suffered from anxiety since I was a kid and recognize how her shoulders tense and her brows dip. Add in the way she's clutching her necklace like it's a life-line and she's easier to read than a stop sign. *Shit.* I didn't mean to push a button hard enough for her to shut down and go on the defensive. I just wanted to give her a little taste of her own medicine. But a frown looks *wrong* on her somehow and I hate that I was the one who put it there.

I take a sip of the scalding hot coffee, burning the roof of my mouth in the process. Karma for being a dick, I suppose. "Well, what have you been doing between that job and this?"

"Watching *Law & Order: SVU* reruns and selling photos of my feet on the Internet," she says with no inflection in her voice. Her shoulders seem to lose some of their tension at the topic change. "This pays better, although you're starting to make me second-guess if it's worth it."

I snort in response. Looking through my list of questions, my eyes laser focus on one that's sure to bring out that fiery attitude of hers. "Are you single?"

I stalked her Instagram and she seems close to this guy named Jack, but there were no obvious signs of them being in a relationship.

"Is that seriously on your list of questions?" The disbelief in her voice has a hint of annoyance.

"Yep. My interview, my questions."

She mumbles something under her breath before saying, "Yes."

"Cool. Then how do you feel about a friends-with-benefits situation? It'll make this whole interview process a hell of a lot more enjoyable for us both, that's for sure. Figure it's a good way to get out any tension we have."

The *friends* part of friends-with-benefits is a stretch at this point, but my other option was *bum chums*, Theo's favorite way to describe casual sex. I lean back in my chair and link my hands behind my head while I wait for her answer.

Then, as if some internal switch has been activated, she bursts out laughing. All-consuming, belly-holding laughter. "Are…you…I…oh, you've got to be fucking with me, Hollis."

She's the one who's got to be messing with me. I've been breaking hearts and backs since I grew facial hair, and I've never seen someone look so simultaneously offended and perversely entertained by the idea of sleeping with me.

It takes her a few more seconds to stop laughing, but when

she does, she stares at me as if I suggested we stick our hands in a garbage disposal for some type of twisted bonding activity. "Regardless of if you are or aren't," she adds with downturned lips, "I'm going to have to politely pass."

I scan her face to try to get a better read of what's going through that pretty little head of hers. "Why? Casual sex between two consenting adults isn't a big deal."

Sex is the only thing where coming first is the worst and second is the best for me. I make sure every woman I sleep with leaves more than satisfied.

Ella shakes her head back and forth as if she's in a stunned state of disbelief. "Uh, we work together. I'm not putting my job in jeopardy just so you can get your rocks off. You need to respect me as a person and as a professional, Blake. And even if we didn't work together, I'm not the hump-and-dump kind of girl. I don't do casual sex. Based on the number of women you've brought back since I first got here, I don't think those are things you're interested in. Plus, aren't you a little old to be sticking your thingy into holes like it's playing Whac-A-Mole?"

Thankfully, I'm wearing black, so the coffee I spit out doesn't stain my shirt. "My thingy? Are you serious?"

She takes a long sip of her coffee-flavored milk. "Were you serious when you point-blank asked me if I wanted to fool around with you and had some unrealistic expectation I'd say yes? Because if so, then yes, I am absolutely serious."

"I don't do relationships," I say without further explanation. "I'm more than happy playing Whac-A-Whatever with my thingy."

God, I cannot believe I just called my dick a thingy.

"Well, enjoy your games. I won't be participating. But just a word of advice"—she shoots me a wicked smile—"you may want to brush up on your Whac-a-Mole skills because the redhead from the other night was definitely faking it."

I'm honestly not sure how much more my ego can handle. My brain short-circuits and I can't get a single word out.

"Our hotel rooms are next to each other," Ella reminds me. "Her name is Natasha, by the way. She's really hoping you call her. We took the elevator down together the next morning."

The waiter appears and asks for our orders. Ella takes her sweet time asking about their different kinds of pancakes and what veggies they have for their omelets. If I didn't know any better, I'd think she's some sort of restaurant critic.

I'm still speechless when Ella says, "Now what's your next question?"

Who is this girl and why does she throw me off my game?

"Uh, yeah, okay." I cough awkwardly, trying to recover. "Why do you think I'm a bad driver?"

"I don't think you're a bad driver. I think you're an extremely talented driver." She gives me a funny look. "Not sure if you listened to the episode or not, but I spent about ten minutes talking about how flawlessly you adapt to whatever conditions you're thrown in, no matter who your competition is."

"You questioned if it was me or the McAllister car winning."

"I questioned it. I didn't say that's what I thought. But I'm sorry." A faint flush tinges her cheeks. "I shouldn't have been so harsh, and I apologize. So, can we call a truce?"

She moves her hand in front of me and sticks up her pinky. Is she seriously about to make me give her a pinky promise? I look at her, trying to gauge if she actually expects me to do it. *Bollocks.* As much as it kills a tiny piece of my soul to admit this, maybe Theo was right and I just need to give her a shot. The issue is that the closer Ella gets, the more harm she's able to do, and the easier it is for her to see how damaged I already am.

Sighing deeply, I wrap my pinky around hers, cementing

the promise. The look she gives me in response sends a bolt of lightning straight to my dick. *Traitor.*

She answers the rest of my questions thoughtfully. Based on her résumé, writing, and George's glowing review, I know Ella's smart. But hearing her talk confirms it. We're sort of like Millie's favorite movie: *Beauty and The Beast*. A gorgeous, independent woman forced to spend time with a selfish, arrogant prick. Unfortunately—or fortunately, depending on how you look at it—for Ella, I'm not equipped for the emotional rollercoaster of falling in love. And sadly for me, she's not interested in the ecstasy of falling in lust.

SEVEN
ELLA

IT'S NOT that I had high hopes that Blake was going to be the easiest person to work with, but suggesting we fool around was out of left field. He said it so casually that he may as well have been asking me to split an Uber with him. When I told Poppy, she said I was an idiot for shooting the idea down. She kept going on and on about how it'd be great if I could include his skills both on *and* off the track in the book. *Whatever*.

I wasn't lying to Blake when I said I couldn't do casual sex. I've tried and it doesn't work for me. I like emotional intimacy too much. To his credit, he took my refusal with grace and hasn't made me feel uncomfortable in the slightest since.

Our conversation did allow me to pass whatever weird test he was giving me. He's sticking to his pinky promise and finally allowing me to spend time with him. We're walking around the Canadian Grand Prix circuit, something Blake likes to do before each race, when he asks me the highest speed I've ever driven.

"I once went ninety mph and got pulled over," I reveal as we near the end of the track. "The officer let me off with a warning, but I haven't sped since then."

"Have you ever been on a hot lap?"

I shake my head. "Nope."

A hot lap is pretty much the closest an average person can get to feeling even a quarter of what a Formula 1 driver does when they're on the track. I'm sure the experience costs more than the car itself, and that's saying a lot.

"How can you write a book about me without having experienced what being in a Formula 1 car is like?"

"Taking a hot lap isn't in a Formula 1 car, though," I point out.

"Close enough." He stops walking and turns to face me. "You need to experience it in order to accurately write about me."

"It's called research. People write about astronauts without going to space. They write about presidents without having been elected." I'm on a roll. "Do you think Eric Carle went through metamorphosis to become a butterfly before writing *The Very Hungry Caterpillar*? No. He did research."

"Ella."

"Blake."

Not a single bone in my body has any desire to go 250 mph in a high-performance sports car with Blake behind the wheel.

"Some people pay upwards of eleven thousand pounds to take a drive with a Formula 1 driver," he says as if this will sway me.

"Yeah, but those people are clearly on crack."

Blake looks at me with the confidence of someone who's used to getting their way. He waves over Josie. She'll have to side with me. McAllister doesn't want to be culpable for my death, right?

"Hi!" Her smile is easy as she jogs over to us. "What's going on?"

"Ella is claiming she has no interest in going on a hot lap with me."

Great, now both Josie and Blake are looking at me like I've lost my mind. She shoots me an apologetic look before admitting, "I'm sorry, babes, but I actually think it'll be great for our social media."

"Traitor." I narrow my eyes at her. "I am *so* watching the season two finale without you."

We've been binge-watching *Game of Thrones* together, although Josie covers her eyes for half of the episodes leaving me to fill in the blanks.

"Don't be mad," she laughs, calling my bluff. "They've been wanting me to push the experience on our channels, and what better way than with a clip of what it's like with Blake behind the wheel?"

He throws his arm around my shoulders. "C'mon, Ella. You can't say no to Josie, and I'm the best there is."

"The best at what? First-degree murder?" I snap, ignoring the flush prickling my skin thanks to Blake's touch. "I'm pretty sure the content will get flagged for violating community guidelines when I fucking die on camera, anyway."

"I'm seriously starting to worry about how much you bring up murder." Now he sounds like my mother. There's a reason that *Law & Order* has won so many Emmy Awards. "These cars have precautions on them. If they were really so dangerous, they wouldn't be letting us take fans out in them. I promise you're going to be safe."

He sticks out his pinky, but I promptly smack his hand away. Excuse me for wanting to keep my organs in place and intact. They both spend the next ten minutes convincing me I'll have the best time of my life. How the speed will make me feel invincible and it'll give me an adrenaline rush like never before.

"Fine," I reluctantly give in, glaring at a very pleased Blake. "I'll do it. But if I throw up all over myself, I'm taking your credit card and buying myself a new wardrobe."

His dark eyes settle on mine before he winks. "Whatever you want, love."

Josie hums along to "Eye of the Tiger" as we make our way over to the Hot Laps tent. My heart is pounding in my ears. Everyone there is wearing so many lanyards, I feel unfashionable with just my single McAllister one.

"Do you want water?" Blake asks, tilting his head. "You look kind of faint."

"If you want me to pee in my pants mid-drive then sure, I'll take a water, Blake."

There's no way in hell he wants to be my fuck buddy now. I've mentioned throwing up, peeing in my pants, and shitting myself about twelve times on our walk over here. Nothing turns a guy off more than female bodily functions.

Fans paying for the experience lose their minds when Blake walks into the tent. He's not one of the drivers set to take people out today, so his presence is an added bonus. Given the tight schedule for the track on race weekends, I'm surprised he's able to get us a vehicle. I'm asked to fill out a waiver just in case anything should happen to me. Nothing makes me feel safer than signing my life away. You'd think I have chronic asthma with the way strangled air is fighting to leave my lungs as we walk over to the car. Its black paint glints angrily in the sun.

Blake tugs a helmet onto my head, making sure it's snug. The way his fingers graze against my cheeks isn't making breathing any easier.

"It's going to be fun, okay? Trust me." He lightly taps the helmet. "Safe and secure."

Josie sets up her GoPro camera on the dashboard to capture my experience. It's strapped down more securely than I am with the measly seat belt I click into place. I think my stomach is going to fall out of my ass. White knuckles grip the console as Blake checks the mirrors and makes sure everything is good to go. This is where it ends. *Do I even have life insurance? Or a will? I never told Josie to clear my search history. Shit.*

"You ready?"

"No."

I try to whip my head around to face him, but the chunky weight of the helmet prohibits the movement as we speed forward. Blake takes the out lap on the track "slow" because 160 mph is apparently a great way to ease into the circuit. I scream at the top of my lungs the entire time, only stopping to incorporate some swear words into the mix. It isn't until we get to the first full lap that he really nails the pedal to the metal.

The acceleration is so violent I feel like I'm being launched out of a slingshot. My stomach fully hits my spine as the car rockets forward. It's like my entire body is in free fall even though we're level with the ground we're blazing over. Completely disorienting doesn't even begin to cover it. The car's engine rumbles through the seat, my helmet bouncing around like a stupid bobblehead.

"Having fun yet?" Blake asks.

"No!" I scream. "What part of my kidney and uterus switching places is fun?!"

In the second lap, I try to anticipate the braking force of the turns by leaning left or right and fail miserably. The way the car reduces speed so effortlessly knocks the wind out of me each and every time. I manage to turn my head to look at Blake and he's cool as a cucumber. Only one hand is on the steering wheel, the other resting next to mine on the console.

"Ten and two, you maniac!" I shout. "Keep your hands at ten and two! What sort of driver's ed did you go to?"

He makes no move to adjust his position. "Want to go faster?"

"This isn't the fastest this thing goes?" I squeak out.

"We're barely skimming the surface, baby." He flashes me a

grin that makes me press my legs together. "Get ready to burn some rubber."

Blake happily rearranges my perception of what fast means. The high pitch of my shrieks as the wind blurs past us rivals only the squealing of tires against the asphalt.

"Finally ready to admit that I'm the best?"

I ignore him. He presses down on the accelerator, launching us through the straight faster than my brain can comprehend.

"What about now?"

My vision blurs as I'm pushed back into the cushioned seat, trapped by the force of an invisible hand. *How is this thing still speeding up?*

"Fine! You're the best driver in the world!" I shout. "Everyone should bow down to how fucking fantastic you are! You're a god among men."

"You sound a little sarcastic," he notes.

I'm going to kill him if he doesn't kill me first.

"I, Eliana Jane Gold, hereby pronounce that Blake Hollis is the best driver in the entire universe. I will forever be impressed by the way he majestically handles a car! Happy?!"

"Very," he says. I don't even need to look over to know that fucker is wearing a shit-eating grin. "I thought you were a screamer. Glad I can now confirm."

"Glad you now know what real screams sound like! Unlike Natasha the fake porn star."

Blake's amused laugh and my ear-piercing screeches cancel each other out as we finish the final lap. When we pull back up to the pit lane, I'm mentally, physically, and emotionally drained. Getting out of the car, my legs are like jelly. Blake has to unbuckle my helmet because my hands are too shaky.

Josie's giggling at her phone where she's been watching our drive in real time. "I have to edit out seventy-five percent of it thanks to Ella's screaming and swearing, but this is high-quality content. You did it! Congrats!"

The only congrats I deserve is one for not throwing up all over my shoes. I shoot her a thumbs-up. She snaps a photo of me, although I'm probably so pale I'm translucent. Josie's been attempting to convince me to let her "run" my Instagram. She says that no matter what I want to do post-Formula 1, I need to build a brand for myself and use Instagram as my résumé. I refuse to give her my login information, but I will let her take photos of me.

"I knew you'd have fun," Blake says. "I sure as hell did."

The corners of his lips tug up in a boyish sort of grin. It's the happiest I've seen him since we met and I can't help but savor the view. My parents warned me about drugs when I was a kid. They didn't warn me about how addictive a smile could be. *Ugh.*

EIGHT

ELLA

IT TAKES three hours in Monaco for me to realize Blake's rich. It takes three more hours to realize that Blake's filthy rich. I know that Formula 1 drivers can make millions upon millions, but seeing it in person is different. He's got major "fuck you" money. I think the soap dispenser in one of the guest bathrooms costs more than my college tuition did. After some Internet sleuthing, I found out he bought the property for a whopping 7.2 million. Chump change when you've won as many championships as Blake.

Did I mention he has two other homes? This isn't even his main residence; he just comes here when it's dreary in London. I'm subleasing my apartment in New York while he owns multiple properties across the world. Love that for us.

When Blake told me he was coming here to relax before the next race, I told him to count me in. The surprise on his face was quickly replaced with exasperation. Too bad, buddy. If I'm supposed to learn about you, that also means learning what you do during your time off.

I've only been in Monaco for a few days, but I've spent each morning interviewing Blake. I finally feel like I'm making headway. It's about time. George accounted for some initial pushback from him, so we're still on schedule to meet our deadline.

Sitting across from Blake at his kitchen table, I get today's interview started. "Have you ever peed in your race suit during a race?"

In all honesty, I'm just curious. I've read about it, and even though it might not be the most professional question I've ever asked, I think Blake will find it amusing. I'm starting to learn that he does have a sense of humor, even if it's drier than I'm used to.

"That's what you're choosing to start with today? I thought you wanted to talk about the Junior World Karting Championship."

"My interview, my questions."

I shoot him a sugar-coated smile, mimicking his interview rule. He rests his hands on his toned stomach, the muscles outlined through his shirt.

"No, I haven't. But I know a few drivers who have."

Equally interesting and gross. I'm sure if I ask Theo, he'll go into a detailed explanation on whether he has or hasn't. Good luck to his future biographer. If Blake doesn't say enough, Theo says too much.

"What do you do if you get nervous before a race?"

I don't even like being in the middle of an intersection waiting to make a left on a two-way street. These drivers travel up to 260 mph, can go from 0 to 100 in 2.5 seconds, and experience 5Gs of force while braking. That's more force than a shuttle launching into space needs. It takes a certain kind of sociopath to not only be comfortable driving under those conditions but to actually enjoy it. The ability to fine-tune the magic of a Formula 1 car into a tactical weapon is no easy feat.

"I don't get nervous."

I wait for him to continue, but he doesn't. We stare each

other down, silently daring the other one to break. At least the view is nice. *Whatever*. If he wants to assert his dominance, fine. I'll be the bigger person.

"Try again." I sigh.

"Why? I answered the question."

"Blake. Do I look like a dentist?"

His brows furrow in confusion. "Uh, no."

"That's because I'm not. So I'd appreciate it if I didn't have to sit here and pull teeth trying to get you to talk. Try again, please."

He chuckles and leans back in his chair.

"I struggled with nerves in my early years, but I guess I've just adjusted to it. I feel most myself out on the track, so knowing I'm going to be out there soon always calms me down. I'm never scared or anything like that."

"Some people say being scared means that you care," I note with a shrug. "It's not always a bad thing."

"Being scared is fatal in F1. Any fear makes you second-guess your instincts, and my instincts are what make me the best." He winks at me. "They don't call me a Formula 1 legend for shits and giggles, love. I earned that title and I'm going to keep winning more championships."

"There's a difference between confidence and cocky," I tease lightly. "You know that, right?"

"Oh, I'm very cocky." He shoots me a smug smirk. "I'd be more than happy to show you just how cocky if you want."

I let out a long laugh. "Oh God, has that line actually ever worked?"

I've made it *very* clear that I'm not interested in sleeping with him. I mean, I'm obviously attracted to Blake. I'm a woman with 20/20 vision—*well, when I'm wearing contacts or glasses*—but I'm not going to be his fuck buddy just because he wants me to be.

"It's not a line I've ever used before."

"You should probably keep it that way." I press my coffee mug against my lips to cover the smile fighting to break free. "But back to business. What do you think makes you the best? Besides your instincts, of course."

The tips of his fingers drum against the table absentmindedly. "I don't think people realize that being a good driver is more than just good instincts and being fast. There's a difference between driving fast and being able to push your car to its absolute limits. And if winning is the goal, which it absolutely is, you have to be dedicated enough to get there. And sometimes that means being ruthless and taking risks regardless of what may happen."

"What if your risks don't end up working out?"

"Losing isn't an option." He pauses thoughtfully. "Because if I do lose, even if that means missing podium by one-tenth of a second, people start to say, 'What happened to Hollis? He used to be so good.' The margin between success and failure is almost imperceptible."

Now I understand why he doesn't like being called out. What he just said is exactly what I did to him. His driving didn't meet the extremely high expectations I'd put on him, and I immediately questioned his skills. My cheeks flame with embarrassment.

"But a lot of the time, the reason you, or any driver, lose is because of things that are out of your control," I argue. "An engine overheating, someone clips your wing, a pit stop gone wrong. How do you handle that type of pressure?"

"Just have to crack on. It's a shame, but I can't really focus on anyone or anything else but me and my team."

"Even Harry?"

"I don't have an issue with Harry." Blake rumples his hair with a large hand. "We may not be friends off the track, but I can appreciate him as an opponent. I remember what it's like having to fight for your first championship. You get eager and emotional, but he'll learn. He'll have to."

If his honesty surprises me, I don't let it show. Blake seemed anything but appreciative of Harry's competitive edge during the previous season.

"As you said," he continues, "I was a little off last year, but contrary to what people think, it had nothing to do with Harry. He's a good driver. I respect that. I obviously don't want him to win over me, but I don't mind a challenge."

Blake's more at ease talking about racing than himself, but I don't think he realizes how intertwined the two are. Getting behind his mask may be challenging, but I think the notoriously enigmatic sportsman will pleasantly surprise people.

THE HARD PART about writing a biography with a planned release date just a few short months after the season ends is that we have to do everything simultaneously. Research. Interview. Write. Edit. Interview some more. Edit a little. Write a lot more. George's motorsport expertise allows him to easily identify the aspects of Blake's life and story that might be worth exploring more in depth, and I dig deep to find the details we need to fill the pages. We're working through a shared document so we're able to collaborate in real time, but it's still exhausting.

After another few days of my routine, I decide to take a break and relax. One afternoon reading by the pool won't kill me. Poppy thinks I'm a workaholic and she's not wrong, but it's what gives me purpose. Right now, I need that. And the views of the French Riviera definitely don't hurt either.

I find Blake out by his pool in a plush lounge chair, his tan body contrasting with the white and blue towel underneath him. I'm not sure if I'm more surprised by his presence or his swim trunks. They're so unbelievably short, my eyes don't know where to focus—his thighs, his abs, his arms, his face. I'm thankful that my sunglasses are already on, so he can't see my eyes going haywire. If Michelangelo had lived five centuries later, I can guarantee he'd be sculpting Blake's body instead of David's.

Blake's been spending his afternoons anywhere but his house, so I'm not sure why he's here today, but I'm too rattled to ask. I settle into a lounge chair a few away from him, not wanting to invade his personal space. He nods in greeting then looks back at the newspaper in his hands. It takes me a second to recognize that he's doing a crossword puzzle. I'm a journalist and don't even read a physical newspaper, yet here Blake is filling out the tiny squares with a stubby pencil. *Stars, they're just like us! They do daily crosswords while lying out at their million-dollar mansions in Monaco!*

Tapping his pencil against the paper, his eyebrows knit in frustration. "Do you know a three-letter word for the clue: you may need this to go on?"

Thanks to the heavenly mix of his cologne and sunscreen, I can barely remember my own name. "Um…no idea. Can I phone a friend?"

He chuckles, a curl to his lips. "Thought you'd be good since you like words."

"Writing them," I clarify. "Not guessing them based on confusing clues."

Blake glances up, his eyes settling on my bikini-clad body. My heart plummets to my stomach. I don't want Blake sitting there, analyzing my body as if that's the most interesting thing about me. *Been there, done that.* Plus, he's slept with models, whereas I don't even have a thigh gap. I have a body that rolls when I sit and bloats when I eat one too many fries. If I knew he'd be out here, I would've worn a one-piece or a burlap sack.

"Whoever makes these clues is the bane of my existence,"

he grumbles, looking back down. "Swear they make half of this shit up."

Trying not to laugh at his frustrated frown—which is very adorable—I take out my book and leave Blake to his puzzle. I'm so used to seeing him in his racing suit, or an actual suit at sponsor events, that it's hard to stay focused on my reading. His thighs are a major distraction. I've reread the same page of Emily Henry's newest release maybe ten times already because I'm too flustered. A frustrated growl escapes my lips and I freeze, praying that it was inside my head. No such luck.

"All good?" he calls over.

I keep my eyes trained down even though I can still see Blake out of my peripheral vision. He's looking at me with mild curiosity.

"Yep! Just a part in my book."

Nice save, Ella. I mentally high-five myself.

"You're a terrible liar."

Or not.

"You know…if you want me to keep telling you things, you're going to have to tell me things too."

Um, contractually, I'm going to have to do no such thing. I don't answer him but track his movements as he makes his way over to the seat next to mine. Apparently, the courtesy of not invading one another's personal space does not extend to me. For the eleventh time, I reread the same damn page of my book. His near-naked body is too close for me to concentrate on anything but remembering how to breathe. In and out. In and out. There should be a fucking Lamaze class for how to breathe when an extremely gorgeous man is a foot away from you while wearing the world's shortest shorts. I'd pay good money for that.

"That page in your book must be really interesting."

"Mm-hmm."

"Care to share what it's about, love?"

Ugh. I hate how he so casually uses the pet name *love*. It's frustratingly charming.

"Nope. But you can borrow it once I'm done if you'd like."

That may be in four to five years depending on how many times I can reread the same page, but oh well. He continues staring at me and I continue fake reading, finally flipping the page although I still don't know what happened on the last one. My cheeks are flushed from the sun, so he's unaware of the effect his intense gaze is having on me.

After ten minutes of him blatantly observing me, I've had enough. If we go on like this, I'll have to finish the book without reading a single word.

"Can you not? You're distracting me."

He cocks his head to the side. "I haven't said anything."

"Okay, well, you and your thighs are in my area and it's distracting. So, if you could remove yourself from my bubble, that'd be greatly appreciated."

"My thighs?"

The laugh that comes out of Blake is loud and raw. It's not helping me feel any less attracted to him. I debate drowning myself in the pool after that embarrassing admission.

"Yes." I put my hand out, pretending to cover the lower half of his body as I glare at him. "In America, men tend to wear swim trunks that don't reveal quite so much. They're a bit more modest."

"Last time I checked, you're American and your bathing suit is anything but modest." Blake has a sassy grin on his dumb, handsome face. "Some may even say distracting."

I immediately cover myself with the folded-up towel I've been using as a pillow. I feel way too exposed in my bikini, even though it's completely appropriate.

Maybe not for a nun, but the bottoms give my ass a decent amount of coverage and the top isn't about to go *Girls Gone Wild* on me.

"It's not my fault you're so used to surrounding yourself with fake boobs that you find real ones distracting."

Blake may be good at bantering, but I'm better. It's my favorite sport and I always go for gold.

"I've seen the girls you hang out with, Blake," I continue, a victorious smile painted on my lips. "There's so much plastic in them that they're unknowingly saving the ocean's turtles."

I have absolutely no problem with women doing what they want to look and feel their best. I'm all for it. But it's nearly impossible to *not* tease Blake for having a type.

He mutters something under his breath while shaking his head at me. I comfortably settle back into the chair and return to my book. Blake doesn't move, but he does put in his earbuds and close his eyes. It's kind of sweet how he tries to hide a smile sometimes.

NINE
BLAKE

I'VE ALWAYS LIKED BEING ALONE. There are no variables I haven't accounted for, nothing that can throw me off. I can depend on myself, and life is predictable. Ella staying with me in Monaco is a shock to my system. And to my house. Her shit is all over the place—a purse on the kitchen counter, a stray sweatshirt on the recliner, a book left open on the patio. Don't even get me started on the strands of hair everywhere. It's like having a goddamn shedding dog.

I've let Ella interview me every morning for the past week and although I hate to admit it, George was right when he said she's the best person for the job. Her interview style suits me. She's straightforward but respectful. She knows when to push and when to pull back. She makes it feel like a conversation instead of an interrogation.

I don't like when she rolls her eyes or tells me to "try again" when I give her a short or half-assed answer. And I definitely don't like when she bites her lip in concentration. It makes me want to push her up against a wall and kiss her until she can't think straight. It also makes my pants uncomfortably tight, so my right hand has gotten a massive workout this past week.

Especially when I saw her in a bikini the other day. Bloody fucking hell. I have no idea how I managed to hide the tent in my pants.

I've been spending my afternoons away from the house and yes, Ella. Taking my boat out, grabbing drinks with friends, going on insanely long runs. All because I don't know what to do with someone in my space. Am I supposed to hang out with her? Pretend she's not there and ignore her? Give her a tour of the town? Offer her snacks? Make sure the air conditioning temperature is to her liking? I fuck women; I don't…cohabitate with them. I'm completely out of my element.

For the third afternoon in a row, I make my way down to the dock that houses Lucas's pride and joy: his sailboat. He owns a place down the street from me—which has been very convenient this week—but spends more time out on the water than in his own bed.

"Ahoy, Hollis," he calls out from the bow of the boat. It's eighty degrees out, but he's wearing a long-sleeved Under Armour shirt and holding a beer can in each hand.

"New tattoo," he explains as if reading my mind. He's annoyingly perceptive like that. He rolls up his sleeve to show me the latest addition. Right above the Roman numerals representing his parents' anniversary date is his niece Madison's name in cursive script.

"Looks good," I comment. "Assuming you told her you weren't flying in for her birthday?"

If I told Millie I was missing her birthday, I'd never hear the end of it. My sister would drive to my house in London and drag me by the ear to a princess-themed party. Lucas's family lives in Boston and doesn't have that same luxury.

"Yep." He flicks up a brow. "I'd rather deal with my parents' disapproving looks over FaceTime than in person."

I take a moment to study my friend. "Listen, I know I'm not one to speak on family shit—"

"Then don't." The sharpness of his voice surprises me, but I don't mention it. Luc's never pushed me to talk about what led to my "shit-show of shenanigans"—thank you for that lovely description, Ella—so I won't push him either. I go to therapy; Lucas gets new tattoos. We all deal with our shit differently.

We spend the next few hours cruising along the shoreline, sipping on beers. Whereas Theo loves to fill any silence with mindless chatter, Lucas is happy to sit in comfortable quiet and leave me to my own thoughts. Unfortunately, my mind keeps circling back to the American journalist with an annoyingly cute dimple. *Cute?*

My stomach gives a curious twist at the memory of Ella trying to help me with my crossword the other morning. I wonder what she's doing right now. Reading on my patio? Exercising in my at-home gym? On the phone with her friend Poppy? The most likely scenario is she's sitting cross-legged on the couch, working. When I left for Lucas's boat, she was making edits to a chapter called "The Art of Karting."

Since I've started letting her interview me in-depth, she and George have made massive strides. The two of them work well together, bouncing ideas off one another, giving constructive criticism. Not that I've been eavesdropping on their calls, but Ella talks loudly and she wasn't wearing headphones. *Sue me.* Both Keith and Marion praised my cooperation after George sent us a detailed chapter-by-chapter outline.

Turns out Ella spent her afternoon watching basketball. I got the cross-legged part right, though.

"Hey," I say, settling on the couch next to her. "Who's playing?"

"Utah Jazz versus the Lakers." She briefly glances away from the TV to greet me with a smile before focusing back on the game.

There's that dimple.

"Anthony Davis may've just lost me some money."

"You gamble?" I ask, surprised.

"Low stakes with my brother and his friends," she admits with a laugh. "I won the pot last year."

I let out a low whistle as I check out the score. Ella's more entertaining than the actual game. Her alarmingly astute and comical commentary reminds me why her podcast was so successful. When she calls a forward on the Lakers the "human equivalent of period cramps," I nearly fall off the couch with laughter. *Who says shit like that?*

Once the game is over, I crack my knuckles and gear up to ask a question I may quickly regret. "Are you busy tomorrow night?"

I cough to hide how awkward I feel. I don't think I've ever asked a woman to hang out with me unless I know we'll be making each other come. *Get a grip, mate.*

"I have a date with Elliot Stabler." She sucks in air between her lips as if debating something. "But I can cancel if you have something better in mind."

How does she have a date with someone in Monaco? When did she meet them? Why do I even care?

"No need to cancel," I respond gruffly.

Ella looks at me with fascination. "Do you watch any TV or are you Patrick Star?"

When I don't answer, she covers her face with her hands. "Patrick Star is from *Spongebob Squarepants*," she explains as if that means absolutely anything. "Spongebob lives in a pineapple under the sea and Patrick's his best friend. He lives under a rock, which clearly you do too."

"Have you been doing drugs or something?"

"C'mon, you're a nineties baby!" She laughs and shakes her head. "You should know this stuff. It's a Nickelodeon cartoon, Blake."

It's not one Millie or Finn have ever watched. What a weird children's show.

"Elliot Stabler is from *Law & Order: SVU*. Well, he actually has his own spin-off now, but I digress." Ella flashes a cheeky smile. "Moral of the story is yes, I'm around."

I hate the immediate relief that floods my body. "Cool. Do you like fish?"

"I've never conversed with any personally, but I've heard they're very lovely creatures."

My head drops into my hands to cover a chuckle. "I was going to have my chef grill some halibut if you wanted to do dinner. Maybe at like seven-ish?"

"Count me in!" she says, her eyes lighting up. "Do you want to pick me up?"

I snort in response. "Sure, Ella. I can pick you up."

MY CHEF KNOWS damn well this isn't a date, but that doesn't stop her from going all out. We're eating on the terrace, the table has tealight candles on it, and we're being served a four-course meal. Ella's surprisingly in an outfit that shows off her curves rather than hides them. When I comment she looks nice, her face turns bright pink and she shifts in her seat. For someone who has confidence, she doesn't do well with compliments. Chef Nicola winks at me as she pours us each a glass of my favorite 1997 Merlot.

Ella takes a small sip before nodding in appreciation. "I don't know if I can ever go back to Trader Joe's two-buck chuck after this stuff."

"What's that?"

"Trader Joe's is a grocery store chain," she explains. "It's the best, and they have this wine that they sell for two dollars. They call it two-buck chuck."

"Two quid for wine? That sounds…really horrible."

She shrugs, unbothered. "In comparison to this, yes."

Nicola brings out mini croque monsieurs as an appetizer and we both dig right in.

"So, why'd you eat here tonight?" Ella asks, leaning back in her seat. "No late-night meetings or dinners with friends?"

"I live here." The scowl I'm used to wearing reappears. "Are you going to spend all of dinner interviewing me?"

"I'm not interviewing you," she scoffs. "News flash, but conversations usually involve two people talking. That includes asking questions."

I mumble some sort of half apology.

"Has anyone ever told you that you can be quite hostile?" Ella asks.

"No. What? No."

She swirls the wine in her glass around and laughs at my bristling reaction. "You may claim you're good at everything you do, but I have a feeling you'd be terrible at first dates."

"This isn't a date."

She rolls her eyes to the high heavens. "Christ, Blake. I wasn't implying this was."

"Oh. Okay." I settle into my chair. I don't want her to think I can do anything more than a friendship. She's only here for the season, then she's leaving. Just like my mum, just like my dad. I closed the door on the idea of a relationship years ago; there's only so much rejection someone can take before it hardens their heart to stone.

"I honestly can't remember the last date I went on," she admits with a shrug.

I tilt my head as if I just learned classified information. "Really?"

"Yep. It's not that I don't date," she continues. "I've just had bigger priorities than that the past few months."

"Got it." I want to know what she's been focused on instead but keep my mouth shut. "Makes sense."

"I mean, if you know a guy who thinks with the head on his shoulders instead of the one in his pants, by all means, send him my way."

I release a low laugh. "I've read your stuff, you know," I confess. This seems to surprise her, but she doesn't comment on it. "Your writing doesn't indicate you have a dirty mind."

"Did you expect me to write about Travis Kelce's tight ass?"

"He has a tight arse? I've never noticed." I may not get a lot of her television references, but I do understand her American sports ones.

"It's why I liked podcasting so much. I love writing, don't get me wrong, but there's only so much subjectiveness allowed. Podcasting is a lot more flexible. It allows me to talk about whatever I want, however I want."

"Including my season last year?"

She grimaces, her brows knitting together. "I didn't mean to go so hard on you."

"It's okay. Comes with the territory," I say, waving off her worry. "Plus, I wasn't at my best last year. I can objectively say that."

"It doesn't make it any less hurtful."

"Well, I also read your article about my Monaco win from a few years ago. That helps soften the blow."

She knows exactly what I'm talking about. My win had been "nothing short of astonishing"—her words, not mine. It was a true testament to my driving skills over the car's performance, thank you very much. The Monaco circuit is wedged into the narrow spaces of city streets with nonstop twists and tight turns. There's no run-off area to correct yourself if you've made a mistake. One error and you kiss the wall and your chances of winning goodbye. Pole position tends to dictate the winner and with a P3 starting position, it was expected that Mateo

Bertole would win. It was me who ended up securing first place instead.

"Your driving speaks for itself." Her cheeks turn a shade similar to the wine. "You don't need me telling you that you're the best."

Refilling her empty glass, I give her a small smile. "It may not be the best, but your podcast isn't half bad either."

I've almost binged every episode of *Coffee with Champions*, but I don't feel like admitting that.

"Yikes. Was that your attempt at a compliment?" She cocks her head to the side. "Because it sucked."

I roll my eyes. "So, how'd you get into sports journalism? Tough industry."

"My family's always been big on sports, so I grew up around it. I've always liked writing and asking questions, so sports journalism seemed like a natural fit."

"Well, you're a good journalist. Your podcasting and writing styles are different. It makes you versatile."

Ella doesn't say anything. She just pushes the vegetables around on her plate. She may be open about some things, but she shuts down immediately over most things related to PlayMedia.

"Would you ever do your podcast again?"

She simply shakes her head.

"Why not?" I probe.

"It's not my podcast." She fiddles with the fork in her hand. "I mean, yes, it is, but legally no, it's not. It was developed and created by a PlayMedia employee"—she points to herself— "for PlayMedia. Meaning that they own it. The intellectual property and copyright are theirs."

My wineglass stops in front of my lips, and I peer at Ella over the rim of the glass. "I thought you left amicably?" That's what I gathered after my detective work online. PlayMedia tweeted: *We are very appreciative of all the hard work Ella Gold has done over the years, and we wish her the best in all future endeavors.*

"There was nothing amicable about how I left," she says wryly. It's the first glimpse she's given into her sudden departure. "It's a shitty situation, but it is what it is."

"But you seem okay."

"I mean, I accepted a job to follow around a guy I barely know for a year," she answers, parroting my earlier interview words back to me. Theo uses humor as a defense mechanism, so it's easy to spot that Ella does as well. "So I don't know how okay I actually am."

She sips her wine, averting eye contact. "Do you collect postcards? You have a bunch on your counter."

Yup. It's clear she wants to talk about anything but this. There's a lot more behind the dimple and loud laughs than she lets on. A soft smile passes across my face as I tell her about Finn and Millie. I may not like Ella digging into my past, but I am starting to like spending time with her. I'm starting to like it a lot.

TEN

ELLA

TODAY'S GOING to be a good day. I know it. I didn't snooze my alarm, the coffee I'm drinking is phenomenal, and my pants fit despite the copious amount of calories I've consumed in the past month. They're definitely tighter, but they still fit. Blake's in a great mood considering he's going into the Chinese Grand Prix with another pole position. He even offers to give me a tour and show me his car before the race. All Blake will tell me is that his car's name starts with a "T" and it's not a human name. So far I've ruled out T-Rex, Tarantula, Titty Twister, Tupperware, Tuba, Tsunami, Toothpaste, Tornado, and Tums.

We spend some time walking around the motorhome, with Blake giving me an exclusive look into his suite. I don't mention that I had to charge my phone in here during the last race, so I've technically already seen it. Just going to pretend like it's my first time ever being inside of his special, private room. It's sparse, to say the least. There aren't many "personal" items besides a TheraGun, his laptop, and a photo of him with his niece and nephew. Oh, and food—if you can even call it that.

Blake's snack choices are appalling. He has every nut in existence (and none of them are salted), whole-grain lentil chips, rice cakes, crackers made with organic oat flour, and a variety of protein bars with flavors ranging from rhubarb custard to ginger carrot.

"Are you, like, on a weird diet or something?" I'm trying not to look completely turned off, but it's kind of hard.

He shakes his head before tossing me a protein bar and tells me to look at the ingredients. It's all healthy nuts and fruits. This further proves my point. Where is the junk food? The candy? The "I just had a bad day and need to eat my feelings" snacks? All I'm seeing is bland, blander, and blandest.

There's a minifridge under the desk in the room and I make my way over to it. All that's in there is Greek yogurt (spelled "yoghurt"), hard-boiled eggs, and celery juice. Not apple juice or cranberry juice. Celery juice. The most flavorless of all the vegetables.

His pantry in Monaco had been *stacked*—a Costco-level abundance of snacks and food—but now I realize that may've been because he wasn't sure what *I* liked to eat. The thought of it sends a flutter deep into the pit of my stomach.

"Here I was thinking I was writing about an athlete." I close the fridge and stand back up. "Turns out, I'm actually writing about a sociopath."

His chuckle is throaty.

"These are survival foods, Blake, not snacks." I sigh. He looks adorably confused. "If you were on a stranded island, then yes, I would totally understand wanting hard-boiled eggs and nuts. But you're not. Snacks are meant to be enjoyed."

"I do enjoy them!"

There's no use attempting to hide the absolutely horrified look on my face. Blake enjoys cardboard. Good to know. What chapter in his book should I file that under? Remember how Blake celebrated a Grand Prix win by snacking on some dry rice cakes and then washing them down with some freshly squeezed celery?

I list off a variety of snacks to see how brainwashed he is by his healthy-eating ways. He's never had white cheddar popcorn or a Pop Tart. He's also never bothered trying a Double Stuf Oreo because "how can it be that different from the regular ones?" He doesn't even know what a Ho-Ho is and thinks I'm kidding when I ask him. It's not that I only eat junk food, but at least I don't just eat rabbit food. Sam needs to loosen the reins on his diet.

"Do you need a bit of fresh air, love?" Blake laughs at me. "I can crack a window if you'd like."

My body drops onto the small couch in his room. I check my forehead to see if I have a fever. The dramatics may be unnecessary, but imagine having gone through that many years of your life without knowing the true joy of a Girl Scout cookie. I know that's quintessentially American, but it's not doing much to help his case right now. My reaction seems to have entirely overwhelmed Blake.

"If my snacks are so horrible, which ones do you consider good?"

I can't help but laugh. "We'll need about five to seven business days to get through that list."

The conversation on our way to the garage revolves entirely around Blake's eating habits. I'm intrigued. It turns out he prefers chocolate milk to regular milk and not just out of a glass, in his cereal, too.

"Blakey and Goldy!" Theo greets us as we enter the pit. "Here to hang out with me?"

His eyes look extra blue this morning. Is being attractive a prerequisite for being a Formula 1 driver? The fucking accents alone are enough to send me over the edge.

"Blake's showing me around," I explain.

He quickly picks up on the warning look I give him. His

lips are sealed; he won't tell Blake he's already done this tour with me.

"You're fine with him calling you Goldy?" Blake frowns. "Because I hate when he calls me Blakey."

I don't think he cares about the nickname. I think he cares that Theo and I have gotten to know each other well enough to even have nicknames.

"It beats sweetheart or babe."

Theo ruffles my hair playfully. "I thought 'muffin' was a cute nickname."

After about two weeks of him calling me a variety of pet names, we had a little chat. Unless my parents legally change my name to "babycakes," he isn't allowed to call me that. When he started with "Goldy," I accepted it. The only cutesy names Theo hasn't called me are "princess" and "angel." Those seem to be specifically reserved for Josie.

I stick my tongue out. "Call me 'muffin' again and I'll shove one where the sun doesn't shine, *sweet cheeks*."

It's hard not to smile when Blake laughs. It's deep and makes the corners of his eyes crinkle. The butterflies in my stomach come out of hibernation. I take a baggie of trail mix out and pop some in my mouth. All the snack talk from earlier has my stomach grumbling.

"See, Blake?" I shake the bag in front of him. "This is how nuts should be eaten. Surrounded by chocolate, raisins, and cereal."

"Are there even nuts in there?" He squints his eyes and peers into the baggie. "Do you even know what a nut looks like?"

There are very obvious peanuts and cashews in my trail mix. The ratio is just not in their favor.

"Trust me, I definitely know what nuts look like." *Welp, that sounds obscenely sexual.* "Want to try some?"

"Of your nuts?" Blake shakes his head. "No, thanks, love."

"Why not? Are you scared of my nuts, Blake?" I tilt my head, leaning into the mess I've made by turning my trail mix into a sexual innuendo. "Scared they're bigger and better than yours?"

He grunts in amusement. "Has anyone ever told you that you're impossibly exhausting?"

I give him a dazed look of bewilderment, exaggerated confusion clouding my eyes.

"Exhibit nine hundred," he says.

"You looking at me like a murderer when I said your snacks looked like you were preparing for an apocalypse is exhibit nine hundred of why you need a higher education in the world of sweet and savory."

"A murderer? Who says that instead of I don't know—any other word? Do you have a criminal record or something?"

I rub my hands together and laugh like I'm Dr. Evil.

Blake mutters under his breath. "You're insane."

"Insanely smart, insanely amazing, or, your third option, insanely impressive?"

Theo's head is bouncing back and forth like he's watching an intense tennis match. "I'm glad Blake's finally talking to you, but you guys fight like an old married couple."

Blake shoots me a roguishly handsome grin. "Probably because just like an old married couple...we're not fucking either."

Not this again. I thought we left this behind us.

"When are you going to let it go? I'm not going to apologize for not sleeping with you. I'm a professional, not a porn star, Blakey." I know my use of Theo's nickname for him is going to grind his gears.

"Says the girl who just asked if I wanted to eat her nuts," he shoots back.

The snort that comes out of me is anything but cute.

"Uh, I think I missed a season or two," Theo cuts in with a

devilish smile. If there were popcorn in front of him, he'd be shoveling it into his mouth by the handful. Interesting that Blake hasn't told his bestie that he propositioned me for sex. Okay, well, it wasn't propositioning, but it was close to it.

Blake shrugs. "Ella doesn't like sex."

"Whatever helps you sleep at night, bud," I say in a consoling voice.

Theo throws Blake a puzzled look, trying to read his friend, but Blake is giving him absolutely nothing to work with. He's too focused on surveying me. I don't think he's ever been turned down in his life.

"Now, if we're done here, Blake was about to show me his cock—cockpit. The inside of his cockpit. His car's cockpit. Inside of his car…that he drives."

Talk about a Freudian slip. Blake shoots me a smug look as if he can read my innermost thoughts. The most annoying part of how good-looking he is, is that he knows how good-looking he is. I don't think he knows what the word *humble* means.

As the late and great Formula 1 commentator Murray Walker once said, "I should imagine that the conditions in the cockpit are totally unimaginable." I couldn't have said it better myself. Blake's cockpit is going to stay very unimaginable and very inside his pants.

ELEVEN
BLAKE

MONACO IS PACKED with celebrities from all over the world flying in to enjoy the race weekend. The city begins to smell like Chanel No. 5 as hordes of models, actresses, and singers flood the streets. And don't even get me started on the men. If you're not dressed from head to toe in Armani, Gucci, or Louis Vuitton, you may as well not be here. It's a whose-dick-is-the-biggest competition, and although I'd most definitely win, I have no interest in participating.

I'm focused on the race. I start in P2 but move into first after Theo rams into the wall on a turn, damaging his car and requiring an early retirement from the race. After the two-hour circuit, I secure my sixth consecutive Monaco Grand Prix win. It feels fucking fantastic. Harry congratulates me and I thank him without any malice or sarcasm. The humming from my car and the cheers from the crowds as I take my victory lap match my own energy.

The VIP section of the ceremony is jam-packed with glitz and glam. I spot Ella leaning against the railing, deep in conversation with Josie and one of the Hemsworth brothers—I'm not sure which one. I hope it's the married one. Or are both of them married? Isn't there a third one? I'm not sure. I make eye contact with her from the podium, and she gives me a big wave. She's wearing a McAllister hat featuring my name and number. It somehow makes my win even better. *Suck on that, Thor.*

The festivities are in full swing by the end of the press conference. This means I'm exchanging a race suit for a navy suit almost right away. I'm slated to attend some party where Diplo's performing. The club is a shitshow. Sweaty bodies everywhere, drinks spilling left and right. Not that I don't have a good time rubbing shoulders with the female fans who throw themselves at me all night, but right now the entire situation is giving me a migraine.

Lucas and Theo are thriving. I'm pretty sure Theo's getting a handy as he sticks his tongue down the throat of some fake blonde at our table. No amount of bottle service can erase that from my mind. I quickly divert my attention away so I don't see any more. How he can yell at me for eating a crisp off a table but then go and do shit like this is beyond my wildest imagination.

Around midnight, we head over to the second event of the night. It's an invite-only party hosted by Dom Perignon. Scoring an invitation means you've made it, or you're rich and famous enough to buy your way in. I've gone every year. I scan the crowd, taking in the impressive array of people. I've already spotted George Clooney and Naomi Campbell when I see Josie talking to some people by the bar. Ella's never too far away from her new bestie. Theo must have seen Josie too because he's off without another word. Lucas and I trail behind him like lost puppies.

"If it isn't my favorite Formula 1 female." Theo sweeps his eyes up and down her body. "Lookin' good, Jos."

Josie's not my type, and she's also not single, but she does look gorgeous in a red minidress.

"I always look good, Walker." Her tone is playful as she flips her hair over her shoulder. "How was the club? Full of sexy women and sloppy guys?"

Theo launches into a five-minute detailed explanation of his now-confirmed under-the-table handjob. Josie looks positively nauseous. Theo may win races, but he is not winning Josie's approval anytime soon.

"Where's Ella?" I sip my drink coolly, trying to come off like I'm not dying to see my writer in a little black dress. I'm dying to see her naked, but this will do in the meantime.

"She's not here." Josie gives me an imperceptible look. "She left after the podium ceremony."

My head flinches back. "What?"

Theo tries to shove a vodka shot into my hand, but I ignore him. I'd spoken to Ella right before the race, and she said she'd see me later. She wanted to interview a few celebrities to get some quotes for the book, and Ella wouldn't miss out on that unless something was seriously wrong.

"She just didn't want to come." Dark blond hair twirls around her finger as she studies me. "Not that big of a deal, babes."

Why would Ella lie about where she was going? And how hadn't I noticed she was lying? She widens her eyes like she's surprised whenever she's not telling the truth. I play back our conversation in my head, trying to pick up on the cues I must have missed.

"Why are you lying?"

"Hollis. Chill." Theo places a hand on my chest, pushing me away from Josie. I didn't realize how in her face I was.

Josie looks at me with a desperate appeal in her eyes. "She's fine, Blake. She went to your place. Just let it go, okay?"

Yep. I offered to let Ella stay with me…again. The first time, I hadn't offered. She'd pretty much forced her way there.

This time is all me. Honestly, I don't mind her company and Chef Nicola keeps asking about her, anyway.

Before my brain knows what my fingers are doing, I'm texting my driver to meet me out front. And before my legs register the command, I'm walking into my house. I don't know why I'm so worried. Or mad.

MUSIC ECHOES off the walls as I make my way to the kitchen. Maybe she's listening to it while she works? I don't know why she'd be working right now, but she's a workaholic, so it wouldn't surprise me too much. All I know is that if she brought a fucking bloke back to my place, I will absolutely lose any ounce of cool I have. I should've checked to see if Elliot Stabler was actually a fictional character or not.

Not much can prepare me for what I see.

Ella is dancing barefoot on the granite island in the middle of my kitchen like it's her own personal stage. The way her hips shake is absolutely tantalizing, rooting me in my spot. I can't move. My feet become cinderblock, stuck to the floor, impervious to my mind telling them to fucking walk. Singing into a kitchen spoon, rocking her hips to a Britney Spears song, she looks positively carefree. Wild hair falls out of the pink scrunchie trying to keep it in place. She missed the party of the year for a dance party of one.

I've never been so grateful my kitchen is open concept with no door. It allows me to watch Ella from the comfort of the shadows. She's too lost in her own world to notice me anyway. I'm not sure how many songs I stay there for. Two, three? Five? All I know is I've seen Ella dance to pretty much every genre of music, from Broadway show tunes to Y2K rap.

I finally cough to announce myself, but it backfires terribly. She jumps back, smacking her head on a hanging pendant light. The rough sound mixes with the music and I'm in front of her instantaneously.

"Shit, are you okay, love?"

"I may have a concussion." She massages the back of her head where a bump will undoubtedly form. "So, ask me again in ten minutes."

Ignoring my offer to help her off the island, she instead chooses to hop down and almost break her ankle in the process. We stare at each other for a full thirty seconds without speaking. I'm not sure which of us is more surprised by the other's presence. Her nipples poke through her shirt and I can't help when my eyes drift down. She crosses her arms over her chest in response.

"What are you doing?" I finally ask.

"Nothing." Her cheeks burn bright red. "Have you ever heard of knocking?"

"It's my house."

She fights the urge to sass me but quickly loses. "Well, it's my dance party."

There's no use trying not to laugh. Her smart mouth never ceases to keep me on my toes. "Your dance party?"

"I'm not waving around a spoon for fun. It's my microphone." Everything about her face says *duh*. Ah, of course. Silly me. I notice her eyes look red and puffy; she's been crying. "What are you doing here? I thought you had a night of partying."

I'm not sure what I'm doing here. Making sure she's okay? Finding out why she's at my house instead of out? Avoiding the party because as much as I hate to admit it, it's getting a little old? I answer her question with a question. "In the mood for an adventure?"

Her teeth trap her bottom lip as she considers it. Is it really that hard of a decision? Continue dancing half naked in my kitchen by herself or go on an adventure in Monaco with me, an extremely attractive man, *with an accent*.

"Okay." Uncertainty marks her words, but it doesn't stop a grin of practiced charm from flitting across my lips. "Just let me put on pants."

"Are you sure?" I'm quite enjoying the view of her tanned legs peeking out from underneath the oversized Chicago Cubs shirt hanging on her petite frame like a dress. "Those are optional."

"If I didn't invite you to my dance party, why would I want to go to a no-pants party with you?"

Bare feet pad across the floor as she power walks to her room. Not her room, my room. The room in my house that she's currently staying in. *Whatever.*

The incessant roar of fireworks makes it hard for conversation, so I settle into the back seat of my car as my driver pulls out of the driveway. From my vantage point, I have the perfect view of Ella's profile as she rests her head against the window. I'm not sure if it's the way she carries herself, or how gorgeous she is, or the fact that the only action I've gotten in a while is from my hand, but I can't look away.

Ella taps her pointer finger against the cold glass. "Doesn't that one kind of look like…you know?"

I lift my brows and wait for her to give me some sort of explanation.

Huffing out a sigh, she says, "Sperm."

"Sperm?" It comes out dumbly as if I've never heard the word.

"Do we need to have the birds and the bees talk, Blake?" she teases. "Look! Look!"

The powerful burst of white does indeed look like drips of jizz. I'm more concerned that she notices this than that she's right.

"It sort of does."

"Definitely does."

The tip of her nose presses against the glass for the rest of the drive. She enjoys her view, while I enjoy my view of her. We park at a private harbor on the outskirts of the province where the smaller of my two yachts is anchored.

"So was your plan to lure me away from your house so you can murder me and dump me in the sea?" Ella questions me as we walk down the dock.

"Considering you said my looks kill, if I wanted to murder you, all I had to do was glance your way."

She lets out a laugh, smooth as silk. "I think we can both agree you're quite brooding."

"Most women I know find brooding men sexy."

I've been told this more times than I can count. I don't have the heart to tell them I'm just not interested in anything more than playing Whac-A-Mole. I can't give them more than that.

"Well. I hate to disappoint you, Blake," Ella says with a brief smile, "but I'm not like the other women you know."

I don't bother telling her it's not a disappointment. It's a problem because I don't know how to handle it.

TWELVE
ELLA

WE'RE on the smaller of Blake's two boats and it's the size of a starter home. Who has multiple boats in Monaco? The dock fees for just one could fund a presidential election, for fuck's sake. I fight the urge to Google what professions I can switch to (that aren't stripping or OnlyFans—no judgment, I just don't have the confidence or coordination) in order to make enough money for this type of lifestyle. His boat not only has a pool table, it has a *spa*. Oh, yeah, and a treadmill. I enjoy a good run as much as any non-marathon running human can, but who comes out on a yacht to *run*?

Blake seems relaxed sitting next to me on the end of the boat. His feet skim the top of the sea while mine dangle in the space above. The lights of Monte Carlo are small dots from the spot we're anchored in, but the velvety sky still glitters from the dazzling display of fireworks.

To say I'm shocked Blake left the party to check on me is the understatement of the year. He's been hyping up the event for days, telling me I can't act like a weirdo when I see celebrities. Of course, then he bristles that I'm not rattled by him since he's a "world champion," but to me he's just Blake.

Everyone else may see him as only a Formula 1 driver, but I'm getting to know him as the man who watches more documentaries in a week than the average person watches in their lifetime. The man who spends close to an hour in the hotel gift shop at each Grand Prix, picking out the perfect postcard to send his niece and nephew. The man who still has a physical newspaper delivered to his house every morning just so he can do the crossword. And he refuses to Google any answers. He'd rather leave it incomplete than "cop out and cheat." The down-to-earth side of Blake is softening me like butter. Josie was right when she said he's a good guy once you get past the rough exterior; he just takes time to open up.

We've been passing a champagne bottle back and forth for the past hour, asking each other ridiculous and arbitrary questions. I appreciate the fact that he's not pushing me on what's going on. I wish I could act like nothing's wrong, but one look at me and you can tell I'm off.

I start to pass the bottle back to Blake before remembering the fact that he walked in on my private cabaret show. If he saw my dramatic reenactment of *Hamilton*, I will immediately throw myself overboard. I take another large gulp.

"Have you ever skinny-dipped?" he asks, interrupting my thoughts with his question.

I nod in response. There's no need for him to know I skinny-dipped when it was pitch-black outside and there were no boys in attendance. I'll let his imagination run wild instead.

"In that case, I dare you to skinny-dip now."

The champagne I've just taken a sip of shoots out through my nose, burning as it drips down my chin. "I'm going to pass on that one. But you're more than welcome to." My hand waves for him to dive right in. I think I'll keel over and die if he does, so I'm not going to encourage it, but I'm not going to discourage it either.

"You just want to see if I'm packing heat or not."

It's a warm night, but the smirk he gives me sends goose bumps down my arms. "False."

"So if I stripped buck naked, you wouldn't be at all curious?"

"Maybe." I casually shrug despite my rapidly beating heart. "But as I've said, I don't mix business with pleasure."

"Aha!" He has a shit-eating grin plastered on his face. "So you do associate my dick with pleasure!"

Without so much as a thought, I push him into the crisp, cool Mediterranean Sea. I can't believe he actually falls in. He's made of pure muscle; I can't even lift a fifteen-pound dumbbell at the gym without getting sore. But I need him to stop talking about his dick, so shoving him into the water to shut him up seems wise.

His head pops up moments later, sputtering water. I collapse in a pile of giggles as he floats there with a look of pure incredulity. The laughter quickly turns into yelps as Blake tugs my legs, pulling me into the water with him. The disbelief on his face was worth it.

"You said you wanted to go swimming!" I remind him.

I'm dog-paddling like there's a real danger of drowning even though we're no more than ten feet away from the boat. A splash of water hits my face before Blake's strong hands push my shoulders down, immersing me underwater once again.

"I'm no Michael Phelps!" I yell when I come up for air. "Don't drown me."

We're face-to-face, our bobbing heads inches apart. *Don't look at his lips, don't look at lips.* He's too sexy, I'm too tipsy, and we're a little too close. If I wasn't already wet, looking at Blake's white dress shirt clinging to his muscles as water drips down his exposed skin would've done the trick.

"Are there any sports you're good at?"

"First of all, it's rude to assume I'm not athletic," I chastise him. "Second of all, I won a hot-dog-eating competition when I was seven, so I have a trophy with my name on it."

He chuckles before disappearing into the dark blue water. My brain catches up to my body and I flutter kick my way back to the boat with Blake following closely behind. I'm desperate to change out of the shirt that's glued to my body like a second skin and am grateful to find his steward left out towels and dry clothes for us. The sweats and shirt are *way* too big on me, but I like baggy clothes. They're comfortable, and after the grossly inappropriate comments on my figure at my last job…it's a protective layer. The shirt smells like Blake—masculine and delicious.

"Do I look like a trash panda?" I point to my face. Mascara is definitely smudged under my eyes. Blake's forehead creases as he frowns in confusion.

"Trash panda is another name for a raccoon," I explain exasperatedly.

He lets out a low, gravelly laugh that vibrates through his chest as the two of us settle onto the sleek leather couch in his boat's salon. A variety of food and drinks sit neatly on the coffee table in front of us, and I waste no time ripping open the bag of Tostitos. The corners of Blake's mouth tug up. He can't seem to get over how much I love snacks.

Theo's been calling Blake nonstop since we stepped onto the boat and Blake's ignored him each and every time. After call number twenty, I insist he answer his phone. What if Theo's in danger or something? Turns out the only thing in danger is our eardrums. The music's deafeningly loud. Blake cringes at the sound too, holding his phone away from him.

"Where the fuck are you?" Theo shouts.

"Out on the boat. What's up?"

"Well, you need to come back." He's almost impossible to understand thanks to the vodka slurring his speech. "Amelie's here. And she's horny for you, Hollis."

Well, that was crystal clear. I quickly slap my hand over my mouth.

"Josie should start a 'Horny for Hollis' trend on Instagram," I joke quietly so only Blake can hear.

He rolls his eyes at me. "Go enjoy the party, Theo. We'll talk tomorrow."

I tuck my knees up under me as Blake attempts to get off the phone. There's no stopping Theo once he has an audience, but he's not making much sense. When he finally cuts Theo off by unceremoniously hitting "end" and then turning off his phone, Blake presses his thumbs into his temples.

"Christ," he mutters to himself.

Keeping my eyes trained on the floral arrangement opposite the couch, I work up the nerve to ask, "So why did you leave the party? Since Amelie's so horny for you and all."

Amelie's probably blond and tall and has massive mango boobs. I bet she's on the Peloton leaderboard and shops exclusively at Whole Foods, or whatever the European equivalent is, and eats only vegan, gluten-free, and keto foods. And I'm sure she can separate sex from feelings and have fun, casual one-night stands. She's the worst and I hate her.

"Amelie is bat-shit crazy. Restraining order level," Blake admits with a nonchalant shrug. "I'm not sure why Theo selectively forgets that part."

My face manages to stay neutral, not giving away that I'm extremely happy Amelie is a psycho stalker instead of an Instagram baddie.

"So you left because…"

He can't avoid my question that easily. And I won't let him get away with answering it with another question again.

"The party's the same every year. Not missing much." He shrugs before winking. "And I wanted to make sure you weren't stealing from me."

"Yeah, because I definitely want to steal your weird blue painting, Blake."

He has a massive piece of so-called "art" that's literally just a canvas painted blue. That's it. I can finger paint something more artistically creative. He mumbles that it's an original Rodolfo. No idea who that is, but it probably cost him more than this boat did. Maybe I'll paint a canvas red and claim it's a Rodolfo, too. Highly doubt he'd know the difference.

"Why'd you decide to dance in my kitchen instead of surrounding yourself with celebs?"

"I was planning on going," I admit, "but saw on social media that some old work colleagues were there."

I'm in such a better spot than I was a few months ago, but the thought of running into someone from PlayMedia brought on a fresh wave of emotion I wasn't expecting. Hence chugging wine straight from the bottle and having a solo dance party. Josie offered to keep me company, but I told her to enjoy herself. At least one of us should stay in case Harry Styles does show up to the party; there was a rumor floating around.

"You don't have to tell me anything, but I'm here if you want to talk," Blake says softly.

Maybe five people know the real story about what happened at PlayMedia, and I'm not about to go screaming it from the rooftops. Blake and I may be friends now, but we're not "spill your trauma" friends. Talking about it always makes me feel like I'm diving headfirst into the past. Part of the reason I even took this job was for a change of pace, a fresh start. New York is too small for Connor's big, lying mouth.

I don't realize I let out a heavy sigh until Blake asks me, "Are you okay?"

His eyes are wide with worry and he's fidgeting, tapping his foot against the ground at an increasingly aggressive speed. His brown eyes are filled with such open sincerity.

"Yeah." I give him what I hope is a reassuring smile. "It's a long story."

"We're in the middle of the Mediterranean at two in the morning," he points out. "I have nothing but time for a long story."

Well played, Mr. Hollis. "Fair enough."

"So, what happened?" he asks calmly.

"You know *Trash Talk*?"

Blake nods. "Yeah, that guy Brixton hosts it. He's some ex-NFL player's son, right?"

I'm not surprised. Everyone knows *Trash Talk*. There's a reason it has over one million listeners an episode and has been ranked the number one sports podcast for three years in a row.

"Yep, that's the one. Connor thrives on this chauvinistic attitude of praising toxic masculinity and feeding into the stereotype of over-sexualized, submissive women." The acidity of his name burns my tongue. "I never worked with him when I was just writing, but when I started podcasting, we were together almost every day. He helped produce my show."

There's a special place in hell for guys like him. Host of *Trash Talk*, producer of *Coffee with Champions*, and director of my nightmares.

"One time, we were a chair short in a meeting and he told me I could just sit on his face. Not his lap…his face. And everyone just laughed like it was an okay thing to say."

My sigh is weighted, holding uncomfortable memories. I don't tell him about the time Connor told me I have dick-sucking lips and asked if I'd give him a blowjob to relieve his stress. Or when he told me he thought of me while fucking some chick because we wear the same perfume. I can write a book longer than Blake's biography with all the examples of harassment I experienced at PlayMedia. The constant belittling and demeaning attitude got emotionally exhausting very quickly.

"I finally worked up the nerve to go to HR," I admit with a shaky voice. "Connor found out I reported him for harassment and long story short…I didn't stay much more after that."

"Did he touch you?" Blake asks, his voice tightly wound. He's flexing his fingers as if fighting the urge to punch a wall.

"He sexually assaulted a girl I worked with last year." A lump rises in my throat as I say the words. It's not a lie, but it's also not the whole truth. It's easier to talk about if I don't have to admit that the girl was me. I unconsciously bring my fingers up to my neck, remembering the feeling of his hand closed around it, squeezing the air out. The surprise of his actions mixed with the intense pressure left me completely shocked. *Deep breath, Ella.*

Blake rubs his forehead, massaging away the stress crease. "What happened?"

"I don't know the details," I tell him, choking out the words. "The police didn't press charges, though."

"Bloody fuckin' hell." I watch his face harden; jaw locking, the muscles ticking. "That's bullshit. And work didn't do anything either? They just let him get away with it?"

"Do you know how much money his podcast generates for PlayMedia? In advertising revenue alone he pulls fifty thousand dollars per episode and he does two episodes a week." The noise that comes out of me sounds like a strangled laugh, covered in sarcasm and dipped in insincerity. "He's connected and powerful in the industry. No one wants to mess with him— or his dad."

My podcast may have been successful, but it is nowhere near *that* successful. Not many podcasts are.

"Christ, Ella," Blake mutters. "That's awful. I'm assuming she left the company?"

"Mm-hmm." I exhale deeply. I don't know why the hell I told him all of that. This may be the first time I've talked about it without crying, though, so that's a win. "I'm happy I don't have to dread going to work, but I'm pissed I was forced to give up a job I really loved, you know? I finally felt like I found my thing with the podcast."

The frightening force of his glare relaxes when he looks at me. "I'm so sorry you dealt with all of that, love."

"It's okay." I'm willing my words into existence. Manifestation or whatever. "I mean, no, it's not, but I'm okay. Really."

"Is that why you carry pepper spray?"

My eyes widen in surprise. Looks like Blake's more observant than I gave him credit for. I nod before changing the subject.

Blake doesn't mention or bring up what I told him for the rest of our time in Monaco. When I wake up on my last day there, I see a text from him saying he left me something.

I skip to the kitchen, praying he left me a yummy treat from the bakery down the street. Chef Nicola has been bringing us different pastries from there every morning, but it's her day off. Their blueberry muffins are heaven on Earth. Instead, I find a beautifully wrapped box with a giant bow on it. *Definitely no baked goods in here.* I eagerly tear the pale-yellow wrapping paper off. Inside, I find a portable podcasting set. It has all the essentials: a microphone and stand, headphones, a shock mount, a mixer, a pop filter, and an audio interface. I read the attached note, the sound of my heartbeat pulsing in my ears.

Ella,

I won't be your co-host, but I do hope you continue doing what you love. Fuck anyone who tries to take that away from you.

xx,

Blake

P.S. I lied when I said your podcast wasn't the best.
I've listened to every episode.

The work I've put into Blake's book may be good so far, but how much I'm starting to like him? That's one plot twist I didn't see coming.

THIRTEEN
BLAKE

ANOTHER GALA I don't want to attend, yet here I am. I chug my whiskey before the bartender slides a new one in front of me. I'm watching Ella from across the room. She's deep in conversation with Keith, nodding animatedly. Every time I think about her being harassed at work, which has been nonstop since she told me, anger thrums through my veins. It takes strength to walk away from something like that, to walk away from a job you love because of some prick who can't keep his dick in his pants.

Ella called me immediately after finding the gift, thanking me repeatedly. I still feel helpless about what happened to her, and I'm not sure if she even wants to podcast again, but at least the portable podcasting set was something I could give her to bring a smile to her face. And damn, is her smile beautiful. Plus, friends do stuff like buy the other one presents to cheer them up.

Keith makes his way across the room toward me. *Fuck.* I quickly down the rest of my drink. It burns my throat. My manager's in the process of locking in a massive brand partnership and the executive vice president of the company is in attendance at tonight's event. A good word from him will expedite the deal, and it's a bloody good endorsement considering Keith flew in for the French Grand Prix.

I've met the bloke once before and didn't particularly like him. He acts like he's God's gift to Earth and everyone should be honored to be breathing the same air as him. *Wanker*.

"Ah," Keith says, appearing next to me at the bar. "There you are. Thought you were avoiding me."

Not avoiding, but not going out of my way to announce my presence.

"Avoid you, Keith? I wouldn't dream of it."

"Well, good"—he chuckles—"because Jean-François is here and I want you two to chat for a bit."

I nod and follow his lead. Jean-François is hard to miss. He looks like the villain in every Disney movie that Millie's ever made me watch. Tall, dark, and handsome with a side of malice and a hint of evil.

"Blake," Jean-François greets me. "Pleasure to see you again."

The smile he gives me doesn't quite reach his beady eyes. He doesn't make a move to shake my hand. Does he expect me to bend down and kiss his shiny Valentino shoes?

"Jean-François. How have you been?"

"*Magnifique*. We just signed David Beckham for an upcoming project."

I guarantee he had nothing to do with Beckham signing with them. I swallow my dislike for the man and let him brag for the next fifteen minutes about how successful he is. If my endorsement goes through, I pray I never have to work with him. He's insufferable.

"So, tell me how you're doing."

"Things have been good." I cross my arms over my chest defensively. "The season is shaping up nicely so far."

His mouth jerks into a sardonic grin. "Much better than last season."

My jaw immediately tenses, and he knows he's hit a nerve. I'm about to knock this piece of shit out. I breathe in through my nose, out through my mouth, just like my therapist told me to. I wish I hadn't finished my drink because I could use one right about now. He drones on and on about my less than stellar season last year and I'm *this* close to breaking his nose when a hand lightly touches my arm.

"Blake," Ella greets me. "There you are! I've been searching everywhere for you."

"'Ello. This is Ella. She's—"

"Blake's biographer," she cuts in.

The smile on her face is the same one my sister used to give me that means "shut up and just go with my plan." I have no idea what she's playing at or what she's doing over here, but I stay silent. There's not much more of this conversation I can handle on my own.

"*Bonjour.*" He couldn't be more obviously checking her out. "I'm Jean-François. You're quite the beauty, Ella."

Hell fucking no. Is he kidding? If I didn't want to knock him out before, I definitely do now. I don't like how he's eyeing her one bit. When Ella holds out her hand to shake his, he presses it to his lips for an uncomfortably long amount of time. She shoots me a grossed-out look and I stifle a laugh. The moment he releases her hand, she tucks it into the crook of my arm. The action both calms me and sends a bolt of desire straight to my dick.

"Blake here was just telling me about last season."

I work to unclench my jaw. *This fucking bloke.*

"Amazing, right? Not only does he have the highest winning percentage the sport's ever seen, but he holds the record for most wins of any Formula 1 driver. Did you know he averages eighteen points per race? It's no wonder he has the all-time most career points."

Ella goes on and on, listing my achievements, going into detail about my most impressive wins. She even talks about some of my races from last year, focusing on what I did right, rather than how I fucked up. Undercutting to bring myself up to P3 from P8 at the Australian Grand Prix. Insisting on finishing the Hungarian Grand Prix on wet tires versus changing back to slick tires, securing a podium win.

"Sorry about rambling on." Her smile is as sweet as the candy bars she loves so much. I know she's not one bit sorry. "Blake's just so impressive! Don't you think?"

Her hand squeezes my arm as she waits expectantly for Jean-François to respond, which he does with a quick nod.

"Anyway. I didn't mean to interrupt." She's an awful liar, but he's not a pro at reading her face like I've come to be. "But I just wanted to let Blake know that the CEO of Puma was looking for him. Something about a campaign for their new activewear line. I'm not really sure, but I said I'd pass along the message if I found you."

This catches his attention. Fuck, I wish I could kiss her. Not only has she stupefied Jean-François with a brief rundown of my career highlights, but she's also planted the seed that his competitor is trying to poach me. There's no one from Puma even at this party.

"It was a pleasure meeting you, Jean-Paul," Ella says with doe-eyed innocence.

"Jean-François," I correct, although she knows damn well what his name is.

"So sorry! Of course. Jean-François."

"The pleasure was all mine," he purrs, giving her another once-over.

Ella shoots me a "good luck" smile before walking away, her hips swaying in a way that hypnotizes me. Thankfully, the conversation doesn't last much longer than that. After Keith praises me for impressing Jean-François, who said I was "exactly the type of person they want to partner with," I search for Ella. I have her to thank for the endorsement not falling apart at the seams.

She's chatting with Josie and Harry at the bar, the three of them laughing at something. I suck up the fact that I'm going to have to socialize with Harry and head over to them. I may respect him on the track, but that doesn't mean I want to spend time with him off of it.

"I owe you big time." I lightly bump Ella's hip against mine. "How'd you know my arse needed saving?"

"You were giving him the same look you gave me when we first met."

Josie's subsequent giggle makes me realize that she's aware of my outburst in Bahrain. Lovely. Ella shoots me an apologetic look, but I deserve it. I'd gone in hard on Ella without giving her a chance. Harry doesn't say much; no doubt because he thinks I'm going to rip into him if he opens his mouth.

"I appreciate it."

"Anytime." She waves off my thanks. "That's what friends are for, right?"

If one friend constantly thinks about the other friend, then sure, that's exactly what friends are for.

"As your friend," I inform her in a serious tone, "I'm obligated to tell you that I know the best steak and frites place in town. Any interest in going after the race? My treat to thank you for your service."

Ella doesn't speak a lick of French, but she damn well knows the translation for French fries. The smile she shines on me is sultry and sweet. I like being the one to put a smile on her face because for those few seconds, I know I've made her happy...and fuck if that doesn't make me happy, too.

. . .

ACCORDING TO THEO, I've broken "bro code" by not going out with him and Lucas after the race. He's acting as if I've committed a crime against humanity. I try to tune him out, but he's seated next to me at the post-race press conference; he placed third behind me in first and Lucas in second. Reporters are still setting up their cameras, but Theo's keeping his voice low, so our mics don't pick up his words.

"Mate," he whispers solemnly from next to me. "You're pussy-whipped and you're not even getting any pussy."

Lucas overhears his comment and chokes on his water. A slew of people look to see what the commotion is, but the stares don't faze Theo, who continues his one-sided conversation. "Your actions are forcing Luc to waterboard himself. Is this what you want, Hollis?"

My lips twitch up. His dramatization never gets old. He's been this way since we met when I was eight.

"We can't just be lettuce and tomato," he whines, switching tactics. Sticking out his lower lip, he slugs me in the arm. "We need our bacon."

Ever since Ella pointed out that our initials are BLT, like the sandwich, Theo won't stop referring to us as such. He's seriously tried catching my attention by calling out, "Bacon!" I'm not sure if I dislike that or Blakey Blake more.

"Call me lettuce one more time, Theo," Lucas complains under his breath.

There's no one who dislikes press conferences more than me, but for once I'm ready to get the show on the road. Anything to get Theo to stop bothering me about how it's not "just dinner." I'm not sure how many times I can repeat that it is *just dinner*. It's simply dinner with a friend who happens to make my dick throb uncomfortably.

I've all but forgotten about Theo's insinuations as Ella and I are seated at dinner. The restaurant is small but stylish, bottles of wine lining the walls, black tablecloths and candles decorating the tables. It's understated in just the right way. They don't have a menu and the only thing they ask you is how you want your steak done. Simple. Ella's in heaven since they have unlimited fries. Yeah, I now sometimes call them fries because of her. *Whatever.*

Despite the small menu, our waiter continues to stop by our table every ten minutes. I'm thoroughly enjoying the whiskey I'm drinking, but if he looks at Ella like *that* one more time, I'm going to smash my glass over his head. Or maybe I'll just break the glass and then use a shard to cut his dick off. I don't mind getting creative. He's eye-fucking her as if I'm not sitting right here. Even though she's only a friend, so I have no right to get angry, it's still impolite. I don't blame him considering how turned on I get just from being around her—the chase or something like that—but that's beside the point.

"Is everything to your liking?" he asks Ella, dutifully ignoring me. It takes everything in my power not to wipe the cocky smile right off his face with my fist.

"He's flirting with you," I comment after he leaves. "Big time."

Ella scrunches up her nose. "He's definitely not. He's just being friendly."

"Would you like to hear about our *delicious* Montepulciano d'Abruzzo?" I mimic the waiter, deepening the pitch of my voice. "It's got a *deep* color and *juicy* flavors with *soft*, *supple* tannins. It'll absolutely *delight* you."

She rolls her eyes. "You're crazy."

The owner of the restaurant comes over to our table to greet us. I've been here before, and he remembers me. He takes an instant liking to Ella, who spends twenty minutes asking him about his life story. Journalism was the right career path for her given her thoughtful questions and genuine interest in his responses.

Halfway through dinner, Ella tells me she has a *really*

important question. Hesitantly, I nod. I'm never fully ready for any question she asks me. I quickly swallow a piece of steak, not wanting to choke on it in case the question catches me off guard.

Her eyes blaze with excitement. "Okay, what would your death-row meal be?"

Whatever I'd been expecting her to ask, I can assure you it wasn't that. A shocked laugh escapes my lips, and once it does, I can't hold back. I'm doubled over, my abs constricting as they do after an hour in the gym with Sam. When I finally get a hold of myself, Ella's looking at me adorably. Her head's tilted and her eyes twinkle with delight.

"You know what death row is, right?" Ella asks. "Like when they're going to kill you because of your crimes?"

"Yes, Ella. I know what death row is. I'm British, not dumb."

Ella makes a *tsk, tsk* noise and shakes her head slowly. "After your race earlier, I have to disagree with you. Overtaking Lucas in lap fifty was extremely risky. Almost got you a five-second penalty and then you wouldn't have placed podium. And what the hell was up with you boxing out Theo on lap twenty-two? Kind of a dick move."

A minor flush creeps up my neck, threatening to make my pleasure at her words evident. There's something so unbelievably sexy about Ella talking about the race. It may be her job, but I enjoy knowing that she keeps tabs on my progress throughout the circuit.

"A win's a win." I'm choosing to focus on that part versus her calling my driving dumb, which it absolutely was. Andreas had ripped me a new one on my radio during the race and then again after the champagne spray.

"Anyway, a death-row meal is essentially what you would choose as your last meal on Earth. Nothing is off the table. But you only get two appetizers, one main, two sides, one dessert, and two drinks. Well, those are the rules I follow, anyway."

Hm, interesting. This is a question I can get behind. Although based on how Ella treats most of my snacks, I have no idea how harshly she'll judge my meal. She gagged when I put pea protein powder in my smoothie. It's not like I put sand in there.

"Oh, and although this isn't a test, if you say La Croix, you're automatically blacklisted in my book. Because it tastes like flavored static electricity and anyone who claims to like it is a liar."

I snort as I contemplate my options. Shit, this is harder than I thought it'd be.

"And—"

Groaning, I push a hand over my face. "Are you going to give me a moment of silence to think?"

"Just one last thing! Promise." She pauses dramatically before lowering her voice. "You can't say *pussy*." Her cheeks flush adorably. "That's not a valid answer for a death-row meal."

The water I'm drinking sprays out of my mouth. "Has anyone ever told you that you have a wildly dirty mouth?"

"Nope. I've never even had a cavity."

"Who in the hell said that as their death-row answer?"

I bet it was her friend Jack. *Cocksucker.*

Her nose crinkles at the question. "You don't want to know."

I collect my thoughts before listing out my "death-row meal." Fried calamari and crispy Brussels sprouts with bacon for my appetizers, lamb chops as my main, potatoes au gratin and spring rolls—from my favorite restaurant in China—as my sides, my sister's banoffee pie for dessert, and green tea and whiskey for my drinks. It's surprisingly harder than I thought it'd be. After I say it, I already want to swap out one of my appetizers and change a drink choice.

"That was such a good death-row meal! I'm seriously impressed. You even included a restaurant name, which is, like, five hundred bonus points."

It's baffling how something as simple as a death-row meal can brighten her face as if she'd just won the lottery.

"I thought this wasn't a test."

"If you lost, I wouldn't have let you know. Want to know mine?"

I don't have time to say yes before Ella launches into a long-winded explanation of her meal. She's seriously thought this out. There are even rotating options based on the season or the type of mood she's in. When she finishes, we're smiling at each other like idiots. For the first time since my mum left, I wish that cookie-cutter fairy tales were written for guys like me. But they're not. They're written for girls like Ella. The ones who *deserve* a happily ever after.

FOURTEEN
ELLA

BLAKE'S in a mood from the second I see him in Austria for the next Grand Prix. Snappy and closed off, his hand permanently rakes through his hair in an agitated state. I try asking him if he's okay, but he waves me off without a word. To make things worse, his practice sessions on Friday do not go well. It seems to be problem after problem with his car. The camber on his back tires isn't right for the circuit conditions, there's too much grain, something with his engine is off. His team makes changes to address the issues, but I don't think anything can snap him out of this funk.

By the time Saturday rolls around, he's in no better of a mood, yelling at everyone from the mechanics to Andreas. I keep enough distance between us so that I can oversee and overhear everything without being an inconvenience. Apparently, not enough distance because after he lands himself P9 at qualifying, which is the worst position he's yet to start in, I become his personal punching bag.

He growls at me in front of the entire pit crew. "Christ, do you have to write *everything* down, Ella? Enough is enough. Move out of their way and let them do their job."

I'm standing off to the side, taking notes on my iPad, not bothering anyone. His jaw clenches and his brows knit together in frustration.

"Sorry," I mumble, wishing I could hide behind the stack of tires next to me.

"Can't you find something more meaningful to do than follow my every fucking move?"

Color storms my cheeks in embarrassment. After a few more similar instances, I'm *this* close to losing my shit on him, but people always surround us. He might not care how he sounds, but being here is my job, and I have no intention of losing my professionalism because of his temper tantrums. I make myself scarce the rest of the weekend to avoid him. He has yet to say sorry for being a dick and I have a feeling I'm waiting on an apology I'm not going to get.

I spend Sunday with Andreas, the team principal. He's the heart and soul of McAllister. Nothing happens that he doesn't know about, so he's a great source for the biography. I've spent some time with him before, but not a ton. Everything he says sounds like he's mad even though he's not. He's indifferent about my presence as long as I don't interrupt what he's doing because there's a lot going on.

After stopping by the pit garage for some conversation about tire compound for the circuit, it's just the two of us. I've already hit 10k steps on my fitness watch and it's just a few minutes before noon. He shoots me a small smile, a knowing glint in his gray eyes. "Wondering how I deal with Blake when he's a pain in the arse?"

"Lots of patience…and alcohol?"

Andreas has muttered about five times already that he needs a drink. I can probably use one too considering Blake's snarky attitude and menacing glares.

"This weekend's been a walk in the park compared to last season."

"I can only imagine."

"He has a fire in his eyes that I haven't seen in some time," he says thoughtfully. "And I'd be remiss not to think it has something to do with you."

"Oh, well, I—"

"I know you're here to help with his book but don't think I haven't noticed your friendship."

"He's a good guy when he's not being…well, when he's not being a complete asshole. Pardon my language."

"Just don't give up on him," Andreas tells me. "He's a tough egg to crack, but he's worth the scramble."

Well, that's a new expression.

I'm still mulling over Andreas's comment as I make my way back to the paddock. I run directly into Blake. The force of it knocks me back a few steps and he grabs onto me before I fall. It's like a scene out of a poorly directed, low-budget Lifetime rom-com.

"Shit. Sorry. Are you okay?"

Sorry for running into me or sorry for being a dickhead?

"Yeah." My voice is flatter than my chest was in sixth grade. "All good."

Scratching the side of his face, he focuses on me for the first time all weekend. He has circles under his eyes and his face is paler than usual. I don't know if I want to pull him in for a hug or smack him upside the head.

He gives me a rough semblance of a smile. "How're you doing?"

His hand is still on my waist and I'm having trouble pushing air out of my lungs. I seriously think I may be asthmatic. Why does the smallest touch from him make me feel like my entire body's on fire?

"I'll be doing a lot better once you remove your hand and let me do my job."

I take a step back, walking away before he can say anything

else to me. It's more than him being rude to me. I can handle that. But doing it in front of his team? When I'm just doing my job? Until he gives me an apology, I have nothing to say to him.

JOSIE and I are hanging out in my hotel room after the race when she tells me she has a "positively brilliant" idea. She's absurdly British sometimes.

"Okay." Josie claps her hands together, tugging at the necklace she's wearing. "What if we recorded something just for the hell of it? Something fun."

I still haven't touched the podcasting set Blake got me. It's not that I don't want to; I just don't know how to without it bringing up everything that happened at PlayMedia. I've been trying to move on from my past and this feels like kicking that door wide open and inviting in a lot of shit I'd rather forget.

Josie picks up the podcasting set from my suitcase with a hopeful smile. I know her efforts are well-intentioned because after a girls' night with way too much cheap wine, I told her why I left my last job.

"Something fun," I repeat back, staring at the equipment like it's a ticking time bomb. "Like what?"

"Just something to get the ball rolling. Get you used to the whole idea of even recording stuff again. Not a podcast *at all*, just two girls chit-chatting and having a good time."

I raise an eyebrow. It's not the worst idea I've ever heard. It's like dipping my toe into the podcasting kiddie pool.

"We can blind taste test wines and see if we know which kind they are," she continues, getting more excited by her own idea. "Oh! Or we can get multiple pints of ice cream, all from different brands, and try to guess which is which!"

I'm thankful Josie loves ice cream, wine, and lounging in pajamas as much as I do. She can tell I'm considering the suggestion and before I can protest, she's out the door and running to the nearest corner store. She's back shortly after with six different white wines, three different brands of vanilla ice cream, and a *lot* of chips. Or crisps, as she calls them. Those are to cleanse our palates. Have I mentioned how much I love Josie?

It takes me almost twenty minutes to set up the podcasting set, but once I do, my hands start shaking and my heart pounds in my chest, the sound pulsing in my ears. I know it's just a dumb fucking podcasting set, but it feels like it's too much, too soon. What's the point, anyway? Even if I can manage to podcast without panicking, I'll never be able to reach the same success I did at PlayMedia. I don't know if anyone else will even hire me. No one wants to work with someone who's "high-maintenance, unprofessional, and rude," which thanks to Connor, is what everyone thinks. It's a lost cause.

"I can't do it," I tell Josie resignedly. "It's—I just can't. I'm sorry. I appreciate what you're trying to do, but I can't right now."

"There's no need to apologize," she says, waving me off. "The fact that you traveled with it from London shows that there's a part of you that wants to give it a go. That day's just not today. But it'll happen. Your horoscope says so. It also says you should be open to new love in unexpected places. Cough, cough, Blake."

I ignore the not-so-innocent smile she's giving me. Josie fills me in on the press conference I chose to skip out on earlier as we disassemble the podcasting set. The asshole still managed to place third even with his shitty starting grid position. It was pretty impressive. Not that I care to tell him this. I guess he snapped at multiple reporters during the press conference, even telling one to "either ask a new question or bugger the fuck off." At least it's not just me taking the brunt of his anger.

"I thought Blake was going to flip the table over. It was like a reality TV show. I wish you had seen it."

I spoon ice cream into two bowls for us. "Yeah, well, he's making me angry."

"Angry with desire?" she teases with an exaggerated wink.

"More like angry with a desire to punch him in the throat."

Opening up a bottle of Pinot Grigio, I take a sip straight from the bottle. It's one of those nights. We spend the next hour getting way too tipsy off cheap wine while devouring a substantial amount of ice cream and playing the game Fuck, Marry, Kill. Or as Josie calls it: Bang, Smash, Dash.

Josie can't stop giggling and barely manages to get out her words. "Chandler, Joey, Ross."

I lick my spoon clean as I think. "Marry Chandler, fuck Joey, and kill Ross. I feel like that's the only right way to answer."

Her blond head shakes in agreement. She's going to either love or hate my next one. "Blake, Theo, Lucas." I spoon a ginormous bite of vanilla ice cream into my mouth as Josie squeals. The brain freeze is worth it.

"The Formula 1 fuckboys? Pass."

"Gun to your head."

She starts singing La Roux's "Bulletproof" and then sticks her tongue out at me, which is white from the ice cream. "You'd probably choose Blake for all three."

I narrow my eyes at her. Admitting how I feel means I'm putting it out into the universe and despite what my horoscope says, I'm not sure I'm ready to do that quite yet. Do I like spending time with Blake? Yes. Even though his favorite facial expression is a scowl, when he does smile? I swear it could end a war. He's clever and always willing to have a debate with me. It doesn't matter whether it's over hot dogs being considered sandwiches (Theo's question), Ronaldo being named the greatest footballer over Messi, or which

Taylor Swift album is the best—obviously *1989 (Taylor's Version)*.

Our conversations are easy, and we genuinely want to hear what the other one thinks. He's surprisingly thoughtful, too, and even started keeping Double Stuf Oreos in his suite for when I need an emergency snack. And God knows we have enough chemistry to create another *Breaking Bad* spin-off. But he's made it crystal clear he doesn't do relationships, and there's no way I can just casually sleep with him. There's no point in wanting to order something that's not even on the menu.

"It's obvious you have a crush on him," she continues, adjusting the clip that's holding back her hair. "And he likes you too."

"Blake likes women in general," I remind her.

"When's the last time you saw him bring someone back?"

She has a point. Blake and I pretty much spend all our free time together. I can lie and say it's all for the book, but he went to Paris with me after the French Grand Prix to do a tour of the Jewish Quarters. He listened to the tour guide intently, asking thoughtful questions, even though he's neither religious nor Jewish. That's not the kind of stuff you do for an interview. That's the kind of stuff you do with someone you want to spend time with.

Speak of the devil.

BLAKE HOLLIS

If you're around, can we talk?

I've listened to Blake talk for the past three days and nothing he's said has been nice. I toss my phone onto the couch. Out of sight, out of mind. Turning back to Josie, I hit her with my next Fuck, Marry, Kill combination.

"Fred Flintstone, Elmer Fudd, and Tony the Tiger." If real-life men suck, may as well go with the fictional ones.

FIFTEEN
BLAKE

WAKING UP HUNGOVER IS BRUTAL. Waking up hungover because fifteen stones of pure muscle are pouncing on me? Bloody horrific. My head is pounding, my throat's dry, and I have no idea whose bed I'm in. I open my eyes and see Theo's face hovering over mine. I realize I'm in his. *What the fuck?*

"Good morning, sleeping beauty!" His voice is cheery and aggressively louder than necessary. "Do you know where you are?"

"It smells like shit, so probably your room."

He ignores my jab—which isn't even a real insult considering Theo's a clean freak and his room smells like fresh laundry—and continues pestering me. "You practically had me breaking and entering last night, mate."

A faint memory of dragging Theo to Ella's room so I could apologize at 2:00 a.m. flashes through my mind.

"Sorry about that," I mumble, mildly embarrassed. "I was a little drunk."

"A little? You couldn't make it back to your own room, so you crashed here."

Fuck. I hadn't meant to get so drunk. Well, I had. Anything to numb the pain of the weekend. Even after placing P3, I'd still been in a piss-poor mood. One drink turned into four turned into a lot more. I knew there'd be hell to pay this morning for my decisions, but I didn't care too much last night. I let the liquor flow through my veins like I was on an IV drip. I'm sure my phone is full of texts and missed calls from Keith and Marion yelling at me for being publicly intoxicated.

I haven't had an anxiety attack in months, yet I found myself doubled over and gasping for air an hour before my first practice on Friday. This weekend always reopens a lot of old wounds.

One cup of coffee and a hot shower later, I'm standing awkwardly outside Ella's room. My knock is so weak, I'm surprised when she opens the door. Instead of her usual over-sized T-shirt, she's in a form-fitting workout top. I manage to keep my eyes trained on her face, not wanting to piss her off even more by staring at her cleavage. The look she's giving me is hard to interpret. I can't tell if she's annoyed, pleased, or indifferent.

"Uh, hi," I say, a stammer rising in my throat as I speak. She opens the door, leaving enough space for me to walk in. "I owe you an apology."

"For what?" She quickly throws on a sweatshirt before sitting on the couch. "Banging on my door at two in the morning or PMSing?"

"PMSing?"

I sit on the couch next to her and place my drink on the coffee table. Why didn't I think to bring her a coffee as a gesture of good faith?

Her dark brows rise ever so slightly. "It's when a girl's on her—"

"Christ, Ella, I know what PMSing is," I quickly interrupt her.

"Okay, well, it sounded nicer than 'your nasty attitude and

extremely rude behavior.'"

"PMSing it is." I shuffle my feet against the carpeted floor. "I was unacceptably rude to you, and I'm sorry for that."

I usually don't apologize for how I act because I don't care enough to do so. You can tell by how uncomfortable I sound. Ella tucks a strand of hair behind her ear, something I now recognize as a nervous habit of hers.

"Listen," she finally responds in a resigned tone. "Everyone has rough days. But to ream me out in front of your team for doing my job? That's really low, Blake. Even for you."

It's the "even for you" that makes my throat thick with guilt.

"And just a heads up"—the corners of her soft lips quirk up —"being a dick won't make yours any bigger."

Leave it to Ella to soften her censure with a teasing comment. Like a ray of sunlight peaking its way through storm clouds.

I stifle a laugh. If I wasn't still walking on eggshells, I'd ask if she wanted to put that theory to the test. "You're right," I say instead. "I was a dick, and it won't happen again. I mean it, El."

She cautiously peers at me before nodding to herself as if my apology passed her test. "Thank you. I appreciate that."

I sit there for a minute, unsure whether I should stay or leave. My desperation to get rid of the silence between us is the only reasonable explanation I can find as to why I blurt out, "I have generalized anxiety disorder."

My spine stiffens as Ella's hazel eyes meet mine straight on. I'm not sure which one of us is more taken aback by my confession. I wait for the world to come crashing down around me, but it doesn't. Everything stays the same. My head doesn't burst into flames for admitting my biggest secret, and the sky doesn't open and swallow me whole.

"I've been on anti-anxiety meds since I was a kid and it

works wonders," I continue with a deep breath, "but this weekend was the anniversary of my dad's death. It triggered some stuff."

"I'm sorry about your dad, Blake." An empathic frown settles on her lips. "If I'd known, I wouldn't have—"

"You did nothing wrong, Ella." I give her a tired smile. "I have a bit of a temper to begin with and when I'm anxious, I get more irritable. It doesn't take much to make me lash out. I shouldn't have been a dick, though."

I don't like talking about any of this, even with my therapist. Nothing good ever comes from it.

"Thanks for telling me." She places her small hand in mine, giving it a light squeeze. "I don't have anxiety, but I've struggled with my mental health since things at work got...bad. I started going to therapy, which has really helped."

Her understanding and openness make my chest fill with a lightness I haven't felt in a few days.

"Do you still go?" I quickly realize how invasive my question is. "You don't have to answer if you don't want to. I go to therapy too, so I was just curious."

"Not right now. I'm here, she's there"—Ella waves her hands in front of her—"and it'd be a bitch with the time difference, anyway."

I chuckle under my breath. "I'd imagine."

"Were you guys close?" she asks quietly. "You and your dad?"

"It's—it's complicated. My mum left when I was a kid, so he was all we had, but he wasn't around much. And when he was there physically, he wasn't there mentally." I know I don't need to tell her about my family, but for some reason, I want to. "He pawned us off to nannies because he couldn't be bothered to care. His death always brings up all those feelings I had when I was a kid. We were never a priority for him, so I finally gave up trying to be one."

"You didn't give up, Blake, you just realized what you deserve. You deserve to be a priority."

A deep sigh leaves me. I hate getting upset over my dad. "Thanks."

There's no judgment in her gaze when she asks, "Can I ask you something? As a friend, not a journalist."

I take a minute to think it over. I've already told her about my anxiety, so at this point, I don't think anything she'll ask will send me into a tailspin. "Go ahead."

"I know stress can trigger anxiety and you have one of the most stressful jobs…the pressure to perform, social media scrutiny, the physical demands. How do you handle it? I'd probably try to move into my therapist's house if I were you."

Only Ella could make such a loaded question sound approachable.

"Lexapro and therapy," I admit with a laugh. "My anxiety's well-managed for the most part, and if something triggers it, Sam's there to help me. I meant it when I said I don't get nervous before races."

I'm pretty sure I took at least a year off his life with the worry I caused him last year. We're chalking it up to an anomaly.

"That makes sense," she muses thoughtfully. "I can't pretend to understand what you're going through, but if you ever want to talk about anything, I'm always here to listen."

"Thank you," I mumble, not sure what the right thing to say is. "Good to know."

Ella bounces slightly in her seat. "Want me to cheer you up?"

When she bites her lip in anticipation of my answer, I can't stop myself from saying sure. I know it's not going to be a blowjob, but you bet your arse I still say a silent prayer that I'm wrong.

SIXTEEN

BLAKE

BARCELONA'S one of my favorite cities—the people, the culture, the food. I always make sure I spend a few extra days here after the Grand Prix. I was pleasantly surprised when Ella asked to tag along with me. Part of me was expecting her to keep her distance after my temper tantrum at the last race in Austria, but she seems determined to prove that everyone's allowed to have bad days. Even if my bad days make me act like a "petulant four-year-old who lost their iPad privileges." Her words, not mine.

It's also nice to have the company after losing the race this Sunday. I'm aware that coming in P2 is technically a win since I still placed podium and secured eighteen points, but it's not the win I wanted.

Ella's never visited Spain before, so I take her to all the touristy hot spots. Park Güell, Casa Milà and Casa Batlló, Ciutadella Park, La Sagrada Familia. Her eyes widen in child-like appreciation at everything we see. The amount of sugary sweet churros she consumes as we tour the city is mildly concerning. I swear she has one in her hand in almost every cheesy photo she asks me to take of her. She takes photos of me too. Not because I ask her to, but because fans recognize me and ask if she'll snap a picture. It amuses her more than it annoys her.

I invite her to hang out with Theo and me at the beach today, but she and Josie are going to Girona for a *Game of Thrones* tour. I guess they filmed some scenes there or something. They meet us at dinner instead, showing up almost twenty minutes late. It's very unlike them both. Josie always says she'd rather show up at the airport three hours early than risk being five minutes late for a flight. I've never had that issue since I fly private.

Ella settles into the open seat next to me. Her cheeks are highlighted with a sunburn, her eyes twinkling.

"The tour was *so* cool." The familiar curve of her smile appears. "You guys should've come with us."

"We even got to try a *Game of Thrones* inspired ice cream flavor!" Josie adds. "It was amazing."

It's a toss-up which one of them loves ice cream more. Sipping sangria, we listen to Ella and Josie joyfully tell us about the tour. They might as well be speaking gibberish, but it's hard not to be excited by Ella's excitement. She can get me interested in paint drying.

"Have you ever thought about podcasting outside of sports?" I ask Ella.

She hesitates before answering. "No, why?"

"You'd be good at it." I place a *croqueta* on my plate, my fingers getting greasy. "Take today for example. You could do an entire episode with the tour guide you met and talk all things *Game of Thrones*."

"Yeah," Ella says slowly. "But what if people don't find that interesting?"

"Who cares?"

"Uh, sponsors, the audience, the studio. Me."

"I'd totally listen to a *Game of Thrones* podcast," Josie adds encouragingly. "I'd listen to any podcast you do, babes."

Ella shifts in her chair, swirling the straw in her drink as if it's the most interesting thing she's ever seen. I know Play-Media left a bad taste in her mouth, but I don't know why she's so hesitant to podcast again. It's clear she loved doing it, and she must know she's good at it. Right?

"Well, I think you should at least try it," I suggest. "You have all the podcasting equipment after all."

"Do you want me to give it back?" Ella asks. Her mouth draws into a tight line as her body goes rigid. "Because I will if you're pissed I'm not podcasting with it."

The table gets unnaturally quiet, the only noise coming from Theo slurping the remains of his drink. I'm not trying to be a dick. If anything, I'm trying to help Ella find her footing again.

"No. It was a gift, Ella. I'm simply saying you should think about it."

"Noted." Her tone is flat and sends a chill down my spine. "Can we move on now?"

"Anyone want to play 'Never Have I Ever'?" Theo breaks the tension. "I want to know if Josie's ever had sex in public."

Josie scoffs with an eye roll. "Bugger off, Walker."

No one's more thankful for his distraction than Ella, who quickly kicks off the game. Three rounds later and we're all tipsy. Ella messes up numerous times, putting a finger down when she hasn't done something versus when she has. The first time is when she puts a finger down after Theo says, "Never have I ever done anal." I nearly fall out of my chair before she quickly declares she has not, burying her face in her palms from embarrassment. After that, she keeps a finger up when Josie says, "Never have I ever lied about my body count." A few seconds later, she swears and puts a finger down.

"In my defense"—Ella shrugs—"there are some people I don't want to count."

I wish we never played this game because I'm lying my arse off. Never have I ever had a sex dream about someone at this table. Lie. I've had numerous about Ella. Never have I ever thought about another person while fucking someone else. Lie. Thought about Ella while fucking the redhead she claims faked an orgasm. Never have I ever lied during this game. Lie. Please see above.

Josie and Theo get into an intense argument about the semantics of what constitutes sending a "nude." He says Snapchat doesn't count because it disappears. She claims if it can get you hard, it counts. The two of them are bickering like it's a mock debate of the United Nations. If Josie didn't have a boyfriend…she'd stand no chance against Theo's flirting. Andrew seems like a nice enough guy, but I think she can do better.

"Do you think they'd even realize if we got up and left?" I whisper to Ella, testing to see if she's still upset with me.

She digs her fork into her paella as she considers this. I wait patiently for her answer, pulling out the fleshy meat of a mussel and popping it into my mouth.

"We can put it to the test," she proposes. "Want to go get ice cream? Jos and I passed a place on the way here that looked really good."

I stare at her in disbelief. She's eating seafood paella and is somehow craving gelato at the same time? I wish this is the most surprising thing she's ever said to me, but it's far from it.

"I didn't realize clams and chocolate went together."

"Is that a no?"

"It's a yes," I confirm. Theo can cover the bill. "Count of three?"

"Last one there buys?"

She grins at me, knowing damn well I have no idea where

we're going, so I'm obviously buying. She's up and out of her seat before I even count to one. I've got to hand it to her, though, the shop she leads me to is amazing.

"I didn't mean to make you uncomfortable earlier," I tell her as we walk down the cobblestone street. "About the podcast."

"It's okay," she says, a flush creeping across her cheeks. "I'm sorry for being rude."

"Yeah, that's kind of my thing, love," I tease her. "I'll grant you my forgiveness if you answer a question for me, though."

"Theo asked me what'll happen to him if he 'accidentally ate a birth control pill,'" she says, struggling to keep a straight face. "So as long as your question isn't as concerning as that... ask away."

As much as I'd love to know how my idiot friend "accidentally" swallowed birth control, I can't focus on that right now. Understanding Theo takes an extreme amount of brain power.

"Did you apply to other jobs before accepting George's offer?" I'm only slightly worried she'll bite my head off. "As amazing and handsome as I am, I can't imagine moving across the world to interview me was your first choice."

"A few, but not ones I was super interested in," she admits. "I signed a non-compete agreement with PlayMedia, so when I left the company, I was limited in where I could actually apply."

I lick my ice cream to hide my surprise. That rules out all the big sports and media companies—ESPN, Barstool Sports, Sports Illustrated, Fox Sports. Those are just a few of the ones I know and I'm not even American. "How long does the non-compete last?"

"One year, but there's a chance I'm blackballed anyway, so I'm not sure that matters." She snorts although I'm not sure I find the humor in the situation. "Connor told me he was going to ruin my career, and he's well-connected enough to make good on that threat."

My mouth opens and closes. The fact that my cone is still in one piece is a miracle. Ella's chin dips down as she stares at her fingernails. I hate how her confidence dissolves the moment Brixton the bastard or her old job come up.

"When I called George for advice and he told me about your biography"—she waves her free hand in front of us—"I decided some time away from everything was a pretty good idea. Get back to writing and build up my résumé so people don't actually think I'm lazy and difficult to work with."

I don't even have to ask to know that's what Connor told people. I'm going to fucking kill the little prick. "What a bloody cocksucker."

"You don't know the half of it."

"Jesus Christ," I mumble. "I'd never want to be a journalist after all of that."

"Blake." Ella chuckles, the dimple I'm so used to seeing making an appearance. "You'd make a horrific journalist."

"Would not!"

"Um, yes, you would. Your interview skills suck." She deepens her voice and starts talking in the worst British accent I've ever heard. "Why do you smother your coffee to death with milk? Do you even know what a biscuit is? Good God, must you be so bloody rude about my celery?"

Before I can help myself, I'm laughing so hard I'm having trouble not dropping my ice cream. "If I sound like that, please just shoot me and put me out of my misery."

"Nah." She nudges me with her elbow. "You can be a massive dick, and I may find you obnoxious at times, but I'm not going to shoot you."

I refrain from adding that I also happen to *have* a massive dick. Instead, I say, "I find you obnoxious at times, too."

"Have you been working on your compliments, Blake?"

Ella shakes her head in mock annoyance, her brown hair shining under the streetlights. "They're slowly getting better."

"I know how to compliment!" I hold my hands up in surrender. "Just don't want you trying to sleep with me if I give you too much positive reinforcement."

"It's cute that you think everyone wants to sleep with you." She seductively licks her ice cream while maintaining eye contact in a tantalizing way. It sends a direct message straight to my dick. "Because I don't."

"So if I kissed you right now, you wouldn't want to tear my clothes off?"

She snorts. "I promise your clothes would stay on."

"Want to make a bet?"

It's a quiet night, making Ella's lack of response even louder. She stops in the middle of the street before turning to me. Conflicting emotions plague her face.

"You really think if you kiss me right now, I'm going to want to pull you into an alley and bang your brains out?"

I nod. *Yes, yes, I do.* The chemistry between us is undeniable. She may not want to be my fuck buddy, but she wants me. I've caught her admiring me more times than I can count. It's not like I don't do the same, although my cheeks don't turn a vibrant pink when I'm caught.

"What do I get if I miraculously manage to keep my hands to myself?"

I try not to let the shock show on my face. I did not think she would take the bait. My dick twitches in my pants. "I won't complain about you interviewing me."

"Deal."

I don't have time to respond before Ella wraps her arms around my neck and pulls me toward her. I have to bend to meet her lips. They're softer than I imagined, and I've imagined them a lot. Her kiss is light and gentle. I run my tongue against the seam of her lips, silently begging for entrance. She parts them just enough for me to slide my tongue inside and taste her. Vanilla, just like her ice cream. Mine's a goner, dropping onto the ground as I wrap my arms around her waist. I lower and lower my hands until I'm squeezing her arse. Bloody fuckin' hell, it's a great arse.

She explores my mouth tentatively with her tongue, growing more determined with each moment that passes. Fuck, I want more. I need more. The quiet moan she releases lets me know she wants more too. My hands grip her waist, pulling her against me. I don't give a fuck if she can feel how hard I am. I want her to know how hard she makes me. Our tongues wrestle, trying to gain dominance over one another. My mind is in overdrive trying to focus on the feel of her. She bites down on my bottom lip, causing an animalistic growl to escape my throat.

The kiss is electric and delicious and over way too soon. Ella pulls back, staring at me with angelic purity.

"Sucks that you dropped your ice cream." She laughs with a gleam in her eyes.

How the actual fuck does she still have hers in her hand? I'm frozen in place. That is *not* how you kiss someone you don't want to sleep with. That is a kiss that leaves someone breathless and overwhelmed and wanting more.

She continues to walk down the street as if nothing's just happened. "You coming?"

I'd fucking like to be coming, but clearly that's not going to happen.

SEVENTEEN
ELLA

I'M grateful that Blake prefers to spend time in his suite alone before each Grand Prix. After spending most of the day signing hats and shirts, taking photos with fans, and answering questions from the media, all he wants is peace and quiet to get into the zone. Sometimes he watches tapes of previous races at the circuit to prep and sometimes he listens to music. He'll even go crazy and watch a documentary from time to time. I don't care what he's doing before the Azerbaijan Grand Prix, as long as it's away from me and my idiotic lust for his lips.

Nowhere in my contract does it specifically state "don't make out with the subject of your work," but I think it's implied. Now I know why. Every time I see Blake, my stomach flutters at the memory of his lips pressed against mine. He hasn't brought up what happened between us and I sure as hell am not reminding him about my momentary lapse in judgment. Especially when I'm the one who drew that line.

I usually hang out with Josie before the race, but today I spend some time with Theo. He has more than his fair share of stories about his early karting days with Blake. I interview Theo for an hour or so before he convinces me to play Mario

Kart. Video games are his pre-race ritual. Little does he know I grew up playing with my brother and Princess Peach is absolutely going to kick Bowser's butt.

Theo frowns after I win the first game. "You low-key don't suck at this, Goldy."

"What a lovely, backhanded compliment, Walker."

Theo snorts and nudges me with his elbow. He may be a World Champion in Formula 1, but I'm the virtual karting champion.

"Question," he says, putting down his controller. "What's the deal with you and Connor Brixton?"

I almost jump out of my skin at the question. "What?" I demand. "Why? Who wants to know?"

"Don't get your knickers in a twist, Goldy. Blake just asked me and Lucas if we knew anything about him." He shrugs like it's no big deal. "Lucas said he'd met him once at some party in New York. Blake got all moody and...well, you know how he can get."

I should've kept my mouth shut. The last thing I need is Blake getting involved in anything Connor-related. "What's that have to do with me?"

"Lucas said Blake should ask *you* about him since he produced *your* show," he answers, narrowing his eyes at me as if I'm an idiot for not putting two and two together. "I thought Blake was going to knock him out for suggesting it."

I bite my lip to stop my mouth from hanging open. "Uh, I'm not on the best terms with him anymore."

I'm leaving it at that. I don't need Theo, or anyone else, knowing about the situation. There isn't even a situation. It's over and done with.

"Ah." He doesn't press me any further. "Well, don't mention I said anything. Don't want him getting all pissy at me, you know?"

I reassure him that I won't, the nervous knots in my

stomach slowly unraveling. I'm eager to start another game so I can focus my mind on something else. Theo's happy to oblige.

"Blake's going to burst in here soon," he tells me a few minutes later. "Just so you know."

"Doubtful." I pick up speed and pass him up on the virtual circuit. "He likes his quiet time."

"Unless someone else is encroaching on his territory. Us playing video games?" He dramatically places the back of his hand against his forehead. "Betrayal."

"I'm not Blake's territory." He's too concentrated on the game to see me roll my eyes. "Grow up."

"You're his writer," Theo points out. "Want to make a bet?"

My cheeks heat at the memory of the last bet I made.

"Sure." I sigh. It's easier to say yes to Theo than spend twenty minutes arguing with him. "Let's make a bet."

I cross the finish line and Princess Peach prances across the screen for the second time in a row.

"If Blake comes in here in the next ten minutes…" He taps on his chin in thought. Theo's classically handsome, but being around him doesn't make my stomach flip like flapjacks. Only Blake's presence does that. "You have to tell Blake that I told you about us Eiffel-towering some bird in France."

"Um, ew." He can't be serious. I thought he was going to say I have to buy him dinner or wear his number to the race.

"And if he doesn't," Theo continues after seeing my apprehension, "then I'll let you read my DMs on Instagram."

Oh, damn. He's got me there. While Blake's Instagram is run almost entirely by his team, Theo is a loose cannon. He live-streamed himself doing nothing for eight hours straight the other day. The things he comments on Instagram model's bikini pics…so dirty even I blush reading them. Josie and I asked what it would take to read his DMs—they've got to be full-blown sexts—and apparently, I just found out.

We shake on it and no fewer than five minutes later, Blake waltzes into the room without knocking. He looks extremely hot in his red racing suit, and it makes me feel very bothered. "Whatcha guys doing?"

Theo smiles at me with obvious enjoyment. *Fuck*. I'm sure the only reason Blake came in is because he could hear us through the thin walls and didn't like that we were ruining his peace and quiet.

"I was here to interview Theo," I say. "But we got side-tracked by our dear friend Mario."

"We got some interviewing done." Theo gives me an exaggerated pout. "Don't throw me completely under the bus."

"True. Theo did tell me about that threesome you guys had in France. Kind of cliché to Eiffel-tower someone in Paris, no?"

I'm a woman of my word, even if I'm cringing on the inside. I look at Blake to gauge his reaction. He stares back with blank confusion before shaking his head slightly.

"Wasn't me," he says slowly. "Pretty sure I'd remember that."

Relief flows through me like lava. The idea of him and Theo doing that…no, thank you. The culprit can't keep it together and breaks into a fit of hysterics.

"Oi, I can't believe you followed through, Goldy," he wheezes. "Good stuff, mate."

Blake narrows his eyes at us and crosses his arms over his chest. Uh-oh. Looks like we're in trouble.

"Let's head down to the pit garage for the race," Blake says while Theo gets control of himself. "I'd like to kick your arse in a respectable manner."

Theo leaps up from the couch and the two of them sprint out of the room to race each other to the garage. It's like they're twelve years old. I stay in Theo's suite for a little longer to finish typing up my notes so I don't forget anything. By the time I head down to the pit, everything is in full swing. Blake's standing off to the side, watching the mechanics ready his car, but he's still the center of attention. The energy in the room shifts to wherever he is.

Blake nods in greeting as I approach him, not taking his eyes off the car. Aromas of dust, sweat, and fuel cling to him, adding to his own sensual grime. I usually like a clean-cut man who smells like cologne, but for him I'll happily make an exception.

"Teletubby all good?" I ask casually.

A smile flickers at the edges of his mouth. "You really think I named my car Teletubby?"

"Worth a shot. So, as I was asking, is Testicles all good?"

He lets out a laugh that mixes with the low buzz the tire warmers are emitting.

"Testicles is an interesting guess, but not even close." He briefly glances at me. "My car's doing great, though."

We're nearing race time and I can see the nervous energy building. Even though the drivers and cars are well equipped to drive in the rain—there's a whole tire set for wet conditions—it's not ideal because it makes the track trickier to anticipate. It's been coming down for the past hour and the race has already been delayed once.

"You watching the race from the paddock or here?"

"If there is a race, I'll be watching from here," I say. "If I watch from the paddock, I'll choke to death on the smell of expensive cologne."

I'm rewarded with a knowing look. Blake may love racing, but he doesn't love sucking up to sponsors. An engineer approaches us to let him know they've gotten the go-ahead to start the race. They really should just cancel it. This is fucking risky. There's no way the visibility is good.

"Time for the world to scream your name," I joke. "Your favorite part."

"I'd rather it was you screaming my name, love, but this'll do for now."

He shoots me a sinful wink. I don't have time to respond or wish him luck before he's sauntering off to the pit lane.

Josie joins me right before the start of the race. We watch the drivers take their positions before peeling off as soon as the gantry lights go out. Blake starts the race behind Theo, who's in pole position, but quickly makes it out front. Lucas's launch is outstanding, and he easily catches up to his friends, with Harry not far behind him. The Everest, McAllister, and Alpha-Vite drivers are always at the front of the pack, trying to beat each other to the top podium positions.

It's not until halfway through the race that things start to heat up toward the front. The cushion Blake built between himself and Harry is quickly dwindling as the Everest driver slowly but surely bites into Blake's lead. The two of them drive tire to tire for an entire lap with Blake finally getting the upper hand. As the race continues, the rain starts coming down harder. There have already been two crashes between midfield drivers. I have no idea how any of them can see a thing.

It all happens so quickly I almost miss it. Harry loses control through an uphill sweep of one of the fastest corners, clipping Blake's right rear wheel with his left front wheel. Blake's car rapidly spins out before slamming into the barrier at a brutal angle. His car jerks back into the track and moments later, another driver slams into the rear of Blake's car, adding insult to injury. Chunks of twisted metal lie in front of the crushed barricade. My knees buckle as the entire garage falls silent. No one moves a muscle. The only sounds you can hear through the entire circuit are panicked yells and gasps. The race is immediately red-flagged, the drivers out on the circuit notified to make their way back to the pit lane.

"Are you okay?" Andreas's voice crackles through the radio. "Blake?"

Time moves in slow motion as we wait for him to respond. I feel utterly and completely helpless. We all do. We're bystanders unable to do anything but hope Blake's fine and that the safety car reaches him quickly. It's an out-of-body experience—hearing panicked noises, seeing blurs of people running by, smelling fuel, feeling scared, but also not recognizing any of those sensations happening to *me*. I don't even realize I'm holding my breath until Josie wraps her arm around me and tells me there's a reason the Halo safety device and other precautions are put in place to protect the drivers. Her eyes tell a completely different story than her lips and I can see she's just as freaked out as I am. Blake's been involved in his fair share of crashes, but this is by far one of the worst.

"Can you let us know if you're okay?" Andreas tries again. "The safety car is on its way."

Ten more excruciating seconds of silence.

"Blake? Let us know if you can hear us. Are there any injuries?"

Another few seconds go by before we hear Blake's voice crackling through the system. "Fuck, fuck, fuck. What a bloody fucking mess. I'm sorry."

Only Blake would apologize for a crash that's not his fault. His team means the world to him and they're going to have to put in a lot of work to get his car back in shape for the next race. The relief that floods my body is so overwhelming I sit down on the pit garage floor. I don't give a shit if my jeans get covered in fuel, grease, dirt, grime. Blake's okay. He's okay. Thank God.

I've never hated a sport more than I do in this moment.

EIGHTEEN
BLAKE

I'M FUCKING ANGRY, but I'm fine. My ego's more bruised than I am. The car can be rebuilt; my points can't be recovered. Harry's slowly creeping up behind me for the World Championship title this year and that makes my head hurt worse than getting hit with 5.6Gs of force. At least no one got points given the red flag that ended the race. They shouldn't have let the race happen with the heavy rain and low visibility. The FIA is no doubt scrambling to come up with some sort of statement explaining why the bloody fuck they kept the race going for so long.

I'm usually able to brace for impact to lessen the blow, but Harry knocked the fucking wind out of me. The crash isn't entirely his fault thanks to the weather, but he'll still be penalized for it. No one can predict how the rain will affect our cars, no matter how much we try to prepare for anything.

I'm anxious to leave the medical tent next to the circuit, but I know I can't until the doctor gives me clearance. All drivers who are hit with a certain amount of force are required to come here to ensure they're okay. I sit on the foot of the stiff medical bed I'm stationed in, answering a text from my sister, when I hear Ella's voice.

"I am allowed in there too. I have a badge and rights, you know."

I can't help chuckling at the scene before me. Ella's waving her McAllister pass in the face of a young nurse. The guy can't be older than twenty-three years old and seems confused about whether he should feel threatened or not. He looks around for help, but everyone else is preoccupied. *Poor kid.* Ella's McAllister pass doesn't mean much to him, but she's putting on an air of importance.

"I'm sorry, miss," he stammers, the tips of his ears turning as red as his hair. "No visitors until he's cleared."

"Visitor my ass," she fires back. "Do I look like a visitor to you, buddy?"

Oof. Ella means business when she calls somebody "buddy" or "buddy boy."

"She's fine to come back," I call out to where they're standing.

I shoot Ella as much of a smile as I can manage, but it looks more like a pained grimace. I don't want her to be here, to see me weak, but I also don't want to be alone. She pushes past the flustered kid and rushes over to the medical bed I'm in. Throwing her arms around me, she buries her face into the crook of my neck. I'm surprised by her public display of affection.

"Careful, sweetheart," the doctor warns. "He's a bit bumped and bruised."

She quickly releases me, jumping back as if my body's on fire. It may as well be with her being so close.

"It's okay. Don't think she can hurt me much considering she weighs no more than eight stone."

The doctor gives a short laugh before giving us some space.

A frustrated noise escapes Ella's lips as she turns her

attention back to me. "How much is eight stone in pounds? I don't know the metric system and it's rude to talk about a woman's weight, you know."

She slowly scans my body, looking for any obvious injuries. There's nothing sexual about the way she's looking at me, but my body heats under her intense gaze. She looks flustered and stressed, her hair falling out of her scrunchie, and the laces on her trainers (or gym shoes as she calls them) undone.

"I'm glad you're okay." Her voice is barely audible.

"Hey," I coax, pulling her toward me, "look at me."

We're face-to-face, her body nestled between my legs at the edge of the bed. I revel in the intimacy of having her so close. She bites her lip, avoiding eye contact.

"Don't worry about me. Stuff like this has happened before and it'll most likely happen again. Just part of the job. I promise I'm okay."

Nobody likes crashing, but there's always a chance of it. It's a risk we take every time we get into the car, whether it be a practice, test drive, or race. It's hard to explain, but crashing is a very small price to pay for the chance to get behind the wheel. With all the new safety features the cars have, it usually looks way worse than it is.

"Ever consider a new career path?"

"Ha." My body starts to relax. "Not a chance in hell, love."

She leans her forehead against mine for a brief second, causing my breath to catch in my chest. It's intimate and unexpected. Her scent is intoxicating, a mix of vanilla and honey. My hands snake around her waist like it's the most natural thing in the world.

I pause, staring at her. Is my head more fucked up from the crash than I originally thought?

"Why are you looking at me like that?" she asks, tucking her hair behind her ears.

"Did you cry?"

"Of course I cried, you idiot. Your car spun out, like, a million times and then you got fucking body slammed. Did you expect me to laugh?"

She frowns as if I said something offensive.

"Don't worry, El. Seriously." I offer up my signature smile, trying to lighten the mood. "Me and your paycheck are A-OK."

"You mean more to me than a paycheck and you know it. So don't minimize my feelings."

I mumble an apology, trying to hide how her words affect me. I know she cares, but fuck does it sound good to hear. I've never had an Ella before. Someone who waves her badge and goes full-blown Karen at a Ron Weasley looking kid just to make sure I'm okay. And who cries because she's worried I got hurt. It's starting to freak me out how much I like being around her.

Before I can think too much about it, Theo barges into the tent. The redhead doesn't even attempt to stop him.

"Holy fuckin' hell, mate." Theo swears loudly as he makes his way over to me. Given his intense fear of hospitals and doctors, I'm surprised he came. "Are you all right?"

Ella immediately takes a step back upon seeing Theo. My arms feel empty as they release her body and fall back to my sides. I wish I could pull her back, but I'm already playing with fire. And she seems embarrassed by her out-of-character display of affection.

"I'm all good," I promise Theo. "Just going to be sore as hell tomorrow."

"You just always have to one-up me, don't ya?"

I roll my eyes. Theo's crash in Singapore last season was brutal. And naturally, everything is a competition between us, so the only reason I could have possibly gotten hit was to outdo his crash.

Theo turns to Ella and winks. "I wouldn't put it past him. He's a sore loser."

"Why can't you guys just one-up each other by seeing who shotguns a beer quicker?" She rolls her eyes and shakes her head. "You're both insane."

"Insanely handsome," Theo corrects her. "We already know that, Goldy."

ELLA HASN'T LEFT my side since finding me after the crash. She took up residence in the medical tent, waiting patiently for the doctors to release me. I couldn't help but chuckle when she told the nurse I requested a small snack and then proceeded to eat the Jell-O and saltines they brought. Her face is etched with worry, giving me glances every few minutes to make sure I'm not going to suddenly keel over and die. There's no point in reassuring her that I'm fine. I've tried and failed numerous times. She even follows me into my hotel room because apparently, I can't walk through a door without my unlicensed nurse by my side.

I leave Ella and head to the bathroom, turning the shower to the hottest temperature. Shower, eat, sleep. That's all I want to do. The steam blissfully envelops me as scalding hot water pounds down, massaging the tension out of my body. I don't realize how long I've been standing there until my fingers resemble raisins.

Stepping out of the bathroom, a petite brunette lying comfortably on my side of the bed greets me. Her hair is sprawled out on my pillow, the white case barely visible under her thick hair. She's sporting an extremely oversized red sweatshirt and what I hope are some type of shorts underneath.

"That may've been the world's longest shower." She flips through the channels on the TV, not even glancing in my direction. "I found a movie that looked good, but it's not in English and I can't figure out how to get the subtitles on."

I thrust an impatient hand through my hair. "What are you doing here?"

"I swiped your room key and changed when you were in the shower so I could spend the night here."

Yeah, because that explains everything.

"Like bloody fuckin' hell you're sleeping here." I need a good night's sleep. Not one where I'm up the whole night hyperaware and painfully turned on knowing her body is in my bed when she may not even be in fucking shorts. I'm getting hard just thinking about it and am momentarily thankful she's not looking at me as I readjust the towel around my waist. I also don't want her to see me take my medication. Knowing and seeing are two different things.

"Yes, I am," she argues.

"Seriously, El," I growl, my displeasure apparent. "You're not sleeping here. I'll carry you out if I have to."

"And I'll bite you if I have to." Her voice carries the same level of annoyance as mine.

I smirk. "I'd rather enjoy that."

"Kinky."

She finally turns my way and I wish she hadn't because the look in her eyes is so innocently sultry it unnerves me. She unabashedly rakes over every inch of my body with her gorgeous eyes.

"You kind of look like a cologne model right now."

"How does someone model cologne?"

The bed bounces as she smacks the empty space next to her. "Settle in and I'll tell you."

"I sleep naked, you know."

"Congrats." Her eyes focus back on the TV, attempting to figure out where to find closed captioning.

"And I like to cuddle," I try again.

"Great, there's an extra pillow right here you can spoon with."

"Has anyone ever told you you're incredibly exasperating?"

"My parents and therapist in not so many words." She shrugs, unbothered. "Oh, and Sal. He owns a bagel shop by my apartment building in New York. He says it's a good thing I'm sweet because I drive him insane. But same thing."

I bury my face into my hands, groaning loudly.

"I don't have women sleep over unless we're fucking." My voice is once again serious. "I'm not about to change that because you want to have a slumber party, love."

She pauses at this and I briefly worry she thinks I'm propositioning her for sex. Again. Yeah, I want to fuck her, but none of the circumstances I have imagined that happening in (and there are many) have played out like this.

"And I'm not about to stay up all night worrying if you're okay. So just let me annoy you for one night. Then I'm back to my own bed and you can bring back as many women as you'd like to fuck and cuddle and sleep naked with."

Now I feel like a bloody bastard. *Fuck.* I can tell my aversion to the situation makes her uncomfortable. The clicker lies untouched next to her as she watches TV, although it's obvious she can't understand a word of what's being said. A few moments pass before I break the silence, asking if she wants to order room service.

"Get me my own plate of fries, please," she requests.

"As if I want you eating all my chips." The room phone is on the bedside table next to where Ella's lying. I walk over and pick up the receiver, leaving a healthy amount of space between the two of us. I'm in my towel and still can't tell if she's wearing anything under her sweatshirt. I pray to God she is.

Ella spends almost thirty full minutes convincing me to watch an episode of *Law & Order: Special Victims Unit*. I ask her why she loves it so much. It's crime and murder, which is straight up depressing shit. Her answer? She likes when victims get justice. Fuck if that doesn't rip my heart right in two. It's cute when she happily hums along to the theme song and yells "bum bum" at the end. We watch a few episodes but end up spending most of the show just talking.

It's comforting to see Ella cuddled in my bed, clearly at ease, trusting me not to take advantage of her like Brixton probably would. I may come across as an uncaring arsehole in the media, but I'm not a monster. I'd never do anything that wasn't completely consensual. I care about Ella too much to "hump and dump" her.

We call it a night when Ella can no longer hide her yawns. I honestly can't think of the last time I had a woman in my bed and we didn't have sex. There's usually not much talking that goes on between the sheets besides dirty talk.

She snuggles under the covers, looking at me expectantly. "Okay, do you want me to turn around now or what?"

I stare at her blankly. Turn around for what? The devilish look in her eyes makes my throat dry.

"I'm giving you privacy to get undressed." She shoots me a sweet smile, testing how far I was going to take my lie. "I thought you slept naked."

"You'd like that, wouldn't you?"

She shrugs indifferently. "You're the one who wants me to know if you're packing heat or not."

Insane. This girl is going to drive me insane and yet I can't get enough of it. I peel my shirt and shorts off, keeping my boxers on. "Don't even say it."

She now has the answer to whether I wear boxers or briefs, something she questioned on her podcast episode about Formula 1. Pretending to zip her lips, she nestles into the pillows. I absolutely hate sleeping on the left side of the bed, but she's fully claimed the right side as her own. Her glasses, water bottle, and phone all rest on the bedside table. I'm not going to sleep much anyway, so I leave it alone.

"Night, Blake. Sleep well."

"Good night, Ella."

I'm wide awake and staring at the ceiling an hour later when I suddenly feel a warm body next to me. *Lord help me*. If Ella wants to screw around right now, it better be over the covers and with the lights on so I can admire every inch of her naked body.

I wait a minute to see where she's taking this but realize she's out cold...she's snuggling me in her sleep. The rhythm of her breathing is steady as she curls up against me, resting her head on my chest. I carefully wrap my arm around her, pulling her closer. She sighs faintly, completely comfortable with the arrangement. I eventually fall asleep to the sound of her soft, shallow breathing.

NINETEEN

I WAKE up wrapped around Blake like a spider monkey. If I want to, I can strain my head forward a little and lick his nipple. My knee is inches from his dick, my arm's resting on his abs, and my head's on his chest. That's how close and personal I'm talking. Not that I mind his body because, holy hell, but I don't need to be on top of it with morning breath. Inch by painfully slow inch, I edge my body off his. He mumbles slightly in his sleep and my heart freezes. *Please don't wake up.*

I've been so focused on making sure he didn't die, I didn't really think through the whole sleeping-in-the-same-bed-together thing. I definitely didn't think we'd end up cuddling the whole night. My intentions were purely to ease my own mind that Blake wasn't going to die of a brain aneurysm overnight. I'm genuinely worried about him being okay.

And last night? We were up until almost 2:00 a.m. talking about nothing and everything. My family and growing up in Chicago, Blake's favorite places to travel, our biggest pet peeves, strangest dreams we've ever had, the most controversial opinions we have, our weirdest habits.

I like Blake. I like Blake a fucking lot. I'm thoroughly

screwed, and we haven't even screwed. The irony isn't lost on me.

There's no way I'm letting him wake up and see me looking like the corpse bride, so I tiptoe into the bathroom. The eight million hair products he owns are surprising. It's like a salon in here. I didn't even know they made Olaplex for men and here he is with three different bottles. Does he purposefully make himself look like he has a perpetual case of bedhead?

I open a jar of pomade on the counter; it's a masculine mixture of leather and cedar. It smells just like Blake. The thought of him massaging it through his hair turns me on more than it should. Not that I'm trying to notice, but there are no strands of female hair on Blake's brush. So either he hasn't had a sleepover guest besides me in a while, or he recently got a new brush. Why oh why do I have to notice these things? I try to make myself look more presentable then quietly open the bathroom door.

Blake flashes me a sleepy smile. His eyes are half-mast like he's still waking up, dark hair sticking up in a million directions, the waves not knowing which way to point. The covers rest below his hip bone and the sight of his V wakes me right up. Who needs coffee when you have Blake's body to jolt you awake?

"And here I was thinking you hated cuddling." He shoots me a devilish smile. "Telling me to use a pillow and then invading my side of the bed like that."

"I mean how could I resist? Your rock-hard muscles are so much comfier than a pillow."

He laughs, clasping his hands under his head, looking casually comfortable and incredibly irresistible. "How'd you sleep?"

"Besides your boner poking my back every other hour? Fantastically."

He has the decency to look mildly embarrassed until I can

no longer keep a straight face. He throws a pillow at me, missing by a solid two feet.

"You look hot," Blake comments, raising his eyebrows.

Heat travels from my head to my toes. "Uh…what?"

"Your sweatshirt," he clarifies with a flick of his hand. "Isn't it making you warm?"

Oh. Of course. My sweatshirt, not me. I shrug. "Not really."

Blake squints as he gives me a once-over. I wish I could disappear into the fabric. "You're almost drowning in that thing, love."

Sitting on the edge of the bed, I tuck my hands into the sleeves of my sweatshirt. "It's comfortable."

Blake nods and I take the pause in conversation to change the topic. "How do you feel?"

His voice is raspy and tired. "Like I got hit by a car."

"Too soon." I peer at him to make sure there are no obvious injuries. "I'm already nervous enough about the Monza circuit."

The thought of him crashing like that, waiting helplessly as the safety car comes to rescue him…nope. Not something I want to see again anytime soon.

"How about we make a deal?" He looks positively beside himself, like he's just had a stroke of genius. "If you don't stress about Italy, and I mean it, not even a line of worry on your forehead, I'll…cook for you."

I've never gotten Botox before, but I'm wondering if there's anywhere close by that can take me for a last-minute appointment. Not a line of worry? My forehead's going to look like a fucking maze with all the worry lines. I also don't even know if Blake can cook. He has a full-time chef, for God's sake. His idea of cooking could mean heating up a frozen pizza or making boxed mac and cheese—both of which are perfectly acceptable, but not for this kind of deal.

I sigh dramatically. "What kind of food?"

"I'll cook you an Italian feast," he decides, clapping his hands together.

"Okay, love the enthusiasm here," I say slowly. "And not to burst your bubble or anything, but I feel like maybe we should eat Italian food cooked by, I don't know, Italian people in Italy?"

Blake points to the door. "I'm kicking you out."

I stick my tongue out. "Fine! An Italian feast in Italy."

All I have to do is stay chill in Monza, hope that Blake doesn't spin out in his car again, and he'll cook me dinner. I can do that. I can at least *try* to do that. *Hopefully*.

JOSIE and I drive the thirty minutes from Monza to Milan and spend the morning at the Pinacoteca di Brera, one of Italy's renowned galleries. I've never been huge on art. Blake's blue painting that cost an arm and a leg is a perfect example. Why is *that* considered art? It's not that I don't respect it, but I don't necessarily understand it. Neither does Josie, so we decide to do a guided tour.

"It's larger than I expected," Jos whispers as we circle a marble statue of Napoleon Bonaparte.

I stifle a laugh behind my hand. "Poor guy kickstarted the Napoleon complex when he could've originated big dick energy instead."

We walk around for another hour before splitting up. Josie has meetings all afternoon, but I stay in Milan to do some more exploring. I find myself at the nearby Brera Botanical Garden. Located behind the austere Palazzo di Brera, it offers a slice of peace and quiet in an otherwise bumbling city. I FaceTime Poppy while I relax on one of the benches overlooking the garden.

I can hear cars honking outside her 35th Street apartment the second she answers.

"Elly Bean!" Poppy greets me with a raspy voice. She sounds just as hungover as she looks with her black hair in a messy bun and last night's lipstick staining her mouth.

"Hello to you, too, Popcorn."

She laughs, snuggling into her comforter. "Where are you today?"

Flipping my camera so she can see my view, I smile at her appreciative "oohs" and "aahs." Each place I've traveled to with McAllister has gorgeous views worthy of one of the many postcards Blake sends.

"God, I'm jealous," she says when I turn the camera back on my own face. "Eating gelato, drinking wine like it's water, drooling over Italian men. You're doing all my favorite things without me!"

"I'll try to have a miserable time while doing them," I tease. "Don't worry."

"Is one of the things you're doing a private tour of Blake's naked body?"

Poppy's not shy about letting me know I should get rid of my qualms regarding casual, meaningless sex and follow the instructions of the customized condoms: ride a driver.

"Nope! My tour guide couldn't fit that in today's list of activities." I pause before waggling my eyebrows. "Although we did have an interesting night together."

The scream that filters through my earbuds temporarily deafens me. I may be the journalist, but Poppy starts asking questions like she's fucking Diane Sawyer. *Ugh.* I meet her dissecting gaze with a glare, wishing I'd kept my mouth shut.

"You had a chance to seduce Blake and you slept in a men's extra-large sweatshirt," Poppy states with a groan. "What is wrong with you?"

"I don't own lingerie." I roll my eyes. "And even if I did, I wouldn't have worn it. I'm not trying to sleep with him, Pop."

"You're unbelievably stubborn." She shakes her head at me. Being scolded by Poppy, even through a phone, is never fun. "And you're saying Blake cooking for you in one of the most romantic cities in the world isn't a date? You spend pretty much every day together whether you're working or not, Ella. It's definitely a date."

I'm seriously regretting ever telling her about our "deal."

"He's only cooking for me if I can keep my cool during the race," I huff. "It's purely platonic."

Blake has no way to check if I'm nervous or not while he's racing, which kind of makes it seem more like a date, but nope, not going there.

"I need more platonic friends like yours, then. None of mine offer to make me dinner or willingly travel to tourist traps in every city."

She's got a point, but I refuse to let her inside my head. If I can sleep in a bed with Blake without anything sexual happening, I'm sure I can handle a dinner with him.

TWENTY

BLAKE not only places first in Italy, but he beats his own fastest lap time. I worry the entire race, but how's he supposed to know that when he's driving 250 mph on the circuit and I'm watching from the comfort of the pit garage? As far as he knows, I was cool as a cucumber. It looks like we both won.

I know it's not an official date, even though it sort of may be, but knowing this still doesn't do much to calm the butterflies having a rave in my stomach. And when he opens the door to his car for me and tells me I look beautiful, the butterflies decide to snort cocaine or something because they are losing their fucking minds.

I spend the drive with my face pressed up against the window, taking in the rolling hills dotted with cypress trees and vineyards. Thirty-five minutes later, we pull up in front of a rustic villa. It's exactly the type of home you imagine in the Italian countryside—exposed stone walls interrupted by pietra serena frames, a classic terracotta roof, and lush gardens overlooking a never-ending sea of towering trees.

Blake seems pleased by my reaction. "Pretty, right?"

Pretty is the absolute bare minimum of how I'd describe

this place. I step out of the car and slowly turn, taking in my surroundings. "Who lives here?"

"You know Rossi? The pasta?"

I manage a brief nod. Everyone knows Rossi Pasta. It lines the shelves at every grocery store boasting its claim of being the number one Italian pasta and ready-to-eat sauce brand. As much as I'd love to say I handmake my pasta, let's be real; waiting for the water to boil takes enough time as it is. I've been using Rossi spaghetti for as long as I can remember.

"Their grandson lives here," he says casually.

"Okay." I'm still confused, which Blake seems to be thoroughly enjoying. "And we're doing what here?"

"We're having dinner." Everything about his voice says *duh*.

"But I thought you were cooking."

"I am." He grins in not-so-secret triumph. "I'm just getting a little help."

Cool, cool, cool. So, apparently, the heir of Rossi pasta is helping him cook me dinner. That's completely unexpected, but somehow very on-brand for Blake.

As if on cue, a man in his mid-thirties comes out the door with arms wide open. His longish black hair is slicked back, he sports a neatly trimmed beard and mustache, and his olive-colored skin is sun-kissed. Everything about him screams that he enjoys the finer things in life, as would I if I had enough money to live in an Italian castle.

"Blake! *Benvenuto!*"

The man pulls him into a hug, placing exaggerated kisses on both of his cheeks. The two of them start talking in rapid-fire Italian. Yep. Blake's bilingual. Technically, he's trilingual since he speaks French, too. What can't he fucking do? And why does everything have to make me like him more?

Italian Stallion finally turns to me. "You must be Ella. It's a pleasure." He grabs me by the shoulders and pulls me in, smacking two kisses on my cheeks before I can even say hello.

"Nice to meet you," I say, my cheeks growing pink.

Is it possible to get high off the smell of someone's cologne?

"It's a pleasure to have you here. I'm Gabriel." He turns back toward the house and motions for us to follow. "Come, come."

"You can stop blushing." Blake gives me a funny look. "He's married...to a man named Alejandro."

I smack him on the arm and walk extra fast so he's a few paces behind me. Not before I see his satisfied grin, though. Gabriel leads us through his home, talking about its history. It's the size of a small liberal arts college. Each room we pass through has the perfect blend of modern decor and antique accents. It's elegant and comfortable. I would bet my savings account that *Architectural Digest* has featured this home at one point or another.

We finally stop in the kitchen after walking for what feels like ten minutes. *Oh. My. God.* The massive island in the center of the room is barely visible underneath the mountain of ingredients covering it. Flour, fresh eggs, olive oil, carrots, celery, red onions, tomatoes, garlic, fresh parsley, sage, and rosemary.

Gabriel puts on an adorably cheesy apron that says, "Kiss the Cook." He tosses Blake an even better one with the naked figure of Michelangelo's *David*. I swallow a laugh as Blake pulls it over his head and ties it behind his back.

"Ella, do you want to grab a wine from the cellar?" Gabriel asks. "Whatever red looks best."

I buy my wine based solely on which label I like the most, but I don't think that's what he means. His wine cellar is massive. Rows and rows of every wine imaginable, from Albariños to Zinfandels. I land on a Chianti Classico because Blake gave me a history lesson in the car all about the Chianti region in Tuscany. Naturally, he knows all of this from some documentary he watched on the Medici family. The wine's from 2001, so at least I'm not dipping into the twentieth-century wines.

Blake and Gabriel are arguing about the chopping technique of a carrot when I walk back into the kitchen. Imagine two six-foot men, both in novelty aprons, and each holding a knife and waving it around like they're conducting an orchestra.

"If you guys are going to kill each other, can you do it after we eat and after I've left?"

Both men stop talking and stare at me.

"I'm hungry and don't want to get framed for your murders if you end up stabbing each other," I admit, pouring three glasses of wine.

Blake places the onion on the table, grandly gesturing for Gabriel to take over and show him the correct technique. Gabriel flashes me a handsome smile. "Your Blake's a stubborn one. I'm glad he has someone to keep him in line."

I've never taken a sip of wine so quickly. It slides right down my throat without hitting my taste buds. I try not to read into the fact that he just called Blake mine. *Not a date, Ella.* But then again, he could've boiled a pot of Rossi boxed pasta and called it a day. Instead, he drove me to Gabriel Rossi's home to have him help cook me a full-blown, home-made Italian dinner. How do I not read into that? I'm only human, after all.

The next hour passes quickly, the conversation between the three of us easy. Blake and I both offer to have Gabriel join us for dinner, but he bows out, claiming he has plans in town. So it looks like it's just Blake and me. It's fine. I'm fine. Totally not reading too much into this. We've eaten plenty of meals together. Is there more wine?

We eat outside on Gabriel's patio. The view is so beautiful it looks hand-drawn. And the food? Best damn meal of my life.

I twirl pasta around my fork. "This is my new death-row meal."

"You'd change your death-row meal to my cooking? I'm flattered, love."

Rolling my eyes, I take a bite. Yep. Definitely adding it to the rotation. Blake takes a sip of his wine, swirling it around in the glass afterward. "How'd you even come up with asking people their death-row meal?"

"You know Hinge?"

His brows burrow in confusion and he gives me a blank look. "Like a door hinge?"

"No…like the dating app." I'm not sure why I even bothered asking. Of course Blake doesn't know what Hinge is. He's not looking for a relationship. And if he were, he'd be on Raya, not Hinge, like us mere mortals. "Anyway, they give you prompts to choose from and then you answer them and they appear on your profile."

"And one of yours was asking people their death-row meal?" He shakes his head back and forth. "It's no wonder you're single."

I narrow my eyes. "Excuse me, but if I remember correctly, you found the question wildly amusing."

Blake shares a playful wink, leaning his elbows on the table. We end up spending over three hours outside. It still feels too short. Our conversation flows with no awkward lulls or pauses. We're both eager to fill up every second with a story, a thought, a comment. When pesky bugs finally interrupt our evening, we decide to head inside with our empty plates.

"Isn't the rule I cook and you clean?" Blake asks innocently.

"According to what rulebook?"

"Kidding." He chuckles. "Gabriel said not to worry about it. His housekeeper is coming early tomorrow morning."

Flour hits my face without warning as I finish placing my

plate in the sink. It takes me a few seconds to recoup, but I grab a handful myself and blow it so it lands all over Blake's shirt. Soon enough, we both look like we've failed horribly at our mission to sneak a kilo of cocaine over the border and now it's all over our clothes instead. I admire my handiwork as Blake laughs at the two of us looking like a pair of snowmen.

"You've got some flour on your face," he notes.

His rough fingers trail my cheek, unguarded desire brightening his brown eyes. I throw all caution straight out the fucking window as my mouth meets his. My body reacts before my mind can process what's actually happening. He cups his hands confidently against my cheeks as he kisses me hard and demandingly.

His tongue meets mine, swirling and dancing around, a shameless moan escaping his mouth. It's months of pent-up tension demolishing the carefully defined boundaries we just blurred into nothingness. He kisses me as if he were starving for me, the burning intensity of it making heat spread through my body like wildfire. It's urgent and unrestrained. Blake's more dominant, leading the kiss, but I do some pushing and pulling of my own. My hands wander through his hair, making their way across the nape of his neck then down his arms. He smells the way he always does—like cedar cologne and expensive leather. I've never been kissed like this, with such desperation and desire.

Warm lips kiss down my neck when I finally snap out of the stupefied trance I'm in. I move quickly, stepping away from the counter to put some space between us. It takes a second to find my voice. A million thoughts are running through my head, the most obvious being what the hell just happened.

"Blake," I breathe out. "What are we doing?"

"Exactly what we should be doing."

He steps forward to continue where we left off, but I gently push him back. The full impact of his hungry stare is almost enough to let him keep kissing me, but I stand my ground. I need to stop this before it goes too far. The tension in the air is so thick, it may suffocate us both.

"Seriously. What's going on?"

My hand motions to the scene around us. The straps of my sundress hang off my shoulders and Blake's shirt is halfway unbuttoned. Our lips are both swollen and red. He looks as mystified as I feel. His normally messy hair is on a new level, sticking out funny. I swallow back the lump in my throat as my eyes fall down to his lips—why do I want to feel them against mine again so desperately?

"We're obviously attracted to one another. You can't pretend we don't have insane chemistry. I've been thinking about kissing you again since Spain, so why deny what we both so clearly want?"

He runs his thumb over my bottom lip, pulling it down. Those dumb teddy-bear brown eyes of his are soft and I know what he's trying to do, but it won't work. It can't. I turn my head away, forcing his hand to fall back to his side.

"Because maybe I want more than just that."

Right as the words leave my mouth, I want to pull them right back in and then swallow them so deep that they never see the light of day. The look on Blake's face is so painstakingly tormented and panicked that I know his answer without having to hear it. I've not only committed the worst sin of all, but I've also said it out loud. I knew falling for Blake was a bad idea long before he ever kissed me, but that doesn't make the rejection any less painful.

"I've said since day one I don't do relationships, Ella." He rakes his fingers through his hair. I watch as the locks fall back into place almost immediately. "I can't give you more than this."

"What? Fuck buddies?"

His voice is tight as he says, "I didn't say that."

"Ah, let me rephrase. Friends with benefits, casual, slam piece, another notch in your belt. Should I go on or do any of those work?"

"Jesus, Ella." He glares at me, eyes dark with frustration. "You know it's not like that. Not with you."

He doesn't get to be pissed; I get to be pissed. Fuck that. Who makes someone a homemade Italian meal with a famous pasta person and doesn't understand how that's not leading someone on? I know people who have been proposed to in less romantic ways than this, for God's sake. This is Kardashian-level shit.

"Then what's it like, Blake? Please, enlighten me."

"I don't know." He kicks the toe of his shoe into the floor in aggravation. "Forget it."

The embarrassment and hurt coursing through my body are blinding. Suddenly, the room feels like the walls are closing in. We both stay quiet and the silence is deafening. Not that anything else he could possibly say would make me feel like less of an idiot. There's no one to blame but myself for the situation I'm in.

"I think we should head back," I say, my voice painfully awkward.

Blake licks his lips, staring down at me as he registers what I just said. He pulls his brows together tight, narrowing his eyes a bit while he shakes his head. He's upset. I don't have the time or energy to worry about how he's feeling. All I want to do is cry and I refuse to do that in front of him.

The car ride back is excruciating. Only the radio cuts through the tension, the silence stretching out further than the twisting roads ahead of us. I press my knees against the car door, angling my body as far away from Blake as I can. The door can't open fast enough when we pull up to the hotel.

"I can't give you what you want, Ella," Blake says quietly as I get out of the car. "I'm sorry."

I fight back the tears that threaten to spill onto my cheeks. "What I want is you. You're just too scared to see that I'm what you want, too."

I want red roses and clearly all Blake thinks he wants is the *Fifty Shades of Grey* red room. As much as I'm a hopeless romantic, I'm also a realist and it doesn't get much more real than this.

TWENTY-ONE
ELLA

IT'S the last gala before summer break, so I know it'll be fun. Josie said there's a fire-blower guy and a shaved ice station, but not even that can convince me to go. I don't want to see Blake more than is absolutely necessary. My emotions are ranging anywhere between sad, embarrassed, mortified, and pissed. Choose your fighter! I have no idea how to act normal around him. I don't know what normal means for us anymore. Strictly professional? Friends? Acquaintances?

The Grand Prix is in Silverstone, right outside of London, so George is here for the race. We spend a lot of time going over the outline we have for the biography, highlighting the areas where we need more information and noting what's good to go. A few chapters have changed—we're combining a few, deleting another, adding one. It's amazing seeing all the work we've been doing coming together in a cohesive way. I haven't felt this excited over a project in a long time.

"Have you started thinking about what's next?" George asks as we finish up on Friday afternoon. "Writing? Podcasting? Another biography?"

He looks at me thoughtfully, biting the end of his pen. The

fact that he still has this habit is astonishing. Back when George was my professor, one day in class he bit on his pen so hard it exploded all over him. He had black splatter marks on his face for the next week.

"I think I should definitely finish this biography before considering another," I finally respond. "But other than that, I'm not sure."

"Blake enjoys your interview style," he shares with a proud smile. "Says he likes working with you."

If only he liked me more than that.

"That's good to hear."

The cheeriness in my voice is so forced I'm surprised when George doesn't question it. It's at least three octaves higher than my usual tone. I don't say anything else. Kissing Blake and then telling him I want more than sex isn't the most professional thing I've ever done.

"You seem to like Formula 1," he adds.

My face falls. I can't tell if he means it as a good or a bad thing. "Am I sounding too much like a fangirl in my writing?"

"No! Not at all. It's just apparent how passionate you are about the sport. It's good, don't worry."

Phew. I really do like Formula 1. George is right about that. Nothing beats the high of a race weekend. Granted I'm rooting for some of the best drivers, who I now consider friends, but still. Knowing them makes the sport feel more intimate, like I'm a part of it. I'm not just an outsider looking in. I can wish them luck or compliment their race because I was there, I saw them, I know them.

"Would you have any interest in moving across the pond long-term?"

It takes me a minute to realize he means the Atlantic Ocean. Pretty big pond.

"I don't know," I admit. "I've never thought about it."

"Something to consider. You're good at what you do, Ella. I

see a lot of myself in you, and I think you can be super successful. I'm happy to make some introductions for you. Just let me
know."

"Thanks, George." I lift my head to meet his eyes. "For
everything."

GEORGE IS TACKLING everything work-related this
weekend, so I'm supposed to sit back, relax, and enjoy the race.
Kind of hard to do when my body is on full alert, ready to run
in the opposite direction of Blake at any given moment.
Having George as my human protective shield definitely makes
it easier, though. I make sure I'm always around but never
alone. There's no way I can keep this up forever, but I need to
adjust to being around Blake again. Seeing him sucks. There's
no other way to put it. It fucking sucks. Because we're both still
the same, but things are completely different.

Josie lets me tag along with her on Sunday. She switches off
between singing Lizzo's "Truth Hurts" and Beyonce's "Sorry."
We love a supportive partner in crime. I try helping her come up with
witty Instagram captions for the photos she took this morning
and suggest some good options, but they're all rejected. Apparently, "Which groupie will Blake bone in Silverstone?" isn't an
appropriate thing to say. She also didn't like "Britain's Blake
Hollis: breaking hearts AND records."

I follow her around for another hour until she's ready to
push me into the pit lane. Timing is on her side because a
driver's home race is always a huge deal, so the rest of her day
will most likely be around Blake. No, thank you.

I spend some time in the kitchen with Albie before heading
up to the rooftop. It's become my favorite place to escape the
madness of race days. Looks like someone's beat me to it. Well,
two someones. Two very small someones. I instantly recognize
them as Blake's niece and nephew. He talks about them a lot.

His sister and her family are the only people he talks about in regard to his family. Rarely his dad and *never* his mom. I'm honestly just happy he feels comfortable enough talking about them in the first place.

They spot me before I can quietly *beep beep* reverse my ass right out of here. They may be four and five, but they clearly don't know stranger danger. The two of them are out of their chairs and running up to me in no time. Where are their parents? Is Blake nearby?

"Hi. I'm Millie. Who are you?"

She's a carbon copy of Blake's sister with the same light brown hair, bright blue eyes, and button nose I've seen in photos. Her shirt has a sparkly unicorn on it and she's wearing cat ears. *Oh, to be young again.*

"I'm Ella. It's nice to meet you, Millie." I kneel so I'm at their level. "What's your name, buddy?"

I already know his name's Finn, but I can tell he's not as outgoing as his older sister. He's hiding behind her with his small hand clasped tightly in hers. Only his blond curls are visible from behind her shoulder.

"Finn," he squeaks out.

"Whoa! That's such a cool name. Did you pick it out yourself?"

"No!" Millie giggles. "He was just a baby when he got it! He couldn't name himself."

Her pigtails bounce as she shakes her head. Finn steps out from behind Millie and places his small hand on my knee. He blinks at me with the same blue eyes as his sister.

"Is Ella short for Cinderella?" he asks sweetly.

Ella definitely isn't short for Cinderella considering my glass slipper got tossed right out a window like a dirty Converse sneaker. "No. I wish it were, but it's short for Eliana."

Millie nods as if considering this. "That's a pretty name."

"Thank you. I think your name's pretty, too. I've never met another Millie before."

"Really?" Her face lights up in excitement. "So in the whole wide world I'm the only Millie you know?"

"Yep."

"Do you know anyone with my name?" Finn asks with wide eyes.

"Hmm." I pretend to think. "I don't think I do! You guys are the only Millie and Finn that I know."

This seems to be the coolest thing they've ever heard. Kids are easy to impress.

"There you guys are! Your mum's been going crazy trying to find you."

I'd recognize that smoldering accent from a million miles away. I quickly stand and hold my hands up defensively. I don't want him to think I was interviewing them or anything horrible like that.

"Uncle Blake!" Millie tugs at the end of his shirt. "Do you know Ella?"

He smiles in that reckless way of his. "Of course."

Millie starts chattering away about a bug she saw earlier, and Blake listens intently, nodding and asking follow-up questions. Why does seeing him with kids make me feel like my IUD is going to eject itself? They look at him like he hung the moon and the stars in the sky. Ugh.

"Can Ella eat lunch with us?" Finn asks innocently.

Dear God. If you were ever planning on revealing the existence of superpowers, please feel free to do so by granting me the ability to become invisible. Thank you and amen.

Blake shrugs and looks at me to try to gauge how I feel about the situation. His eyes are apologetic.

"I can't, but thank you!"

Millie's eyebrows draw together in disappointment. "Why not?"

"I forgot," I mumble.

"Forgot what?"

All right, Miss Millie. What are you? The question police? I can't think of anything. I forgot to take out my tampon? Forgot to pay the parking meter? Forgot I have a doctor's appointment?

"An email," I blurt out. "I forgot to answer an email. It's, uh, very important."

Nice. Totally believable. Blake knows I'm lying out of my ass but doesn't say anything. It's a Sunday, 6:00 a.m. in America, and George is here, so there's not really anybody I'd be emailing.

"Why don't you guys go wait for me at the door?" Blake suggests while ruffling Finn's curls. "I'll be there in a second."

Millie and Finn wave goodbye, so it's just me and Blake. Well, me, Blake, and the awkward tension surrounding us. Now I know what they mean by three's a crowd.

"I want to make sure we're cool," he explains, a frown creasing his forehead. "We haven't talked since Italy."

"We're cool!" I paste a smile on my face even though I'm mentally screaming. "Cooler than an ice cube."

I can't fault Blake for how he feels. He doesn't date. Rejection stings, but I'm a big girl. I'll get over it. I just need about thirty to ninety business days to do so. Formula 1 has a month off starting tomorrow, and you bet your bottom dollar I'll be using that time to lick my wounds. See you at the end of August, Blake! Hopefully, distance doesn't make my heart grow fonder.

TWENTY-TWO
BLAKE

I PRETEND it doesn't matter. I try convincing myself that she's a fever dream I can easily forget. But you don't forget a girl like Ella, whether you meet her in line for Starbucks or spend months traveling the world with her. She leaves that type of impression. Trying to protect my heart with barbed wire is useless when a simple smile from her can cut it straight away.

My nights are spent tossing and turning; it turns out my favorite dreams and worst nightmares both have the same main character. My days are spent strategizing with my team on the upcoming second half of the season, trying to distract myself from the loneliness that's starting to creep in. Being alone never bothered me before. In fact, I welcomed it. But I've gotten so used to having Ella around every day that I feel lonely for the first time in years.

After a week of not eating, barely sleeping, and partying with Theo to try to distract myself, I call my therapist for an emergency appointment. There are too many feelings to process and I'm comfortable enough to say I can't do it on my own.

I've been seeing Paul on and off since I was a kid. Our

relationship switched back to "on" after last season's fiasco. His office is filled from top to bottom with textbooks, the walls adorned with his impressive degrees and accolades. I need those degrees to pull me out of the hole I've dug for myself. A ladder, a rope—anything he's willing to offer me because I'm spiraling.

Each session leaves me emotionally drained and physically exhausted. I dread and eagerly anticipate each one with equal spirit. It's been a trying few weeks. As I lean back into the worn-in leather chair in his pristine office for the second time this week, Paul lightly pushes me to open up about Ella. I have been, albeit slowly, but it's a punch in the gut every time I do. I treated her like she means nothing when she actually means everything. And the worst part is, even though I want to make it up to her, to tell her how much I do like her, I'm not sure I'm capable of giving her what she needs. I'm trying not to hide from my emotions, but sometimes I'm scared to dive in because they're so deep I'm worried I'll drown.

"What if I really let her in and she hates what she sees?" I ask Paul.

I bounce my leg in an attempt to shake off the discomfort gnawing at me. I've opened up to Ella more than I've opened up to most people, but I'm still holding back. Still not letting her see all the parts of me. The part that my mum broke long ago, that my dad did nothing to fix, that the praise from the world barely holds together.

Paul sips his coffee. It's in a "World's #1 Grandpa" cup. I've only seen him repeat mugs a few times. And it doesn't matter if my appointment's at 7:00 a.m. or 8:00 p.m., he always has a cup of coffee in hand. Never tea. It's as much a part of his identity as his combed-over salt-and-pepper hair or his gray-blue eyes.

"It's not easy opening up, allowing people to see the parts of you that you want to keep hidden and private. It's always a risk to expose ourselves emotionally. A lot of people struggle with vulnerability, Blake. You're not alone in feeling this way. Far from it."

"Really?"

"Really." His smile is annoyingly sincere. "Sharing the most honest version of yourself—cracks, cuts, and scars—that's scary. But opening up, letting people know the *real* you, not the you that you want them to see...that's the foundation of forging intimate relationships that last. That vulnerability allows us to find the people we want to be in our lives."

"I want Ella in my life." Her name tastes sweet as sugar in my mouth. "As more than just a friend. I just...I don't know. It's not like I have a great example of what a relationship should look like. Or how to get someone to stay."

"Tell me about her."

"About Ella? What do you want to know?"

Paul never misses a beat. "Anything you feel comfortable sharing."

"Uh, okay. Well, she's beautiful. Not just physically beautiful either. She has this contagious energy that brings a smile to everyone's face. You know those people who just light up a room when they walk into it?"

I pause barely long enough for Paul to nod.

"Ella walks into a room and fucking blinds everyone. She has this type of beauty that doesn't only demand attention, it requires it and sucks you in until you can't see anything else. I've never met anyone like her. She wants to spend time with me because she genuinely likes me. It's not because of my job or my money or what I can do for her. She shows me she cares without even having to say anything."

My entire face is warm with embarrassment. I don't think I've ever said that much to Paul about anything, ever. He's great at keeping his face blank as a slate, so I have no idea what he's thinking.

"And how have things been since Italy?"

I'd filled him in on that situation two sessions ago.

"Not great. I didn't see her until the race in London and it was awkward. George was there, so we were never alone or one-on-one. She's not ignoring me, but she's not *not* ignoring me if that makes sense."

Ella's stubborn as hell. Most of the time, I respect it, but her determination to act like she doesn't care that things are off between us hurts.

He nods in understanding. I'm praying he doesn't go cliché therapist on me and ask how that makes me feel.

"Why do you think you might be hesitant in being with Ella?"

He waits patiently while I come up with how to verbalize what's going on in my head.

"What if she leaves like my mum did? What if I'm not good enough for her either?"

I rest my face in the palms of my hands, trying to compose myself, but it's no use. Oh, how the media would have a field day if they saw Blake Hollis, King of Formula 1, crying in his therapist's office. Paul hands me a box of tissues that seems to appear out of thin air. I don't question it, instead gratefully taking the tissue box.

"It's been well over twenty years since she walked out. Why can't I just be fucking over it already?"

"Sometimes the ones we think we need the most are the ones who let us down the hardest, Blake, but that doesn't make you any less capable of giving or receiving love. Coping with the loss of someone isn't linear."

The only thing I can do is shrug. If I talk, I'll start crying again.

"Imagine your grief like a ball in a box, and in that box is a button that represents pain. In the beginning, the ball takes up most of the box, hitting the button constantly. It's demanding and exhausting, a relentlessly overwhelming feeling. Everything is a reminder of your loss."

I nod along to indicate I'm following.

"Over time, the ball gets smaller. It doesn't mean the grief goes away, but it hits the button a lot less. You have more time to recover in between bouts of sadness. And the ball will always be there. It just becomes easier to manage over time."

"But then finding my mum last year, not that she deserves that title, and hearing that she doesn't care enough to have a relationship with me"—I struggle to get the words out—"I feel like it added another ball into this hypothetical box. And so even though my grief may have gotten smaller or whatever, now this ball is constantly bumping my button."

I cringe at how sexual this hypothetical sounds but suck it up and keep talking.

"So it's this constant reminder that my grief is still there, and then I'm forced to hit the fucking pain button again."

Paul applauds my ability to apply the situation to his analogy. It feels good that he notices the work I'm putting in.

"Exactly. And the ball will always be there. It's just a matter of how we handle that pain when it does hit."

"Hitting people with my car felt like a pretty good way to deal with it."

One of the biggest downfalls of being a public figure is that not only does my therapist hear about my shitty life decisions from me, but he gets to watch them on TV and read about them in the paper. A three-for-one deal. Lucky him.

"But you decided to finally come back to therapy on a regular basis after that. You realized you weren't coping in a healthy, productive way."

That's for fucking sure. Drinking myself into oblivion and driving my car like I was a player in Mario Kart (thanks for that one, Ella) was the furthest thing from healthy or productive.

"I feel like I'm broken, and if I let her in, I'll just end up breaking even more."

"You're not broken, Blake. Don't be so hard on yourself for taking time to heal. You've been through a lot of shit and no one's expecting you to come to terms with that instantaneously."

"I guess I'm just scared," I admit. Saying it out loud makes me feel like I'm going to pass out. Calloused hands push into the seat of the couch as I count how many textbooks are behind Paul's head.

"Being scared isn't always a bad thing. It can also mean you care."

I groan loudly, leaning back into the couch. That's what Ella said during my first interview with her.

"Ella deserves the world and what if I can't give that to her? I'm scared of losing her because I'm not enough. I feel like I've already lost her and I'm fucking miserable."

"Why do you feel like you've lost her already?"

Paul waves at the floor, letting me know I'm more than welcome to pace. It's how I think best. I'm up and striding across the room without another thought.

"You know phantom limb syndrome?" I don't wait for him to answer. "I watched some documentary about war veterans, and they talked about it. They described it as this, like, twisting ache that comes in a quick flash or spark. That's sort of how it feels. Like she should be here, with me, but she's not."

He looks sincerely impressed with me and I glow under his attention. Hell, I'm proud of myself too. I've been known to walk out halfway through a session if I don't like where the conversation is going.

"My advice? Stop worrying about those who've hurt you and start focusing on those who heal you. Who you know will stick with you through hell and high water. Based on what you've told me about Ella, she doesn't sound like someone who's going to run away just because things get hard. Wouldn't you agree?"

I spend the rest of the break continuing my sessions with Paul, sim driving at McAllister's HQ, seeing my sister and her family, and yep, stalking Ella on social media. I've officially become that guy. She spent a few weeks in Chicago with her family before heading to New York.

I chuckle at a photo of her and her brother eating hot dogs together at a Cubs game. I watch her take the phrase "dance like no one's watching" to a new level at a bar with her friends. I listen to her drunkenly explain to Poppy why appetizers are just as important to dinner as dessert. I grin at a picture of Ella and her bagel guy, Sal. I can't get enough of her. It's like watching her life through a crystal ball when all I want to do is live it with her instead.

Paul is worth the 250 pounds a session and then some because I end the summer break with a determination to fix things with Ella. I'm willing to put in the work to be the kind of man she deserves. The kind who can give her the world. I want to be vulnerable with her, no matter how much time it takes to get there. I don't know what will happen, but I know I'd be doing a disservice to myself by not trying just because I'm scared. That's not who I want to be.

She has a magnetism that easily draws you in—and the closer you get, the harder it is to pull away. But I'm done trying to fight it. Someone better get out the checkered flag because I'm ready to win back what's mine.

TWENTY-THREE
ELLA

I CAN'T EVEN GO to therapy without seeing Blake. I'm flipping through a *People* magazine in the waiting area, only to find his dumb, handsome face smiling up at me. It's a red-carpet photo from some Marvel movie premiere he went to last week. *Fuck that.* The room's empty since it's a Friday night at seven o'clock—the only time my therapist could squeeze me in —so no one sees me dramatically toss the magazine in the trash.

"Ella," my therapist Cindy greets me. She's wearing a deep brown lipstick, but somehow there are no smudges of it on the mug she's holding. "It's great to see you."

"You too." I follow her into her spacious office, noting the potted plants that have taken up residence on her windowsill. The soft lighting of the room eases my nerves as I settle into the gray couch facing her chair.

I spend the next twenty minutes giving her a condensed recap of my past five months. She nods, occasionally asking questions while jotting things down in her notebook. Once I'm done speaking, I take a deep breath. I feel like I just gave a commencement speech or something.

"How do you feel about seeing Blake next week once your break is over?"

"Nervous," I say. "I mean, overall I feel great…besides that. For the first time in a while, I feel like I'm in a really good spot professionally *and* personally. I just don't want my feelings for Blake to affect that, you know?"

I cringe at my own words. It sounds like I'm in fifth grade complaining about a stupid boy not liking me back.

"I'm pissed that I thought he could want more than just sex," I admit. "We have such a great time together. It's just…I don't know how to explain it. Everything with him is just easy. It feels so right. But God forbid he forms any sort of an emotional attachment."

My words sound just as bitter as they taste. Blake's made it clear where he stands with the paparazzi pictures of him leaving clubs with Titty Titty Bang Bang and Ms. Silicone Valley two days into the break. I may not be able to mute him in real life, but at least I can mute celebrity gossip sites on social media. Can't escape a *People* magazine, though.

"I get why that would be frustrating," Cindy says, her voice soothing my annoyance. "Relationships require a lot of responsibility and Blake may not be at a point where he knows how to value something deeper."

"I wear oversized shirts and sweatshirts most of the time," I point out. "And he *still* only sees me for sex. How is that even possible? It's not exactly great for my self-esteem."

"Physical connection is common, but mental connection? That's rare. It's why it's a lot harder to find."

She sounds just like my mom. I wonder if they colluded before my appointment.

Cindy crosses her legs before asking, "When you kissed, did you feel like you were in control of the situation?"

I take a moment to think about it. After everything with

Connor, the idea of putting myself in a vulnerable position with a man holds zero appeal. "I didn't feel like he would take advantage of me or anything like that. It was obvious he wanted me to be cool with a casual bang, but once I said no, he respected that."

"That's great." Cindy smiles at me. "Even if the situation didn't end how you wanted it to, you were given an opportunity to regain your sense of personal control and you took it. That's big, Ella."

For every negative thought I have, Cindy's always there to give me two positive ones.

"George suggested I apply to jobs in London at the end of the season," I say, pivoting the conversation away from Blake.

"Would you be interested in moving to London?"

"I'd definitely consider it," I say, surprising even myself. "Getting away from this city was probably the best thing I could've done for myself, but moving there full-time is a big commitment."

"It is," she agrees. "What kind of jobs would you be interested in pursuing?"

"Blake got me a portable podcasting set," I admit. I'd failed to mention that in my recap. "I tried using it once and panicked, so I don't think podcasting is a viable option."

"Why do you say that?"

"I can't even hit record without freaking out." I tuck my hair behind my ear, an overwhelming sense of dread creeping through my bones. "How can I podcast if that's how I react? I just want to move the hell on already, you know?"

"Wanting to let the past be the past is a normal part of the recovery process, Ella," Cindy reminds me. "But eventually, we need to deal with our fears in order to heal and take control of our lives. If you could podcast without those feelings of fear and panic, is it something you would *want* to pursue?"

Listening to a podcast is like hanging out with friends while they discuss your favorite things. Being the person to create that? Fucking magical. I miss it.

"Yes, but I'm scared," I reveal after a minute of silence. It's somehow simple yet so complicated. "Connor is an absolute piece of shit, but he's also the reason my podcast got so big. What if I'm not successful on my own? What if I can't do it without *him*? What if he somehow ruins podcasting for me all over again? I don't know how I'd handle that."

"You define your own success, Ella," Cindy states matter-of-factly. "Success to you may mean getting X number of downloads, but it could also mean scoring your dream guest. Hell, it could even be just hitting record on the set that Blake got you. You're in charge of setting goals for yourself."

It's no wonder I'm paying her the big bucks that thankfully my insurance covers.

"I feel like I have a before and an after," I admit. "Sort of a B.C. and an A.D., if you will. The B.C. is PlayMedia, Connor, and my podcast. The A.D. is Formula 1 and writing. I'm not sure how I feel about mixing the two."

Cindy purses her lips in thought. "If we put areas of our lives into tiny boxes and keep them locked away, one day all those boxes are going to pop wide open and we're going to be left with a really messy floor. I think if we can acknowledge that parts of our past can productively flow into our present or future, we're setting ourselves up for success."

I feel like she's Ebenezer Scrooge making me look at the past, present, and future. "So like a Venn diagram instead of a box?"

"That's a great way of thinking about it." She nods, pieces of hair falling out of her clip. "Let's reframe it. Instead of thinking about what you lost, think about what you stand to gain if you get back into podcasting without PlayMedia."

Cindy stays quiet, giving me time to think. "Um, I guess I'd have more of a say in who I choose to interview. And I could work with sponsors whose products I actually use and like. I'd also have complete creative control, which would be really nice."

"Those are all great things." Her smile is supportive. "Rather than seeing podcasting as something you need to leave behind in order to move on, I challenge you to think about how to adapt it to what you want to do and who you want to be."

"What I want to do is get a drink." I sigh, sinking back into the couch. Therapy is simultaneously the best and the worst. "This is a lot to think about."

We spend the rest of our session discussing ways to neutralize podcasting as a trigger so that I can make it my own and regain a sense of power over it. I leave Cindy's office and head to SoHo to meet my friends at our favorite bar. I find a glass of wine waiting for me. *Home sweet home.* I take a long sip before greeting them.

"I'm taking it you had a fun time with Cindy?" Poppy asks, raising an eyebrow. Anyone eavesdropping would think we're discussing a good friend of ours. Not someone I pay to listen to me vent and cry.

"An absolute ball." I elbow her lightly in the side. "What've you guys been up to? Did I miss anything fun?"

I immediately regret asking the question when it's revealed that Poppy and Jack think that me flirting with random guys will help keep my mind off Blake. According to Pop, it's the perfect way to prove I'm over him. *Screw a glass of wine. I need the whole fucking bottle.*

"What about him? He's cute."

Poppy points out some finance bro in a Brooks Brother button-down and Hermes belt. She knows I don't do casual hookups, but she's insistent that the best way to get over someone is to get under someone else. Flawed philosophy in my opinion.

"If he's so cute, then why don't you talk to him?" I reply with an unamused smile.

"He looks like he'd talk about his fraternity bros for an hour," Jack adds. "Or would ask you about Nasdaq and try to explain Bitcoin to you."

Every guy she's tried to push me toward, I have an excuse for. Is he handsome or does he just look like he has a house in the Hamptons? Is he attractive or does he just have a sense of style? Is he hot or is he just tall? I'm asking the hard-hitting questions as per usual.

"You're making it extremely difficult to cheer you up." She sips on her drink, slamming the glass back down on the table. "How about the guy in the blue polo drinking the Manhattan?"

"He looks like someone you'd see on *Dateline*," Jack muses with an eye roll. "I'm going to have to pass on Ella's behalf."

"I'm fine," I interject. "I don't need to flirt or sleep with someone to prove that. I just want to have a fun night out with my two best friends. Can we do that?"

"We are having fun," Poppy argues. Suddenly, her eyes widen. Nothing good can come from that look. "Okay, a really, really cute guy just walked in."

Jack lets out a low whistle. "I agree with Poppy on this one. He's just your type, El. Tall, dark, and handsome. Sort of a mysterious vibe going on."

"Oh! Does he also have a devilish smile and a rumbling laugh?" I ask, feigning interest. "Or what about a jawline that could cut glass? Does he have that? Let me know if he has an accent because I'm a sucker for those too."

"Ugh," Poppy moans, "No! We weren't trying to remind you of Blake."

"He's trouble, Ella," Jack comments with a pointed look.

It takes me a second to remember that Josie's back in London and isn't about to belt into "I Knew You Were Trouble (Taylor's Version)" or "Bad Reputation" in response to Jack.

I sigh with a shrug. "Well, at least I didn't waste a customized condom on him."

TWENTY-FOUR
BLAKE

SUMMER BREAK IS over and I'm back. Definitely not back and better than ever, at least not yet. That'll happen once I convince Ella I fucked up and want to be with her. I know her flight to Hungary got in on Tuesday morning, but I don't think ambushing her while she's dealing with jet lag is in my best interest. So I wait a full twenty-four hours before making it my mission to find her. Even if we don't have "the talk," I want to at least see her. I've missed her.

She doesn't make it easy. Ella's smart. She knows the less she's in the paddock or pit, the less likely she is to run into me. No one's seen her. Not Theo, not Andreas, not the twelve mechanics I ask. I even stake out the dining area during lunch because she's a sucker for Albie's food, but she doesn't make an appearance, and Albie says she hasn't come for breakfast either. If she hasn't been to the dining area in three days, then where the hell is she? I try asking Josie, but I'm on her shit list right now, so that proves to be useless.

I finally find her on the motorhome's rooftop between practice sessions on Friday. It's chilly out, so I hadn't thought to look here before. She's tucked away in the corner, secluded behind the greenery brought in for each race. If I had to take a wild guess, she purposely chose to place herself in a very hidden spot.

Seeing her sucks all the air out of my lungs. My heart speeds up, each beat thumping like a bass in my ears. All I can do is stare and commit each curve to memory. Fuck, I missed her. Her skin is tan, cheeks freckled from time in the sun. In usual Ella style, she's bopping her head to whatever she's listening to on her earbuds as she types away on her computer.

I'm not sure if she doesn't see me or doesn't bother looking when I approach the table she's at.

"Hey," I greet her.

Lifting her head, our eyes meet over her computer screen. It cuts straight to my core. I even missed her eyes, for fuck's sake.

"Hi. Sorry." She pulls out an earbud. "What'd you say?"

"Just hey." I shoot her a charming smile. "What are you up to?"

Nice, Blake. Really fucking smooth. You haven't seen her in a month and that's what you lead with? Not how was your break, how are you? This is what happens when I haven't talked to a fucking female in over a month.

"Responding to an email. Some Saudi prince offered to marry me if I wire him ninety thousand dollars, so I'm sending over my banking information."

My chuckle comes easily. Her ability to deadpan so flaw-lessly is astonishing.

"Weird, I just got an email saying I won a free cruise if I send them my National Insurance Number."

The barest hint of a grin flashes, causing her dimple to wink. "Wild world we live in. How was your break?"

"It was okay. How was yours?"

"Good. Hung out with my family and saw some friends."

I know damn well who some of those "friends" are. I've

never met Jack Feinstein and he better hope I never do. When I stalked his Instagram, I didn't like what I saw. A photo of him and Ella sitting *way* too fucking close in a booth at some bar. Her cheek pressed against his while his arm sat comfortably around her shoulders. And the caption? *The babe came back for a quick visit.* Jealousy spread through me like a fever. I've never been a jealous guy. Never had any reason to be. Now it might as well be my defining personality trait. Theo told me Jack's gay and has a boyfriend, but I really don't give a shit.

"Want to hang out this afternoon?" I sound like an awkward kid asking a girl to a school dance. "Should have some time between meetings."

"Uh, depends on how much work I get done." She points a finger at her computer. "I owe George some edits."

She may as well be saying "leave me alone already." Ella's not being bitchy. She's being indifferent. She's tolerating my presence but would prefer me to be anywhere but here.

"Gotcha!" My voice is sugar, spice, and everything nice. "Well, let me know!"

Her earbud slips back into place as she gives me a glint of a smile.

The rest of the weekend goes no better. It's fucking torture having to watch Ella talk and laugh with everyone else while she tries to subtly avoid me. I debate throwing the Grand Prix just so I can see something other than blank disinterest when she looks my way. I obviously don't because that'd be fucking dumb, but the fact that I even considered it speaks volumes. How am I supposed to win her back when she won't even look at me? It's really hard to move forward with my plan when I can't get past stage one, which is getting her to bloody talk to me.

I make sure I'm doing things with my friends every night in case Ella decides she wants to see everyone, but she doesn't. It's not until after the race on Sunday that she makes an appearance. When she waltzes into the bar we're at, I have trouble breathing. *Bloody fucking hell.* Her breasts press against the material of her shirt, tugging the fabric taut. Well, there's no way it can be considered a shirt. I've seen lingerie with more coverage. It hugs her waist, accentuating every curve. I've never seen Ella wear anything so revealing, and I want to take off my own shirt and throw it over her. No male with a pulse is going to have whiskey dick with Ella around.

Theo thrusts a drink into my hands. I'm well aware I'm ruining the mood, so I take it to appease him. I quickly realize it's straight vodka. Christ. I know getting drunk isn't the best idea, but I can't handle having her so close yet so far away. *Bottoms up.* Theo sighs dramatically, drumming his fingers against the table.

"I've never seen you like this over a girl, mate. It's kinda refreshing, but kinda alarming."

I grunt in response. *I've never been like this over a girl because none of those girls were Ella.*

"I'm not going to lie to you, though, you're an idiot," he continues. "You clearly like her heaps, so just tell her already. You're being extra dark and moody, mate."

"There's the supportive and caring friend I know and love."

I can feel his blue eyes studying me, trying to figure out where my head's at. Right now, it's shoved so far up my ass, there's no way he's going to get to it.

"Is your plan to just stare at her across the bar all night like a lovesick puppy?"

Maybe. Ella is having the time of her life. She's dancing with Josie, laughing as she expertly moves her hips to the beat of the music. I don't know if she's purposefully trying to make me jealous or not, but it's working either way. She looks gorgeous. Every guy at the bar seems to notice too, and she hasn't gone out of her way to turn them away when they talk to her or buy her a drink. My heart rate is dangerously high. I'm supposed to be on my best behavior this season, but if someone lays a hand on her, I have no problem throwing a punch or twelve. I ignore Theo and continue my sulking.

When Josie disappears to go to the bathroom, leaving Ella alone, I make my move. Maybe the liquor's loosened her disdain for me, if only a fraction of a centimeter.

"Hey."

"Oh." She looks like a deer in headlights, not sure how to act with me so close. "Hi."

Without realizing what I'm doing, I'm resting my hand on her forearm, absentmindedly moving my thumb back and forth. I hear her breath catch in her throat. She feels it, too. I know she does. The heat between us is enough to burn the place down.

"I fucked up, love," I murmur, leaning in close. "I know I did. Please talk to me. Tell me that you're pissed, that you hate me, that you're upset. Anything." My voice cracks. "Anything is better than you pretending like you don't care."

"Maybe I don't care." The alcohol seems to have removed the protective mask she's been wearing all weekend because her tone doesn't match her words. It's like she's saying what she thinks she should be but can't get herself to believe it.

"I know that's not true."

She doesn't disagree, instead choosing to stay quiet. Her perfume makes my head spin. How does everything about her turn me on?

"I want you, Ella."

Her laugh is tightly wound. "Wanting me and wanting to be with me are two very different things."

Fuck. That's not what I meant, so I try to backtrack. Maybe I shouldn't have had that drink. "I mean I want to be with you. I want to try."

"I'm not an ice cream shop where you can just try a sample

to see if you like it, Blake. Go to Baskin-Robbins if you want to try something. They have thirty-one flavors, so I'm sure you'll try something you really like."

An extremely irritated Josie interrupts us. Her blond eyebrows are furrowed and she's tapping her high-heel-encased foot against the sticky floor.

"Can you move?"

She snaps her manicured fingers at me and points to the other end of the bar. When I don't immediately leave, she throws her arm around Ella like a guard dog. I have to bite the inside of my cheek. She looks like an angry Barbie doll with her blond hair tied in a high pony and her bubblegum pink nails.

"Josie!" Theo shouts at her. "Come look at this!"

She shoos him away with her hand, knowing he's just trying to give me one-on-one time with Ella. Her eyes don't leave mine. I ignore her and look at Ella, trying to see what's going on inside that beautiful head of hers. She wraps her arms around Josie's waist and looks at her shoes like she's never seen a pair before. That right there proves she still cares because she knows if she keeps looking at me, she'll give all her thoughts away without saying a single word.

I give them both a warm smile before walking away. She might've just told me to go to an ice cream shop, but she loves ice cream more than anyone I know.

Our time at the bar seems to stretch on forever. I just want the night to be over. I'm exhausted. I can't go out like I used to and to be honest, I don't want to. What I want to do is curl up next to Ella and hear about her trip back home while she runs her fingers through my hair.

Theo's given up on trying to put me in a better mood, which is saying a lot, but Lucas is still at it. As the dad of our trio, he's the most responsible and gives the best advice. I'm not listening to a word he's saying, though. I'm laser focused on the guy Ella's talking to at the bar. It looks like a relatively friendly conversation, but I don't give a shit. Until he walks away, my eyes are staying right where they are.

"Relax." Lucas chuckles. "She's just having a good time, man."

"Oh, trust me. She's been having a *very* good time this past month, babes," Josie pipes in.

She's been on Luc's other side faithfully ignoring me. I've tried speaking with her, but she's Team Ella or bust. I can appreciate loyalty, but she's making things bloody difficult for me.

"What the fuck's that supposed to mean?" I snap.

Josie looks at me with a hostile gleam in her eyes. Why did she put emphasis on *very*? Not that it'd change me wanting to be with her, but I'm sick to my stomach just thinking about another guy kissing Ella. She said she doesn't do casual sex, but what the fuck do I know?

She gives me a look of infuriating smugness. I'm doing everything I can to control my breathing. It's not working. I down my drink in three large sips before slamming it on the table. There's no point in hiding my anger.

"Let's calm down, everyone." Luc throws his arm around Josie's shoulder. "Can we just have a good time tonight? No need to bring out the claws."

Josie tips her face up to him. "Just because your friend doesn't know a good thing when it's right in front of him, doesn't mean other blokes are just as stupid."

Her face isn't full of anger, it's full of pity. I'm not sure which one I'd prefer more. Maybe anger?

"I know I had a good thing, Josie." I sink further into the seat. "I know I fucked up. If anyone would listen to me for a second, they'd know that."

She looks surprised by my admission. Sighing, she slinks

out from under Luc's arm and moves over to the empty seat next to me. "Then you really are a bloody twit."

"I know. What do you think I've been trying to tell Ella the past week?"

"Probably something to try to get in her pants."

I deserve the barb even though it stings. My reputation precedes me once again.

"I like her, Josie," I say earnestly. "I'm trying to prove it and make things right, but I can't get her to talk to me."

"You rejected her and now you won't leave her alone. That's confusing, Blake."

My plan depends on Ella's willingness to listen to me. Given how she's avoided me this past weekend, I know I need to bring in reinforcements. I spend the next fifteen minutes outlining my plan to Josie. The way her eyes light up makes me feel like I've done something right for the first time in a while.

"I can help," she agrees. "But what she decides is up to her."

It's a step in the right direction. Theo rejoins the table and hands me a new drink. I happily accept it. Leaning back in my chair, I have a front-row seat watching Ella's electric smile from across the room.

CONSIDERING I drank enough tequila to incapacitate a linebacker, it shouldn't surprise me when I wake up at 5:00 a.m. with a splitting headache. Bits and pieces of my night come back, including Josie wrestling me into my pajamas. I absolutely did *not* need those extra two shots of tequila last night, but not much I can do about that now.

My flight back to London isn't until tomorrow morning, but there's no way I can be productive today. Besides a few quick bathroom breaks and a much-needed scalding hot shower, I spend the entirety of my day in bed. Between my parents, my brother, and me, we have access to every streaming site. It's both a blessing and a curse. Right now, it's a blessing because I manage to get through over half a season of *Law & Order: SVU*.

Josie's supposed to come over for a lovely room service dinner, but she cancels at the last minute, saying she forgot she has plans with some marketing people. I'm too tired to think about it or care. Half an episode later, I hear someone at my door. I immediately know it's Blake. He has such a specific way of knocking. He uses the heel of his palm rather than his knuckles, making the sound less harsh. I immediately hit pause on my computer. Maybe he just got here and hasn't heard a perp yelling at Stabler?

"I can hear your TV, Ella. Can you open the door, please?"

No such luck.

"Yes, I can." *That doesn't mean I'm going to.*

Moments go by before I hear Blake sigh. Welcome to the club.

"*Will* you open the door, please?"

I bite back a tender smile, knowing he noticed my grammar catch. Blake's not going away until we talk. He's made that much clear based on how many times he's tried to corner me in the past week. I know we need to because I can't avoid him forever considering my job quite literally depends on speaking with him. Sighing, I reluctantly get out of bed. I take my time putting on my slippers before dragging my feet to the door. I swing it open aggressively.

Blake's in a tuxedo, looking like he's walked off the cover of *GQ* magazine. His hair is handsomely styled, his face freshly shaven. Forget about his just-rolled-out-of-bed look, this is his take-me-to-your-bed-so-we-can-roll-around look. What is it about men in tuxes? I miraculously manage to keep my expression flat.

I lean against the doorframe to block him from waltzing in. "Did you run out of clean shirts or something?"

He chuckles softly and holds out the most gorgeous bouquet bursting with purple, yellow, white, and pink flowers. They smell like spring. If Marc Jacobs is looking for a new perfume scent, this would be it.

"For you." Blake coughs and hands the flowers to me.

"They're beautiful." I take them from his hands. "Thanks."

We stand there awkwardly, neither of us saying anything. I finally step back, allowing him inside the room. Part of me wishes I'd tidied up a bit. It looks like I've been robbed, with clothing still strewn across the floor leading to the bed. I'm pretty sure there's a thong on the lamp.

I place the flowers in the small kitchenette. They still look pretty even without a vase. Blake makes himself comfortable on the couch, positioned between the jeans I wore last night and a pair of leggings. I'm not sure where to sit. I don't trust myself to be next to him when he's looking like that. Meanwhile, I probably look just as horrible as I feel. The coffee table seems like a safe bet, so I sit on the far edge, leaving a healthy amount of space between us.

Blake runs his fingers through his hair, messing up the coiffed styling. "I've been so focused on getting you to talk to me, I didn't really think about how to start."

"I've been talking to you." Not very often, but words have come out of my mouth. "Sort of."

"You've been avoiding me."

"I've been adjusting to the time change."

If Blake had a bullshit meter, it would be going off right about now. I've gone from his biographer to his hide-and-seek opponent.

"You won't even look at me."

"What are you doing here, Blake?" I sigh, giving him the eye contact he wants. "I told you we're all good."

"We're not all good."

He taps his foot against the floor. I'm not used to seeing him so visibly nervous. It's refreshing, but not doing much to ease my own nerves. He's the confident one, always so sure in everything he says and does.

"I don't blame you for how you feel if that's what you're worried about." He's not going to compromise on his end, and I'm not going to compromise on mine. "Yeah, things are a little awkward right now, but I'll get over it."

"I was wrong when I said I can't give you more. I know I can and that I want to. I've been positively miserable not being able to talk to you. I kept picking up the phone to call you when something happened over break because you're the person I want to share things with, whether they're good or bad."

Um…what the fuck? He looks at me, wanting and waiting for me to say something.

"You looked *super* miserable with your tongue stuck down that one chick's throat. Was that one of the times you wanted to call me? Or was it when that Kylie Jenner lookalike straddled you at the club? Probably hard to get your phone out of your pocket when someone's on top of you."

The petty in me will not let that go. He wants to be with me but also wants to fuck socialites and models? I'm not a mathematician, but that doesn't quite add up. Blake looks so uncomfortable I almost feel bad. Almost.

"I didn't sleep with any of them." He leans forward with a sincere look in his eyes. "I swear to you. I was trying to convince myself that casual was what I wanted, but I was wrong. None of them meant anything and I'm an idiot for thinking they could even remotely compare to you."

"What do you want me to say? That I'm glad you've decided what you want?"

I'm not trying to be rude, but I'm hungover and extremely thrown off by this entire conversation.

"What I want is you, Ella. I'll do whatever it takes to prove to you that I want this. That I'm serious about us. Christ, I even talked to my therapist about you."

There's no point in hiding my surprise. I already know Blake goes to therapy, but I'm dumbstruck that I came up as a topic of conversation. Our therapists should get together to compare notes.

"Says he's never heard me talk so passionately about anything besides Formula 1 until you."

I bury my face in my hands. My mind is going a million

miles an hour, not sure what to do with what he's saying. I've spent the past month wishing this is what he'd said, but he didn't. And now that he is? I still like him, but what's changed? I'm not prepared for this.

"Have dinner with me," Blake says softly as if it's that simple. "You can tell me every reason you shouldn't be with me, and I'll tell you every reason you should be."

I barely wanted to open my door for him and now he wants me to go to dinner with him while I'm in my pajamas?

"You're in a tuxedo," I point out. "I'm wearing boxers."

"I'll change," he says. The look of hope on his face is unusually bashful. "We don't even have to leave the hotel. We can just eat in the dining room."

He's using my love of food and pajamas against me. Sneaky. My stomach betrays me by growling. Blake hears it— there's no way he doesn't—but he makes no comment.

"Okay," I relent. "But just dinner."

He knows the way to my heart is through my stomach and I've got to give him brownie points for that.

TWENTY-SIX

BLAKE

THE LOOK on Ella's face when we walk into the dining room is worth every hour of planning and every pound I've spent. If I could bottle up her smile for all my dark days, I'd be sitting under sunny skies needing sunscreen. Her eyes are unblinking as she takes in her surroundings. The room is filled top to bottom with floral arrangements, featuring the same flowers I'd brought to her earlier. It rivals the Royal Botanic Gardens in Kew. I've never bought a woman besides my sister flowers before, so this is a first for me.

"How did you—" Her face crumples into a scowl. "Wait. Did you just assume I'd come to dinner with you? Is that why you were wearing a tuxedo?"

"Josie told me I'd look more distinguished and serious in a tux," I admit with a chuckle. I don't mention that she also canceled their dinner plans tonight, so I knew Ella would be available. "And it's been like this since Wednesday."

I cashed in a lot of favors to get celebrity floral designer Paolo Berlusconi to bring my vision to life. Well, my vision was filling the room with a ton of flowers. Paolo's vision was to bring Ella's personality to life through flowers. He's used to creating floral installations for celebrity events and royal weddings, so this was a walk in the park for him. Lucas claims I've cleared out every flower in the entire country to make this possible. He may not be wrong, but I'd do it again in a heart-beat. I'd chosen yellow tulips for how happy she makes me, purple hyacinths for forgiveness (and it's her favorite color), amaryllis for her beauty inside and out, and white camellia for affection and adoration.

Ella walks around the room slowly, her amazement grow-ing. She keeps glancing back at me, confirming she's not imag-ining everything and that I'm still there. Convincing the hotel manager to shut down the dining room for the past week was no easy feat. And then making them put every table but one in storage so Paolo could work his magic…I don't think McAl-lister will be allowed to stay here ever again.

"They're beautiful, Blake."

"You're worth it."

She stays silent as we make our way over to the sole table in the center of the room. She's in boxer shorts and a sweatshirt with mismatching socks peeking out of her hotel slippers. Her hair's in a haphazard bun and she's not wearing an ounce of makeup. She's still the most beautiful woman I've ever laid eyes on.

I love that she didn't feel the need to change into something different. It was me who had to insist on changing for dinner. We'd been in the elevator down with a group of girls who looked like they were going out for a night at the club. They'd given Ella a not-so-subtle once-over and she couldn't have cared less. She even complimented one of their purses.

She's unapologetically herself and that might just be the sexiest thing about her.

There's a McDonald's Diet Coke waiting for her when she sits down. Finding Diet Coke instead of Coke Zero in Europe was a challenge; finding a McDonald's Diet Coke instead of

Coke Zero…nearly bloody impossible. But Ella says their "pop" is superior to all other forms—plastic bottles, glass bottles, aluminum cans (both mini and full-sized), liters—so that's what I got. There's a ranking system I'm completely unaware of because I don't drink soda.

I don't need to see Ella's legs to know she's sitting cross-legged. She happily sips on her drink as four waiters come out from the kitchen carrying trays of food. I wait patiently. They set down spinach artichoke dip, matzo ball soup, spaghetti and meatballs, garlic and parmesan roasted smashed potatoes, cornbread, and every single flavor of ice cream known to mankind. Two appetizers, one main, two sides, and dessert.

Her face lights up, making the hundreds of flowers look dull in comparison. It sends a jolt of warmth straight into my stone-cold heart.

"My death-row meal for when I'm sad," she says softly.

It sounds ridiculously morbid out loud. As if this colorful room is really a ruse for a hidden electric chair.

"Can we just call it your favorite meal? 'Death-row meal' sounds entirely unromantic."

"Nope."

Her eyes move back and forth between me and the food like ping-pong paddles during an intense game.

"You were right when you said I was too blind to see what was right in front of me"—I break the silence—"but I really hope I'm not too late."

She rests her cheeks in her palms. "What's changed, Blake? Because a month ago you were dead set on staying single. I meant it when I said I can't do casual with you."

I nervously push my fork around in the pasta. *Inhale. Exhale.* Ella puts her spoon down on the table, giving me her full attention. Knowing I beat out matzo ball soup pushes me forward.

"You know how I said my mum left when I was a kid?"

Ella nods but stays quiet.

"I-I guess I always felt like it was my fault or something I did, y'know? Then my dad pretty much gave up on being a parent, so I always thought something must be really wrong with me if neither of them wanted to be in my life. It was easier to push you away than pull you close because I didn't want you to realize what they both did. That I wasn't good enough or worth sticking around for...then you'd leave too."

Ella gazes at me softly, her head tilted slightly to the left. "Of course you're good enough, Blake," she says affectionately.

"Am I?" I shrug. "Couldn't get two parents to stay and they're the ones who are supposed to love you unconditionally."

The beautiful girl in front of me is out of her chair faster than I can ask her what she's doing. Ella curls up in my lap and snakes her arms around my waist, squeezing me tight. I feel like a ton of bricks has been lifted off my back. My arms instinctively wrap around her, pulling her against me. It's a puzzle piece finally falling into place.

"It's ridiculous how enough you are, Blake Hollis."

Her words calm my rapid heartbeat. Ella's a terrible liar and right now her face is completely open and honest. I intertwine my fingers behind her back, keeping her close.

"My sister hired a private investigator to look for our mum last year," I admit slowly. "After having kids of her own, she wanted to understand how she could just up and leave us like that. I know my dad wasn't the greatest guy, but to leave *us*? Just didn't make sense."

"Did she find her?" she asks gently.

"Turns out she's remarried and lives just outside London. Even has a few stepkids. All this time, she was less than a three-hour drive away but never tried to reconnect." I take a moment to collect myself. "I always held out this ridiculous hope that she'd show up and apologize, ask how we're doing, say she's proud of us, and want to have some sort of relationship. Now I realize how terribly pathetic that was."

"It's not pathetic," Ella answers. "Not at all."

I'm not sure I can even get words out. The air feels too thick to swallow.

"We reached out to her," I say after a minute of silence. "Want to know how that went?"

Ella rubs the back of my neck, her fingers expertly massaging out the tension that's building.

"She's glad we're both happy and well, but she doesn't think reconciliation is in her best interest," I whisper. "She only wants to focus on the future, not the past. The past, meaning us. As if we're not important. Like we're collateral damage or something."

"Look at me." Ella places her hands on either side of my face. "Anyone who doesn't fight to have you in their lives is a damn fool, okay?"

I nod slowly, not sure how to tell her that those words mean more to me than anything. "It really fucked with me and that's why last year…" My words trail off.

"It's okay," she tells me. The sigh I release is grateful; I really don't want to dive further into what a mess I was. "I figured something happened. I just didn't know what."

"Then you come along and you're all smiles and sarcasm and sweet and sexy. And it scared the shit out of me how much I liked you, how much I wanted you to like me. I've been scared of falling for you, and you breaking my heart. I'd be lying if I said it still doesn't scare me. But what we have is real and special and yeah, pretty fucking scary, but not having you in my life is even scarier. I'm ready to admit how much you mean to me. I'm still working through a lot of shit, but I want to do it so I can be the guy you deserve."

"And you're sure you don't just want a fuck buddy?"

Her voice sounds nervous, like I'm going to suddenly

change my mind. It may have taken me an extra few weeks to realize it, but now I've never been so sure of something.

"I promise you I don't want casual. Or friends with benefits, or no strings attached. I want so many strings attached we'll look like marionettes."

I can see the bottled-up doubt inside her fading away. "Or a tangled-up ball of yarn."

"There's a lot of shit I don't know, but I do know for certain my life's better with you in it."

Ella suddenly scrunches up her nose. "Dating your biographer isn't going to be good for your image."

"It'll look better than me humping and dumping my biographer," I point out. "I'm not worried about how you'll affect my image, El."

"What if we get into a fight and I write mean things about you?" she argues. "I bet you'll worry then."

It takes every ounce of control I have not to roll my eyes at her. "Ella, are you seriously playing devil's advocate to try and convince me to *not* want to be with you? It won't work, love. I'm all in."

She bites her lip. "Then I'm all in too."

Happiness spreads through me like nirvana, releasing me from the past month of stress and worry. Ella tips her head up, looking at me with those sparkling eyes. She rewards me with one of her stomach-flipping smiles. Knowing it's because of me? Better than winning a damn Grand Prix.

The air crackles with electricity as I cup her jaw, searing my lips to hers, kissing her with all the words I can't say, but need her to know. To think I almost missed out on this. No-holds-barred kisses just as pure as her heart and dirty as her mind leave me wanting more no matter how much I have already. If I wasn't such a gentleman, I'd have Ella out of her clothes and on the table by now.

"You have no idea how badly I want you."

I'm aching with need, the bulge in my pants impossible to ignore.

"Here's the thing." Ella shoots me a mischief-ridden look. "You have no idea how badly I want to finish that matzo ball soup."

The force of my sudden laughter knocks my head back. I'm not sure if I should be offended or not. Ella's commentary used to throw me off my game, but now that I don't need any game, I can just enjoy it. She leans into my chest, the weight of her like a security blanket, then leisurely kisses a trail down my cheeks, my neck, my jaw.

"It tastes just like my grandma's recipe."

I groan. "Can you not talk about your nan right now?"

She smacks my arm playfully, happily dipping a pita "chip" in spinach artichoke dip. The chip versus fry and crisp versus chip issue has reached a standstill.

"It is your grandma's recipe, by the way."

The chip drops out of her mouth and onto the plate. She doesn't seem to notice. Her face changes rapidly from surprise to confusion, not staying on one for too long before jumping to the other.

"What? How?"

"I asked." I'm enjoying this way too much. "Your mum requested me on Facebook a while back and I accepted. I sent her a message asking for it."

Mrs. Gold didn't believe it was me. I guess Ella told her there was no way it was my real Facebook, so when I asked for the recipe via messenger, she wanted proof it was actually *the* Blake Hollis. So we FaceTimed. I spent about thirty minutes explaining what an idiot I'd been and once she seemed satisfied that I was serious about Ella, she gave me the recipe.

"I seriously can't believe you did all of this."

"Believe it, baby." I grin, undisguised charm weaving its way through my words. "I'm down to finish dinner, but can we take the dessert to go? I can think of a few more ways to show you how sorry I am."

Her bubbly laugh vibrates through the otherwise quiet room. It sends a burst of warmth straight through my veins. If I could mainline the sound, I'd happily stay high for the rest of my life.

TWENTY-SEVEN
ELLA

IF YOU'D TOLD me four hours ago that instead of ordering room service for dinner I'd be eating one of my death-row meals with an unfairly attractive Formula 1 driver...I'd question your sanity. Or ask if you were dropped on your head as a child. Or if you were taking recreational hallucinogenic drugs. So yeah, it's been an interesting—but very welcome—turn of events, to say the least.

"Ella?"

I'm completely spacing out. Busted. "Hm?"

"I asked if you wanted to come up to my room." He tilts his head before grimacing. "But that doesn't sound great, does it?"

"No, it doesn't," I agree before adding, "But yes, I will."

Blake aggressively pushes the up button, willing the elevator to come faster. When it arrives, I'm practically dragged on, my feet barely touching the floor. As soon as the doors close, his lips mesh with mine. There's no rush as we hum into the kiss, both of us wanting more, but biding our time.

When the doors open, we're breathless. I blindly follow

Blake, letting him lead me to his room. My mind is in over-drive realizing what's about to happen. I started off my night in bed, by myself, while wearing pajamas. I'll be ending my night in bed, with Blake, while naked. I'm so nervous I could puke.

"Are you okay?" Blake stops in the middle of the hallway, planting his feet on the ground. "You're being quiet."

His voice is extremely loud, carrying down the hallway. Quickly untangling our fingers in frustration, I glare at him. "Shh! People are sleeping."

"I don't care." He doesn't bother lowering his voice. "What are you thinking about?"

Uhhhhhhh. "How Rihanna hasn't released an album in about six years."

Before I can stop him, Blake picks me up and throws me over his shoulder like a sack of potatoes. I let out a surprised yelp and smack his backside in protest as blood rushes to my head. He ignores me and walks down the hallway.

Only when we're in the security of his room does he toss me carefully onto the bed like he's scared of breaking me, which is obnoxiously hot as hell. I immediately sit up, the glare still ever-present on my face.

"Well?" He waits expectantly as his light brown eyes search mine.

"You've slept with models who look like real-life Greek goddesses."

It's not a question, it's a statement. He looks mildly panicked; like I'm trying to trap him and he's going to get in trouble no matter what he says or does. Blake opens and closes his mouth. To be honest, I don't know what I'd say to me either.

"And you've had sex with enough people to fill the House of Representatives," I add.

What the fuck? I don't even know where that came from.

"I'm British." He sits down on the bed next to me. "I don't know how many people are in the House of Representatives."

I'm American and neither do I.

"A lot." I nod emphatically and rack my brain, trying to think of the exact number. American History was never my strongest subject. "Four hundred twenty-nine."

There's a very high chance my number is way off, but I have a feeling Blake isn't going to fact-check me. And the number seems to drive my point home. His eyebrows fly up in surprise.

"You think I've slept with that many people?" He sounds appalled, which makes me feel slightly better. "Christ, Ella."

I frown, daring him to correct me. "Am I wrong?"

It takes him a moment to find his voice. "I may have slept with a lot of women, but I hardly think the number's in the four hundred range. And they don't matter. You do. I want *you*, Ella."

I don't say anything in response.

"What's really going on?" Blake pushes. "Talk to me."

Nerves ripple low in my stomach as I eventually say, "I haven't slept with anyone in a while."

Not since before what happened with Connor. I shake my head, not wanting that rat bastard to ruin a night of amazing sex with the world's most gorgeous man.

"We can take it as slow as you want to." Blake cups my face; his eyes filled with tenderness and lust. It's an oddly satisfying combination. "Whatever you feel comfortable with, yeah?"

I take a deep breath, reminding myself I have nothing to worry about with Blake. I trust him. "Okay...you may orgasm me now."

He crosses his arms over his stomach as peals of unrestrained laughter fill the room. "Orgasm you?"

My arms wrap around his neck and I pull him in. Blake's

smile is simultaneously sexy and affectionate as his lips brush across mine, teasing my mouth open lightly. My tongue hesitantly meets his, and he must sense my nerves kicking back in because he threads his fingers through my hair, drawing me closer to him. I let out a moan and he hungrily swallows it, kissing me deeper.

Blake's phone starts ringing, and he momentarily pulls away, a brief look of irritation shining in his eyes.

"It's okay if you need to get it," I say, the words dragging themselves out of my throat.

He shakes his head. "It's just Marion. I'll call her back tomorrow."

"You sure? It could be important."

His eyes slide up and down my body, making my limbs tingle with heat. "Not more important than this."

"Okay."

I barely get out my whispered reply before his lips are on mine. The screaming colors of glittering and burning fireworks flash through my mind as I eagerly tug on the hem of his shirt. Fuck fabric. I want it off his body and on the floor. He happily indulges me and pulls at the material behind his neck with one hand, lifting the shirt over his head. I lick my lips in appreciation. A breathy chuckle bounces against his already messy lips.

Taking full advantage, my fingertips trace the contour between the hills and valleys of his muscles. His skin pebbles under my touch. I count eight—yep, eight—ab muscles and let out an appreciative whistle before rolling my eyes at his grin. I've been wanting to do this since Monaco, and it was well worth the wait.

"Your turn." His voice is husky.

I wiggle out from under his body and Blake tugs my sweatshirt over my head in record time. My self-consciousness begins to evaporate at the strangled sound that escapes his lips and the unbridled lust in his eyes.

"You haven't been wearing a bra?"

I shrug sheepishly. It's not like I was expecting company.

His breathing is ragged. "Are you at least wearing panties?"

"You can find out if you want," I say shyly.

Blake quickly shimmies me out of the rest of my clothing, kneeling on the edge of the bed so he can view every inch of me. It's almost like he's not sure where he wants to touch first. Watching in silence, I see his pupils dilate in pleasure as he skims his fingers across my skin. Knowing how badly he wants me just makes me want him more.

He rubs two fingers against me, feeling how wet I am. My back arches off the bed in response, desperate for his touch. Lazy kisses make their way down my body. When Blake lies between my legs, wrapping his arms under my thighs with his hands clasped across my stomach, I'm drowning in desire. If I were wearing my Apple Watch, the Genius bar would be contacting 911 over my dangerously high BPM. I can't take my eyes off him as he presses his tongue, as pink as his lips, against me. He licks slowly, savoring the taste. His eyes are closed, a dip to his brows indicating his concentration. I want to save the image forever.

It doesn't take long before I'm grinding against his mouth, greedy for more. The things Blake can do with his mouth would have anyone writhing in pleasure. It's the one and only time I'll be grateful for the women who came before me. He knows damn well what he's doing, listening to my moans and expertly changing the pressure just when I need him to. My body is on fire, just waiting to explode. As he latches his soft, wet lips onto my clit, I know I'm not going to last long.

"So close." My hands curl into the soft mess of his hair like it's a lifeline. "Don't stop."

When he slips a finger, and then another, into me, I see the stars, the moon, and the sun. My orgasm rolls through me slowly. Before Blake, I'd never come from a guy going down on me. I just thought I couldn't. Turns out I can, but only if it's Blake's head pushed between my legs.

No inch of skin is left untouched or untasted as Blake makes his way back up my body. Unintelligible sounds slip through my lips; I'm overstimulated by his touch, yet I can't get enough.

"Fuck, I missed you," he whispers, flicking his tongue into the shell of my ear. "So fucking much."

"Your turn," I pant, mirroring his earlier words.

My desire to touch him, to feel him, is making my body ache with a need I'm unused to. I slip my hand into his waistband, wrapping my fingers around him before immediately pulling my hand back out.

"Blake." I scramble to sit up, but his fingers dig into my hip, making it impossible to move.

"What?" Pure panic is etched across his chiseled features. "What's wrong?"

I stare at him in disbelief. *What's wrong?* Has he never seen the size of his dick?

"You will physically break me in half with that thing," I frantically prattle. "I thought you were packing heat, not smuggling a goddamn anaconda in there. Do they not stop you at customs when you travel? Did you not have to register that thing as an exotic animal?"

Blake stares at me in that smug, masculine way of his before howls of uncontrollable laughter ripple through him. The room reverberates with the sound. His body drops onto mine, the dead weight making it difficult to breathe. At least I don't have to look at his face after accusing him of having a snake dick, though.

He pushes himself up onto his forearms, kissing me gently. "I mean it, El. We don't have to do anything you don't want to."

"No, I want to," I confirm with a hearty nod. "I just may

need you to buy me a wheelchair in case I can't walk tomorrow."

He chuckles before wrapping his lips around my right nipple. I let out an involuntary whimper. My breasts have always been sensitive, and Blake quickly realizes this, teasing them with flawless fervor. I press my chest further into his mouth as his teeth graze softly against the now hardened buds. He switches between the left and right, releasing each one with a pop and a heavy, panting breath.

I gently push him off me. A frown forms on his swollen lips until I hesitantly pull down the sweatpants hanging on his hips. Eyes heavy with lust watch me as I guide the material off his legs. He rolls onto his back, letting me see him in his full naked glory. *Holy fuck.* A delicious hiss pierces the air as I lightly wrap my hand around him once again. It's warm and pulsing, and just as thick as I thought it was.

"Should I have a safe word for, uh, you know?" I give the "you know" in question a light squeeze.

"If you want." I can tell he's desperately trying not to laugh. "But I promise you'll be more than okay."

"You seem awfully confident that Indiana Bones isn't going to cause internal bleeding."

"Did you really just call my dick Indiana Bones?" His voice is incredulous.

"I can call it something else if you'd like. Long Dong Silver, Jurassic Pork, The Dicktator, Cocktapus, King Dong—"

He covers his face with his hands. "You're crazy."

"But you like me."

His lips crash into mine, proving just how much he likes me. I lean into his touch as his calloused hands cradle my cheeks. We're both messy with need. The kiss is sloppy and wet in the best kind of way. Blake leans back and gazes at me, the unguarded desire in his eyes sending a new wave of want down to my core. A question burns in his eyes, and I nod in response. I desperately need him.

He hops out of the bed with the speed of Usain Bolt. His Olympic abilities end there as he fumbles to open the bedside drawer, frantically looking for a condom. He mumbles to himself, struggling to tear the plastic wrap off a box of Trojans. I'm relieved to see it's a new box because that's far more preferable to a half-used-up one from his collection of one-night stands.

"I'm going to sue them." Blake's still unable to get into the box. "Is this bloody childproofed?"

"King Dong is the size of a small child, so probably not." I motion for him to toss me the box. Effortlessly, I tear the plastic off, take out a condom, and rip open the foil packaging.

Blake gets back into the bed, breathless as I slowly roll the condom over him. I'm surprised the rubber doesn't snap in half. My palms are sweaty with nerves, and he immediately notices my hands shaking.

"Hey." He peppers my face with sweet kisses. "Say the word and we can stop whenever you want, baby. I'll go slow."

My throat's dry—caught somewhere between nerves and need. Blake balances above me as I guide him between my legs. The crease in his forehead, a sheen of sweat beading on his skin, shows just how much he's restraining himself. Our mingled breathing is the only sound as he slowly pushes inside me.

When he's seated fully inside me, he releases the most carnal sound I've ever heard. We lie there, not moving, just feeling the heat of one another. It's the most sinful torture I've ever experienced.

"More." My voice is desperate and demanding. There's no need to ask him twice.

"You feel so good," he growls as he leisurely rocks into me, mouth dropping open. My brain's in overdrive, unable to get any words out. Soon I'm gripping his ass, silently letting him know I can take more. That I need more. He takes my cue, thrusting into me at a quicker pace that allows him to free some of the pent-up passion he's desperate to share. I lift my hips up, matching his fluid movements.

I moan brazenly, not giving a single fuck if the room next door calls the front desk with a noise complaint. All I can focus on is the warmth of Blake's solid body grinding into me, the sound of our groans drowning one another out, the feel of him stretching me full, the familiar smell of his cologne.

"You're taking me so well, love." His voice is thick with lust, hot breath hitting my already sweaty neck. I tighten my legs around his waist, allowing him to get deeper inside me. He continues to pump in and out, and soon I'm completely unaware of anything but the building heat between my legs.

"I'm close," I gasp. "Yes, right there."

"That's it," Blake coaxes. "Come for me, baby. So fucking beautiful."

At his words, I unravel, my body pulsing with unrivaled ecstasy. My heartbeat pounds in my ears, making it impossible to hear the incoherent noises we're both making. Confessions slip from Blake's lips, making it no secret that he's close too. I kiss him deeply as he pumps out his own release, a groan vibrating from the back of his throat.

We're both breathing heavily, sweaty limbs tangled together. My entire body is slick with sweat, stuck to Blake's like glue. He doesn't seem to mind. His lips curl into an easy smile and he kisses me. It's passionate yet gentle and so unbelievably perfect. I nuzzle into his touch.

"We weren't each other's firsts," Blake says, "but I sure as hell hope we'll be each other's lasts."

TWENTY-EIGHT
BLAKE

THE GARAGE IS jam-packed with mechanics working on my car, which is severely dented after I took a turn too quickly and smashed into the barricades during the first practice at the Dutch Grand Prix. Usually I'll watch them as they tinker with my car and magically bring it back to life, but right now my eyes are focused on Ella. She's nodding at something a track-side engineer is saying, balancing a coffee in one hand and her iPad in the other.

If you'd told me I'd have a girlfriend six months ago, I would've called you a bloody twit. Now I'm falling asleep with Ella in my arms every night, kissing her awake every morning, grabbing that peach of an arse whenever I damn well please. And I damn well please a lot. Ella did make me call George for his "blessing" before allowing me to officially call her my girl-friend because "a writer sleeping with their source is completely against the code of ethics." She listed off a bunch of scandals and I happily shut her up with a kiss. And then another kiss. I can't stop bloody kissing her.

The rest of the weekend is a blur. Grand Prix weekends always are. Each moment bleeds into the next, creating a never-ending stream of meetings, media interviews, and fan interactions. The excitement of getting out onto the track, even if I'm only behind the wheel for a few hours, fends off any bit of annoyance or exhaustion I feel. And then there's Ella. Just being around her gives me the energy I need to endure any excruciatingly long press conference.

I find her blow-drying her hair in the bathroom when I get back from a post-race meeting. We kept our own hotel rooms for a few days but quickly gave that up. There was no point when neither one of us wanted to sleep alone. She still spends half of her nights at her apartment in London when we're there, but she's become more than just a house guest at my place.

A besotted smile flirts on her lips as I wrap my arms around her waist. I like knowing that I'm the one who makes her pulse quicken just with a simple touch.

She leans against me. "How was the meeting?"

"It was good. William McAllister was there." Our team owner only shows up to a few races a year. I'm glad I placed first—with Theo in second—at this one so we were spared any long-winded speeches about the importance of winning. I lower my voice to a calculated sultry tone and say, "Want to hop in the shower with me?"

"Nope! I'm drying my hair, not trying to get it wet again."

I give her a small pout. "But I love it when you're wet."

Placing my lips against her neck, I softly kiss her before sucking the skin into my mouth. I don't do it hard enough to leave a mark. As much as I'd love to give Ella hickeys, reminding her, and everyone else, that she's mine and they can kindly go fuck themselves, I get that they're not the most professional look. She glares at me in the mirror, not budging in her resolve to keep her hair dry. "Sorry, babe. You can't always use your muscular manliness to get what you want."

I make exaggerated kissing noises while blowing raspberries

into the crook of her neck. She squirms to get away, but I tighten my arms around her like a roller-coaster safety belt. I finally lift my head up, a mischievous gleam in my eyes. There's no hiding the fact that I'm aroused. Every time I'm near Ella, my dick springs to attention like a soldier greeting its lieutenant.

"You didn't seem to mind me using my muscular manliness on you this morning. I think your exact words were, 'Baby, that feels so fu—'"

She presses her hand over my mouth to shut me up, but I lick it in response.

"Ew," she shrieks. "Gross!"

"You liked when I used my tongue on you earlier."

"You're a mouthy man, Blake Hollis." Ella ducks out of my reach and leaves the bathroom, forcing me to shower by myself.

The first thing she tells me when I'm toweling off is that Marion called. Three times, to be exact. My face darkens immediately, sullen resentment flowing through me. I can't help it. I know exactly why she's calling. I've been dodging her calls and emails for weeks.

"Everything good?" Ella asks, brows pinched together.

I push out a deep breath of air, trying to calm my nerves. Sitting on the edge of the bed, I wrap my arms around Ella's waist, so she's nestled in between my legs. Her arms automatically snake their way around my neck. "What's going on?"

"I have to do the late-night talk show circuit to promote the book." I lean my head back and stare at the ceiling. "Marion's calling to confirm dates with me."

She's also going to yell at me to stop being a spoiled brat. Yes, I'm aware that presales for the book start a few months before the actual release and I have to help build buzz. No, I don't give a fuck if it's a *Sunday Times* bestseller or not. Blah

blah blah. It's all bloody stupid. The only good thing about this book is Ella.

She skims her fingertips along my jawline, my heartbeat speeding up under her touch. "You're going to be great."

"No, I'm not. I hate doing talk shows," I huff. I don't like putting myself in a position where I know my anxiety can be triggered, and this is a prime example. "I suck at them."

"Do you know how amazing you are?"

"Yeah," I mumble into the material of her shirt. "I suppose I do."

Ella shakes her head. "No, I'm not just talking about the cutthroat, competitive racer the world loves. You're an amazing driver, Blake. There's no doubt you thrive behind the wheel. But you're also an amazing person and I think you forget that."

She presses her lips against my forehead. "You're a guy who's figuring life out, day by day, just like everyone else. You've been through a lot, but instead of letting it make you weak, you've let it make you stronger. So don't go thinking you're not going to be great, okay? You're great without trying. And you're going to be great at these interviews."

I lean into her touch as she runs her hands through my hair. I love when she plays with my hair. Whether she's tugging on it during sex or absentmindedly toying with it like she is now.

"Why don't you have Marion send us over the questions beforehand?" she suggests helpfully. "We can look over them together and come up with answers you feel good about so you're less nervous."

I know my publicist won't object to this even though it's technically her job. She knows Ella will have a lot more luck than she ever will.

"Yeah? You'd do that?"

She kisses me in response. "Of course. What talk shows are you going on? *Ellen*? *Jimmy Kimmel*?"

"British talk shows."

Her eyes widen. "Do you think they'll have other guest stars on the talk shows? Like Tom Holland? Oh! Or what about Harry Styles?"

I practically growl at her question. Weaving my hands through her hair, I urge her lips against mine. It's not an affectionate kiss, it's a greedy kiss, reminding her exactly why it's my name she's moaning each and every night. I know I have absolutely nothing to worry about, but that doesn't mean I have to like other men existing in the presence of my girlfriend.

"I'm kidding!" She gives me a playful punch. The grin on her face reveals her dimple in full force. "I'm all about you, baby. But I'm happy to go with you to be your fluffer."

My head falls into Ella's chest as I vibrate with laughter. "You have no idea what a fluffer is, do you?"

"Do too! It's someone who helps get the talent ready."

"It's someone in porn who helps keep a guy hard in between takes," I gleefully announce. The devilish delight in my eyes is unmistakable. "So actually, I think it's a grand idea for you to be my fluffer. Have a quickie before any interviews to really relieve my anxiety."

She sticks her tongue out in response. "No fluffing will be done."

"Can we fluff right now?"

"Is fluffing the new fucking?"

"Mm-hmm." I hold her tighter against me. I'm getting hard just thinking about Ella's naked body pressed against mine. "And I really fluffing want you right now."

I tangle my fingers in the soft hair at the nape of her neck and pull her in for a deep kiss. My tongue slides over her lower lip and she shivers in anticipation. The way she moves her lips over mine makes a low groan come from the back of my throat. She pushes me down so I'm lying flat on my back as she straddles me. *Jesus, take the wheel.* She slowly tugs her shirt over her head and unclasps her bra. Her soft breasts fall out and are begging to be licked, teased, nibbled. They're hardening at the very tips. It's hard to keep my eyes on Ella's face when her nipples are desperately trying to make eye contact with me. As gorgeous as her eyes are, I'd rather have a staring contest with the set of pale pink buds in front of me.

"Fucking perfect," I moan, feeling the weight of them in my hands.

Ella blushes at my words before trailing sloppy kisses up and down my jawline. She sucks the sensitive skin right beneath my ear, causing me to jerk my hips up in pleasure. Her tongue torturously traces down my neck, drawing out a deep groan from me.

"I want to taste you," she murmurs, nipping at my ear. "So badly."

I rip my towel off so quickly you'd think someone poured acid on it. Ella leans over and places kisses on my chest, then my stomach, then finally on my straining cock. I'm shifting restlessly beneath her attention, my breathing choppy. I can't think straight, my body listlessly craving her touch.

She sucks on my tip, sending me into a frenzy. The noise I make is unintelligible. Ella teases me with a lick, a stroke, a touch, not giving me what I desperately need. This right here, this is heaven and hell. When she finally takes me into her mouth, resting her hands on my thighs, the noise that leaves my throat is animalistic. She looks up at me with sultry eyes and I moan at the sight of her pouty lips wrapped around my dick.

"You're so fucking good at sucking my cock, baby," I croak out. "If this were a sport, you'd be a world champ."

The chuckle she releases vibrates against me and I whimper blissfully. She leans back, making a popping noise as I slide out of the warmth of her mouth.

"Your what?"

"Cock."

"Hm. Don't know what that is."

If I die of blue balls, I would like it to be known that it's because my girlfriend wants me to call my dick by one of her insane nicknames.

"Will you please continue sucking"—I struggle to think of a name because I refuse to refer to my dick as King Dong—"my stick shift."

Ella leans back over, slipping my "stick shift" between her parted lips. She hollows out her cheeks as she bobs her head, twisting one hand around the base of me where her lips can't reach. The pulsing, vibrating need wracking my body is blinding. I'm desperate, arching up to meet her slowly measured rhythm. Incoherent praise encourages Ella to pick up her pace. She's swirling her tongue around me like I'm a goddamn Popsicle on a hot summer day.

"Wait, Ella, stop."

She shoots up with a confused look on her face. I immediately realize my mistake. No man with a fucking pulse would interrupt their girlfriend giving them the best head of their life.

"I want to finish inside you." The hint of a smirk appears on my lips. "Want you to come with me."

Her cheeks redden at my words, but she nods eagerly, leaning over to grab a condom from the nightstand. She rips the packaging open with her teeth, and it's the hottest thing I've ever seen in my life. We both love foreplay, especially Ella, but it's obvious she doesn't care about me returning the favor right now.

She slowly eases down onto me, inch by incredible inch. She feels so tight and warm, I swear I almost pass out from how she's gripping me. I'm trying to think of sad things to distract from the feeling, but the only sad thing I can think of is that she's not moaning in pleasure.

"Interview me."

Her eyes widen in surprise. I'm aware that my ask is insane. I'm inside her and rather than give her what she wants—hell, what we both want—I'm asking her to interview me. The one thing I constantly complain about.

"Did you mean to say *ride me*?"

Her body rocks with laughter and the movement causes my balls to tighten. My hands grip her hips to keep her still. I may bruise her from holding on too tightly. "I'd like to last longer than thirty seconds after that blowjob."

She smirks, very pleased with herself. "Fine. Um, what's your least favorite candy?"

"Popping candy. They make my tongue feel weird and I hate the sound."

The surprise appearance of a devilish grin makes me nervous. "I have a follow-up question."

What follow-up question could she possibly have about popping candy?

"Do you think if I put popping candy in my mouth and then put your dick in my mouth, your dick would get the tingly sensation? Or would it just be uncomfortable? Sort of like gravel?"

It's a good thing I'm not standing because her question would've knocked me right off my feet. Laughter leaves my body at an alarmingly fast rate. Has she seriously thought this in depth about fucking popping candy? And in that capacity? Her weird follow-up question does the trick and I'm ready. So fucking ready.

She lazily rolls her hips, finding a groove she likes. *Fuck.* It takes an insane amount of patience not to take control. Ella wants to go slow and soft, and I want to go fast and hard. But I'll do anything to keep this girl happy and if that means giving up the dominance I crave for a bit, so be it. I love seeing how expressive her face is when I'm inside her, watching her as she bites down on her lip in concentration, focusing on her pleasure. I move my thumb so it's pressed against her clit and her pace falters slightly as she adjusts to the new sensation. Her moans are more angelic than any choir I've ever heard.

It doesn't take long before she's riding out the waves of her climax. Her body melts into mine and she can't do anything but lean against my chest and clutch my arms as I slam into her sloppily and quickly. My hands find her arse, squeezing and kneading until she whimpers in response.

I thrust up, hitting her sweet spot just like I do every time. It's something I'm incredibly smug over—knowing her body well enough to know exactly what to do and where to touch to get her to moan. And there's absolutely nothing more satisfying than bringing Ella to a euphoric state. The air fills with broken pants as I get close to my release. As she gently reaches back to massage me, my balls tighten in her palm just before I explode in pleasure, grunting as I lose control to a shattering orgasm. We're both spent, breathing in short, shallow breaths.

"I'm addicted to you, baby," I murmur into her neck. "Your taste, your noises, your feel."

"Me too." Ella presses her forehead against mine. "Should we check into rehab?"

"Nah." I chuckle. "Fluff that."

TWENTY-NINE
ELLA

WRITING a biography on your boyfriend is a lot harder than writing a biography on some historical figure. I hardly think George Washington's biographer had mind-blowing shower sex with him and then ate Michelin-star sushi in his bed. Not that I'm complaining about either of those things.

I spend the day before the Belgian Grand Prix camped out in an empty conference room—my new unofficial office—rewriting a chapter about Blake's first World Championship win. I've attempted to write in Blake's suite before, but I never get much done when he's around. He's the most handsy person I've ever dated and the minute we're alone and away from prying eyes, it's like white on rice. It's four o'clock when I finally feel satisfied with my work and send George an email, letting him know it's ready for him to read. Fingers crossed he doesn't have too many edits.

As I walk through the lobby of the hotel, ready for a mental break, my phone vibrates with a call from Jack. Time zones and work schedules haven't made finding time to catch up easy and we've been playing phone tag all week. I immediately pick up and greet him with a loud, "Jack!"

"Ella!" he says back with equal enthusiasm. His raspy voice brings a smile to my face. "I'm glad I caught you because I have *very* exciting news."

"You're pregnant," I guess as I wait for the elevator. "You found out Jennifer Aniston is your long-lost mom. Your neighbor is actually a—"

"Before you get all crime and cult-y on me, I'm going to stop you." He laughs. "You know Peter? That guy I'm dating?"

It's hard to keep track of who Jack's dating because he has a never-ending roster of guys, but he's been with Peter for two months. That's essentially marriage in Jack's world.

"The audio engineer at Big Town, right?"

Big Town is one of the podcast networks included in my non-compete agreement. I'm an idiot for signing it, but I didn't think I'd have any reason to leave PlayMedia at the time. That backfired.

"Mm-hmm."

Stepping into the elevator, I tuck the phone between my ear and shoulder and hit floor thirty-seven. "What about him?"

"He told me that Big Town is developing a new podcast series. Think *ESPN Daily* meets Barstool's *Spittin' Chiclets*. They've already locked in Alex Sutherland, but they're still looking to fill the other host position. So…I sort of told Peter to suggest you."

I really wish he had told me his creepy neighbor was the ringleader of a satanic cult instead.

"Did you start smoking crack?" I whisper-yell, trying to keep my voice down. "Why would you do that?"

The older woman who pressed floor forty-four peers in my direction, but I ignore her glare. Societal niceties—like abstaining from loud personal calls in elevators—don't apply when someone drops a bombshell like this.

"Because you'd be a great fit," he says. I can picture him tugging his right ear in anticipation. Never his left ear, only his

right. Five years of friendship make you notice these kinds of
things.

The elevator stops at my floor and I quickly step off so Jack
can understand me loud and clear. "I legally can't work there,
Jack."

And even if I could, I don't know if I'd want to.

"Your non-compete ends soon," he says confidently. "And
this is a great opportunity."

I rub my hands over my face. For someone so smart, Jack
can be really dumb sometimes. He means well, but this isn't a
decision he, or anyone, can make for me. If I podcast again,
it'll be on my own terms and because *I* want to.

I take a deep breath and count to three. "I've had a long
day and really can't think about this right now, Jack."

"I didn't mean to upset you," he apologizes as I near my
room. "I just…I want you to be happy, El. I'm sorry, okay?
Please don't be mad."

I reassure him that I'm fine, promise to call him back later
this week for a real catch-up, and end the call. Sliding the
smooth plastic card into the slot beneath the door handle, I
glide into the cocoon of my suite, the hum of the air condi-
tioner greeting me. *Home sweet hotel.*

"Baby?" Blake's deep voice calls out. His head pops out of
the bedroom a moment later. "Hi, love."

The tension in my shoulders relaxes at the sight of his
smile. It's different from the one printed in magazines and
displayed all over the McAllister motorhome and garage. This
smile is relaxed and playful and just for me. I push away all
thoughts of my phone call with Jack.

That only lasts about an hour.

For the rest of the week, Jack's confession plays on a loop in
my mind. *Do I want to work for a network again?* I'd be rich if I
knew the answer to that million-dollar question.

· · ·

ON THE PLANE ride to the Japanese Grand Prix, while Blake sleeps soundly next to me, I make a pro-con list in the note app on my phone. Throughout the race weekend, I randomly add items to it as they come to me. *Pro: steady salary. Con: potentially toxic work culture/boys' club like PlayMedia.* I don't know if this will help me come to a decision, but it feels like a step in the right direction.

I go back to the hotel after watching qualifying rounds at the circuit on Saturday and sink into the overstuffed, patterned couch in the suite Blake and I are sharing. Grabbing my computer off the side table, I start editing a chapter about race strategy. George suggested I add some detail to the section about Blake's pre-race walks around the circuit. I was supposed to work on this earlier today but got sidetracked when Josie insisted I listen to an episode of her favorite podcast, *Dating and Dildos*. With a name like that, I was obviously intrigued and ended up neglecting my work to binge three episodes.

Blake gets back to the hotel room a few hours after me, already showered and changed out of his racing gear. He landed himself in pole position, so there's no doubt he's in a great mood.

"Hey, babe," he greets me with a grin.

"Hi, handsome. I'll be done working in a minute."

Which means in about ten to fifteen minutes. He relaxes into the couch and brushes his lips against the top of my head. I nuzzle against him and type away at a rapid speed. Blake reads as I write, watching as the words of his life story appear on the page.

"You used the wrong form of the word," he says a few minutes later. "It should be *are*, not *our*."

His finger gently taps the spot on my screen to indicate the mistake. *Holy shit.* Is my mind that preoccupied that I can't use the correct three-letter word?

"What's going on with you, love?" Blake asks gently. "Your head's been in the clouds all week."

My gaze bounces around the room, landing everywhere but on him. He's like a damn ninja mind reader and I don't want my jumbled thoughts exposed like that. There's no denying I've been a space cadet lately.

"I'm okay," I say a moment later. Squeezing his thigh lightly, I give him what I hope is a reassuring look. "Jack said something that's been on my mind, I guess. But I'm fine. Don't worry, okay?"

"What was it?" Blake asks, immediately concerned. A dark cloud of a scowl washes over his features. "What's wrong?"

"It's really not that big of a deal."

Blake stares at me with an intensity I'm not used to seeing off the track. "If it's not a big deal then just tell me."

Before I can argue that he can't demand answers like that, his serious expression turns into a wolfish grin. Without another word, he scoops me up and carries me over to the cloud-like bed, then lowers his body onto mine. I try wriggling my way out because my organs are being crushed beneath his weight, but it's no use. I'm trapped.

"This is the worst hug ever, Blake."

"I'm quite enjoying it."

"Because you can breathe," I cough out. "Do you have an asphyxiation kink or something I should know about? You seem to like suffocating me."

"No." He burrows his face into my neck. "I'm only trying to suffocate the secrets out of you."

After a minute of my squirming, he finally rolls off me, propping himself up on his elbow. He twirls a piece of my hair in between his fingers, watching me with a frown.

"I'm not going to force you to tell me," he says tenderly. "I just want you to trust me, El."

I curl up on my side to face him. "You're the only person

who knows about my secret fear of seahorses, Blake. Of course I trust you."

He lets out a chuckle from deep in his chest. "Seahorses aren't the reason you've been acting off, love. Talk to me."

If the situation were reversed, I'd be just as persistent to find out what was eating at him. Sighing through closed lips, I bury my apprehension. "The guy Jack's dating is recommending me as a host for this new podcast his company's producing."

"People at Little Big Town?"

"Big Town, but yes." He can never seem to remember that Jack's newest boy works for Big Town, not the American country group.

Blake listens intently as I recap the conversation. When I finish speaking, I slowly release a deep breath, the tightness in my chest fading.

"Are you considering it?" His forehead puckers in thought. "I know he only suggested your name, but are you open to the idea?"

"Maybe. I don't know," I mumble. "I made a pro-con list, but I'm not sure any of it matters."

"Why not? What's holding you back?" Blake asks, his voice low and calming. "Your podcast was amazing, El. You have to know that."

My body feels like it's burning from the inside out. It's an inescapable feeling of dread that washes over me and doesn't let go until I push all thoughts of what happened out of my mind. I avoid eye contact like it's my full-time job, so Blake ducks his head to try to catch my line of vision. His eyes lock with mine, and my heart skips a beat. There's so much going on in my head that the words fight to get out, leaving me tongue-tied. Blake waits patiently, running his thumb against my hip in a soothing motion. Will talking about this ever get easier?

"You know how I told you a girl I know was assaulted?" I finally ask after a few minutes of silence. "At work last year?"

"Mm-hmm." His voice is soft, almost like he's scared he'll spook me if he talks too loudly. I twist the sleeve of his shirt between my fingers. "I remember."

"I didn't tell you the full story," I admit quietly. Salty tears fall down my cheeks, and Blake wipes them away with the pad of his thumb.

Realization slowly creeps over his face. "It was you, wasn't it?"

All I can do is nod. Blake releases a heavy breath, clenching his jaw so tightly that he's shaking. I shrink away, wanting to shield myself from his reaction.

"I'm sorry I didn't tell you."

"What?" Blake looks genuinely confused. "You're sorry?"

"You opened up to me about your anxiety and your family, and I didn't tell you about this until now. I don't—"

"Ella, baby, no," he interrupts me. His face crumbles, the hardness in his eyes dissolving. "I'm not angry at you. God, no. I'm angry this happened *to* you."

"You're not upset I didn't tell you before?" I bite my lip to try to stop more tears from welling. "It's not that I didn't want to tell you. I just didn't know how to."

"I'm going to punch a hole in the wall later and quite possibly commit murder," he admits. "But I promise it has nothing to do with you, love. You just shared something intensely personal and private with me. I'm here for you however you need me to be, okay? Thank you for trusting me."

He pulls me against him, and I bury my face in his chest. I feel his heart pounding as he runs his hand up and down my back in a comforting motion. It's like a fucking dam's been broken, everything that's been bottled up and kept tightly under lock and key finally breaking loose. My body shakes as tears soak through Blake's shirt. I haven't cried like this in *months* and now that I've started, I can't stop. I'm not sure how long the two of us lie there with Blake holding me as I let everything out.

I lean back from him sometime later, wiping my nose with the back of my hand. It's definitely not the cutest thing I've ever done. I take a deep breath. "It happened about a month after I went to HR to report the harassment. I was in the studio room—it's on another floor than our offices, so it's a lot quieter —prepping notes for my next interview."

Blake stays quiet, letting me talk at my own pace. The muscles in his jaw tick despite his soft expression. I know I can stop talking right now and he'd be okay with that, but I want him to know. It's not even a want, it's a *need*.

"I'm assuming Connor found out that I went to HR because he showed up and started yelling at me. Told me I'm a fucking prude and shouldn't take things so seriously." I close my eyes in an attempt to hide from the memory. "When I tried to leave the room, he pinned me against the wall. He started groping me and ripped off my underwear and"—I take a deep breath, working up the nerves to finish the sentence—"said no one else was around to hear him fucking the attitude out of me."

I pause again before continuing. "Marcus, a sound engineer, came in as Connor was unbuttoning his pants…I guess he forgot his notebook. I told him I was on my way out and would go downstairs with him, so he waited while I got my things together."

The *what-ifs* still make my stomach churn. What if Marcus hadn't come at that exact moment? What if he hadn't forgotten his notes? What if he was in a rush and couldn't wait for me? What if I had frozen and didn't say anything?

I've never seen Blake look so furious. His eyes are fiery, lips pursed into a tight line. The veins in his neck are popping, muscles pulsing. "Why the *fuck* did they not arrest him?"

"I'm surprised they even investigated him." I hunch further into myself, wishing I could magically disappear. "It's his word against mine and you know who his dad is. The prosecutor didn't think there was enough evidence to move forward with the case, so they didn't."

"I am so sorry, love." Blake rubs his hands over his face before kissing my forehead lightly. "You are unbelievably strong."

"Most of the time, I'm fine, you know? I've worked through a lot of it in therapy. But with podcasting...it's just over-whelming."

I turn my head into the pillow to hide my face as I start crying again. Blake wraps his arms tighter around me. "It's all right, baby. I've got you, okay? I promise I'm not going anywhere."

Feeling safe in Blake's arms is a new kind of intimacy. I'd be lying if I said I don't love him for that.

THIRTY
BLAKE

I REST my hands on the steering wheel, letting the familiar feel of the car's vibrations calm me. The smell of fuel and burning rubber distract me from the white-hot rage twisting through me. It's constantly there, pulsing and threatening to break loose at any moment. It feels like I'm choking on my temper, unable to swallow down what Ella went through. I'm going to kill Connor Brixton. I don't know how or when, but I will kill him. Each *Law and Order* episode I watch with Ella gives me new twisted ways to murder that son of a bitch.

"Everything look good, Hollis?" an engineer asks through the radio.

"Sweating my balls off," I reply grumpily. "How fucking humid is it?"

"Eighty-four percent humidity."

Bloody hell. Even though it's a night race, the Singapore heat is brutal. Add in twenty-three corners on a bumpy street surface and you've got one of the most physically exhausting races.

As I wait for the gantry light to start flicking on, images of Ella's assault play in my mind. The pain in her eyes as she told me what he said to her, what he tried to do to her. The thought of a man double her size pressing her up against a wall. The way she bit her lip to try to stop the tears from welling in her eyes. The knowledge that Connor had the nerve to threaten her career when she got the police involved. Her ability to be so emotionally vulnerable with me despite everything she's been through.

My entire body is burning; the anger boiling through me, ready to crack open and destroy everything in its path. *I need this win.* When the race finally starts, I speed forward with the practiced precision I'm known for. I tail behind Theo, who started in pole position, for the first few laps before finally over-taking him so I'm in the lead. I channel every ounce of rage into the race. It's the first time I've been able to let any aggression out in the past week and a half.

"Stay focused, Hollis," an engineer tells me through the radio. "You've got Thompson coming up behind you."

I quickly glance in my rearview mirror to see the silver paint of an Everest car menacingly glaring under the street-lights. No way am I letting that fucker get ahead of me. This is not the race to mess with me. Harry's finding his footing, but years of experience give me an advantage. He attempts to chase me down, but I hold my position, making it impossible to overtake me. Sparks hit the asphalt, lighting up the ground as the two of us battle it out. I hit the apex of the next turn perfectly, boxing him out.

"Don't open the gap. Keep your pace."

The crackle of the radio pushes me forward. I'm not letting him use the dirty air to his advantage. The only thing that interrupts my silky-smooth driving is the jolt when I change gears. I'm taking turns at 4.5Gs of force like it's the easiest drive of my life. I welcome the distraction with open arms.

"Harry spun out on the last turn," my radio tells me a few laps later. "Took the corner too quickly."

He'll be beating himself up over that stupid mistake later. *Not my problem.*

"What's my lead?"

"You're about seven seconds ahead of Adler. Thirteen laps left."

"I may sweat to death before then."

Lucas catches up to me during the final laps and it's touch and go who's going to cross the checkered line first. During the second to last lap, he brakes a second too late going into a turn, giving me a chance to speed around him.

"Great race, mate. Fantastic pace." The radio buzzes with excitement. "Hard work pays off."

"Fuck yes, baby! Woo!"

I bang my hands against the wheel, relaxing at the security that twenty-five points just went toward another future title. Theo's going to be pissed that he's ending the race in P5 given he had pole position. I'm sure they'll have to bleep out a lot of his radio recordings. Not that that's anything new.

Josie's snapping photos on her camera the moment I step out of my car. "Congrats on the win…again."

I snort at her comment. "Thanks, Jos."

Ella runs toward me, stopping short with wide eyes and parted lips. She slugs me in the arm. "Great race, buddy boy."

"Buddy boy?" I cringe at the nickname. "What am I? Your dog?"

"I bet I could get you to roll over for a treat," she jokes. *Cheeky woman.*

Lowering her voice, she adds, "I'm trying to act casual."

Running my hand through my hair, I blow air out of my cheeks. "I don't want to hide you, El."

She shifts her weight from one foot to the other. "The second the media gets involved, our relationship isn't going to be ours anymore. You know that, Blake."

I hate that she's right. Bloody fucking hate it. *The Sun* ran an article last week called "Blushing Blake" with the tagline, "Fans spot Formula 1 favorite getting cozier with American writer working on his biography." It went into detail about Ella's education and job history. All of that was already public information thanks to LinkedIn, but I understand why it makes her uncomfortable. They also included a grainy photo of us eating dinner at some restaurant in London. My arm's wrapped around the back of her chair and she's resting her hand on my thigh. It doesn't look "casual." Being my girlfriend also means being in the public eye; I don't think Ella realized the implications of that when we first got together.

"You're right." I sigh. "It just means you'll have to give me double the affection later, though."

"That can be arranged…dude." She winks at me before I'm escorted to the designated interview area located under the podium. Lucas is already there, grinning at reporters. The post-race interviews go by quickly, and soon enough we're standing on the podium as "God Save the Queen" plays through the speakers. Hat in hand, I hum the words under my breath. I can't wait to take this damn suit off.

It's going to be a long night. Singapore makes up for the blistering humidity by throwing some of the hottest parties. After a quick shower, I head to a bar with my friends. We're packed like sardines—rich fans rubbing shoulders with top-tier drivers. I see everyone as a threat to Ella. I can't focus on any conversation, keeping my eyes glued to my girlfriend as she dances and mingles. I'm ready to pounce on anyone who so much as looks at her the wrong way. It's not jealousy or posses-siveness, it's a fierce need to protect her. It's so intense it constricts every breath I try to take.

Around midnight, I get a call from my lawyer and step outside to answer, praying it's good news. I told him to reach out at any time if he had an update on the deal I'm pursuing.

His news is that there's no news. I walk back inside with a piss-poor attitude.

I make my way to the table my friends are at, but Ella's no longer there. No one seems to know where she is. The anxiety that's been coiled up tightly inside me lets loose. I take a seat, trying not to stress out, but when she's still not back twenty minutes later, my heart starts pounding. The telltale signs of an anxiety attack creep up on me. A million and one scenarios run through my mind and none of them end well. I lean over, resting my head in my hands to get the room to stop spinning. I can't even get up to find her because I'll fucking pass out if I try.

"Are you okay, babes?" Josie asks me, placing her hand on my shoulder. "Do you want to go outside for a minute?"

"No," is all I can manage.

I know if I stand up, there's no way I'm making it more than a few steps without collapsing. The last thing I need right now is to faint in a goddamn bar. I'm focusing on my breathing. *Deep breath in, deep breath out.* I repeat the motion, trying to clear my mind. Lucas sits next to me a few moments later and hands me a cup of water. I hold it to my forehead to cool myself down; I feel entirely too hot.

"What's going on?" I hear Ella's voice drift into my ear a few minutes later. "Blake?"

Thank God. I slowly lift my head up even though I feel like it's going to float away at any moment. Sitting down, she places the cup of cold water against my lips. I take a few small sips. My friends give us space, so it's just the two of us tucked away at the table. I'm not sure how long we sit there with Ella slowly rubbing circles into my back. I feel fucking pathetic.

"I didn't know where you went and I panicked," I finally manage to cough out. "Thought something had happened."

"Ugh. The bathroom line took forever," she complains. "I'm almost positive people were snorting coke in there. Or they were having a very long quickie. Wait, why would you think something happened?"

When I don't answer right away, a quiet "oh" escapes Ella's lips. I don't even want to fucking say it. The words burn my throat coming out. "I hate him," I say softly. "I hate what he did to you. I hate knowing that you went through that. I hate that I can't protect you from all the bad shit in the world."

"I know." She rests her head against my shoulder. "But it's in the past, okay?"

She opens her purse and rummages around to find something. Pulling out a lipstick, she hands it to me.

"Are you going to kiss an attacker to death?" I twist the bottom to see what color her deadly makeup is. A tiny knife pops up instead. *What the fuck?*

"It's a lipstick knife," Ella explains as if I can't blatantly see the sharp blade in my hand. "Poppy and Jack got it for me before I left. I've never used it, but I keep it on me just in case."

How has airport security not taken that from her? Where did her friends even buy that?

"See? I can protect myself." She takes it out of my hand and tucks it back into its rightful place next to her real lipstick. God forbid she ever gets the two confused. "I've also taken a few self-defense classes."

I'm glad she's taken self-defense, but Ella's petite. Unless she turns into the Hulk when provoked, it doesn't help ease my mind much. I mumble some approving noise, anyway. There's no need for her to worry about me worrying.

"Do your friends know, um, why you freaked out? Because of me?"

"God, no," I reassure her. Taking her hand in mine, my heart rate continues to slow down. "I wouldn't tell them that."

She nods. "I just don't want people thinking about *that* whenever they think of me or my career, you know?"

"Listen to me." I hold her chin in my hand. "What

happened has no reflection on you as a person or as a professional, okay? It isn't your fault, and no one would ever blame
you for it."

Tucking a piece of hair behind her ear, she gives me a
small smile. "Do you feel any better? You're not shaking
anymore."

I hadn't realized I *was* shaking. "I'm doing okay."

She nods and bites the end of the straw in her drink before
taking a sip. It comes sputtering out of her mouth, spraying me
like I'm sitting in the front row at SeaWorld.

"Oh my God. I'm so sorry." Ella slaps her hand over her
mouth. "I wasn't expecting it to taste so bad."

"Ah, well, thanks for sharing." I wipe remnants of her drink
from my cheek. "It's a vodka soda, babe. Did you think it'd be
good?"

"I thought I was tipsy enough not to hate it so much." She
places the shitty drink on the table in front of us. "Let's go back
to the hotel."

All I want to do is take a cold shower and go to bed, but I
feel bad making Ella leave. She was having a great time before
I freaked out. "No, let's stay."

"I don't really want to," she lies. When is she going to learn
that I know her facial expressions like the back of my hand?
"I'm pretty tired."

She stands up and tells everyone that we're heading back
before I can object. I know the only reason she's doing this is
because my anxiety is bad. I'd be lying if I said I don't love her
for that.

THIRTY-ONE
ELLA

WHEN BLAKE INVITES his sister and her family over for brunch the weekend before the Mexico City Grand Prix, I paste on a smile despite my brain nearly setting itself on fire. Besides my brief run-in with Finn and Millie in Silverstone, I haven't formally met anyone in Blake's family. And meeting his sister is a big deal. A *huge* deal. She's the only family he's ever had and it's important to him that we get to know one another. *No pressure.*

I spend all morning yanking ingredients out of the pantry like I'm on an episode of *Chopped*. Blake suggested Nicola make brunch, but that felt impersonal, especially because his sister is bringing over banoffee pie, his death-row dessert. Blake's help is more of a hindrance considering he doesn't know where anything in his own kitchen is. And it took him about fifteen minutes too long to zest a lemon. Now he's assisting by taste testing everything "we" made.

"God, this is phenomenal," he moans. The noises he's making are absurdly sexual. "I love Battenberg."

My eyebrows lift. "Battenberg?"

"That's what this is called." Crumbs fall out of his mouth

as he grins. He takes another bite of the dessert he picked up from the local bakery earlier this morning, which is a cute cake made from different-colored squares and wrapped in marzipan. "Want some?"

"No." I grab the remaining cake and place it out of his reach. "Keep your hands off the food."

Blake waves his arms around his kitchen. There's enough food to feed an army. I ignore him and stand guard in front of the spread so he can't touch anything else until his family arrives.

When the doorbell rings, Blake intertwines our fingers and tugs me toward the door. Finn and Millie launch themselves at me, the foyer suddenly filled with nonstop babble.

"It's lovely to finally meet you, Ella," Ashley says warmly. She pulls me in for a long hug and my nerves slowly dissipate. It's uncanny how alike she and Millie look. "These rascals have been very excited to see you again. They've been referring to you as Uncle Blake's lady friend with the accent."

"It's nice to meet you, too." I turn toward the two munchkins. "Did your uncle Blake tell you that I've been talking about how cool I think *your* accents are?"

This sets off a round of squeals. I notice Ashley smile at Blake as her kids clamor to get my attention. Most of the brunch is spent with Finn and Millie asking me every question that comes to their minds. *Do I have a dog? Why do I say feet instead of meters? What's the grossest thing I've ever eaten? Do I like yellow or purple more? What's my favorite movie of all time? Did I know that it's impossible to sneeze with my eyes open? Can I do a cartwheel?*

After we're finished eating, Blake and his brother-in-law, John, play Chutes and Ladders with the kids. I know it's their way of giving Ashley and me alone time to chat, which we both appreciate.

"I haven't seen my brother this happy in a long time," she tells me. "Last year was really hard on him."

"He's stronger than he thinks," I reply, adoration filling my heart. "It just took him longer to see what everyone else already knew."

"Blake's always had this secret hope that she'd come back." Ashley rakes her hand through her hair, a habit I'm used to seeing him do. "I had a gut feeling she wouldn't."

"What made you want to look for her?" I ask softly. Taking a small sip of my coffee, I stay quiet. If Ashley is anything like her brother, silence is sometimes the best way to get an answer.

A few moments later, she gives me a pained smile. "I owed it to myself. It was never about reuniting with her, though. I mean, obviously, that would've been the best-case scenario, but it was more about proving to myself that I was strong enough to look for her, regardless of what the outcome may be. Does that make sense?"

I nod, unable to find the words to explain just how much I understand.

"I don't regret finding her," she continues, "but I wish the situation had turned out differently, especially for Blake's sake. We just don't fit into the new life she's crafted for herself. I accepted that long before she said it, but for Blake, it was like she was abandoning us all over again."

"I think he's doing okay with it now." I look over at where Blake's sitting on the floor, pointing out something on the board to his niece. "Or better than he was before."

"It's—it's nice to know he has someone." She briefly rests her hand on my forearm. "Now, enough with the heavy stuff. Tell me all the Formula 1 drama. Blake never shares anything, but I know there has to be some good tea."

Soon enough, the two of us are talking like old friends. She and Blake are yin and yang. Whereas he's private and suspicious of newcomers, Ashley is an open book. It turns out she also thinks his Rodolfo painting is ugly. Considering she's an interior decorator, my opinion feels vindicated.

We don't even realize the Chutes and Ladders tournament has ended until Finn runs into the kitchen. He's covered in colored marker. Red, blue, and green shapes take up almost every exposed inch of skin. It looks like he missed the paper and drew on himself instead.

"It won't come off." He pouts, burying his face in his mom's side. "Millie said it would."

I bite the inside of my cheek so I don't laugh. As a sister myself, I've done similar things to my baby brother.

Blake appears moments later with a guilty smile. "My bad," he apologizes while walking over to us. He tousles Finn's hair before plopping into the empty chair on the other side of me. "John was in the bathroom and my lawyer called, so I stepped out."

Ashley mumbles under her breath as she takes Finn to clean up. The moment they've disappeared from the room, I'm greeted with a deep kiss. The kind of kiss that makes me feel weightless. Like I'm levitating off the ground and floating in the air. My lips instantly miss his when he pulls away.

"You and Ashley seem to be getting on well," he notes, intertwining our fingers. "What'd you chat about?"

"Your imaginary pet frog named Roger Ribbit." I'll need to dig deeper into that later; there's a lot to unpack.

Blake narrows his eyes at me. "Anything else embarrassing?"

"Not really," I admit, choosing my next words carefully. "But we did talk about your mom for a bit."

His mom's not an off-limits topic, but I pause anyway to gauge his reaction. He's arching his eyebrows, his full lips slightly parted like he wants to say something but doesn't know what.

"We don't need to get into it," I reassure him quickly. "I just, well, um, Ashley said something that made me think."

"About what?"

"That maybe I owe it to myself to explore my options." If Josie were here, she'd start singing "YOLO" by Drake. "George said I should utilize his contacts, so I was going to see if he knows any podcasters who'd be willing to chat with me."

One of the best parts about this year is the autonomy I've had. Despite the strict time constraints and rigid schedule, George never micromanages me, instead trusting me to do my work, do it well, and do it on time. I'm not ready to give up that independence and freedom.

"An indie podcaster," I quickly clarify. "Not someone at a big-budget media company."

"That's…wow. That's a huge step, baby," Blake murmurs. The boyish grin he's wearing makes my heart beat ten times faster. "I'm so proud of you."

I'm proud of myself, too. I'm sure as hell not the same person I was last year, but I'm okay with that. I'm starting to like this version of me better.

THIRTY-TWO
ELLA

GEORGE PHILLIPS IS one of those guys who knows anyone and everyone. Want to try out a new restaurant but there's a four-month long wait list? No problem—he knows the chef and can get you a reservation at 7:00 p.m. on a Friday. Dying to go to an Arsenal F.C. game? It just so happens that he went to university with the general manager. If I wasn't so impressed, I'd be mildly concerned by his mafia-level connections.

The moment I asked him if he knew anyone in the podcasting space—just so I could ask some questions and pick their brain—he put me in touch with Remi Barnes. The same Remi who hosts Josie's favorite podcast: *Dating and Dildos*. Turns out George's wife plays tennis with Remi's mom. Go figure.

To say Remi and I have different areas of expertise is the understatement of the year—she knows about footjobs and I know about football—but I appreciate that she's willing to sit down and chat. I'm all in favor of women supporting women.

We're meeting for coffee in an hour, and I've changed about ten times already. I take off the sweater dress I'm wearing and add it to the growing pile of discarded clothing on the floor. It's a lost cause. Everything looks like I'm trying too hard or not trying hard enough. Blake walks into the bathroom, and I snatch up my robe from the ground, quickly putting it back on.

"Don't go all shy on me now, El." Blake chuckles gruffly. "I quite enjoy it when you're naked. Did you forget I ate you for breakfast, lunch, and dinner yesterday?"

My cheeks turn pink at the memory. His kitchen table has seen some very explicit things. Hell, everywhere in his house has.

"I'm supposed to be dressed, not naked," I remind him. "I still have to go over my notes, review my questions, and print out my résumé."

My mind is going a million miles an hour, unable to stop spinning.

"It's not an interview, love." Blake walks over to where I'm standing and pulls me against him. "Stop stressing. You're going to be brilliant."

"Did you know there are over two million podcasts? And less than twenty percent of new podcasts survive the first year." Burying my face into his chest, I sigh. "I just don't want to fail again."

"Eliana," he says sternly. I flinch at the use of my full name. He never calls me that unless he's dead serious. "You did *not* fail."

I swallow the dryness from my throat. "What if I start a podcast and then have to compete against Connor?"

A flash of anger lights Blake's eyes at the mention of Connor's name.

"All he does is get drunk with his friends and record himself recapping games and events twice a week. Anyone with a brain and general sports knowledge can do that. What you do takes creativity, intelligence, and an ability to interview people without them wanting to murder you. He has absolutely none of that. You wouldn't even be on the same playing field."

I puff out my cheeks before releasing a deep breath. "I guess."

"Stop fixating on what could go wrong," he says gently. "Focus on what could go right. What if you become the number one sports podcast?"

I like the sound of that. "What if I become so successful that Nabisco wants to be my sponsor?"

"What if you become so successful that McAllister wants to be your sponsor?"

"What if I become more famous than you?"

"Impossible"—he chuckles—"but I like where your head is at."

These what-ifs sit a lot more comfortably in my mind than the ones PlayMedia left me with. Before I can say anything else that'll send me into a tailspin of self-doubt, Blake presses his warm lips against mine. Even a kiss is enough to weaken me. The light stubble on his chin grazes against my face, no doubt making my pale skin bright red. One of his hands slowly slides under my robe and I melt into his touch. My breasts warm beneath his cool touch as he runs his thumbs over my nipples, teasing them to stiff peaks. His hands continue to wander around, caressing every part of my body he can reach. He pulls back, watching me with dark, hungry eyes.

"You are so amazingly talented," he says, his voice husky. "Stop questioning yourself."

His pupils dilate with desire as he traces his fingers down my body, watching as my skin erupts in goose bumps. He pulls my thong to the side, his finger slipping easily between my wet folds. My hips instinctually begin to move, and I spread my legs wider, giving him more access.

"I need you," Blake groans. His words send a lightning bolt straight to my core. I'm not sure if it's how desperate he looks or the little pout I've grown so fond of, but I quickly say yes. Without another word, he spins me around so I'm facing the mirror. Our ragged breathing is the only sound as Blake slips on a condom.

"Want you to watch how sexy you are when I'm inside you," Blake whispers as he slowly rocks into me. His tone is raspy, making my ache for him even stronger. A rush of air leaves my lungs as he stretches me full. My hands press against the counter in front of me, trying to steady myself so I don't pass out from pleasure. His touch has the power to soothe me and set me on fire all at once. It's overwhelming and he knows it. He tugs on my hair, forcing me to focus on the mirror.

"Feels so good, baby," he murmurs, teasing my exposed neck with wet kisses. "Love how wet you get for me."

Each thrust becomes more urgent than the last. I whimper as Blake drags his hand down my body until his thumb is pressed against my clit, rubbing it in circles that match his pace. Some sort of noise slips through my lips, urging him on. I can't think, let alone speak. My brain's shutting down, letting my body do the talking instead. Blake readjusts his stance to support my shaking legs and the new position hits my sweet spot. I'm putty in Blake's hands as he guides my hips back to meet his. He looks stunning. Sliding his tongue over his full lips, watching himself disappear inside of me with each stutter of his hips.

When he looks up to find me staring, he smiles so guilelessly it makes me tighten around him. We're both desperate for release and when our eyes lock again in the mirror, heat floods my body as I'm pushed over the edge. Every nerve sparks and then fades out. Blake holds me tightly against him, not letting my body slump as he continues to thrust into me. Shortly after, he shudders before stiffening in release. He presses a kiss between my shoulder blades before sliding out of me.

I turn around and slide my hands through his hair, capturing his lips for a quick kiss. "Thank you."

"For what? Giving you an orgasm?"

If I thanked Blake after every orgasm he gave me, I'd be a record on repeat. "Sure, but I meant for supporting me."

"Of course, love," he says, kissing my temple. "Anything else I can do for you?"

"What if…you made me pancakes?" I shoot him a hopeful smile. "That'd be nice."

Blake lets out a deep chuckle before heading downstairs to get breakfast started. I finish getting dressed, coming up with as many positive what-if scenarios in my head. There's a chance that my new hypothetical podcast may explode like the Hindenburg. But what if it doesn't?

I WAIT until I see Josie in Mexico to tell her about my meeting with Remi. My expectation that she'll start singing "Happy" by Pharrell or "Oh My God" by Adele is so far off base, it's not even in a baseball stadium. Instead, she hits me with some of Justin Bieber's "That Should Be Me." Not letting her tag along to meet her idol was sacrilege and the highest offense I could've possibly committed.

We're eating lunch in the cafeteria before afternoon practice when Josie says, "I cannot believe you didn't invite me."

She's said the same thing ten times in the past two minutes.

"It was a business meeting!" I argue. I've never been to a business meeting where someone said "nipples" so many times, but there's a first time for everything. I tried keeping a mental count but gave up after reaching eight.

"So unfair." Josie aggressively dunks her grilled cheese into her tomato soup. Red drops splash onto the cafeteria table. "You got to meet with Remi Barnes, and I had to teach a man-child how to do a bloody TikTok dance."

As much as Josie complains about Theo, the two of them are thick as thieves.

"It got over ten million views," I remind her. "That's pretty cool, Jos."

Theo's not a dancer, but the enthusiasm he put into his performance on McAllister's TikTok account was award-winning. It took Josie over an hour to teach him three simple moves, but it was well worth it. I think I've watched the video over a hundred times. Hell will freeze over before Blake participates in anything like that, but at least she has one driver willing to go along with the social media trends.

Josie sighs in defeat. "Was she as cool in person as she is on her podcast?"

"She suggested I let Blake use nipple clamps on me to enhance my orgasms." I cringe at the memory. "And then told me that a lot of athletes like being called *daddy* and asked if Blake was one of them."

If I can survive an interrogation from Remi, I'm positive I'll be able to handle the paparazzi and reporters who will no doubt hound me the moment my relationship with Blake goes public. Remi's questions didn't offend me, but they did almost knock me right out of my chair. The way she casually talked about butt plugs and anal sex made me feel like a prude.

Josie's mouth falls open and her spoon clatters onto the table. "You asked her for sex advice?"

"Shh! I didn't ask," I whisper-yell. "It was an unsolicited recommendation."

"I don't know!" Josie says back, lowering her voice. "Those seem like awfully specific suggestions, babes."

We stare at each other for a solid fifteen seconds before dissolving into laughter, clutching the table as we fight for air. It takes five minutes before either of us can speak without gasping for breath. I don't even know why we're laughing, which somehow makes it funnier.

"Okay, now tell me everything," Josie finally manages to say. She claps her hands together before stealing a few parmesan garlic fries off my plate. Albie's fries have made my favorite pair of jeans a little too tight, but it's so worth it. "And don't spare a single detail."

Warmth radiates through my body as I tell her about how our coffee meeting turned into cocktails. Remi and I have a lot more in common than I initially thought. She's a firecracker who says *dick* as often as people say *because*, but she's business-savvy and smart. I've already downloaded a business plan template she emailed me, and she's connecting me with a free-lance producer she knows.

She reminded me that I've already mastered how to do the hard stuff. Researching and asking the right questions, connecting with the listeners and creating a community, building good rapport with the guests. The things that Play-Media did for me—editing, producing, marketing—can be learned. Or outsourced, as Josie reminds me. She's offered to help me with branding and social media.

"Do you want to have a similar format to your last podcast?" Josie asks after she's satisfied I've given her every last detail. "Or completely start over and do something new?"

My nerves buzz with excited energy as if I just downed a double espresso. In the words of the nipple queen, "I'm not starting over. I'm simply redirecting."

THIRTY-THREE
BLAKE

THERE ARE ONLY four races left in the season. I know a lot can happen in four races and so does Ella, but that doesn't stop her from pacing around the pit garage an hour before the Brazilian Grand Prix. I watch her with devilish delight. She may not put up with my shit, but she's still my biggest supporter. She's asking everything and anything. Are the tires they chose right for today's weather conditions? Is their two-pit strategy smart? How are they going to deal with the fact that Theo landed pole instead of me? There can only be one winning strategy, and I have a much better chance at the Championship, so how does that fare for team camaraderie? Are they going to be using a harder suspension? And what about wing settings?

When she asks an engineer if they're planning on using a low off-throttle differential setting for the slower turns, I step in. The McAllister team loves Ella, but they also love doing their job, and her questions are making it a little difficult to concentrate. I place my hands on her hips and pick her up, walking over to the other side of the garage with her feet inches off the ground.

"I can't believe you just physically removed me." She glares at me in exasperation. "Completely unnecessary."

"You have no idea how sexy it is to hear you talk about overrun, but you're making it hard for them to do their jobs."

"It's exactly because I want them to do their jobs that I'm asking."

"I appreciate it, love." I chuckle. "So does the Tickle Monster."

Ella has trouble keeping her balance as she laughs. It takes her a minute to catch her breath. "You named your car the Tickle Monster?"

"Finn and Millie named it," I defend myself. To be honest, if it weren't for them, I probably wouldn't have even named the car.

Ella looks at me with undisguised affection. "You continue to surprise me."

"Blakey Blake." Theo saunters over to where we're standing, placing himself firmly in between us. "Your girlfriend doesn't want me to have a threesome with you guys, but I think we need to talk about it as a group."

I'm sorry, what? I fold my arms across my chest. Over my dead body am I sharing Ella with anyone else. Especially not Theo. "I don't want to have a threesome with you either, Walker."

"C'mon," he argues with a pout. "You can't deny that I'm a fantastic-looking bloke. You'd be lucky to see me naked."

I've already seen Theo in the nude plenty of times. If there's a chance for his dick to be out, it will be. The man acts like he's bloody Tarzan.

"I'd rather gouge my eyes out with a spoon than see you naked," Ella says, wrinkling her nose like a rabbit. "I'm not having a threesome with anyone."

"Unless it's Pete Davidson and Harry Styles," I grumble.

I've gotten over the fact that if my girlfriend is ever in a threesome, I'm not involved in any capacity. Well, I'm still pissed about it, but I can't be *that* mad considering I've already had a threesome with two of my celebrity crushes.

"You got cockblocked out of a threesome with your own girlfriend!" Theo slaps his hands against his knees as he doubles over. "How the hell does that happen? You got a thing for blokes with tats, Goldy?"

"It's hypothetical." Ella smacks him in the arm before narrowing her eyes at me. "Don't you guys have a race to win or something?"

"I don't need to beat Blake." Theo winks at her. "Looks like Styles and Davidson already have."

I'm going to smash his face in.

"Good luck out there." Ella gets on her tiptoes and gives me a kiss. She's not fully comfortable with major PDA thanks to the cameras on me at all times, but she's starting to warm up a bit.

"Thank you. See you after dinner?"

The last thing I want to do after the race is to entertain sponsors at a three-hour-long meal, but it's not up to me. Ella was invited, but she's skipping out. People won't leave her alone now that our relationship's public. The media is trying to learn everything and anything they can about the woman who stole the heart of Britain's broody bachelor. Ironically enough, it wasn't a sneaky pap photo that exposed us, but my own sister posting a photo of Ella with Finn and Millie on her Instagram. Go figure.

I steal another kiss before heading out to the pit lane. I ended this race in P3 last year, but a five-second penalty for crashing into Thompson dropped me down to P7. I'm ready for an actual podium win this year.

Ella's good luck must have been sprinkled with special fairy dust or some shit because my win is *very* lucky indeed. I place P1 by less than a quarter of a second.

"Blake!" a reporter yells during the post-race interviews. "How are you feeling after today's first place win?"

"I'm feeling on top of the world," I reply, meaning it. The most amazing part? I know the best is still yet to come.

IF IT'S possible to die from boredom, I'm about three minutes away from my funeral. Theo, on the other hand, is thriving. He's a born entertainer who can somehow talk incessantly about himself, but still make you feel like you're part of the story. I've told the big wigs at McAllister that Theo is much better suited for these types of dinners, but they still insist I go. Theo's amusing everyone with one of his outlandish stories, so I slyly check my phone. I see two missed calls from Ella and immediately excuse myself from the table. My heart starts beating faster, my skin crawling with discomfort. Ella never calls during business dinners. She claims that unless she's bleeding or something's broken, nothing is urgent enough that it can't just wait. I quickly make my way outside to call her back.

"Hi," she answers.

"Did something happen?" I ask agitatedly. "Are you okay?"

"Yeah, I'm fine." Her voice trails off. "I-I just wanted to hear your voice, I guess."

"I'll be back twenty."

Before she can argue, I end the call and shoot Theo a text, saying I don't feel well and need to leave. He'll probably love not having to share the spotlight with me, anyway.

Ella's curled up on the couch when I finally get back to our hotel room. She looks like a little burrito with how she's tucked herself under a blanket. I sit next to her, resting my hand on her back as she talks to her mom on the phone.

"My mom wants to know if you'd prefer regular potatoes or sweet potatoes for Thanksgiving," Ella tells me. "And she says hi."

"Whatever she wants to make is good with me," I answer. "Tell her I say hello."

"He's fine with either, Mom." She rolls her eyes at something before saying goodbye. Narrowing her eyes at me, she says, "You shouldn't have left dinner."

Ella watches me warily as I lift up her arms and tilt her chin, looking for obvious signs of injury. When I don't see any, I relax slightly.

"Checking for broken bones or blood," I explain with a shrug. "What's wrong, love?"

"None of that," she says, her lips turning up the smallest amount. "He made *Forbes* Thirty Under Thirty."

She hands me her phone; I find the website already pulled up on her screen. I briefly read through his feature, trying not to crack her screen in half when I read the words "titan in the industry." I don't bother finishing the profile; I already know more than enough about him.

"I started working on a business plan, but then Poppy texted me that," Ella shakily admits. "She didn't want me to hear it from someone else."

I scoop Ella up, wrapping her in my arms. She sighs, resting her head against my chest.

"It's not fair," she murmurs. "He put me through hell, yet he's being praised and I'm what? Starting from scratch and stressing out that he told people not to work with me? It makes me feel like I'm damaged goods."

Her chin starts trembling and she hunches her shoulders, shrinking into herself. If I could take every bit of pain from Ella and suffer through it myself, I would without a second thought.

"You're not damaged goods," I reassure her. "You don't

want to work with people who would believe his bullshit, anyway. It means they're bloody idiots."

"I guess so," she sniffles, her voice cracking. "I hate that it makes me want to cry. I just want to be okay."

"But it's okay to *not* be okay," I gently remind her. "I'm nearly thirty and still dealing with shit that happened to me when I was a kid. You went through something bloody terrible. No one expects you to emerge from that unscathed."

She nods into my chest, and I feel her body shake lightly as silent tears fall down her cheeks. I tighten my hold on her, desperate to let her know I've got her. That she's okay. That she's the strongest person I know. A few minutes later, Ella tilts her head up, blinking those damn beautiful eyes at me. I hate how red they are because of her tears.

"You know when someone massages a knot out of your back? And it really hurts, but you know it'll be worth it in the end because you'll feel better?"

"Yep. Sam once gave me a back massage after a crash and told me he couldn't tell if I was choking or having an orgasm."

Her soft, infectious laugh is the best damn thing I've heard all day. And I won a Grand Prix earlier.

"That's what all of this is like," she admits. "I know it's all part of the healing process, or whatever, but it just sucks."

"I know it does but look at how far you've come. You've traveled the world. You're almost done writing a goddamn book that I know is going to be a massive hit. Not only because it's about me and I'm remarkable, but because you wrote it, which makes it doubly amazing. And you're working on a business plan for a podcast that's going to wow the world. That's pretty impressive shit, love."

She nods to herself, tugging her lower lip between her teeth. "Yeah? You think so?"

"I know so." Pulling her close, I brush my lips against the

top of her head. "You're proof an angel can walk through hell and make burns look beautiful, baby."

THIRTY-FOUR
ELLA

I WOULD'VE MUCH PREFERRED to be at *The Tonight Show Starring Jimmy Fallon*, but *The Elliot Brown Show* isn't too bad, I guess. It's the third talk show appearance Blake's done this month. They've all gone great, but he's still anxious. I'm losing circulation in my right hand because of how tightly Blake's grasping it. His deep brown eyes look over every inch of the studio like it's a torture chamber. The show producer is walking us around, giving Blake a breakdown of the segment. He nods along, half listening, half glaring. Marion's elbowed him no fewer than five times, hissing that he needs to pay attention.

The halls of the studio are lined with framed wall portraits and posters of the famous guests who have appeared on the show before. I spy a photo of Elton John as we make our way to the dressing rooms. The moment the producer leaves to take care of some pre-show checks, Blake starts pacing the length of the room. Marion shoots me a worried look, but I give her a reassuring smile.

Blake only stops his incessant walking when the other guest for today's show bursts in. Gemma Buckley is a health and wellness guru who's launching her own book soon, hence their pairing for this episode. She's a real-life Barbie doll with her honey-blond hair, unblemished skin, and kick-ass body. I may buy her book if it divulges how to look so…flawless.

"Blake Hollis!" she squeals, pulling my boyfriend into a massive hug. "It is *so* nice to finally meet you!"

I wonder if her boobs are real or fake. I'll have to ask Blake considering they're pressed up against him. I've decided I no longer want to read her book.

"Lovely to meet you as well." He takes a step back, keeping a healthy distance between the two of them. "This is my girl-friend, Ella."

Blake gently nudges me forward and two seconds later, I'm enveloped in Gemma's toned, tanned arms. She smells like a rose-filled garden.

"You look so familiar," Gemma muses when I'm finally released from her Velociraptor-like grip. "Have we met before?"

"I don't think so." There's no way I'd forget that. "Maybe I just have one of those faces."

She gently grabs my chin, turning my face from side to side. I awkwardly take a step back so I'm out of her grasp, bumping into Blake, who's watching with amusement.

"I'll figure it out." She nods to herself. "I have to go finish up hair and makeup, but I'll see you out there, Blake!"

"She's nice." Blake chuckles, leaning against the wall after she's left. Nice is one way to put it.

A crew of people comes in to whisk him away thirty minutes later. *It's showtime, baby.*

I'm not sure if Blake's gotten better at being interviewed, or if he's just ready to get this round of his press tour over with, but he's brought his A-game. He's the perfect combina-tion of charming and confident with a side of cheekiness. The audience is loving every minute of it.

"So your girlfriend is one of your biographers," Elliot says with a wink. "Tell us about that. Work hard, play hard?"

I hear Marion sigh frustratedly under her breath. *Same, girl, same.* This interview is supposed to be about Blake and the biography, not the writer he's dating. I'm almost positive I'm listed as a persona non grata on Blake's release form. The audience laughs as Elliot leans forward like he's about to receive salacious information.

"Well, she wasn't my girlfriend when she took the job," Blake responds coolly. He likes not having to hide our relationship, but he's still fiercely overprotective of me, threatening to keep reporters out of the press room if they don't respect my personal space. Having me brought up on live television? Not going to bode well for anyone. "She's a journalist first and foremost and a phenomenal writer, so she's not biased. Just the other day she asked me if I pay extra when I travel since my confidence must take up so much luggage space, if that tells you anything."

"What'd you say?" Elliot asks. The way he's resting his elbows on the desk in front of him makes me roll my eyes. He couldn't be more desperate for information if he tried.

Blake grins, his teeth flashing white against his tanned skin. "I fly private, so it's never been an issue."

The audience gobbles it up like cake, leaving no crumbs left behind.

"Good on her." Elliot nods delightedly. "I can imagine it's hard to be unbiased since it looks like the two of you are in the honeymoon phase."

An image of Blake and me appears on the screen behind them. It's from the last Grand Prix. Blake's holding his trophy above his head with one arm, the other wrapped tightly around my waist. We're staring at each other like we're the only ones in the room. It's one of those photos you would want to add to your Pinterest board titled "J'adore" or something cheesy like that. The audience erupts into a chorus of "awwws."

"Look at you lovebirds!" Gemma places her hands over her heart. "You two are positively adorable."

Blake barely acknowledges the photo.

"In case the audience doesn't know, Blake's girlfriend is pretty successful in her own right," Elliot continues. "She used to host a podcast for PlayMedia, which is one of the largest sport and entertainment media companies in America."

Elliot Brown fucking sucks in comparison to Jimmy Fallon.

Gemma turns toward Blake, smacking him lightly on the arm. "That's why she looked so familiar earlier!"

Blake says nothing, but I see the muscles in his neck tense. Mine do the same. I really don't want to be the topic of conversation anymore.

"We pulled some stats and her podcast received four point seven stars from over seventy thousand reviews. Quite remarkable for a female-hosted sports show!"

"Go fuck yourself, Elliot," I mumble under my breath.

"That is quite impressive," Marion whispers to me, trying to diffuse the situation. "At least it's not mean tweets or anything sordid like that."

"One of PlayMedia's biggest podcasts is blowing up in the UK right now," Elliot continues with a relaxed smile. "*Trash Talk* I think it's called. Have you listened to it? I haven't yet, but I know they've covered some Formula 1 races."

"No," Blake states, his voice flat. His demeanor has changed from relaxed to angry within the span of a question. It's not lost on anyone.

A new image appears on the screen and I blink in a stupefied trance. It's of Connor and me at the launch party of *Coffee with Champions*. It feels like I've been sucker punched. A lump rises in my throat as I look at myself grinning next to Connor like it's the best fucking day of my life. I was excited to learn from him, to have him as a mentor. His arm is draped over my shoulders, a slight smirk on his face. At the time, I thought the worst thing I'd have to deal with was bad reviews on Spotify.

"Where'd you get that photo?" Blake hisses. He's gripping the arms of the chair so tightly he may claw through the fabric. "Take it the fuck down."

"Oh!" Gemma giggles in delight. "Are you jealous?"

"Bloody fucking cock-up," Marion swears. She waves her hands, trying to catch Blake's attention, but it's no use. His eyes are focused on Gemma. He needs to control himself and walk away. My entire body is on edge, my chest tightening. I'm biting my lip so hard I taste blood.

"She's obviously close with him since they worked together," Gemma says, completely oblivious to the effect her words are having on Blake. "Maybe she had a little office romance with him. I'd be jealous of that if it were me."

"An office romance?" Blake spits out. The sharpness of his voice could pierce through stone. "Brixton's a fucking predator."

Adrenaline swirls through my veins, igniting my fight-or-flight instincts. I silently beg Blake to let it go. He's already said too much.

"Just because he worked with Ella doesn't make him a predator," she scoffs critically.

"He's a bastard who harasses and assaults women," Blake states flatly. "He belongs in a jail cell."

This is not happening. This cannot be happening. My body trembles as waves of anger and fear flow through it. Marion places her hand on the small of my back to steady me.

"How do you know he's done that?" Elliot inquires. "That's a pretty big accusation to make. I know you should never judge a book by its cover, but he seems like a proper fellow. The people love him. It's why he's got such a cult following."

He knows his question is going to push Blake over the edge

and he knows what it'll do for his ratings. Hot, angry tears roll down my face as I clutch my hands to my heart.

"Oh my God," Gemma balks, realization claiming her features. "Did he harass your girlfriend?"

"Do you consider him asking her if she wants a dildo that was made from a silicone mold of his dick harassment?" Blake's so angry that he's visibly shakings. "Or how about when he choked her and then tried to force himself on her? Is that considered assault?"

There's a small circle of close friends and family who know what happened at PlayMedia, but that number just grew to include the half a million people tuning in. Gemma's jaw drops and she struggles to regain her composure. Elliot, on the other hand, jumps on the opportunity to probe more. I know as well as he does that this interview is going to go viral.

"That's definitely inexcusable behavior." He nods sympathetically. "Is there proof of her alleged assault?"

Alleged. The word presses down on me like a bruise. Painful and sore. It bothers Blake just as much because he loses any and all restraint. There's no stopping him unless security drags him out, and even then, he'd be kicking and screaming. I stop listening. I can't focus on what he's saying, nor do I care to. I've already lived through this in private; I don't need to hear about it while the world finds out.

It feels as if drops of ice are trailing down my spine as I stumble away from the stage, finding my way outside. The fresh air dries the tears on my cheeks, staining them against my skin. I wrap my arms around my waist, trying to calm my erratic breathing. After a few minutes, I'm able to wave down a cab. I give them Josie's address, knowing I can't go back to my own place.

Josie's waiting for me outside of her building, bundled in a winter coat. She pulls me into a hug, telling me that I'm going to be okay, that it's going to be okay. Nothing about this is going to be okay. She keeps her hand interlocked with mine as we make our way up to her apartment. I'm holding on to her like she's a lifeline, unable to stop my heart from thudding against my ribcage.

She gives me clothes to change into and sits me down on the couch. Fierce sobs wrack my body, making it hard to catch my breath. I feel like I'm drowning in tears, unable to wipe them off my cheeks quick enough before more follow suit. Josie doesn't leave my side, petting my hair and rubbing calming circles into my back. All the memories I've fought so hard to get control of are swirling around in my head, not stopping to let me take a breath. It's like I reverted to where I was a year ago. It's the last place I want to be, but I don't know how to escape it.

Josie takes control of my phone, fielding texts and calls like she's J.J. Watt. There's no way anyone in America will see this before tomorrow, so at least I don't have to deal with Poppy or my parents right now. I don't even know what to say to them.

"Marion texted you, asking if you're all right," Josie informs me. "She said she's working on getting them to scrap the episode, but no luck so far. Blake's also been calling you nonstop."

The last thing I want is to talk to Blake. "Just turn my phone off."

She nods. It may not be the most mature thing, but I can't deal with him right now. Josie makes us tea once I've calmed down a bit, and I sip it gratefully. My throat feels raw from crying, the hot green tea a much-needed antidote.

Theo starts calling Josie incessantly. She turns her phone on silent, letting each one go to voicemail.

"Blake's going to show up here sooner or later, babes." She looks at me for direction on how to proceed. "What do you want me to do?"

"I don't care." I don't have enough energy to care. "I just don't want to see Blake."

She answers Theo's next call on speakerphone with a curt, "Hello."

"Is Ella with you?" Theo greets Josie with a strained voice. "Blake's absolutely losing his mind trying to find her."

"Yes," Josie reveals after a long pause. "She's here."

We can hear him telling Blake that I've been located like he's some fucking secret agent. "Blake's going to—"

"Theo, she doesn't want to see him," Josie interrupts, her voice stern. "The front desk of my building knows not to let him up, so don't bother trying."

I can't help but crack a small smile. Josie lives in a walk-up, but neither of them knows this.

"Um, that's…not going to go over well." Theo sighs. "Will you talk to Blake, at least?"

"I have nothing to say to Blake, so no."

"Josie," he stresses. "The guy's a fucking mess. At least let him know she's okay."

"He's a mess?" Her voice rises with incredulity. "How about his girlfriend? You know, the one he just sandbagged on national television? He can go fuck himself up the arse for all I care."

My jaw drops at Josie's words. I don't think I've ever heard her swear so aggressively.

"Well, I'm not going to tell him that." Theo chuckles quietly. "Please just talk to him."

An uncomfortable silence settles between them. "He has thirty seconds," she decides with finality.

"Josie?" Blake's voice comes through the phone loud and clear. "Is Ella okay?"

"I don't know, Blake," Josie says, each word more sarcastic than the last. "Would you be okay if the situation were Uno-reversed?"

"No, of course not." His voice is so husky it's almost imperceptible.

"So then obviously she's not okay. Is that all?"

"Can I talk to her? Please, Josie."

She cocks her head at me. I take a deep, steadying breath, gathering the little energy I have. I feel each heartbeat pounding in my throat as I turn the phone off of speakerphone and press it against my ear.

"How could you?" I murmur quietly. Every nerve in my body seems to cry out. "How could you do that to me?"

"I am so fucking sorry, Ella," Blake says hoarsely. "I lost it and I know that's no excuse, but I need you to know I did not mean to hurt you."

"Well, you did," I snap fiercely, the betrayal in my voice harsh. "I told you that in *private*, Blake. You know it's not something I like talking about or want people knowing, yet you told the fucking world."

"Tell me how to fix this."

"You can't." I rub my eyes. My contacts are long gone, cried out somewhere in the streets of Waterloo. "It's already out there."

"I'll have them stop it from airing and I'll issue an apology. Or I'll—"

"Stop," I plead, my voice so low it's barely audible. "Please."

"Ella, baby. I'm so sorry. So, so sorry. I didn't mean—"

"I can't do this," I interrupt. "Not now."

"You can't do what?" The unspoken questions hang in the air.

I can't do this conversation? This relationship?

"I don't know." My voice cracks as I fight to get words out. "I need...space."

"Okay," he agrees quickly. "I can get you from Josie's tomorrow and—"

"No." I'm trembling, struggling to find my breath. "I need space from you, Blake."

The silence through the phone is deafeningly loud. My throat is thick with guilt, not wanting to hurt Blake, but not wanting to comfort him either.

"What does that mean?" Blake asks, an eerie calmness in his voice.

"I-I don't know. I just…need time."

Time to mourn the loss of privacy this will bring. Time to figure out how this impacts me and any future career I may have. Time to deal with *everything* without also having to handle Blake's own emotional fallout.

"Okay," he says slowly, voice barely above a whisper. "If that's what you need, Ella."

"Thanks," I say so quietly it's a surprise he can even hear me.

"I'm so sorry, El. I promise I'm going to make things right," Blake continues agitatedly. "I'm here whenever you're ready to talk, okay?"

"Okay," I mumble before ending the call.

Sagging into the couch, I make no attempt to wipe away the tears falling down my face. I try to create a tally of all the shit that's gone wrong in the past few hours, but I don't have enough fingers or toes to count that high.

THIRTY-FIVE
BLAKE

I CAN'T LEAVE my house without reporters shoving their cameras in my face and their questions down my throat. Even though *The Elliot Brown Show* has taken the episode off air after both my team and PlayMedia threatened to sue, it's been a media circus. Some people are applauding me for calling out a predator, especially since a few other women have come out with similar claims following the interview.

Those close to me are calling me an absolute bloody idiot for doing so at Ella's expense. They're right. I am an absolute bloody idiot. There are no two ways about it.

I've been a dead man walking since Ella flew back to Chicago. I don't blame her. I hate myself for what I did, so I can only imagine how she's feeling. I promised her I'd be the kind of man she deserves, yet I'm the reason she's reliving her own personal hell. I lost my cool and may have lost the love of my life in the process.

There is no me without her and the thought of living life without her is the worst kind of pain I've ever experienced. It's been over a week since we last spoke, and there's not enough whiskey in the world to burn the thought of her out of my mind.

I'm pouring myself another drink when I hear banging on the door. I have a pretty good guess who it is, and if I'm right, I'm not in the mood for it. I take my time finishing making my old-fashioned before slowly heading to the door. I find Theo, Lucas, and an absurd amount of beer on the other side.

"It's cold as tits out there, mate," Theo complains. He pushes straight past me into the warmth of my foyer. "You really took your sweet bloody time, didn't you?"

Lucas rolls his eyes at Theo. "What he means to say is 'Hey, Blake, how are you doing?'"

"You should've texted." The deep timbre of my voice is diluted down to a tired, raspy pitch. "I'm not in the mood for company."

"We did text." Lucas walks past me, closing the door behind him. "And we brought beer and pizza. When's the last time you ate?"

His guess is as good as mine. A loud crash from the kitchen indicates Theo's making himself right at home. They're not leaving anytime soon, whether I want them to or not. Lucas and I follow the noise and find Theo sitting on my kitchen counter while a glass pitcher lies shattered on the floor.

"I leave you alone for one minute, Walker." I sigh, rubbing my brow. "And you break shit."

I listen to Theo explain that he's on the counter to avoid getting glass in his feet. They are his money maker after all.

"I wanted to pour the tinnies into a pitcher," he explains. "Like iced tea...but with beer."

I head to the pantry to get a broom and pan rather than tell Theo that may be the single-handed stupidest thing I've heard in my entire life. Lucas takes over cleaning duties as I put the frozen pizza in the oven. Theo watches us from the counter, perched like some sort of handsome Australian gargoyle.

"Grab me one of those, mate?" He nods toward the beer on the opposite end of the kitchen. "Please and thank you."

I toss a can over and sip my whiskey. The ice cube is starting to melt, but I need the liquor to numb the ache that's sitting in my chest.

"We've been texting you all week, by the way," Lucas says as he empties the glass-filled pan into the garbage. "You've just continually ignored us."

"Maybe my phone died." I shrug. My phone's fully charged just in case Ella needs me or wants to talk. Neither has happened so far but wishful thinking and all that.

"Bullshit," Theo chides, calling me out on my fib. "Doesn't matter. We're here anyway."

I don't answer. I'm not sure why they're here. It's not like they can do anything to help the situation. They're good friends—I'm lucky to have them, I know that—but right now I don't want to talk about anything. Especially the one thing they're here to talk about.

As if on cue, Theo says, "Have you spoken to Ella? Since… you know?"

"Since I revealed the fact that she was sexually harassed and assaulted on live television?" I snap before taking another sip of my drink. "For some weird reason, she doesn't particularly want to talk to me."

I run my hand through my hair. Ella's everywhere and everything. I feel the ghost of her lips on my neck, the echo of her laugh in my bedroom. I can't sleep without her warm body pressed against mine, but I don't want to be awake when I'm forced to think of all the hurt I've caused her.

"Don't bite my head off, mate." Theo holds his hands up in surrender. "I was trying to be nice about it."

"I told him to chill with the questions until you're at least a few drinks deep." Lucas chuckles with a guilty shrug. "God forbid he listens to me."

"Being a parent is tough," I add with a small smile. "Especially with a child as disruptive as Theo."

"I'm right here, you know." Our adult kid pouts dramatically. "And I'm just trying to help."

Lucas leans against the counter. "So is that why you asked us about Connor? Because you knew?"

"No." I shake my head. "She didn't tell me about the assault until we were dating. I just knew how he treated her."

Theo mumbles under his breath. "No wonder you almost hit Lucas when he said he'd met him before."

"Sorry about that," Lucas mutters. "I didn't know he was actually a piece of shit."

The two of them talk amongst themselves as we wait for the pizza to heat up. I'm zoning in and out of the conversation, but my ears perk up when Theo tells Lucas he went to a spin class with Josie the other morning.

"Did you ask about Ella?" I interrupt. The hopeful tone of my voice is pathetic, but I'll take any scrap I can get. "How she's doing?"

"You really think Josie told me anything?" Theo slowly raises an eyebrow. "I tried asking, but her lips are sealed, mate. Also kind of hard to chat during a class when a bike seat is crushing your balls."

His answer doesn't surprise me. Josie's barely said a word to me since the interview except when absolutely necessary for work purposes.

"More importantly," Theo continues. "How are you doing?"

The oven beeps and I quickly take out the pizza, grateful for the excuse to not have to answer his question. How am I doing? I feel like life is moving on in vibrant color, but I'm frozen in place surrounded by grays and browns.

We head to the kitchen table, everyone grabbing a slice of pizza. I eat despite the fact that I'm not hungry. I can tell my friends are worried enough given the furtive glances they keep giving one another. Subtlety has never been Theo's strong suit, and Lucas doesn't bother hiding his concern. It's like everyone's waiting for a repeat performance of last year's breakdown. They have no reason to worry; I can barely get out of bed, let alone want to.

"What's your game plan?" Lucas finally asks. "Are you still going to Chicago for Thanksgiving?"

I start to shake my head but hesitate. "I don't know." If she doesn't want to speak with me on the phone, I doubt she's going to want to see me in person.

"So you're just going to do nothing?" Theo rests his elbows on the table, staring me down. "That doesn't sound like you."

"I don't feel like I'm in a position to *not* do what Ella asks of me."

"But she's your better half," he argues in a loud voice. "Or whatever."

She's not my better half, she's my whole fucking heart.

I take my phone out of my pocket to press ignore on an incoming call, but the name flashing across the screen makes me pause. I step outside to answer. My friends are staring at me with wide eyes and curious expressions when I come back in. Theo wastes no time in asking questions. *Who was it? Do I know them? Why'd you have to talk to them outside?* I sink into my seat before a shadow of my old grin appears.

"It was my lawyer." I blink slowly, still in shock. "The deal's going to go through."

The seven-month legal battle I've been in has remained at a standstill for weeks. To be honest, I'd almost all but given up hope. Now I'm damn glad I didn't.

"Good on you, mate!" Theo drums his hands against the table in excitement. "Looks like that shitstorm of an interview was good for one thing."

So much for him trying to be nice about it.

"Did they finalize it because of that?" Lucas lets out a low whistle. "Holy shit, man."

Theo grabs another piece of pizza. "So is it yours? Is it hers? Give us the details, Blakey Blake."

An idea starts forming in my mind. It's borderline crazy, but it might be crazy enough to work. I outline what I'm thinking to my friends and it's the longest Theo's ever stayed quiet in a conversation. Three phone calls, two beers, and one hour later, it's decided. I'm headed to New York City after the next Grand Prix.

THIRTY-SIX
ELLA

MY PHONE'S been buzzing constantly ever since Blake's bombshell of an interview. Reporters asking for an exclusive interview, old colleagues apologizing for not speaking up, friends saying they're here to talk, faceless people on social media either calling me a liar or praising me. It's too much. All of it. The only person whose call I'll answer right now is Cindy's. Today's our second session since I flew back to Chicago. We've been doing video calls because "body language reveals a lot." So far all I've done during our appointments is talk a little and cry a lot. The more I talk about it, the easier it gets, so I'm trying my best.

"How do you feel today?" Cindy asks me. Her blond hair looks unusually dull through my computer screen.

"Tired," I admit haggardly. "Really fucking tired."

"Tired because you're not sleeping well or tired of something?"

"Both, I guess." The timeliness of my yawn couldn't be better. "I'm also pissed, mad, sad, and pretty much every emotion under the sun. It's like I'm completely numb, but also feeling way too much at the same time."

"You're going through a lot, Ella," she says kindly. "There's no right way to respond, and your body is in overdrive trying to process everything."

That's for fucking sure.

"Okay, well, how do I get it to stop doing that?"

"We may be able to send people into outer space, but science isn't that advanced yet, unfortunately." Her cheeks push her glasses up on her nose when she smiles. "If you had to pick your primary emotion right now, what would it be?"

I take a minute to think about it. "Mad."

"Why mad?"

It's a simple question with a complex answer. The *Jeopardy* countdown sound plays in my head as I piece together my thoughts.

"All I've wanted was for Connor to be held responsible for his actions, but when that didn't happen, I just wanted to disassociate from the entire thing," I admit. "I didn't want anyone knowing because if they did, I'd have to think about it and talk about it, but nothing would change. Now that people are realizing he's a shitty person, I'm...I don't even know. Pissed they found out what happened, but happy that they finally know. It feels contradictory."

"When you were assaulted, it consumed you. You were up in arms, ready to burn PlayMedia down. You were *ready* for everything that may happen."

"Yeah." I rest my chin in my hands. "I guess so."

"You weren't ready for this," she reminds me gently. "You went to a talk show to support your boyfriend and left having your personal life revealed to a lot of people. You didn't have any control in that situation."

"So you think it's a control thing?"

"I think that's part of it." She nods. "Not having control is how this all came into the public eye...it's understandable why you're mad. It's hard to make your story your own when someone else tells it. You also felt like you were finally in control over your life, and Blake threw a wrench in that."

"Did you know that if you Google my name, the first two search pages are all about Connor and PlayMedia? I'll forever be attached to them."

"It's something that happened to you, Ella, but it isn't who you are."

She's right, but it doesn't make me feel any better. I sink further into my seat, fighting off tears. I'm not sure how my body is still producing more; I feel like I should be all cried out at this point.

"I don't want Blake to think that what he did was acceptable, even if it wasn't on purpose. The means don't always justify the ends."

"It's more common than you'd think," she reveals soothingly.

"Oh, is it? You have other clients whose boyfriends have gone on a talk show and went into detail about their girlfriend's trauma?" My body flinches back at how harsh my words are. "Sorry…that was rude of me."

"It's okay." Cindy ignores my bitchiness. "A lot of people— whether it be a dad, a sister, a boyfriend—have anger and hate toward the person who hurt their loved one. Unfortunately, they don't realize how their responses can traumatize you even more. It's why a lot of well-meaning people make crappy decisions."

"How would I even go about forgiving him?"

I can't imagine my life without Blake, but I also don't know how to reconcile who he is with what he did. This isn't like he left the toilet seat open or forgot an anniversary.

"Even if Blake didn't hurt you purposefully, it still takes a lot of strength to forgive someone. You're not making excuses for his behavior or condoning it, but you are choosing to accept what happened, acknowledging how you feel about it, and then moving on from it."

All I want to do is move on, but it's like I'm trapped underneath a layer of fog. Everything is heavy and hurts. The ache in my throat grows stronger. I've been getting a lot better at actually allowing myself to feel my feelings the past week, and it's been just as cathartic as it's been painful.

MY YOUNGER BROTHER may be a pain in the ass sometimes, but he's also a secret sweetheart. He told me he's home for the weekend because he didn't have a hockey game, but I know it's really to check up on me. It's nice having him here. He can't solve my problems, but he can keep me company as I hibernate on the couch.

"Morning," my brother greets me. "Want coffee?"

"Yes, please."

Tyler reappears a few minutes later with two steaming mugs. After handing me one, he settles onto the other side of the couch.

"What are you doing up so early?" he asks.

It's 6:30 a.m. I usually sleep until at least 8:00 or 9:00 a.m. on the weekends if I can.

"The race is on soon," I admit with a slight blush.

"And you're going to watch?" I can't tell if he's impressed or bothered. "You're such a masochist."

"Big word for such a small brain," I tease him. "Do you want to watch with me? I could use a buddy."

"Can we cheer if Blake crashes?"

He smiles slyly, flashing a dimple that matches my own. I lean over and smack him on the arm. The memory of Blake's crash in Baku still haunts me even though he's been in a few minor ones since then.

"Kidding, kidding!" Tyler chuckles under his breath. "Have you guys talked recently?"

I shake my head. It's only been a week without talking to Blake, but it's my own personal hell. Dante forgot to write about the tenth circle, but I'm there and am more than happy to fill him in. The worst part about it is that the person I want holding my hand through all of this is the person who put me in this position in the first place.

"You know I've got your back, right?" Tyler says after a few minutes. "I'll kick Blake's ass if you give me the word."

It's a toss-up who'd win that fight. "I appreciate it, Ty."

He releases a deep breath, biting his lip in concentration. "If I were in Blake's position, on that show, I can't say I'd do anything differently than he did. I mean, I probably wouldn't have kept talking, but I couldn't have sat there calmly while someone said that shit about the guy who assaulted you." He pauses. "Remember when I had a one-game suspension last year?"

"Mm-hmm."

Tyler got into a bar fight and ended up breaking someone's nose. No one pressed charges, but Tyler's coach suspended him nonetheless.

"I overheard some guys talking," he says slowly.

My curiosity is piqued since Tyler's never spoken about it. "About what?"

"You."

"Me?"

"Yep." His lips come together, making the last letter end in a popping noise. "You."

I wait for him to say more, but he just sips his coffee. "Well, what were they saying?"

"They told me they liked your podcast," he admits. "Listened every week."

"That's bad?"

"They asked me why you'd leave such a cool job." His voice is strained. "Said PlayMedia was the best and that they'd met Brixton before and he's a fucking legend...the GOAT."

"So you beat the shit out of him?"

"Mm-hmm." Tyler shrugs aloofly. "All I'm saying is I get his reaction. It's up to you if you forgive him or not, but it's obvious how much he cares about you, even if he has an ass backward way of showing it."

My phone dings with a text from Josie. She's been sending me voice memos of her singing a variety of songs including "Irreplaceable" by Beyoncé and "I Will Survive" by Gloria Gaynor. I truly never know what a text from her is going to be, but I appreciate that about Jos. I haven't watched any press conferences from this weekend, but she's keeping me up to date. Apparently, today's is action-packed.

JOSIE BANCROFT

A reporter just asked why you aren't here, and Blake ripped off his microphone and left the room.

OMG. Theo's telling everyone about his skincare routine.

Lucas is now talking about some football game?? I think he means American football, not ours.

These boys do not know how to handle a crisis well. This is comical.

Okay, Blake's back. He's giving his statement. "Please respect and refrain from asking me questions about my personal life. Unless it pertains to the race, it has no place in this conference room."

> Totally get why you're not at the race (fully
> support you), but I miss you, babes!!

I can't help when my lips curl into a smile at her rapid-fire texts. Tyler takes the remote and changes the channel to ESPN. We catch the tail end of the press conference. Seeing Blake, even through a screen, makes my heart flutter wildly. As angry and upset as I am, I still miss him. I miss him so much it feels hard to breathe sometimes. I'm homesick for a person.

The race is a nail-biter. Blake's performance highlights that he's at the top of his career, but Harry drives just as well. I know Blake tries not to listen to what people are saying, but it's hard to ignore the question at the forefront of everyone's mind, including the broadcaster's. Can Blake win a championship that's so close? The last Drivers' Championship that was this tight was a few years back when he beat Lucas by a mere five points. With only two races left in the season, the pressure is seriously on.

I make a last-minute decision to text him after the podium ceremony.

ELLA GOLD

> Great win today. I was rooting for you.

BLAKE HOLLIS

> That means the world to me, baby. Thinking of
> you constantly. I'm here when you're ready to
> talk. I'm so incredibly sorry.

ELLA GOLD

> It was weird not watching a Grand Prix from the
> pit garage.

BLAKE HOLLIS

> It was weird not having you there. I miss you.

I edit my text back to Blake about ten times. I'm a writer and always have things to say, but my mind is blank. It's an unfamiliar feeling—not knowing what to say to him. There are twenty-six letters in the alphabet and I somehow can't think of a single combination that accurately expresses how I feel. So I say nothing.

THIRTY-SEVEN

BLAKE

POPPY CALLOWAY'S easy to spot. Even if I hadn't already met her on FaceTime or stalked her Instagram, she stands out in a crowd. You can tell she's *someone*. It's subtle, but it's there. Everyone at the airport is in comfortable clothing meant for traveling, but Poppy looks like an off-duty model wearing sunglasses even though it's gloomy. She slips them down her nose as I approach her.

I told her I was more than fine taking a car service, but she insisted on picking me up. Now I know why. She's letting me know I'm on her turf, and she has the upper hand. I wouldn't expect anything less from Ella's best friend.

"I don't know if I should slap you or hug you," she greets me, her mouth twisting sardonically.

"Who says you have to choose?"

She gives a breathless laugh at that. When I called Poppy, she seemed totally on board with me coming to New York. I would even go so far as to say she was excited. Now I realize she's trying to kill me before we even get to the city. Literally. Vehicular manslaughter. Or is it vehicular homicide? *Fuck*. Ella told me Poppy grew up in the city, but she forgot to mention the fact that her friend can't fucking drive.

"Do you want me to take over?" I suggest. "I'm more than happy to."

It comes out snappier than intended, but I'm quickly learning she can't handle the delicate stop-and-go nature that traffic requires. I've never been car sick in my life. Not once. And I hit turns with 5Gs of force. There's a first time for everything, I suppose. When the traffic eases up and we start cruising, expletives fly out of my mouth. Poppy accelerates through turns, only braking after we've hit the straight. She'd make a horrendous Formula 1 driver. How can she be so casual and confident in driving that's so catastrophic? It's concerning.

"Oh, relax." She laughs lightly. "I passed my driver's test, you know."

"Have you driven since then?"

She snorts and rolls her eyes. Which should be laser focused on the turn ahead. "Now would be a bad time to tell you I failed the test twice before passing, right?"

"Poppy…" My voice comes out half as a warning, half as a question.

"Kidding!" She quickly glances over at me with a frustratingly easy smile on her face. "I only failed once."

Bloody hell. I managed to survive every Formula 1 crash I've been in, but for some reason, I find it wise to leave my life in the hands of a girl who's failed her driver's exam. I may be the fastest, but apparently, I'm not the brightest.

"The brakes on this car are just sensitive," she notes as we jerk forward.

Or you're just a bad driver.

"If you were an Uber, I'd rate you one star."

"Noted," she responds passively. "You know you're a fucking idiot, right? I feel like we should just establish that first and foremost."

"It's well established and documented. The last thing I ever want to do is hurt Ella."

"Well, I wouldn't audition to play James Bond anytime soon because mission failed, buddy."

I deserve it, so I don't argue.

"I'm assuming you've been following the aftermath of your interview?" She changes lanes and my life flashes before my eyes. This must be some type of fucked-up interrogation technique. I give her a quick yes.

"The girls who have come forward plan on suing him."

"I saw." I'll happily pay for the victims' lawyers if it helps them take that son of a bitch down. Ella didn't want to pursue a civil suit against him, but part of me hopes she'll reconsider.

"At least the attention's moved off Ella." Poppy sighs and glances at me. "Listen, I get it. Trust me, I do. When Ella told me what happened, what'd been going on, I seriously looked up ways to inconspicuously kill someone. I even asked my weed guy if he knew anything about poison."

I release a low chuckle. "How'd that turn out?"

"Well, he's still alive. So not great."

"I fucked up." Thrusting an agitated hand through my hair, I glance at Poppy. "I know I did. I don't think it's possible to have fucked up more than I did."

"That's good."

"That I fucked up?

"No." She shakes her head. "That you know you fucked up. It takes a certain type of man to own up to his mistakes. And not only that but actively try to do better."

"I'll always try to do better for Ella," I say. "Pinky promise."

Pinky promises are the end all be all for Ella, so Poppy knows I'm not fucking around. "Let's go over some ground rules for when you're here."

"Okay, like what?"

"First rule," she begins. "You have to go incognito. No one can recognize you."

That's the reason I flew private. Plus, there's no reason for me not to. I'm also wearing the most inconspicuous clothing I own and am sporting a beard since I haven't shaved in over a week. If fans spot me and take photos, or if paparazzi find out I'm here, it'll be all over social media in minutes. This entire plan hinges on Ella being kept in the dark. Shouldn't be too much of a problem on my end since our communication has been just short of nonexistent.

"Do I wear a wig?" I'm joking, but I can tell Poppy's considering it. "I'll stay undercover. Don't worry."

"Ella definitely doesn't know you're here, right?" she asks with a pointed look. "She can't know we're together."

"You're making it sound like we're having an illicit affair."

"Illicit affairs are more my dad's thing than mine." I can't tell if she's serious or kidding and I'm not sure I want to know either way.

"Rule number two. Do you like bagels?" The confused look on my face makes Poppy sigh. "The rule is dependent on your answer."

Yeah, sure. That makes sense. "Yes, I do."

"Okay, then rule number two is that you're on bagel duty every morning. You can just order delivery to my apartment. Oh, and I take my coffee with lots of cream, two sugars."

Their friendship is starting to make a lot of sense.

THIRTY-EIGHT

ELLA

I'M WATCHING *LAW & Order* reruns and working on my business plan when Poppy texts me an article titled "The Brixtons: Behind Closed Doors." I immediately click it, eyes widening in shock as I skim through. Blake's bombshell interview has spiraled into something way bigger than either one of us. I already knew about the three other women who've come forward with accusations of their own against Connor, but this is about women supposedly settling out of court for an undisclosed amount. No one's contacted me, but there's a rumor that the D.A.'s office may file charges. It's become more high-profile given his dad and the other women speaking up.

"El?" My mom's voice interrupts my reading. "Do you feel okay? Honey?"

"Hm?"

I look up to see her standing in front of me. Her eyebrows are drawn together, worry lines creased into her forehead. She puts the back of her hand against my forehead to check for a fever. "Are you okay? You're white as a ghost."

I turn my computer so it's facing her.

"I saw that this morning." She settles on the couch next to

me, and our dog Murphy immediately jumps onto her lap. He's definitely the favorite child. Putting her arm around my shoulders, she pulls me against her. "I'm proud of you, honey."

"Why?" I scrunch my nose. "I literally haven't moved from this couch in, like, seventy-two hours."

I'm wearing leggings so worn down I'm surprised there aren't any holes, and a sweatshirt that most definitely has a hole in it somewhere.

She gives my shoulder a squeeze. "Do you know how much strength it takes to walk away from a career you've spent so long cultivating? To choose yourself and your mental health? To wake up every morning with a smile even after all you've been through? That's badass. I'm proud of you."

My head flings back as I laugh. *Badass?*

"It's true." She nods emphatically. "You're a fighter, Eliana, but you're not alone. You never have been."

"I know." I rest my head on her shoulder. "I was thinking of flying back to London after Thanksgiving."

Besides the fact that half of my stuff is still there, I have no desire to permanently move back in with my parents. I also don't want to miss the final Grand Prix. There's no need for me to be there from a professional standpoint. I'm done interviewing Blake, and we have everything we need for the book. The only reason I would be there is to support him. I wonder if there's a scientific explanation for how I can miss him so much that it physically hurts.

"What are you ladies talking about?" my dad asks, coming into the room. "Anything fun?"

My mom shoots me a wink. "Oh, just our badass daughter."

"Badass, huh?" A deep chuckle vibrates through his chest. "Well, do my badass daughter and wife want to go grab some lunch? I'm starving."

His face falls when I give him an unconvinced shrug.

There's a *Law & Order: SVU* marathon starting in thirty minutes. Plus, I don't feel like putting on real people pants.

"I'm happy you're finally relaxing, but you can't hide here forever, sweetheart." My mom sighs, ruffling my hair. "At least go outside and get some fresh air. Play some ball with Murphy."

"It's chilly out!" I protest. "I don't want to catch a cold."

"Wear a coat," my dad suggests. "Put on a hat, some gloves. Maybe go crazy and wear fuzzy socks."

"Hey, Dad..." I grin, my lips curling up at the edges. "What happens when someone gets angry in cold weather?"

He rubs his chin in thought. "They complain?"

"They have a meltdown."

My dad's raspy laugh fills the room. The joke wasn't that funny, but he's a sucker for a lame punchline and I feel guilty for shutting down his lunch idea.

"How about you guys go and bring me back something?" I suggest. "I'll take Murphy on a walk while you're gone."

This seems to satisfy them. Murphy instantly jumps up at the recognition of the word *walk*. He runs around in anticipation, so I have no choice but to bundle up against the crispy November weather. He nips at my heels in excitement as I pull on my boots and coat.

"Be safe, hon!" my mom calls out as she and my dad head to the garage. "See you later."

I wave goodbye as I put Murphy into his harness. I'm not important enough to have paparazzi camped outside my house, but that doesn't stop me from holding my breath as I walk out the door. No one's hiding in the bush, and Murphy is eager for a walk, practically dragging me down the driveway. I should've worn fuzzy socks.

Slipping my earbuds in, I put on a playlist Josie made for me called "bad bitches only." The fresh air may be turning the tip of my nose bright red, but it's making me feel more awake and clear-headed than I have been for days.

We're finishing up our walk when a familiar sound interrupts the song I'm listening to. I glance down at my phone and stop dead in my tracks as I see the notification lit up on the screen.

> A new episode of Coffee with Champions is now available!

I don't know whether I should laugh at how fucking horrible this is or cry at how fucking unfair this is. Throwing up is an option too because I'm suddenly extremely nauseous. I stand still as a statue for a full five minutes while looking at my phone, deciding what to do. With Murphy in tow, I sprint up the driveway and back into the house. Settling myself into a comfortable position on the couch, I press play on the episode. Here goes nothing.

Episode 53: Ella Gold

Jack Feinstein: Hey, everyone. I know I'm not Ella and this isn't a usual episode of *Coffee with Champions*, but we're here with her boyfriend, Blake, for a very special episode. It's sort of sports-related since we have a five-time World Champ with us, but—

Poppy Calloway: And you both have balls, and balls are sort of sporty.

Blake Hollis: I completely understand why you and Ella get along so well.

Jack: Uh, anyway, I'm Ella's friend Jack.

[silence]

Jack: Are you guys going to introduce yourselves or…

Poppy: Oh, sorry. Hi! I'm Poppy, Ella's other best friend. You may recognize me from making some appearances on her Instagram.

Blake: How can anyone recognize you if this is a podcast? No one can see us.

Poppy: Don't be so literal. Now introduce yourself.

Blake: Okay, um, 'ello, everyone. I'm Blake.

[Jack whispers off mic]

Blake: Uh…sorry. Blake Hollis. I'm Ella's boyfriend. That is if she decides to accept my apology and not dump me for being an absolute idiot. Seriously. An idiot of the highest regard.

Poppy: Well, we can all agree that you're an absolute dickhead. But on to more important things. Blake, do you want to share today's topic?

Blake: Yes, um, sure. The topic is…

Poppy: No, you have to do the drumroll first.

Blake: Do I really? I've listened to every episode and there's never a drumroll.

Poppy [in a fake British accent]: Do I really? Yes, really.

Jack: I would just do the drumroll, man.

Blake: Fine.

[Drumroll noise]

Blake: Today's topic is Ella Gold.

Poppy: Woo! And before everyone gets too excited, no, we're not sharing our favorite embarrassing Ella stories. Although… I'd be down to do that at another time.

Jack: Oh, I'm so down. I have a very long list. Blake, you in?

Blake: I can't commit to that until I know whether Ella forgives me or not, so let's table it.

Jack: Good point.

Poppy: Blake, do you want to do your thing? Get this show on the road?

Blake: Sure. So for starters…um, the podcast is officially yours again, Ella. Well, if you still want to do it, that is.

Poppy: Blake bought the podcast! That's how we're recording this!

Jack: Peter said he technically bought the intellectual property.

Poppy: Okay, but it's hers now.

Jack: Yep. The entire back catalog of episodes and all future content from this podcast belongs to our Elly Bean.

Blake: So much for me sharing.

Jack and Poppy: Sorry.

Blake: After you told me about the podcast not being yours any longer, I reached out to my lawyers to see if there was a way to buy the rights to it. I felt like it was still yours, and you deserve to be able to decide what you want to do with it.

Poppy: She thought you got her a blueberry muffin when you got her that podcasting set.

Blake: What?

Poppy: When you told her you got her a present, she thought it was going to be a blueberry muffin.

Jack: That's the most Ella thing I've ever heard in my entire life.

Poppy: Right? Remember when she asked me for a gift certificate to Sal's bagel spot for her birthday?

[Blake laughing]

Blake: I can tell you about the details in person, but as Poppy and Jack already said, the podcast is officially yours.

Poppy: I knew you were rich because the Gucci shoes you have on right now are from next season, but I didn't realize you were, like, buy-intellectual-property-or-whatever-just-for-fun-rich. You're sort of like Batman.

Blake: I didn't do it just for fun. I did it for Ella. Wait—how am I like Batman?

Poppy: You're both wealthy and have cool cars.

Blake: Thanks, I guess.

Poppy: You're welcome. Now continue with your groveling.

Blake: Straightaway.

[Blake clears throat]

Blake: I'm sorry for letting my anger get the best of me and for putting you in such an uncomfortable position. It wasn't my place to share your story. I know that. It's your story, not mine. I wish I could shield you from everything bad in the world so I never have to see you sad, but I know that's not possible. I guess I was just trying to defend you and protect you, even though I did it in a rather fucked-up way. And you're strong as hell, baby. You don't need me, or anyone, to do that for you. What I did was inexcusable and I'm so, so sorry. I spoke without thinking, but my intention was *never* to hurt you. All I want is for you to be happy, Ella, and knowing I'm the one who made you unhappy is killing me. I'm so in love with you and—

Poppy: Oh my God. You couldn't have given me a heads-up or something?

Blake: What are you talking about? You knew I was going to apologize.

Jack: I think she's more focused on the part where you—

Poppy: Just *finally* admitted to being in love with my best friend? Yeah. Definitely focused on that. With literally no warning, mind you.

Blake: Oh fuck.

Poppy: Excuse you? What do—

Blake: No, no, no. Of course I love her. I think I've been in love with her since she made me watch an hour of YouTube videos about snacks. But I would've preferred to have told her in person rather than…well, this way.

Jack: Did she make you watch the one comparing European candies to American ones?

Blake: All three episodes.

Jack: He's truly in love then, ladies and gents. Those videos are mind-numbingly brutal.

Poppy: But I feel like you should just roll with the moment, ya know? Keep talking about how you love her and all that cute stuff.

Blake: Right now?

Jack: Why not? The cat's already out of the bag. Just pretend we're not here and that millions of people aren't going to hear this.

Blake: Yeah, no pressure. Thanks, guys. So, uh, as I was saying…I'm maddeningly, hopelessly in love with you, Eliana Jane Gold. I love how you bite your lip when you're concentrating. I love how you can never hide how you're feeling, no matter how ridiculous your facial expressions are. I love your carefree laugh and how you crack up at your own jokes even when they're not funny. I love that you take your coffee with more milk than actual coffee. I love how you can't help but dance whenever you hear music, even if it's coming from a car passing by. I love how your eyes light up whenever you see me and how you say my name. You've never once given up on me, even when I tried to shut you out. You know my flaws and insecurities, yet you accept me as I am. You may drive me absolutely crazy sometimes, but you also drive me to be a better person. I really bloody love you. Fuck, I love you so much, I'd even let you put popping candy on my di—

Poppy: What the fuck! No. Jesus, Blake. Keep it PG.

Blake: Shit. Can you edit that out?

Jack [hysterically laughing]: I have so many fucking questions for you. Is it like foreplay or—

Poppy: Enough! Next topic. Her parents are going to hear this, Blake.

Blake: Jack said pretend like millions of people aren't going to listen!

Poppy: The key word being *pretend*. After this, you need to avoid all microphones and cameras.

Blake: Yep. Agreed. Sorry, Mr. and Mrs. Gold, I promise you that the sex we're hav—

Poppy: Oh my God! Why are you still talking? Move it along, buster.

Blake: I'm going to take your microphone away if you keep interrupting me.

Poppy: I'd like to see you try, Hollis. I go to boxing classes three times a week.

Jack: Can the two of you not threaten each other? Or can you at least move it outside of the studio room? This shit's expensive. I don't want Peter to kill me.

Blake: What I'm trying to say is that spending time with you is the best part of my day, every day, without fail. When I'm not with you, I'm thinking about you, and when I am with you, I'm happy. I love you. Every single piece of you. You're my person. I've already gone twenty-nine years of my life without you and now that I've found you, I plan on showing you just how much I love you every single day for the rest of my life. I'm a little broken and a little messy, but I swear to God I'll love you with every jagged piece of me.

Jack: Okay. Wow. That was…surprisingly sweet.

Blake: Oh, um, I'm not done.

Poppy: For someone who didn't want to say "I love you" this way, you certainly have a lot to say.

Blake: I know tit for tat is never the answer, but I figured I should at least even the playing field a little bit. So here goes nothing.

[extended pause]

Blake: Sorry if this is awkward…I've never, um, done anything quite like this before. Uh, okay, well, my mum left when I was a kid. Never saw her again, and my dad, well, he didn't like being a dad very much. It was just my sister and me growing up. I was diagnosed with anxiety after that and have struggled with it ever since. I go to therapy and take medication, but I'm still a work in progress. I've always kept my private life hidden because I thought if people knew me, the real me, they wouldn't like what they saw. I wouldn't be enough for people. So I decided to just show people the driver because he's confident and worthy of people's attention. Then Ella came into my life like a goddamn tornado, and she turned everything I've ever thought upside down. She's taught me that being vulnerable doesn't make me weak, it just gives me a chance to be strong. So, yeah, that's my story, I guess.

Poppy: Blake, if Ella forgives you, we should talk about custody rights. Oh! Or maybe we just do a sister wives situation. Honestly, that might be ideal. Well, I don't really believe in the construct of marriage, but we can chat about logistics later.

Blake [laughing]: And before we go, or sign off, or whatever it is you do, I know you're still upset with me, rightfully so, but I hope you can forgive me because there's nothing more I want to do than kiss you and—

Poppy: STOP! Do I need to put on a parental warning?

Blake: No. I was going to say, "And tell you I love you in person."

Poppy: Oh, shit. My bad. Sorry 'bout that.

Blake: All good. I think that's it, yeah?

Poppy: Wait. I have something to add. Jack and I had Blake try *both* Ess-a-Bagel and Tompkin Square Bagels. And guess which one he said was better? Tompkin, baby! So I was right. Their bagels are superior.

Blake: You also made me eat two slices of pizza and a cupcake afterward.

Jack: If you're Ella's boyfriend then you should know you're going to have to do all this shit with her anyway. We're just easing you into it. I'm pretty sure it's a scientific fact that you gain weight when you start dating someone.

Poppy: Anyway, I think we're officially done with the episode, right?

Jack: Yep! Happy Thanksgiving, everyone!

Poppy: There's nothing happy about a holiday that celebrates the conquest of Native Americans.

Blake: Yeah, I'm British, so this holiday isn't a thing for me.

Jack: I was talking to the listeners, not you two. But forgive me for breathing. Go to the airport. I have to send this to Peter so he can do all the tech stuff or whatever.

[episode ends]

FORTY

ELLA

IT TAKES a lot for something to render me speechless. I was still able to talk after the *Game of Thrones* finale, so my threshold for shock is damn high. Blake's blown that out of the fucking water. My brain is in overdrive trying to comprehend everything I just heard. I'm holding my phone in my hand like it's a baby; I'm not quite sure what to do with it. Do I call Blake? Text him? Send a carrier pigeon? Or is he supposed to reach out to me? How does this whole thing work? My phone vibrates, interrupting my internal debate.

> **MOM**
>
> Can you grab the package at the front door? It can't stay outside for too long. Thanks, honey.

My mom single-handedly keeps our FedEx delivery guy busy with all the online shopping she does. I rush over to the door, eager to get back to the couch and come up with a game plan. Murphy follows closely behind me, on high alert in case whoever's at the door has a treat for him. Swinging the door open, I find Blake bundled up in a jacket. This is not the delivery I was expecting. He calmly waits for my mouth to stop opening and closing like a fish out of water. There are so many things I want to say and ask that I'm inarticulate.

Since I can't speak, I launch myself into his arms, burying my face in his chest. The familiar smell of him envelops me. He stumbles back a few steps at the force of my embrace, quickly grounding himself and pulling me even closer against him. I lean back a minute later and study him. He looks like he hasn't been sleeping well. If he's been sleeping at all. Week-old stubble and tired eyes exacerbate his slightly disheveled appearance.

"You're here," is all I manage to get out.

"Surprise." He chuckles, switching his weight from one foot to the other. "I'm the special delivery."

"Hi," I breathe out slowly. I drink in the sight of him. I've missed his intense brown eyes. The broadness of his shoulders. The sharp lines of his jaw. I can't tear my eyes away from him.

"Hey," he says back. My stomach does more flips than Simone Biles at the Olympics. "Can we go inside?"

I nod dumbly and step back to let him into the house, shivering at the cool blast of air that sneaks inside. Murphy barks excitedly, running around Blake in rapid circles. He's the worst guard dog ever.

"Hey, little guy," Blake says, bending over to scratch Murphy behind his ears. "You're a cutie, aren't you?"

"You're here," I repeat, still dumbstruck. "In my house… with a beard."

"Quite the investigative journalist." Blake absentmindedly strokes his chin. "I figured we should talk…and I missed you."

"I missed you, too," I say without hesitation. "A lot."

The corners of his eyes crinkle as his lips curl into a smile.

"Let's chat on the couch." Blake shrugs off his coat and hangs it on the rack next to the front door. "More comfortable."

He walks to the family room like he's been here a million

times before. The two of us sit down, sinking into the couch's comfy cushions. We both start speaking, ending in overlapping awkward chuckles.

"You first," Blake offers. His fingers tap against his thighs faster than I can type.

"It's…it's been really hard dealing with everything," I start, my voice unusually quiet. "Especially without you."

"I'm so—"

"I know you weren't trying to hurt me, Blake," I cut him off mildly. "I'm not mad about that. I mean, I am—you're an idiot and definitely shouldn't have done that—but I know you weren't doing it maliciously. You were put in a shitty position and I know I'd try to protect you in the same way. Maybe not so publicly, but still."

"I am a bloody fucking idiot," he says simply.

"Yeah," I agree, "but you just so happen to be my idiot."

"You have no idea how sorry I am." Blake's eyes dart to meet mine, his pupils dilated. "I'm the reason the world knows what you went through. You trusted me and I royally blew it. I'll never forgive myself for hurting you."

"I watched that art forgery documentary you told me about," I blurt out. "I thought it was really good."

Blake runs his fingers through his hair and glances around like he's looking for answers. I'm sure he thinks I'm off my rocker with that sudden topic change. "Glad you liked it, love."

"Do you think the gallery owner knew what was going on?"

"Oh, for sure." He nods animatedly. "There's no way they couldn't have known."

Yep. That's what I thought, too. I tuck my hair behind my ears, trying to work out the best way to explain my feelings. "I guess the point I'm trying to make is that there's no one else I'd watch an art documentary for. Even though I was upset with you, I still watched it because I knew how much you liked it. I wanted to be able to talk to you about it. Relationships are hard and messy, and we're both going to fuck up and make mistakes. That's life. But no matter how complicated shit gets, it's you I want by my side. It's always going to be you, Blake."

I can see the tension in his shoulders evaporating at my words.

"I love you, by the way," I add, not wanting to forget the most important part. In retrospect, I realize I should've led with that. "A lot."

Blake inhales sharply as a flush creeps up his neck. "You what?"

"I love you," I repeat. The words taste sweet as they roll off my tongue. "I'm desperately, wildly, hopelessly, and crazily in love with you."

He echoes it back, making sure he's hearing me correctly. I watch him as the words sink in and it's the purest thing I've ever seen.

"I love you, too." His eyes focus intently on mine, and I've never felt more exposed without losing a single piece of clothing. "We'll get through this together, okay? I made a wreck out of things but I'll be by your side every step of the way."

"Pinky promise?"

Blake interlocks our pinkies together. "Pinky promise, baby."

I always thought love was supposed to be flowers and candlelit dinners, but it's not. It's watching documentaries that bore me to tears just because Blake likes them. It's him ordering waffles when he wants eggs just so I can have a bite. It's fighting over who gets the right side of the bed and leaving parties early to cuddle on the couch. It's the big stuff and the little stuff and all the things in between.

"I listened to the podcast," I continue, realizing we haven't even talked about *that*. "It's probably going to get the most downloads the show's ever gotten."

"Yeah? What'd you think?"

"As far as apologies go, it's a twelve out of ten." I nod in approval. "I can't believe you talked about your anxiety and your parents. I'm really proud of you."

"Yeah, well, love makes you do crazy shit, doesn't it?" he says with an unabashed grin.

The butterflies in my stomach settle down, safe in the knowledge that I get to tell this man I love him for the rest of my life.

"I think it's worth whatever chaos it causes," I murmur, clasping my hands behind his neck.

His lips brush against mine, soft at first, then rougher and hungrier as I open my mouth to him. The feel of him alone scorches fire through my veins. Weeks apart have made us both desperate, fumbling with need. I moan into his mouth as he grabs my hips and grinds into me. I want to be consumed by this man, by his hands, by his tongue. I curl my fingers into his messy brown hair, tugging until he releases a low growl.

"Not to ruin the mood," Blake murmurs as my lips move down his neck, sucking and nibbling on the skin, "but Murphy's staring at me and it's making me quite uncomfortable."

The ridiculousness of his statement makes me collapse against him. I turn around and notice Murphy sitting a few feet away from the couch, staring at Blake like he's the enemy.

"It's because you didn't give him a treat."

I tell Blake where the pantry is so he can get one. While he's getting on my dog's good side, I shoot my mom a quick text to let her know that her package arrived. I'm not surprised she's known Blake's plan for the past week, considering how buddy-buddy the two of them are thanks to Facebook Messenger.

Blake gives Murphy the treat before sitting back down next to me on the couch. Resting his hand on my lower back, I lean into his touch.

"When do you think your parents will be home?" he asks, shaking his leg. "Soon?"

A loud snort escapes before I can stop it. I straddle his lap, grinning at his nervousness.

"Why is that funny?" Blake asks, massaging the back of his neck. "I don't think officially meeting your parents with a hard-on is going to score me brownie points."

"We're two grown adults acting like horny teenagers at my parents' house, nervous about getting caught." I wrap my arms around his neck and swivel my hips, feeling him grow hard beneath me. "It's like high school all over again."

He presses his lips against my forehead. "I never did the whole high school experience, love."

"Making out like a horny teenager? Or trying not to get caught?"

"Both."

"I'm more than happy to teach you," I offer. "But there's no need to worry right now. They won't be home for another hour."

"In that case..." He slides his hands down until he's cupping my butt. "Where's your room? I'd like to properly show you how goddamn much I love you, Ella Gold."

FORTY-ONE

BLAKE

A WARM TONGUE licking the inside of my ear wakes me up. I open my eyes and find Murphy's nose inches from my own. He's wagging his tail, panting in excitement that his new best friend is awake. Ella told me he usually sleeps with her parents, so I must've made quite the impression. I quickly get dressed before making my way to the kitchen.

"Good morning," Mrs. Gold greets me, her voice warm as a cup of tea.

I fight back a yawn. Ella and I were up until 2:00 a.m. talking and "watching a movie" last night. "Morning."

"I went to the store earlier," she tells me. Walking to the pantry, she pokes around before pulling out a few of my favorite snacks. "Ella told me what you liked, so I got you some things. There's also celery juice and chocolate milk in the fridge. I hope you don't drink them together, though."

"I don't," I quickly assure her with a chuckle. "Thank you."

"Of course." She waves me off like it's nothing. To her, it may not be, but to me? It's much appreciated. "Want some coffee? Just made a fresh pot."

"That'd be lovely. Thank you."

She pours me a piping hot mug, slowly handing it over so it doesn't flow over the edge. I take a small sip. *Damn.* Mrs. Gold makes a good cup of coffee. There's the perfect amount of natural sweetness paired with the refreshing acidity I love. I watch as she fills another mug, adding an obscene amount of almond milk to it.

"Will you bring this to the family room?" She hands me the mug. "Ella's working in there."

I consider myself an early riser, but Ella's been up at the crack of dawn the past few days. Heading into the other room, I find my girlfriend sitting with her legs folded like a pretzel on the couch. Her glasses are perched on her nose and she's staring at her screen intently. I can't count the number of times I've found her in this same exact position.

"Why are you working, baby?" I kiss the top of her head. "You're on holiday."

"It's not work," she confirms. Her glasses slide down her nose and she pushes them back up. "Well, it is, but it isn't."

I smile down at her. "Ah, yes. That makes perfect sense."

"It does!" She pats the spot next to her. "I'm working on my business plan."

Carefully sitting down, I place our mugs on the coffee table, not wanting to spill on the cream-colored couch.

"For *my* podcast," she adds, a wide smile stretching across her face.

"Damn straight it's yours."

It took half a fucking year to hammer out a deal with PlayMedia to buy the intellectual property to *Coffee with Champions*. God knows how many hours my lawyer billed. He has three kids and I'm sure I've paid for at least two of them to go to uni. I never thought they'd agree to sell it; they were still generating ad revenue from new downloads of old episodes. It seems my outburst on *The Elliot*

Brown Show changed their minds. They'd look like real arseholes holding her podcast hostage after ignoring both the sexual harassment *and* assault claims she filed with HR.

I give her thigh a light squeeze. "I'm proud of you."

She beams at me, glowing under my praise. Ella walks me through her plan, explaining everything to me in layman's terms. Not that I thought making a podcast would be easy, but I never realized how much stuff a network took care of for you. Monetizing and sponsorships. Growth plans and marketing affiliates. Hosting platforms and equipment. My head is spinning.

She's completely revised the format of the podcast, but the most surprising part about her business plan is that she wants to do two episodes a week rather than one. I make her go back and explain it to me multiple times.

She wants to have one episode a week specifically dedicated to Formula 1. These episodes will feature insights and interviews with the drivers, engineers, mechanics, fans, race officials, and whoever else she damn well pleases. I haven't been able to get a word out in the past five minutes. I'm still wrapping my head around the fact that she's going to be with me next season.

"Hello?" Her hand waves in front of my face. "You're either broken or you think this is the worst idea ever."

"I think it's the grandest idea I've ever heard," I finally manage to say. "And I'm a World Champion, so my opinion is worth about ten times more than the average person's."

"Oh, is that so?" Ella laughs. "Good to know."

Leaning back into the couch, I let out a low groan. "Wait, does this mean if I have a shitty race, you're going to poke fun at me again?"

We've really come full circle.

"I'll play nice," she promises, placing her hand on my

thigh. "If I'm tough on you, I'm sure I can think of a few ways to earn your forgiveness."

"Do you two want breakfast?" Mrs. Gold's head pops into the room. "I made pancakes and eggs."

"I'm starving," Ella says, jumping up from the couch.

I am, too. Coffee on an empty stomach always makes me jittery. The three of us sit at the kitchen table with plates piled high. I'm starting to see where Ella gets her appetite from. Like mother, like daughter.

"Your dad and I were looking at flights last night," Mrs. Gold tells Ella. "I think we're going to fly in for the first race next season and then stay for a bit so we can be in London for the book's release party. What do you think?"

Ella steals a strawberry off my plate. "That'll be fun. Can Dad take off that much time?"

"He'll probably work remotely for a few days," Mrs. Gold says before turning to me. "Blake, are you okay if we come to the first race? I'm sure it's a stressful time for you. Should we come for a different one?"

"Sorry," I cough out. This is all news to me. "What?"

"We want to come watch you race." Her smile is almost identical to Ella's, minus the dimple. "We'll make a family trip out of it."

"Oh, don't feel pressured to come to a race." My words stutter over one another as a flush of surprise marks my cheeks. "I, um, don't want to put you out."

"Of course we're going to come!" Mrs. Gold briefly rests her hand on my forearm, giving it a quick squeeze. "We want to support you."

"Thank you," I murmur with a quick nod. "The first race is great."

Mrs. Gold chatters away about how excited she is to see me in action. The chest-swelling sensation I'm experiencing is unfamiliar. The Golds have shown more interest in my career in the few days I've been in Chicago than my own dad ever did.

"Tyler's flight lands soon," Ella reminds her mom. "Do you want us to go to the airport for you?"

"Thanks, honey, but I'll get him." She stands up from the table, collecting our empty plates. I offer to help her, but she waves me off.

Ella and I exchange a secret look of anticipation. *Home alone? Yes, please.* I've truly gotten the full "high school experience," trying to stay quiet and undetected as we fool around before bed. Our sex the past few days has been unhurried, with slow strokes and whispered "I love yous." It's been amazing, don't get me wrong, but I'm desperate for the full volume of Ella's moans as she comes.

The second we hear the garage door close, we sprint to Ella's room, tripping over one another in a frenzied rush. I kick her door closed with my foot, leaving a whining Murphy on the other side. *Can't say I'm terribly sorry, buddy.*

Clothes drop to the floor as we stumble to the bed. I climb on top of Ella, hungrily capturing her lips against mine. I'm so hard it feels like my dick is going to fall off. Her kiss is insistent, impatient, wanting me to be everywhere.

"I need you," she whimpers, placing my hand between her legs so I can feel how wet she is.

I moan at what a mess she is for me. I slowly dip a finger inside her. Her back immediately arches, her perfect tits rising and falling with desire. My mouth waters at the mere sight of them. I suck her right nipple between my lips, swirling my tongue around the tightening bud. Switching between her two breasts, Ella moans like she's been coded to do so. I add another finger inside her, caressing and curling until she's rocking against my hand for more.

I slowly kiss my way down her body, nipping at the soft skin on the inside of her thighs. The happy sighs slipping through her lips make me lightheaded. Fuck exploring cities. I want to explore Ella's body every goddamn second of every goddamn day.

I slowly drag my tongue against her clit, sucking the sensitive nub the way I know she loves. The combination of my fingers pumping inside of her and my tongue tasting her make Ella cry out in pleasure. It's a damn good thing we're home alone. All I want is to watch her fall apart. To know she needs this just as much as me. My eagerness to coax an orgasm out of her is quickly rewarded. Her thighs tremble as she comes, pleasure pulsing through her body. I don't move until Ella gently pushes my head away, too sensitive for more.

"I'm changing my death-row meal to you." I smirk. "Your pussy is perfect, baby."

She lets out a loud laugh, her body vibrating beneath mine. "That's the one thing you can't change your death-row meal to!"

Placing her hands on the sides of my face, she tugs my lips against hers. Her breathing gradually returns to normal, pupils dilated and lips slightly swollen. I quickly grab a condom, rolling it on before I line my tip up at her entrance. Pushing in slowly, I make sure she can feel my every ridge. She lets out the filthiest whimper I've ever heard.

"Fuck," I groan above her. Sliding into her core is fucking electric. "Always so tight for me."

I thrust deep inside her, my body burning with desire. The rhythm of our clashing hips is frantic, my pubic bone rubbing against Ella's clit at the perfect angle. The noises she's making are sinful and I can't get enough of them.

"Your cock feels so good," she breathes out, her voice desperate and raw. Her nails dig into my back with reckless abandon. "Love having you inside me."

I'll take Ella's praise over the praise of the world any day. She knows the effect her words have on me, and I lose any sense of reality as I pump into her, surrendering myself to the overwhelming sensations. I feel my own release building like a rubber band about to snap.

"Yes," she groans. "Come with me. I want to feel it—"

Ella shudders around me, biting into my shoulder as another orgasm rips through her. That always does it, her begging me. I can't resist the ache in her voice. I utter her name like a prayer as I let go to a jarring, pulsing climax.

I roll over, lying on my back next to Ella.

"I love you." She leans over and places a sweet kiss on my shoulder. "And King Dong."

A happy laugh comes deep from my throat. "We love you, too, baby."

FORTY-TWO

ELLA

SOME FAMILIES DRESS up for Thanksgiving—jeans, skirts, button-downs, blouses. Not my family. Leggings and sweatpants aren't just suggested, they're highly encouraged. There's nothing worse than overindulging and having to sneakily unbutton your jeans at the dinner table. May as well get ahead of it and wear stretchy pants to accommodate the inordinate amount of potatoes and pie you'll eat.

Blake thought I was kidding when I said that every inch of our kitchen would be covered in a dish or platter. When he comes inside after playing "American" football on Thanksgiving Day with my dad and brother, his jaw drops. He's frozen as he watches Murphy follow my mom around, begging for scraps of food.

The five of us are in food comas after dinner. Blake tried everything my mom made, which put the biggest smile on her face, but now he's complaining that even his sweats feel tight. Tyler's sprawled out on the floor, claiming he'll throw up if he moves. My mom doesn't care. Nothing is going to stop our Thanksgiving Scrabble tournament. Not even Blake's inability to spell things the American way. Colour, color. Centre, center. Aeroplane, airplane. Another world war almost breaks out when Blake starts using both British and American spellings for words, choosing whichever fits his tiles more favorably.

"I'm challenging that word," Tyler tells Blake for the tenth time in the past hour. "*Aubergine* sounds made up."

I blow air out of my mouth loudly. This game is going to go on all night if Tyler keeps this up. "It's a real word, Ty. It's what they call eggplants in England."

"They call eggplants aubergines?" The disbelief in his voice is comical. "You're kidding, right?"

"*Gormless* was a real word," my dad interferes neutrally. "I don't think he's making it up."

Tyler huffs and searches the word on his phone. Blake watches him, the edges of his lips curling into a smirk. The two of them have been overly competitive at *everything* since meeting. Football, video games, who can lift more. Now Scrabble.

"Fuck, fuck, fuck," Tyler swears under his breath. "It's a stupid British eggplant."

"Language," my parents warn him.

Blake adds twenty-eight points to his tally for the double word score his tiles fall on. He's now beating Tyler by five points. Neither of them seems to care that I'm kicking both of their asses by twenty points. I'm zoning out as my mom takes her turn when my phone rings. Standing up before anyone can object, I head to my dad's study to take the call.

"Hello?" I answer the phone.

"Ella!" Remi greets me. "How're you?"

"Very full." I sit in my dad's oversized office chair. "I just ate my weight in turkey and cornbread."

"I hope you're getting stuffed in more ways than one," she jokes. Suddenly, she lets out a string of expletives. "Oh my God, it's Thanksgiving! I'm *so* sorry, I didn't mean to interrupt. It completely skipped my mind."

"Don't worry about it," I assure her. "I can use a break from Scrabble. It's getting a bit intense."

Her contagious giggle carries through the phone. "Well, I was just calling to tell you that I read over your business plan and think it's brilliant."

"Really?" I tighten my grasp on my phone so it doesn't slip out of my clammy hand. "I can handle the criticism if you think it's bad."

"It's great, Ella," she congratulates me. "I love the mix of interviews and commentary. And how you want to segment each episode? So clever."

I don't realize I've been holding my breath until it comes heaving out of me. When Remi offered to look over my business plan, I knew it would be dumb to turn her down; she's mastered the indie podcast world.

"I have a few ideas," she continues, "but we can chat tomorrow. I don't want to barge in on your family time."

I can hear Tyler yelling that there's no fucking way *codger* is a real word. Dear Lord. I bite back a laugh when my dad asks if Larry David would be considered a codger. The fact that I can hear them through the door means I'm safer in here than I am out there.

"Trust me, Remi. You're not."

Blake's head pops in sometime later. I'm still on the phone, but I wave him in. He closes the door quietly behind him; leaning against the desk, he waits as I finish up the call.

"Everything good?" he asks after I've hung up.

I glance at my watch; I've been in here for almost an hour. Swiveling the chair so it's facing him, I make sure he's not bleeding or bruised thanks to Tyler. "Sorry for leaving you to fend for yourself. Did you survive your hazing?"

"Your brother's brain may have short-circuited," Blake whispers conspiratorially. "But we had fun. How was your call?"

"It was good. Remi asked me what you meant when you said you loved me so much you'd put popping candy on your dick."

Blake groans into his hands. Out of everything he said on the podcast, people are really focused on what he meant by that. "What'd you say?"

"I told her I'd come on her show and give her the exclusive," I tease, poking his rock-hard abs.

"Hardy har har," he grunts before ruffling my hair. "Now tell me about the call. Did she say you're the most brilliant woman in the entire world?"

"Not exactly," I reply. "But she did finish reading my business plan and said it was really good."

"Of course she did." Blake nods like he was expecting that answer. "What'd she say about still using *Coffee with Champions* as the name even with all the changes and updates you want to make?"

"She thinks it's totally fine," I answer. "She also told me about this co-working space in SoHo that I should look into. There are a lot of entrepreneurs who work out of there, which could be good for networking."

"SoHo is above Tribeca, right? Poppy tried teaching me Manhattan geography."

"What? No."

"Oh." His brows furrow together. "What's it near then? I can't keep them all straight."

"No, SoHo as in…well, I don't actually know why it's called SoHo there, but I'm talking about London, not New York."

"What?" He flinches back slightly. "London?"

"Yeah." It comes out as more of a question than a statement. "Why would Remi know about an office building in Manhattan?"

Blake scratches his cheek, parting his lips like he wants to say something. The way he keeps tilting his head is exactly what Murphy does when you say "treat" or "play ball" in a high-pitched voice.

"I assumed you'd want to be back in New York." He tugs at my hands, pulling me up from the chair. I lean against him, wrapping my arms around his waist. My body molds against his like he was sculpted just for me. "I'd buy a place and we could be there in between races. That's why I was learning the neighborhoods."

My eyes widen in surprise. "You'd do that?"

"Of course." He looks offended that I even had to ask. "I love you, El, and if that's where you want to live, that's where I want to be, too."

I'm not sure how many times I'm going to need to hear him say he loves me before it stops being my favorite phrase of all time.

"I'll miss the bagels and pizza," I concede, "but I've done all I wanted to do in New York. I can always visit. I'm ready for something new. Plus, I'm crazy in love with this cute guy who lives in London."

"Cute? I'd say so ridiculously good-looking you can barely be in a room with him without wanting to tear his clothes off." He squeezes my ass, drawing me tighter against him. A lopsided grin appears on his lips. "I pinky promise you're going to love London. It'll feel like home in no time."

I pull his lips against mine. "You're my home."

"You're mine, too, baby."

EPILOGUE
BLAKE

The grandstands have been packed since earlier this afternoon, the sounds of cheering fans mixing with the rumbling noises of the garage. The last Grand Prix of the season in Abu Dhabi is always madness and mayhem, but I wouldn't want it any other way. I've barely spent time with my family because of all the chaos, but Ella's been with them all day.

"Uncle Blake! Uncle Blake!"

Finn runs at me at full speed, the bulky noise-canceling headphones he's wearing slipping off his head and onto the ground. I quickly put them back on him. He's cried at past races due to the loudness and I don't want a repeat performance.

I pick him up and he wraps his tiny arms around my neck. "How many championships have you won?"

Weird question considering Ella easily knows the answer and he's been with her all morning. In fact, she probably knows more about my career than I do. I ask him if he means Constructors' or World and he wiggles out of my arms and is off without a word.

He's back a minute later, barreling into me breathlessly.

"World!"

"Then the answer is five."

This is not the answer he wants to hear. His shoulders sag forward, disappointment flooding his face. I think five World Championship titles is bloody good considering no one else has ever won that many, but I'll just go fuck myself, I suppose.

"I asked Ella to be my aunt and she said she'll only marry someone who's won at least eight of those." He sighs dramatically. "How long will that take?"

I look over at where my girlfriend is standing in the corner talking to my sister and brother-in-law. There's no stopping a smile from hovering on the edge of my lips. That cheeky woman of mine. I'm glad my nephew's proposing to her on my behalf; not so glad Ella's challenging me while simultaneously turning me down. She catches my eye and shoots me a wink. I motion for her to come over.

"Eight championships, huh?" I slip my arms under her jacket so I can feel the warmth of her skin. "Quite the order, Miss Gold."

"Someone's got to keep you in check." She rests her chin on my chest and looks up. "Win today and you're already at six!"

"No pressure." I chuckle. It's a good thing I don't get nervous. "How many championships until kids are on the table?"

She gives me a gentle kiss. "Let's take it one championship at a time."

"We can have a lot of fun making a baby," I mention. I'm already imagining Ella pushing a pram around the streets of London. "If we have a boy, I hope he's just as well-endowed as me."

Her face falls into my chest as laughter bubbles out of her. "Can we start with a puppy and take it from there?"

"One hour," an engineer calls out. "One hour!"

The pit garage erupts in applause and cheers for our final race. It's been one hell of a season. After today, we've got two and a half more months until we're doing it all over again. Not that our time off will be spent idly. The mechanics and engineers will be back in the garage, working hand in hand on next year's car. Theo, Lucas, and I will be fulfilling our personal sponsorship agreements and meeting at our respective team's headquarters to start strategizing for the upcoming season. We may only race for twenty-one weekends of the year, but we spend all fifty-two weeks prepping.

I pull Ella in for a shameless kiss. Running my tongue over her bottom lip, I hear her release a quiet hum. I don't realize how intense the kiss has gotten until Theo smacks me in the back of the head.

"If you guys are going to bang in here"—Theo smirks—"at least make people pay, so you can turn a profit."

I roll my eyes at him. "Bugger off."

Ella's cheeks flush and she hides her face in my chest. If she knew he's probably heard us having sex in my suite, she'd positively pass out from embarrassment.

"So, Goldy," Theo says. "Were you planning on telling me that Miss Bancroft is single?"

I've known about Josie and Andrew's breakup for a day or two, but there's no way I'm repeating anything Ella tells me in private ever again. Loose lips sink ships and I have no intention of being the Titanic.

"Don't even think about it," I warn him. "Keep it in your pants."

Ella lifts her head up and pokes Theo in the chest. "I have no qualms about cutting your dick off and sending it back to Australia, Walker."

Theo scratches his chin. Ella may be just over a meter and a half, but she can be intimidating as hell when she wants to be.

"First no threesome and now no rebound sex?" He juts out his lower lip. "You're not letting Theo Junior have any fun."

"You named your dick Theo Junior?" Ella's brows knit together. "That's painfully unoriginal."

"Is not!" he huffs. "What would you name it?"

Jesus Christ. I really don't need to hear my girlfriend and best mate discuss names for his cock, so I tune them out. Ella focuses her attention back to me as I finish zipping up my suit and getting on my gear. She loves Formula 1 but loves knowing I'm safe even more.

"Good luck, babe." A smile clings to her lips, causing her dimple to pop up. "I love you."

"More than ice cream?"

"Oof, that's a tough call." She lets out a low whistle. "But yes, I love you more than ice cream."

"Well, I love you more than anything."

"Told you he's a one-upper, Goldy." Theo rests his hands on Ella's shoulders, shaking her gently. "When are you going to learn?"

"I better see you boys on the podium later!" she calls out as she walks back toward my sister. "Go kick some tushy!"

I hear Finn and Millie giggle at the word "tushy." For someone who swears like a sailor, Ella becomes quite child-friendly the moment my family is in range. Finn's giving me a run for my money for Ella's affection, but I think I have the upper hand.

Forty minutes: The pit lane opens and I head out to take my reconnaissance lap.

Thirty minutes: I'm pushed to the front of the grid as soon as I finish my test lap. Part of me feels bad that Theo has to play second fiddle to me once again, but I can't think about that right now. The roar from the stands is deafening and drowns out the sounds of my engine.

Twenty-five minutes: I hop out of the car and wait patiently as my team babies the Tickle Monster, making sure she's ready to go. One minute until the first fire up.

Twenty-two minutes: When I hear a mechanic turn on the engine once again, I let the adrenaline rush through my body. It used to be my favorite feeling. Now it's second to the feeling I get whenever Ella looks at me.

Twenty minutes: Josie yells at the mechanics to move out of her way as she grabs photos of me and Theo in front of our cars. I know she has an arsenal of captions ready to go, depending on if I win or lose.

Fifteen minutes: I'm back in the cockpit after the national anthem. Instead of going to a club later to celebrate the end of the season, I'm going to a family dinner. Ella already looked up the menu online and knows what she's going to order.

Ten minutes: Another fire up. Mechanics swarm my car, monitoring with cables, plugs, and laptops.

Seven minutes: I readjust my helmet and shrug my shoulders to loosen up as the tire blankets are removed from my car.

Five minutes: Everyone leaves the grid. Now it's just us twenty drivers. This used to be the love of my life. Now it's just one of them.

Three minutes: The formation lap goes by quickly. I'm happy with the tires my team chose. I think our strategy is going to clinch me another World Championship title.

One minute: The first light goes on. I take a deep breath in and a deep breath out. I'm ready to go.

Forty-five seconds: Another light flicks on. The thought of Ella cheering me on makes me feel weightless.

Thirty seconds: Three lights.

Fifteen seconds: I hear the crowds chanting my name as the fourth light goes on. The steady sound of it fuels me.

Ten seconds: And just like that, the final light flicks on.

Zero seconds: All five lights extinguish. Let's go get ourselves another World Championship title.

BONUS EPILOGUE

ELLA

I FIND Blake on the mezzanine floor of London's SoHo House creeping around like some sort of cat burglar. I shouldn't be surprised that he's hiding at his own book release party considering he fought Marion tooth and nail on having it in the first place. But here we are at the exclusive venue, surrounded by celebrities and journalists decked out in Gucci and Balmain. They're all eager to get their hands on a signed copy of Blake's book, but giving my boyfriend a Sharpie isn't in their best interest. He's more likely to stab them in the eye with it than sign a book. In his words, *"Isn't the fact that they have a whole bloody book about me enough? They want my signature now, too?"*

The sound of clinking champagne glasses, laughter, and animated conversations mask the sound of my arrival, so I take a moment to drink Blake in. He looks drop-dead-gorgeous in his fitted black pants—that hug his ass like a well-worn baseball glove—and a charcoal dress shirt with the top few buttons undone. He's tanned to perfection thanks to the impromptu trip we took to Fiji last week. Yep. That's the kind of thing I can do now that I'm dating Blake and working for myself.

Making my way toward the man of the hour, I slip my

arms around his waist, hugging him from behind. His tense muscles relax under my touch, and he settles his hands over where mine rest on his abs.

"Hey, love," he greets me in that rumbling British accent I can't get enough of.

"Hi." I press a brief kiss against his back, knowing there's no risk of lipstick getting on him since that wore off about fifty *hellos* ago. "You do know the party's down there, right? And that you can't use the excuse you were looking for the bathroom since there's one on the first floor?"

He turns around in my arms with a smirk on his face. "Exactly why I'm up here."

"Well, it wasn't very nice to leave me all alone down there. Especially because my brother accidentally introduced Finn to the word *fuckwad* and your sister isn't pleased."

"I figured it wouldn't take you long to come and find me." He tucks a stray piece of hair behind my ear. "And I'd hardly call it all alone. Our families plus two hundred other people are down there. Intimate my arse."

I bite back a smile at his grumbling. Now is definitely not the time to tell him that he looks absolutely adorable when he gets all grumpy. "Considering Marion wanted this party to be about triple the size, I'd call this intimate."

He *hmphs* before eyeing the crowd like they're zombies out for blood a week into an apocalypse. I could live without the paparazzi and press maneuvering through the crowd taking photos, but other than that, the party's been great. The canapés being passed around by the waitstaff are delicious and the live jazz band even has my dad—who has two left feet—dancing.

"There's no reason to be nervous," I remind Blake, running my hands up his chest. "They're here to celebrate you, babe. And if anyone asks you a question you don't want to answer, just tell them to read the book and find out. Easy."

The corners of his lips twitch up. "They should be here to celebrate *you*. You're the one who wrote the damn thing. All I did was answer your questions."

"All you did was answer my questions?" I throw my head back and laugh at how casually he says it. "Blake Andrew Hollis. It took me weeks just to get you to answer a single one of my damn questions."

He leans down and presses his forehead against mine. "I was worth the wait though, right?"

"Yeah, yeah. You were."

He tucks me against his chest, holding me as he observes the crowd with discerning eyes. Even though Marion's probably having heart palpitations not knowing where either of us are, I don't push Blake to head back downstairs right away. He's been anxious about the book launch all week, and if he needs to hang out here for a bit to take a deep breath, then so be it.

Blake breaks the silence by saying, "Theo's finally here."

I peer down and spot the blue-eyed Aussie slapping some soccer player on the back in greeting. "Surprised he didn't hire a herald with trumpets to announce his arrival," I tease.

Blake chuckles. "He's probably trying to play it cool, calm, and collected for Josie."

"You really think he's going to pursue her?"

Blake lifts an eyebrow. "Josie's finally single for the first time in forever. He's one hundred percent going for it."

"Hmm," I muse. "Well, if there's one person who can get him to settle down, it's definitely her."

"You got me to settle down." Blake chuckles. "And some may argue that's harder than winning a Grand Prix."

I tilt my head up and mold my lips against his. The butterflies in my stomach do the cha-cha-slide just like they did the first time we kissed and every time since then.

What starts as a quick kiss spirals into a need as Blake's

tongue tangles with mine. He tastes like home and feels like safety, so I sink into the feel of him. My hands slide into the hair on the nape of his neck and I scratch my nails against his scalp in a way that drives him crazy. He replies with a deep moan before directing us away from the banister overlooking the party and toward a darkened alcove behind us.

"Blake," I laugh breathlessly. "We can't stay up here much longer. People are probably wondering where we are."

His lips ghost over mine. "You're forgetting something."

"What's that?"

"I don't care about people. I care about you."

And with that, the conversation is over, and his lips are back on mine. His touch is firm as he sandwiches me between his body and the wall, placing a large hand on the back of my spine. His fingers feel cold against my skin, which is exposed thanks to the open-back style of dress I'm wearing. "Fuck, I want you so badly right now, El."

I swallow a whimper that's fighting desperately to slip out. It'd be a lie if I said I didn't want him just as much and he knows it. Smirking at my lack of response, he languorously licks up the column of my neck.

"Fuck," I swear, resting my head against the wall.

"Oh, we'll be doing a lot of that later, baby."

I roll my eyes and start to admonish his very correct assumption when footsteps clap like thunder on the marble staircase to our left. I readjust my dress and hair to try and look like I wasn't making out with my boyfriend in a corner instead of being a guest of honor at this very fancy party.

"There you two are!" Marion's voice travels a short distance to us. "Blake, Jessica from *The Sunday Times* just got here and wants to say hello. And then there's the—"

Blake groans into the crook of my neck as Marion chatters at rapid-fire-speed about the who's who of the party and what photo ops he has to do. As if on command, the tension in his muscles coil up again.

"You'll be fine," I reassure him, softly enough so only he can hear. "I'll stay by your side the whole time."

"Pinky promise?"

I kiss him with a smile on my face. "Always."

THANK YOU FOR READING!

Thank you for taking a chance on my debut romantic comedy! It means the world to me. If you enjoyed DRIVE ME CRAZY, please consider leaving a review on Good Reads/Amazon or sharing it with your friends!

Stay up-to-date on all of my future releases by subscribing to my newsletter (www.carlyrobynauthor.com/newsletter) and following me on social media (@carlyrobynauthor).

ACKNOWLEDGMENTS

Drive Me Crazy would still be a draft on my computer if it weren't for my amazing support. It's because of them that this story came to life!

To my parents, who encouraged my passion for storytelling from the very beginning and provided unwavering support throughout this adventure. I'll always be grateful for everything you've done—and continue to do—for me.

To Justin, for being my Formula 1 buddy with no questions asked (despite me not having a "sporty" bone in my body) and letting family dinners be "all about me" when I want to talk book stuff.

To my agent, Claire Harris, thank you for loving Ella and Blake and giving them a chance. You're a rockstar and I'm so lucky to have you in my corner. And a huge thank you to Taryn Fagerness, our co-agents at Abner Stein, and the team at Michael Joseph for helping Drive Me Crazy find a home in the UK. Romance and comedy can be felt worldwide and I'm so happy you chose my story to share.

To Kara, your friendship has been a constant source of inspiration. Thank you for indulging my texts asking, "What's a better word for *said*?" and serving as my sounding board during our brainstorming sessions.

To Rochelle, Lisa, Renée, and every other author I've met through the Good Book Fairy, who offered advice, encouragement, and the occasional dose of tough love. Thank you for welcoming me into this wonderful community with open arms.

To Libbs, for supporting my late-night writing sessions and reminding me that writing and having a social life aren't mutually exclusive. You're the matcha latte to my iced coffee.

To my friends, who provide me with a constant source of laughter and inspiration. Your habits and anecdotes have slipped into these pages more times than you might realize. I'm #blessed to do life with you at my side.

To my beta readers, who read the early drafts of Drive Me Crazy that may or may not have resembled fan faction. You helped shape this story and I appreciate the time and care you took to help me create the best story for Ella and Blake.

To you, the reader, who chose to spend your time with these characters and their journey. I hope this story brings a smile to your face and warms your heart, just as writing it has done for mine.

To the characters in this book, you may be fictional, but you've taken on a life of your own, and I thank you for your quirks, your humor, and your willingness to surprise me at every turn.

And last but certainly not least, to me. Pour yourself a crisp glass of Diet Coke, put on some Taylor Swift, and give yourself a round of applause because YOU DID THE DAMN THING. I'll forever be proud of you.